Ask the Cat

by

Kathleen F. Ewing

Table of Contents

More from Kathleen F. Ewing

The Importance of Moments – made available as an ebook in 2016

Acknowledgements

To my husband, Handsome Harry, who came into my life at age 17 and has helped make all my dreams come true. You have given me everything I ever wanted in my life and I love you!

To my son Tim, his wife Nici, and my grandchildren; Cody, Laci, Addyson and Greyson. You have all helped keep me busy and young at heart. The antics of your little family have given me many ideas for stories yet to come.

To my son Nick and his wife Sonja, thank you for your continued encouragement to "go for it." You remind me every day that all things are possible if one is willing to work. You give me the "it is never too late" speech and I believe you and want to make you proud. I hope I have!

To my family, friends and co-workers – thank you for letting me tell you about my dreams and for your wonderful words of encouragement.

And finally, to my parents, Mom here on earth and Dad watching from heaven. Thank you for letting my creativity soar and giving me just enough praise to let me know I needed to grow further.

Pinesdale

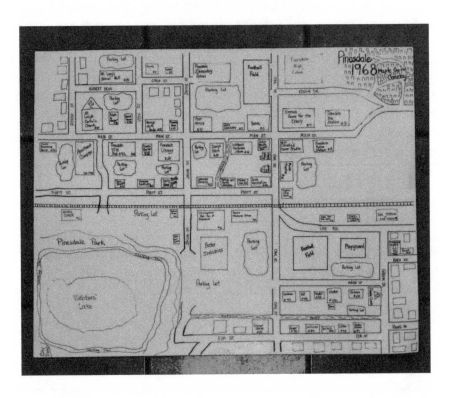

PROLOGUE

This was the lead story of the Pinesdale Review newspaper on October 5, 1951:

Pinesdale Mayor Henry Winter found dead

Mayor Henry Winter was found dead in the garage of the home he shared with his sisters, Miriam and Lina Winter. A complete autopsy will be performed when Coroner Ben Gregory returns from his annual hunting trip at Cook's Forest on October 7th.

At 7:48 pm Thursday evening, a call to the dispatcher was placed by Miss Miriam Winter requesting an ambulance at her home at 102 Maple Street. She reported that her brother, Henry was in the garage and ill.

Patrolman Jim Dowdy was first on the scene. Upon entering the garage, he reported he found Henry's car running and Henry lying on the garage floor near the door. He was unresponsive.

Within minutes, the volunteer squad arrived and pronounced Henry dead at the scene. The body was taken to the Bricker Funeral Home.

The family will post a complete obituary. Henry Winter was 46 years old. He was a lifelong resident of Pinesdale. He was a 1923 graduate of Pinesdale High School with a business degree from Penn State College awarded in 1927. He owned and operated Winter Accounting Firm and became Mayor in 1944. In 1939, his family suffered a house fire that took the lives of his wife, Marie and son, Paul.

Further information and the official cause of death will be published following the autopsy.

Well, hello there. If you just read the old newspaper clipping regarding Henry Winter, then I know what you are thinking; the story sure didn't tell the reader much information. It left out many pertinent details. I scoured the archives at the Pinesdale Public Library for any follow up story covering the dates of October 6th and beyond, but I could find no mention of old Henrys' final cause of death. I did find his obituary but it conveniently did not mentioned a cause of death.

So, I did my own form of research. I wish I could tell you all about the case of Henry Winter right now because it is pretty interesting and I do know the answers. It is just this; there is a lot to the story and so many details you need to understand in order for it to all make sense. It has been a few years now since the big event happened and I will say this; there were more than a few people involved in the crime.

There, I did tell you a little bit....yes, there was a crime! Also, I really do feel if I did try to give you just a quick answer, you would think it wasn't much of an answer or even much of a story.

So I think I better just let the story unfold for you just as it did for me. Along the way I will tell you about me, about the move and about the mistakes that were made; you know, the history.

I thought about introducing myself to you .... right now. But I decided....I shouldn't. At least not yet. I promise I will at some point. And if I should happen to forget to mention it by the time you get to the end of the story, do me a favor and just ask the cat. He knows everything!

SABRINA

Chapter 1 - 1968

Did I even tell you why I didn't want to move into old Aunt Elsie's house?

Well, first of all, it came as a complete surprise. I mean Daddy just said at the dinner table that as soon as we finished eating Mommas' good roast beef, taters and green beans dinner and each had ourselves a huge sliver of her prize-winning double chocolate cake, we were going to have a family meeting. Well, I was all for that because the last time Daddy said we were going to have a family meeting was two years ago when I was only nine and he told us we were going on a camping vacation to Burr Oak. It was a great time being out in the woods, well except for the humongous rainstorm.

There we were, our whole family, Daddy, Momma, me, my three sisters and little brother Davey all jam-packed inside a brand new, bright blue family-sized camping tent trying to get settled in to get a good night's sleep. Suddenly, and I mean suddenly, a huge rainstorm blew up. Just that quickly the rain poured down and the wind started whipping around shaking up everything. Just like they say in storybooks, I really could hear the whistling of the wind as it whipped through and thrashed at the smaller tree branches. It blew so hard well let me tell you, that tent all but about blew away.

When I tell you that Momma was not a happy camper, it is no exaggeration. She said we should have never went camping, but I think she was wrong. I really liked it and I think Momma would have too if it

3

hadn't rained. But, I guess Momma had a harder time camping than me. My little brother Davey was scared and he cried and cried and didn't want to go to sleep. Back then, he was just a little guy. Now that he is four, he would probably like camping too.

My little sister JoJo was a lot like me in that way; she loved camping. Most of the time, JoJo was more like our big sister, Audrey. They were both real pretty. They both looked a lot like Momma. I think I look more like my Daddy. Anyway, JoJo and I both thought it was super cool to be able to lay against the cold hard ground and snuggle down inside our brand new sleeping bags. Yep, Daddy got us each our own sleeping bag; brand new! I wished mine would have been red, but hey, you can't have everything. The bags were all exactly the same, blue and green plaid. I remember the smell that came from them. It was a smell I can't quite describe, but I remember it was different. Maybe it was supposed to smell different…. Kind of outdoorsy. Momma said we could have just used our regular old bed blankets, but Daddy said no. He said this was a camping adventure and we were going to do it right. He also bought a special camping stove and a gas lantern that glowed like a hundred summer fireflies stuck on one of Dr. Timm's tongue depressor when Daddy lit it that first time. I loved staring at that lantern.

Come to think of it, camping probably did seem like a lot of work to Momma. I guess for her it wasn't like she was on much of a vacation at all. She couldn't just sit like me and watch the glow of the lantern.

She still had a lot of regular chores to accomplish each day and a big worry for her was keeping track of Davey. And besides all of that was the fact that she really didn't even like to go fishing or to eat fish!

Daddy said JoJo and me were his best campers. We were good at helping Daddy pick out the best spot to put the tent and we helped him stretch it out across the ground. We kept track of the different tent poles and took turns handing Daddy each one as he yelled out for a straight piece or a curved one. Once all the poles were in place and the tent was standing, we took turns hammering the small silver stakes into the ground. I guess we did a really good job on that part because when that rainstorm hit, it got really windy but the tent stayed anchored down.

4

We also both liked fishing, just like Daddy. Neither one of us was afraid to bait the worm onto the hook. Daddy had taught us how to hold the worm and curl it around the hook and jab it a couple of times in different sections of the worm to keep it secure. Those dang fish wouldn't be able to bite a chunk of our worm off before we could hook them. And we were both very patient. Daddy said we could sit as still as the best of his buddies and stare at that bobber, watching for the first signs of a nibble. When it happened we could hook 'em and reel 'em in while holding a net in the other hand ready to scoop them up and with a little bit of help, get the hook out and put them into our fish holder that was tied at the shore and floating in the water.

Luckily, Momma didn't have to do anything but cook the fish. Daddy was in charge of all the cleaning and filleting. He was really good at it and fast too! And those fish tasted so good. My favorite was the bluegills. Daddy said some folks called them copper nose, but I like the sound of bluegill a whole lot better. I don't much like the idea of thinking about their noses.

My older sister, Audrey thought more like Momma. She wasn't happy about the idea of camping and she started complaining as soon as Daddy had mentioned it. She said she didn't want to be that far away from home and miss the summer fun with her friends. She thought we should have a family vote on the idea.

Well, Daddy put a stop to that right away. He said camping was already decided by him and Momma and an 11 year old was not about to change that decision for the whole family. I thought it would have been smart of him to say, "OK, let's vote." Me, JoJo and Davey would have voted yes with Daddy. Momma, Audrey and maybe Holly would have all voted "No" and it wouldn't matter, we would have still won 4-3. He must not have been thinking about how easy he would have won and he simply said "No vote."

I think it used to be hard in our house for Daddy because we were all girls for such a long time. But, finally he got a boy when Momma had Davey. He was probably extra glad to have a boy because Momma had said he could be named David after Daddy. If Davey had been a girl,

Momma had planned to follow her Audrey Hepburn obsession and name the baby, Eliza.

Did I tell you about Momma's obsession with Audrey? Oh my goodness, she LOVES her! I mean to tell you, she really loves her. It all started when Momma got to take a trip to New York City with Aunt Sara and Uncle Richard. Uncle Richard was an insurance agent with Metropolitan Life Insurance and he had won some sort of contest. I think he was named best salesman or something like that and the prize was to attend a big business meeting in New York City for three days. He was allowed to take his wife and their hotel expenses were covered as part of the prize. He was going to be busy during the days with meetings to attend, so Aunt Sara asked Momma if she would like to go along to be her companion. While they were there, they of course wanted to see a show on Broadway. Momma says that anyone who goes to New York City must see a Broadway show. It is still just the thing to do. They walked the streets in the Broadway section and studied all of the many marquees and posters. They finally decided to try to buy tickets to see a show called, "Gigi," starring a new young actress. And yes, you guessed it; that actress was Audrey Hepburn.

You should hear Momma tell the story about that day. She can tell you all about the theater, the music, the colors of Audrey's outfits and even the way she wore her hair. She describes the ease with which Audrey moved about on the stage, like she was gliding on air. She says she was totally mesmerized and still feels like it was only yesterday that she was sitting in section C, row 3, seat #15 of the Fulton Theater at 210 West 46th Street. So, with that new obsession came Momma seeing every movie Audrey was in ever since 1951. Momma says Audrey is a great role model for all women. She is a fine example of beauty, grace, elegance and a kind heart. So, Momma made sure that we all share her connection to Audrey.

My older sister is 13 and, as Daddy would add, going on 18. Daddy didn't get much of a vote on taking part in naming his first child, that is, unless it was a boy. If it was a boy, the name would be David. Momma totally took control of selecting the girls' name. And as it turned out their first child was a girl. Momma named her Audrey Kathleen directly after Audrey Kathleen Hepburn. I think Audrey was the absolute perfect name for her because if you ask me, even though I would never say this to Audrey, she is pretty perfect. She has long brown hair that has soft curls at the ends even though she doesn't try to make it curl. She has really pretty green eyes that shine like my grandmas' antique emerald ring and a nice solid smile with straight white teeth. There are lots of boys that like her but I know she is sweet on one named William. I know that cause she has his name written all over the inside of her math notebook. She has a big heart drawn around it, so I would say he is the one on her mind.

As for me, I am Sabrina Marie. I am 11 years old and pretty tall for my age, taller than most of the boys in my class. My hair is yellow, well blonde, but nothing special. It is long enough so that I can pull it up into a ponytail to keep it out of my face. I was named after Sabrina Fairchild, from the movie, "*Sabrina.*" I don't love the name Sabrina but I do like that in the movie, she is a tomboy. That part kind of suits me.

My younger sister is Jo Ellen but I like to call her JoJo and she is nine years old. Her Audrey character is from the movie, "*Funny Face,*" and don't think I don't tease her about that one on a regular basis. I tell her, "Momma must have took one look at you and thought, "Oh….Funny Face! Yes we will name her Jo." JoJo, as I call her, doesn't think it is funny at all but, in truth, she really does have a pretty face. She actually looks and acts a lot like Audrey with the same long brown hair. They are both really pretty, I guess pretty like Momma and Audrey.

My littlest sister is Holly. She is six and has brown hair that she wears in cute little pigtails. Right now she is missing a couple of teeth in the front so when she talks it sounds a little funny. She is named after Holly Go-Lightly from the movie, "B*reakfast at Tiffany's.*" Just like her namesake, she has a magic touch with cats. Not just our cats, Sister Luke and Tiffany, but all cats. Tiffany and Sister Luke love to curl up on her lap and calmly sleep while she pets them. They never nip at her like they do to me. They also follow her all around the house as if she has a fish hanging out of her pocket.

7

As I already told you my little brother is four years old and finally, on the 5th and as Momma says, final try, Daddy got to name a baby. He is named after my father, David, but we call him Davey. I think it is kind of funny that in the movie, *"Sabrina,"* Audrey thinks she is in love with David. And who plays the part of David? That would be the handsome actor, William Holden. And what is our last name? Yep, you guessed it. It is....Holden! I just think that is really funny.

And, it doesn't end there. Our pets are also blessed by Momma's obsession. We have a really old Collie named Gigi. Gigi is like a hundred years old and mostly lays around and sleeps. We also have a little tiny poodle that we got about two years ago and Momma named her Fair Lady. I know, that one is kind of strange, but that is what Momma wanted to call her. We all shorten it to Lady, except Momma. Our cats, like I already told you, are named Sister Luke and Tiffany and they are really related. Tiffany is actually one of Sister Luke's kittens. I wanted to keep them all, but Momma said we could only keep one. There won't be any more kittens. Momma had Daddy take both of them over to Doc Pritchard and he "fixed" them. Momma said it was the right thing to do. I wondered if Sister Luke could talk, if she would have agreed. I figured she probably did cause it would be really hard to have six or seven babies and then see someone give most of them away.

Our Daddy doesn't think about Momma's Audrey fascination too much and I guess the name choices weren't too big of a deal for him because he never uses our given names. In his eyes, we are, in order: Princess, Stinkweed, Possum Belly, Munchkin and Tiger. The dogs and cats, well, he doesn't really ever call them by name......he just kind of yells a little and they come.

Oh, I got way off course. I started to tell you about Daddy's after supper meeting and instead I jumped to camping and how all of us kids got our names. Sorry about that. Now about that meeting.

Well, this time, it wasn't near as much fun. It wasn't one of those ideas or adventures that I got excited about right away. Matter of fact, I didn't get too excited about it at all. I actually got a little sick to my stomach and as I looked around the table, I think everybody was sick to their stomach. Well, maybe everyone except Davey. He didn't care, because he probably didn't really understand what Daddy was saying at the meeting. This would have been a good time to ask if we could take a vote because I think the vote would have been all girls – five, against all boys – two.

But, I knew better. This was not a vote type idea. I had a feeling this was already a done deal before Daddy even opened his mouth. This was our new reality, we were moving. We would be leaving our nice, quiet country home where our closest neighbor was almost a half a mile away. We all loved our small farmhouse. We had a long tree-lined lane and the house sat up on a hilltop as if we were king of the mountain. Now Daddy was telling us that not only were we leaving the country, we were going to move into Pinesdale. We knew Pinesdale, it was a small town of about 650 people. It was where we went to buy food, to get ice cream and to go to school. It was where Daddy had his Barbershop. It was where we went to church at St. Lucy's. It was where we went to the movies and to the library. So, that wasn't the problem, we all knew Pinesdale. Our address was Pinesdale, but we never felt like we really lived there. We didn't live in town. We lived in the country.

One scary part was just that we were going to be leaving our home. Our house at 7479 Rt. 16 was the only house I had ever lived in and I didn't really want to leave. I didn't like the idea of that at all. The other scary part was we were going to move into Daddy's Great Aunt Elsie's house, a house that was big but also very dark. It was a large three story home, but to me it was just an old mansion. I am sure it was beautiful or at least pretty in its day, but now it was ragged and tired looking. Did you happen to see the Doris Day movie, "Please Don't Eat the Daisies" that came out a few years ago? If you did, do you remember when Doris bought the big run-down house in the country and David Niven hated the idea of the house and of living in the country? Well...that is kinda how I feel about Aunt Elsie's house; but I would prefer to live in the country. In the movie they fixed it all up and it was magnificent....but that was a movie. I know my Momma is a determined woman and very creative, but when it came to turning this house around – I wasn't sure it was possible. I guess it isn't as falling apart as the house in the movie, but there just wasn't one thing cheerful about it. It reminded me of something out of one of my old fairy tale books. You know what I mean. It was like a big dark castle with over-sized looming peaks stretched out over the windows and high pointed crests on the roof. And besides the house, I also worried about the other thing Daddy said….that we would move so that we could all help take care of Aunt Elsie. All of that was a lot to absorb for my 11-year-old head.

It was all such a shock to me. I never once, I mean not ever once, thought that I wouldn't spend all of my life in our hilltop house. I just never imagined that there would ever be any need to move. We all loved our little home. We all loved our trees, our yard and our big porch swing. Oh…our porch swing! We had spent so many wonderful nights watching the lightening bugs flicker in the dark while we chit- chatted on our porch swing. So many thoughts started jumping through my head. So many memories. I looked around the table. I saw my sisters, JoJo and Holly were looking worried just like me. I saw Audrey all smiles and looking excited. I saw Momma smiling at Daddy and I saw Daddy….and he was talking. Oh my! Daddy was still talking. I completely zoned out. I needed to listen. I needed to figure things out.

Aunt Elsie is Daddy's only relative left from that older generation. She wasn't just his aunt, she was his great aunt. So I guess that makes her my great-great aunt. We have always visited her on every special occasion. You know what I mean, Christmas, Easter, her birthday, those kinds of days. She is really old and I probably shouldn't say this, but I have always thought her great big house smelled kind of stinky. You know what I mean; like old people's houses smell. A kind of a combination of stinky and musty; like it had a pair of old wet dirty socks lying around in the corner of every room. If I didn't know that we had been over to visit; at least six or seven times a year; I would have guessed that she hadn't opened any of her doors or windows for about 10 years. Momma has one special closet at our house that smells like mothballs. Aunt Elsie has a whole house that just plain smells.

So...now I am not thinking about missing our porch swing, I am thinking about stink. I think we are all going to stink like moth balls. And I know my Momma is not going to like all that stink.

As if Momma was reading my mind, she waited for Daddy to take a breath and then she says, "Children, this is going to be a big change for us, I mean a really big change. But the truth of the matter is Aunt Elsie needs our help. You know she has always had Miss Eulalie by her side doing all the cooking and cleaning and taking care of Elsie, but Miss Eulalie has just gotten too old. Aunt Elsie is 86 now and Miss Eulalie, God bless her, is 77 and needs to just retire and take care of her own self."

She stopped and then looked at Daddy.

"Aunt Elsie's mind isn't always working at its best anymore," Daddy said with a sad-look on his face. "She has what they call hardening of the arteries, so she forgets a lot of little things, but she also forgets a lot of important matters so it just isn't safe for her to be alone. She is also dead-set against moving into Hilda Mae's Boarding House. She just wants to stay in her own house. My Great Uncle Otto died a long time ago, before any of you were born. He was a great man. He was a very smart businessman. He started his own very successful company and he and Aunt Elsie had a great life. They liked to travel and gave wonderful parties at their home for as long as I can remember. It was a very sad day when he died. It was an accident. One day he was up on his ladder cleaning the gutters along the side of the house when he fell. Aunt Elsie had been in the house and heard it happened and ran outside. He must have landed very hard and hit his head against the paved walkway or basement window protector. He died instantly."

"Yes, it was very sad," he said with his head hanging slightly downward as he remembered it. "I was 21 at the time. I remembered what a shock it was to everyone. I remembered everyone worrying about how Aunt Elsie would do without him. Her brother Herman and his wife Nancy both had died many years ago. And remember, Elsie and Otto were never blessed with any children, so right now, it is just us. We are all she has here in Pinesdale or anywhere for that matter. So, we are her family and it is up to us to help her; to do for her the things that need done and make sure she is well cared for now and until, well, until she doesn't need us anymore."

Everyone sat quiet for a minute or two. I think we were all kind of stunned. I was thinking about Aunt Elsie and wondering if I was "crazy" when suddenly Audrey spoke up.

"But Daddy," she said, "what about here, what about our house? I mean I like the idea of moving into town and being closer to my friends and school and, well, and to everything.....but what will happen to our house?"

Daddy looked pleased to have an answer all ready to go. "Well, Princess, I am glad you asked. We planned to rent this house and I actually have already found someone and they have signed the papers. Gus Gratton and his family are going to live here and they are pretty excited. That was to be the rest of my news. So, today is May 18th and Gus already signed a contract in which I told him they could move into this house on June 1st. So, my little Holden crew, that gives us 13 days to get our stuff out of here and into Aunt Elsie's."

Now everybody had questions, everybody except Davey. Everyone was talking at once and finally Daddy held up his hands to stop and even gave us one of his very loud whistles. It worked. We stopped.

Daddy said, "One at a time....please. Now Munchkin, how about we start with you. Do you have a question?"

Holly looked at everybody sitting around the table. First she looked embarrassed and lowered her head, but then just as quickly, she lifted it upright, looked right at Daddy and said, "Well, I have two. Where am I gonna slth-eep in Aunt El-thie's hou-slthe and isth Gigi, Fair Lady, Sth-isth-er Luke and Tiffany coming with us-th and where are they gonna slth-eep?"

Everybody laughed. She looked at all of us and seemed a bit mad at first, but then she finally broke into a smile. When we all finally settled down, Daddy got a real serious look on his face.

He bent down to be somewhat at eye level with her and said, "Well my little Munchkin, Aunt El-thie's house is a rather big house." He smiled at her then looked back to all of us.

He continued, "Her house has many large rooms in the downstairs but it also has many large rooms upstairs. There are five rather large bedrooms and she only uses the one on the first level. I am sure there will be one of those four other bedrooms that will be perfect for you and maybe Possum Belly to share," he said looking back at Holly.

He looked toward Momma for agreement and then returning to Holly he said, "And as for our comical crew of animals, Aunt Elsie will welcome them into her home as long as they all get along with the crown prince of her household, Mr. Mertz. He is very old and Mr. Mertz is very special to Aunt Elsie and our little guys must behave. So, maybe you could be in charge of making them use their manners in the new house. You will need to remind them that Mr. Mertz has lived there a very long time and he rules the animal world at the Becker house. Munchkin, could you do that for me and Momma?"

After that, we all felt a little better. The rest of the meeting had many more questions but Momma and Daddy answered them all well enough to make us all feel a little better about the big news. Momma said before we start moving any of our belongings, we would need to spend a time scrubbing and cleaning. She said she was thinking that maybe we could even paint a few rooms as long as Aunt Elsie likes the paint colors we choose.

Aunt Elsie's house had a lot of rooms with big flowered wallpaper and dingy old curtains in faded shades of blues and grays. Those drapes were probably pretty shades of blues when they were new and for a few years afterwards, but now they looked like they had been washed about 100 times They were frayed and totally discolored. All the downstairs rooms had carpeting, except the kitchen. The kitchen had really and I mean really old linoleum with some sort of a color-block pattern that was probably pretty and popular in its day but now had only some vague color left under the cabinet edges that was no longer distinguishable at all in the main walkway path. It was also speckled with deep stepped-on type grime, especially in front of the oven. At any rate, back to the carpets. I remember noticing that the carpets were all pretty ugly. None were soft and smooth carpet, like it is when it is new.

They all felt stiff. The rug in the living room looked like it needed a really good sudsy bath. Can you give rugs a bath? I don't know. In our hilltop house we had wood floors or linoleum that you washed with a mop. Our only rugs were just small "throw" ones that we hung on the clothesline and hit with the side of a broom to clean. I always hate when Momma gives me that job. It starts out being fun at first, like for the first 5 swings but then my arms get tired and I want to be done but Momma doesn't agree.

I usually hear, "OK Sabrina, now you need to hit them from another angle."

Oh well, Momma will know how to fix Aunt Elsie's carpets. Momma is really smart. Next, Daddy wrote down a list of things we needed to do at our house to be ready for such a big move. The list was long and our time was short.

1. Make phone calls we need to make to stop the different utilities- Momma in charge
2. Sort our belongings into piles: give-away, throw-away or keep - Everybody
3. Deliver the give-away items for the needy to the church – Daddy in charge
4. Haul the trash to go to the city dump – Daddy in charge
5. Clean Aunt Elsie's' house – Momma in charge – Audrey to assist
6. Move our bigger items that need to go to Aunt Elsie's house – Daddy in charge – everybody help
7. Prepare to have a big household tag sale – Momma in charge

Daddy said to think hard and make the tough decisions. Each item we touch has 3 choices: 1. we don't want it or need it, so give it away or sell it; 2. we want to take it with us to our new home at 104 Maple Street; or 3. it has served its purpose and is no longer any good, so throw it away. As Daddy told us about 15 times during our family meeting, it was going to be lots of work, but we could do it. He said we were his mighty moving crew and he was counting on each of us to do our part.....without complaint!

The meeting was over. As I sat looking at my family I saw; my sisters were gabbing about I don't really know what, as they moved from the table, but I did notice Daddy's face. He looked real happy, but more than just happy, he looked proud. I guess he was pretty excited about moving his family into such a big house. He looked over at Momma and then, just like that, he gave her a little wink. She looked real calm and peaceful and winked back at him. Then they both smiled.

So I decided to be glad about Daddy's big news. Glad for Daddy and glad for all of us. It was going to be very different, but I knew it was going to be okay.

SABRINA

Chapter 2 - 1968

For the next 13 days, we all worked our hind ends off. We worked like a team and went through the whole house one room at a time sorting, pitching and sorting and pitching again until we had it all down to the minimum of what we needed to take into town with us for the big move. We did it just like Daddy had told us to with his three choice decision method. And...it worked! It was funny to think about it but we were moving from a small three-bedroom house at the end of a long private lane to what looked to me like a five bedroom mansion on Maple St., but yet we were throwing out so many things. Then I remembered an important fact. The house was still filled with all of Aunt Elsie's furniture and belongings, so Daddy was right again, we had to get rid of things.

About one week before the scheduled move, I was helping Daddy carry in some smaller boxes and I noticed as soon as we walked inside that the house was smelling better. Momma and Audrey had been spending a lot of time there scrubbing, well, just about scrubbing everything! Momma said Miss Eulalie had been a very loyal worker and a good friend to Aunt Elsie, but that her days of doing hard scrubbing must have ended a few years ago because there was sure a lot that had to be done in every room of that big house. I was happy that Momma didn't ask me to go along when they took the buckets, mops, sponges, sweeper, brooms and dustpans. They looked totally worn out every

16

time they returned home, but it sure did help, because all that musty old stinky socks smell was about gone. I was surprised that Audrey went along so willingly, but then I realized that she was planning to have a much more active social life once we were living in town. She could walk to her friends, to the library, to the Five and Dime, and Sue's Dairy Isle. She must have felt like a prisoner does when they finally get released from jail. She didn't mind the work because she thought it was going to bring her some new freedom. Maybe she was right, only time would tell.

As I walked thru the kitchen, I was surprised to see all those grimy spots were gone from the floor and you could actually see some of the different colors. Don't get me wrong, the linoleum was still ancient looking and the worn out path was still obvious but Momma couldn't change that no matter how hard she scrubbed. I gave old Mr. Mertz a quick rub on the head as I passed him in the dining room. He looked me over cautiously but I could tell he appreciated the rubbing. He started to follow me as I headed for the stair steps, but changed his mind quickly when he realized I was really going upstairs. He was kind of a lazy cat, but I guess that is okay since he is like a senior citizen in the animal world. I was thinking that I should have brought along Sister Luke today. After all, Sister Luke was six-years old, the oldest of our cats, so I thought it would have been proper to introduce her to Mr. Mertz first. But maybe it was better to just wait and spring it on Old Mr. Mertz when we finally all move in and everybody arrives at once. It might shock him, but then he will see we are all staying and he might as well get used to ALL of us; Sister Luke, Tiffany, Fair Lady and Gigi. Wow, that was going to be a day!

I helped Daddy place the boxes in the rooms where we thought they might belong. Momma and Daddy were taking the biggest bedroom on the 2nd floor. It was a beautiful room. I knew Momma was going to love being in this room. This room was twice the size of her and daddy's room at our house. It had a wallpaper on it, that was old like everything else in the house, but since it had probably been Aunt Elsie and Otto's room at one time, the paper was real pretty. It was a very delicate pattern that reminded me of a party dress Momma had that was made of pale blue dotted-swiss material. This paper had that dotted-swiss look with an added faint thin stripe in a soft powdery white color. The pattern repeated itself around the room. The blue had probably lost some of its color over the years but it didn't look dingy just very soft and pale which was appealing. The room had two nice big windows that faced the back of the house. Each had a pale baby blue crisscrossed country curtain with a white sheer showing underneath. The sheer looked old and worn so I was sure Momma would make a new pair once we got settled. The room had a good-sized closet, but they would definitely still need Momma's prized dresser and vanity that she brought with her when they married. It had been in Momma's family for I guess about two hundred years. They were given to her Momma by her Great Aunt Flora, who lived in what Momma referred to as the "Old Country," so I guessed that made them real special pieces. I was thinking as I put down the box filled with shoes, that those pieces will look real nice in here.

I was standing there looking around at all the space in this room and realized the room also has some real pretty wood all over the place. Not like our bedrooms back home, this house has wood all around the top of the walls like to connect it to the ceiling. I think Daddy called it molding. It was a soft shade of medium brown with a few darker colored stripes and small spots running through it, but not over-powering. I am not at all sure what it would be called, maybe maple, maybe pecan, maybe hickory? Daddy could tell me. But anyway, it was nice.

I knew just where Momma would put her vanity. It would go right between those two windows. I can imagine Momma sitting there, staring into her mirror and carefully putting on her brightest red lipstick, smacking her lips lightly together and then gently patting the surface with a tissue. I can picture her doing everything sitting there like she always does when doing her makeup, but this time feeling like a queen in her big new room. I like the way she always cocks her head slightly to the right and stares at herself in the mirror a few extra seconds. Then with an approving look, she pats her hand across the smooth vanity and gets on with her day. I wonder if when Momma is sitting and doing her makeup, if she pretends she is Miss Audrey Hepburn. Probably not, but ...maybe.

Just about then, Daddy yelled to me to get a move on; that there were more boxes to unload. I pushed the box of shoes a little closer to the wall and headed back downstairs. Now, I notice that the stairway railing and steps are made from that same pretty wood and has the same dark stripes. It really is nice and feels so smooth against my hand. Momma must have spent some time of this staircase. As I climb downward, I looked across the massive old living room with its very high ceilings and massive windows and thought no wonder Daddy and Momma were acting pretty excited about moving here. Now that it was almost all washed down, dusted and I guess you could say, scrubbed inside and out, it really looked like it had potential. I knew Momma wouldn't be able to do much about the old worn carpeting. As Daddy always says, "money doesn't grow on trees." But Momma was very clever. She will soon change out the curtains to something more cheerful. Curtains....Momma can make. Carpeting....she can't.

I also notice Mr. Mertz is now perched on the end of the railing waiting for another head rubbing. I stand for a few seconds rubbing his old head and wondering how he hopped up there since he was a pretty chunky cat. As I start to walk away, he purrs a little and I figure that he now knows I will be his friend. I give him a nod and say, "Cool Beans Mr. Mertz!"

I head through the living room and Mr. Mertz hops down and moves to the big wide window ledge. Very quickly he curls himself up and begins to sun himself on the windowsill. I give him a quick wink and keep moving.

Just as I am ready to exit the room, I hear Aunt Elsie holler from the library. I freeze on the spot and just listen. I wish Daddy was still inside. I don't usually visit with Aunt Elsie without one of my parents being right there to say the right things. Daddy is already outside so I realize I am on my own. I say a quick prayer that she doesn't call out again, but before I can finish, I hear her.

19

"Who is that out there....is that you David?" she says from the other room. I know I must answer her. If I didn't Daddy would be very upset with me. I answered back, "No Aunt Elsie, it is me, Sabrina."

"Who?" she yells and I can hear her trying to scoot her wheelchair.

I realize there is no easy escape, so I walk toward the room. I reach the doorway and I can barely see her sitting in her big old black wheelchair. The room was dingy dark since she had the heavy curtains pulled shut covering the two big windows at the front of the room. There was only a small table lamp lit in the far corner near Aunt Elsie.

Once Miss Eulalie retired, Daddy hired a home health person to come in every morning to get Aunt Elsie up, sponge bathed, dressed and fed a good breakfast. Momma and Daddy have been taking care of lunch and supper while we have been getting the house ready. One of those ladies comes back in the evening to get her changed and comfortable in her bed for the night.

I imagine Aunt Elsie gets tired of sitting in that yucky chair all day. I sure would. But as of right now, she seems alright. I was still standing in the doorway looking around her and the many books in her library when she said, "Well come in here child so I can see which one you are, I know David has a whole truckload of you young'uns."

I walk further into the room. I see the same ugly carpeting that looks like it has never seen a sweeper even though I know it has because Momma has been here. Aunt Elsie looks old, really old. Older than the last time I saw her or maybe I just wasn't this close the last time and missed seeing some of those heavy wrinkles in her face, neck and hands. She has on a dark green house dress and a heavy black sweater with silver buttons that I guessed used to sparkle but now had stones missing from many of them. She wore black old-lady pumps that laced up the front and had on heavy dark hosiery. I was thinking it is a safe bet to guess she no longer bothered to wear a girdle. I wondered if she wore one of those things like Momma does that snaps onto your stocking so they don't fall down, or if she just rolls them up and her heavy legs hang onto them. I was still wondering all that when she spoke again.

She said, "Come closer child I want to see you. Which one are you?"

"I am Sabrina Ma'am. I am here with Daddy unloading some boxes and I really do need to go back and help him." I was almost begging to get back to work.

"Now you hush child and come closer, I want to show you something," she said.

As I walked a little closer and got close enough to the light, I could see she was holding something in her hand. It was something small like a letter or a picture, yes it was a picture.

"Yes Ma'am," I said as I was finally close enough.

She leaned forward from her chair and studied my face. I wanted to tell her she could see me better if she would open the curtains and allow some light into the room, and just then, she said it.

"Girl," she said, "go open that curtain over there. I want to see your face. After all if you are going to live here I better get to know you."

"Yes Ma'am," I said obediently and walked over and opened the drape. Immediately light rushed into the room and I could see now that there was still some color left in the old rug but I could also see Momma and Audrey had not yet tried to clean the bookshelves. There were dusty looking shelf edges and just from the swish of the curtain movement I could now see tiny dust particles dancing throughout the room wherever the light was shining. I walked back toward Aunt Elsie and now it was easy to see it was a picture she was holding.

"I want you to see this picture," she said. "This is your Uncle Otto. Isn't he a handsome man? It says on the back 1933. He is older now," she says as she is smiling down at the picture. "Since you are going to be staying here with us, you should get to know him. He is away right now on a business trip but he'll be home soon. He will be quite surprised, but pleased to see all of you. I didn't tell him yet about David bringing his family here, but he will be fine with it. He always liked David."

I wasn't sure what to say so I just said, "Yes Ma'am."

"Where is your father, did he leave?" she asked me as she was again trying to scoot her chair.

"No Ma'am," I said, "he is outside waiting for me. Did you want to talk to him? I can go fetch him for you."

21

"No..no...no child," she said, "Don't you go and do that. He is probably working hard. You just push me out and into the living room so I can watch that old neighbor over there. I don't trust her any further than I can throw my shoe. Actually, I would really like to throw my shoe at her. I don't exactly remember why, but I don't like her."

I obeyed and pushed her chair out into the bigger living room. She was not a small woman so pushing the chair took a little effort on my part. I parked her right near the window just as she had asked.

"Is there anything else you need Aunt Elsie before I go?" I asked sheepishly.

"Yes," she said, "Where is Mr. Mertz? You haven't let him outside have you? I don't want that awful neighbor to get her hands on my precious cat."

"No Ma'am," I answered quickly. "I just saw him. See, he is over there on the other window ledge. See....right there. He is sun-bathing." I said with a chuckle.

"Yes, I see him," she said unapologetically. "Okay then young lady now quit dolly-gagging and go help your father. I am sure he is more than tired of waiting for you."

I was more than eager to get moving and I did.

"Alright, good-bye then Aunt Elsie." I said as I heading out of the living room. I passed through the smaller dining room and skipped into the once bright yellow kitchen and out the back door to Daddy's old blue truck.

I grabbed another box that wasn't too heavy and headed back in. I see there are about four or five more boxes marked for my parents' bedroom. So a few more trips for me, but that is okay. We are making progress. As I was walking back inside, I heard a noise to my left. I looked over and saw a strange older man next door at the Winter house. He was walking thru her back walkway that was kind of overgrown with some sort of trellis type growth. There are green leaves everywhere but not in a pretty way. They look unkept and heavy. I could picture in my head that at one time when they had not been overgrown and it was probably very pretty. Like one of those pictures in Momma's House and Garden magazine. Now, it looked like something I pictured from the book, *The Secret Garden*, where things could easily be hidden amongst the thick greenery. It looked rather evil. I caught another quick glimpse of the man and saw that he was looking right at me. He looked so creepy so I turned my head quickly back to the house and hurried inside. I noticed as I went thru the living room that Aunt Elsie is staring too...directly out the window toward the same garden that I was studying. I wondered if she was looking at that man. She was staring so intently, that she didn't even realize I had re-entered the room so I kept moving.

When we finished unloading the truck, Daddy went in and said his good-byes to Aunt Elsie. It was time to head back home now and see how they did with the packing up of the kitchen. Daddy laughed and said, "Once it is packed, we will probably be eating peanut butter and jelly sandwiches until we get moved into the new house."

I think to myself that would be okay, I love peanut butter and jelly.

Then Daddy said, "We have to have another family meeting tonight and it is all about bedrooms."

I hopped into the truck and I didn't say anything, but I was wondering which bedroom I would get and who would I have to share it with....maybe Audrey??

I asked Daddy about the creepy old man. He said, "What old man?"

I said, "The one walking around outside the Winter house. I have seen him walking around her yard before when we were visiting Aunt Elsie. I never knew his name or who he was and I was hoping that you do Daddy. Is he related to Miss Winter or a friend of her sister?"

As we pulled away, Daddy looked over and said, "Who? Oh...him. That is Tram Keller. He is harmless. Just an old man. As far as I know he is not related to Miss Winter, he is just a friend. Actually, I don't recall that he is related to anyone in Pinesdale. I mean he had family here at one time, but I think they may have all passed on by now."

"Ok, I guess," I said. "I wonder what he is looking for over there. But, I suppose he is okay, if he just walks around....."

I stopped mid-sentence and turned my head to look again as I caught a glimpse of him entering her big oversized garage. The door shut quickly.

I admit, I was more than a little fascinated with him and I wasn't sure why. Is he a boyfriend of Miss Winter or her sister?

On the ride I told Daddy what Aunt Elsie had said about Uncle Otto. He reminded me about Aunt Elsie have trouble remembering things and said it was something we would all have to get used to and to pretend everything was okay. He said peoples' memories are important to them and that there was no point in correcting her. It would just upset her and we were moving there to make her life better not worse.

I knew he was right, but I thought about me when I get old. How would I feel if everything I thought everyday was the wrong thing? I think I would want someone to tell me. I would want to know. But for now, I would listen to Daddy.

Daddy was now whistling as he was driving so I knew he was done thinking about Aunt Elsie. He was in a happy mood. The tune was *Camptown Races*. I love when he whistles. It is infectious. I started singing along and before I knew it, we were in our driveway.

When we went inside, I was relieved to smell dinner cooking and thought I could even smell chocolate, so maybe even a yummy dessert. Momma might have been packing the kitchen, but she hadn't packed everything, at least not yet. And I was right, Momma made a super dinner and there was even chocolate brownies. We ate and then all started to do the cleaning up, all except Daddy. He was sitting at his big desk, shuffling through a huge stack of papers. I hoped for all our sake that it wasn't all bills. If it was, he would be real grouchy. We hurried to finish cleaning up and then all returned to our seats around the table. Daddy was still checking papers at his desk, so we all sat very quiet and waited patiently. Tiffany hopped up and stretched herself across my lap so I sat stroking her fur until Daddy finally returned to his seat at the table.

I knew right away those papers must not have been bills, at least not all of the pile, because he called our family meeting to order, and he smiled. He had drawn a map of sorts, of the bedroom layout and marked the rooms 1-4. He began by reminding us that Aunt Elsie's' bedroom is on the first floor. There are two big bedrooms and two smaller bedrooms on the 2nd floor.

It was a no brainer that Momma and Daddy got to have the best and biggest room. That had already been decided and I had already started putting all of those boxes in there today. So, we started with Davey. He had two factors in his favor; he was the youngest and he was the only boy. We all agreed to give Davey his own room. He glowed like a big shot when he got to pick which one of the smaller rooms he wanted to occupy. He, of course, picked the one closest to Momma and Daddy. Daddy wrote his name on bedroom # 2 on the map.

Next was Audrey. Being the oldest, Momma said she felt Audrey should have her own room. So, after a nod in agreement from Daddy, she got the other big room, which thrilled her to death. She jumped up from the table and squealed like a baby pig! Daddy wrote her name in Bedroom # 3.

And then the dilemma came. One small room left and three girls still waiting. I wondered, did they really think we should have that small room for me, JoJo and Holly?

We quickly found out they did not. Daddy got a grin on his face, winked at Momma and then said, "We thought you three adventure girls might like to have your own special space."

I thought to myself....What?? Wait? Where??

He had all of our attention. We three all leaned forward anxiously awaiting his next sentence. He looked back at Momma and smiled a big smile. He pulled out another piece of paper....with another hand-drawn map. One we did not recognize from our many trips to the house.

Then he said, "Your Momma and I thought you might like to have the 3rd floor.....all to yourselves!"

A look of shock flashed amongst all of us, but especially between me and my two younger sisters. I had not ever remembered being on a 3rd floor at Aunt Elsie's. I thought quickly, how do you get to it, where are the steps, is there some sort of a hidden passageway somewhere. I had too many thoughts buzzing, so instead I jumped up and blurted out, "YES!" as Tiffany went flying off my lap.

And I followed that with a quick, "How do we get to the 3rd floor?"

Everyone laughed and then Daddy said, "Well Stinkweed, how about you sit back down and I will explain."

I sat back down. All eyes fixated back on Daddy. He told us that the 3rd floor had not been used by Uncle Otto and Aunt Elsie for anything except storage. It was a very large attic, but a very old and dirty one. No one, including Miss Eulalie, had been up there for years. Daddy and Momma had checked it out and found that the space was definitely safe but in need of a good clean up. It was filled with old trunks, blankets, boxes of clothing, garment racks and boxes of memorabilia. It would take some time to sort it and clean it up, but it could be done.

I shouted, "Cool Beans!" and quickly asked again, "But how do you get to the 3rd floor?"

Daddy said the stair steps were kind of hidden. There were inside the hallway closet. The one that faced the front of the house, toward Maple St.

Before my two little sisters could answer, I shouted again, "Cool Beans! We'll take it and…. we will even do all the cleaning up!"

Holly and JoJo gave me a quick questioning look.

Then Holly said, "Really….we will clean it all up….just us?"

I gave her back a super quick, "Yes, it will be fun. I can't wait to see all the stuff in the boxes and trunks and even the old clothes. It is all probably really old…like a 100 years old. When can we start Daddy?"

Daddy said, "First things first. … Do you three girls all agree? Is this going to work to give you your own floor?"

I eagerly looked at Holly and JoJo's faces. "Come on girls," I said. "It will be ours, all ours. Momma, can we decorate it ourselves?"

She shrugged a yes kind of shrug, so I went back to my sisters.

"Did you see that?" I said. "She meant …Yes! Are you in….are we going to be the 3 Musketeers….or maybe ….what…the 3 Nancy Drews?"

With that everybody laughed and my sisters nodded in agreement to take on the 3rd floor with me. Daddy wrote on the map….The 3 Nancy Drews. Then he folded it and put it aside and went back to the map of the 2nd floor.

I was so excited, that I wanted to end the meeting and drive right into town to see the space, but Daddy said it was too late to bother Aunt Elsie and we had one more thing to discuss.

I accepted his answer, but found I could hardly sit still and listen. My mind was wondering, thinking about the trunks, wondering if there were any fur coats on the garment rack, diamond tiaras or maybe even a treasure map tucked inside a crack in the wall.

Daddy must have been reading my mind, because he looked right at me and said, "If we can continue." I gave him my attention.

He said, "That leaves one small empty bedroom on the 2nd floor." Daddy pointed to Room #4 on the map.

Daddy said that we all remember Aunt Elsie has some medical problems. She doesn't walk very well now and prefers to move around in her own wheelchair. So climbing the stairs would not be an option for her, which is why a ramp was built at the back door of the house a few years ago, even though she very seldom wants to go outdoors.

He continued that her mind doesn't always work too well. It has been a problem for the last three or four years. She is forgetful and often repeats the same phrases over and over again. He reminded us that we might even hear her talking to Uncle Otto sometimes, as she often forgets that he passed long ago. He says he regularly catches her talking to Mr. Mertz as though he is a real person. She complains to him about her dinner or she gossips about the neighborhood as though he can understand and respond. He reminded us that Aunt Elsie has changed quite a bit over the past few years but she has always been very kind to us and is being very generous by having us live in her home. He said we would ALWAYS be kind and respectful to her, but that there would certainly be times when a break from the situation may become necessary.

Daddy said, he and Momma decided to make the extra small bedroom #4 into what they would call a "get-away" room. It would be a space that we could go to as a family, or alone, if it had been a time "when Aunt Elsie was kind of getting on our nerves" type of day. We would call it "The Library." We would fill it with our books, playing cards and family games. It would be our secret little escape area.

Then he said, "We would never ever want to hurt Aunt Elsie's feelings, but we also expect there to be times when we all might need a little ....well, "escape." Aunt Elsie had been an avid reader in her younger years. She would be happy to know we created a library of sorts.

He finished by asking, "Does everybody understand?" We all nodded yes. "Is everyone happy with their room assignments?" Again we all nodded yes. "Well then, we move in 1 week so rest up. Meeting adjourned!"

I bounced up to my room and flopped onto my bed. Tiffany had followed me up the stairs and leaped onto my bed too. I pulled her over to me and laid back resting my head on my pillow. I let my head fill with all kinds of amazing thoughts of those special hidden stairs up to the 3rd floor, the magnificent size of the huge room and the treasures that might be stored in there waiting for me to find.

SABRINA

Chapter 3 – 1968

So, now you are all caught up. Now you know it all. You know why I initially didn't want to move into old Aunt Elsie's musty-smelling house and now you know why I can't wait to move into old Aunt Elsie's house!

The week before the big move we were crazy busy. I set my alarm clock an hour early so I could get a few things done in the morning before I had to leave for school. I tried my best to convince Momma and Daddy that moving was much more important than to be there for the last day of school. I told them not one thing of any importance happens during the final day. We would turn in books, watch a movie and have a longer gym class.

They listened, half-heartedly and then said in a joint response, "No, go to school!"

School seemed to be twice as long today as normal and the final assembly, well, it just went on forever and ever. Every kid just wanted out! Finally it was 3:20 and the bell rang. Everyone ran out the door as if the school was on fire.

When we got off the bus, I practically ran the whole way up the lane. I couldn't wait to get home, change my clothes and head in town to see my room. Thank goodness, Momma and Daddy were both there waiting for us. They said they had been at the new house all day. Daddy said he started by knock down some of the cobwebs in the attic for us, but then remembered that we wanted to do it all by ourselves and stopped. He laughed and said, "So duck your heads when you first go in. Some of them webs are pretty big!"

We loaded a few things into the truck cab and then all piled in and headed for Maple Street.

Daddy parked and I was ready to jump out and run into the house when Momma said, "Whoa there girl. Let's remember this is Aunt Elsie's home. She has lived here a very long time without dealing with the noise of children. Let us act like civilized people as we enter the house."

Momma was right. I calmed myself as best as I could and slowly walked to the back kitchen door with JoJo and Holly right behind me. Once inside, Daddy and Momma went in to speak with Aunt Elsie and we three ran up the steps to the 2nd floor. We went straight for the hallway closet. I reached for the doorknob. I paused. I turned and looked at my sisters.

"Well," I said staring into their excited faces, "is the Nancy Drew threesome ready?"

They each immediately nodded their heads with a yes and I slowly turned the handle.

As the door opened I could vaguely see the steps in the dark. There was a small stream of light coming from above, but it was not sufficient to light the way. All I could see in that skinny little stream of light were tiny speckles of dust floating around like I had just shook Momma's old rooster shaped salt shaker over my steaming hot ear of corn on the cob. I did love my salt and butter on my corn. But, getting back to the doorway, I slid my hand along the side of the wall hoping to come across a light switch. I did not feel one. From behind me, JoJo suggested instead of a wall switch, maybe it was on a pull string. I started to wave my hand in front of me and felt nothing.

JoJo said, "Higher! Come on Sabrina. Try to reach up higher."

I did as she suggested and sure enough, there it was within my reach. I grabbed it and yanked on it. A bright light sprung on, so bright it almost hurt my eyes, but it illuminated our path. There were five steps up, slightly smaller than normal stair steps and then a small landing. To the right and up three more steps and then there it was in all its dust-filled marvelous glory. Our room! I looked around in amazement but still saw lots of darkness in the corners. I saw there was another single bulb in the center of the room. I carefully walked around the obstacles on the floor and pulled the string. Again, it was a very bright light. Now we could see quite well everything in the room. I looked at my sisters. JoJo had the same excited expression as I did, but Holly looked like she wanted to cry.

I headed back to my sisters and grabbed Holly by the shoulders and said, "I promise you Holly, I will do most of the work. It won't take long and it will be wonderful, I mean absolutely spectacular when we are done. I promise."

She had tears welled up in her eyes. JoJo put her arm around her and said, "Holly don't worry. You know how crazy and determined Sabrina is when it comes to her ideas. I do believe she will make this room great. I will help her. How about you, can we count on your help too?"

Holly's little watery eyes searched the room from one side then to the other. She studied the different mounds of old stacked boxes, the zipped garment bags hanging on the two different racks, the dust-covered mousetraps in the corners, and two old travel trunks with rusted looking locks.

With her eyes teary and her little lip trembling, she said softly, "How can we fix this?"

We both chimed in with bubbly enthusiasm repeating our thoughts and promises until Holly finally said, "OK....I guess I am in. I have no place else to go unless I want to share a room with Davey or sleep in our new library." And then, she even grinned a little which made both JoJo and I feel better.

Holly and JoJo were still hugging each other when they suddenly heard a loud banging sound. They turned and saw me almost jumping down the stair steps.

I yelled back to them as I headed down the stairs and through the house. "Time to get started. I'll be right back."

In a flash, I was out to the truck grabbing the cleaning supplies I brought and ready to zip back up the steps and begin. I remembered what Momma had said about Aunt Elsie not being used to children in her house….and I made myself walk back into the house. Mr. Mertz gave me a quick look as I started up the stairs. I looked his direction and said a quick, "Sorry….no time for a back rub today Mr. Mertz. I have things to do!"

All three of us dug in and started. Holly grabbed a broom and started sweeping in the far corner. JoJo took the dustpan over and was peeking through the garment rack while waiting for Holly to form a pile to scoop up into one of the boxes I brought over to her.

I, on other hand, headed over to the other side of the room; the northwest side. I just stood and looked around at the wooden walls and the wood slats on the floor. I was trying to picture the changes that we could do in this huge space. I pictured our beds with three different but colorful quilts. We could each take a corner and have our own little library in the 4th corner. The room was massive with its high pitch in the center and then the low sides all the way around the room. We had six small windows, one on each of the north and south walls. They were the standard size and usual placement. Then there were four smaller windows, two on each the east and west walls, that were low to the point of touching the base of the flooring.

I was still excited beyond belief! I was looking around and realizing this was all ours. This was about the Coolest Beans ever! We could create our totally own space with different paints, decorate it however we wished and place our furniture wherever we wanted. I was scanning my eyes across the west side wall when I caught a movement. I went closer to the window. It was him. It was that Tram guy. There he was again in Ms. Winters' backyard. He was walking with his head down. What in the heck was he always looking for in the wild garden?

I moved closer to the small window. I actually laid down on the dusty, dirty floor and put my face right up to the glass. The glass was dirty with more than just dust. It had patches of grime on it that was pretty heavy, cobwebs and more than 1 petrified spider. It was hard to see, almost like I was looking through a puzzle. I couldn't get a really good look so I couldn't tell what he was doing. His head was still down, so I assumed once again, that he was looking for something. I told the other girls to come look.

JoJo came running over and said, "Oh yuck. He is gross looking."

Holly was still sweeping and ignored our comments. JoJo egged her on.

"Holly," she said, "come see him. He reminds me of a troll. Remember that story we used to read about the troll and the goats. That is what he is, he's a troll."

I said, "Dad said he is just an old man. His name is Tram."

"Tram!" said JoJo, "What kind of a name is that? Isn't a tram a trolley car?"

"Yes it is....and I don't know if that is his real name," I said, being the oldest and maybe the wisest, "Maybe his name is really something like; Tramble, Tramson, Trambert or maybe Bertram. Isn't that a name?"

"Sure, Bertram, that's what it is" said Holly. "I have heard of that! And I think," she continued, "that Daddy is right. He looks like a nice old man to me."

JoJo and I just looked at each other. How could she think that? He is creepy #1 in my book. Oh well, back to work.

I started to move some of the smaller boxes over to the corner. Most were dusty and the cardboard was rumpled looking. The box lids had long ago been folded inward so they were never closed properly. I figured most of the stuff inside was probably a yucky mess. I lifted a corner and tried to peek inside. The corner was too dark. That light in the center of the room was good and bright, but with the way the roof sloped downward in all four corners of the room, I just didn't have enough light. I would have to fix that by putting a small stand in the corner with a table lamp. But for now, I needed to head back under the light. I moved toward the center carrying the box. Now that I could see, as I lifted the lid, I saw it was filled with books. Right on the top was a small book called *The English Poets* by Lord David Cecil. I noticed a musty smell as I ruffled through the pages. I was kind of worried about sticking my hand back in the box, maybe there were live spiders or bugs in there! I touched the next book and I saw under that was an old

33

sewing pattern. It was for a dress. It showed 2 views of a dress with short sleeves, a round neckline, a very small tight fitted waist and a full skirt. Printed on the top corner was size 6. Under that there was another pattern, again size 6 and it showed a full apron and a half apron.

Under the patterns I saw a spiral notebook. Looking deeper, I saw not just one… I saw there are about five or six of them! As I flipped through the first one, I saw it was filled with hand written pages, lots of pages. I grabbed the next one and it was the same, so was the next one. I went back to the first one and looked better at page one. Right at the top of the page was written, Oct. 11th 1951. Knowing the date that it was written was very cool. Imagine that! 1951 was forever ago. I tried to think fast…it was 16, well, almost 17 years ago. The pages were crisp and ancient feeling, and luckily, the person wrote in ink and not pencil. If it had been pencil, I bet I wouldn't have even been able to read it. Pencil marks start to look smeary when they have been on a paper for a long time. The ink was clear and I could see now that the handwriting was very neat and smooth, almost like a river flowing. I figured the person who wrote this must have really paid good attention when learning to write cursive letters. And then I thought I should try harder next year to write like this too. My papers always looked pretty sloppy. And I usually got a C on my report card in Handwriting. Daddy and Momma would like to see that be a B, but if it would be an A they would be crazy happy.

I get back to actually trying to read the notebook. I read the first line and my eyes freeze. I read it again. I slowly look up and stare across the room at my sisters. I know who wrote this. I immediately know whose book I am reading. I look again. It says:

Today is my first day in the house when I realize I am truly alone. My Otto is really gone and my heart is broken. I shall never forgive Mitzi, not ever.

Oh my….. I instinctively close the book very carefully. I sit very still for a minute, feeling like I am about to be caught stealing or something. Why do I feel like a criminal? It is silly. I reopen the notebook. I flip through some pages, and read a word or two on each. This is Great Aunt Elsie's journal. I mean, it is like her diary. I have found a box of her life.

I know immediately I should put these notebooks all back in the box and let Momma and Daddy know I found them, but I just can't. I want to read them. I know that sounds bad. But I do. I want to read about her life. I mean she is really old. It would be so cool to read about how things were 17 years ago. It would be like a history lesson. I want to know things about her, to know about all the things she can't remember to share with any of us now. It was wrong. I knew it was wrong, but I hid them.

I looked at the girls. They were not cleaning, but looking through the garment bags, unzipping and peeking inside each bag. I saw JoJo was already wearing some of the things. She had on a short red jacket with some sort of fuzzy looking fur around the collar and it was hanging off her shoulders. It was about five sizes too big for her! The good news was they were paying no attention to me. I put everything back in the box in just the order that I found them. I put the box back in the dark corner and look back at the girls but I see something new.

There in the open doorway I see Mr. Mertz. He wasn't there a minute ago, I know he wasn't but he is there now sitting very still and staring right at me. I wait for him to move, but he doesn't. I slowly move back toward the center of the room and his eyes follow me. I sit on the floor. He doesn't move. He doesn't look at my two giggling sisters; only at me.

Admittedly, this made me feel very weird. Is he really watching me? Does he know I did something I shouldn't have when I opened and read the journal? No! I was being silly. He is just a cat. But he is a cat that seems to watch my every move. The way he looks at me makes me think he is an old smarty cat and that he hasn't made up his mind whether to trust me or not to trust me. Does he feel the need to somehow protect Aunt Elsie? Does he think I am going to hurt her or does he know I might discover something that might upset her? Or does he think I can help? Does he sense that I am a future detective? Has he been waiting for someone to come to this house and help her? Oh I

35

wish he could talk. I wish he could just tell me all about Aunt Elsie and this old house but maybe the journals will tell me those things. But as for right now, this is creepy. I wish he would either help me or stop staring at me! He chooses to stare at me for another two minutes then he slowly gets up and starts tiptoeing down the steps.

I decided I was getting, what do they call it, paranoid? I told myself to snap out of it!

I jumped up to join my sisters. I pretended to laugh and giggle and "Oooo and Ahhh" along with them as they opened each dusty bag but my mind wasn't on these old coats and dresses, it was on those journals and Mr. Mertz. I move quietly to the landing and peek down the stairway. No one is there. No one like Mr. Mertz that is. I join back in with my sisters. I step into one of the flowered dresses with a full skirt and I twirl around and around making Holly laugh as she joins in with me. Both of my sisters are laughing. We are making good memories. This is definitely fun, but I still want to read the journals. I can't wait to learn about Aunt Elsie's life. Hopefully my little sisters will tire soon and head back downstairs. I need some alone time. I need to sit down and figure out how I can get some alone time to read. I might have to wait until we get moved in to really read. Luckily, I am more of a night-owl than either of my sisters and that may be my answer. I will need a flashlight. Then it will be under-the-covers, late night reading for me! I can't wait to get moved into this house. I just can't wait. The Nancy Drew in me is busting to get started.

SISTER JEANETTE

Chapter 4 - 1968

I had taken numerous bus rides over the past three years, but this one had to top the list as the most uncomfortable. I knew someone in my vocation should not complain about missing such luxuries as a soft seat, but the coils in this one must have broken many a trip ago. There were dull worn looking pieces of duct tape with frayed dirty edges stretched across the length of the seat in the shape of a big X. The floor under my feet seemed to have something sticky spread across it as though someone on a previous trip had spilled a sugary drink and it had eventually dried and stuck in all the tiny crevasses in the dark black flooring. The back of the seat immediately in front of me had tiny tears scattered throughout the material and a darkened line defining the top ridge of the seat. The air throughout the bus was pungent with rough, damp smelling sweat. And strangely enough, every once in a while, I could smell a faint scent of roses drifting in the air from the woman's overly applied perfume on the other side of the aisle. To top off all the other annoyances, there was a persistent haze of cigarette smoke that spread throughout the bus like a fog setting in on a rainy fall morning.

Yes, this was going to be a very long ride. The original information from the bus terminal said it would be a seven-hour trip with scheduled stops along the way to, of course, allow some passengers to depart at their specific destination and others to come aboard. At this point, I was three hours into my journey to the small community of Pinesdale. It was definitely not an ideal travel option, but one that was necessary when a church did not receive an abundant surplus in their weekly collection basket.

Actually, I was looking forward to my new assignment at St. Lucy's Catholic Church. I had been told it was a small town with a good size congregation. I would be living in the convent with two other nuns. Sister Charlotte, an older nun with a long history of teaching in the primary grades and Sister Bergan, who was a trained nurse and had served in the military prior to entering the order. It had been suggested due to my newness to the order and the fact that Sister Bergan was also fairly new, that both of us would learn a great deal from Sister Charlotte.

The ride continued, moving swiftly thru some areas and then dragging along much slower on the roads that were not in the best of conditions. The bus traveled through many towns with names that I did not recognize. I watched people climb aboard and search for seats as others grudgingly awoke, gathered their belongings and departed the bus. The stops grew tiresome and seemed to be very much out of the way of Pinesdale. There was plenty of time for reflecting when the stops were stretched with many miles between them and apparently from the landscape out my window, many farming communities. During those periods, I noticed most passengers slept with their heads dangling downward onto their chests or they simply sat and stared out the bus's filmy windows.

I could see the perfume woman was filling her time oblivious to her unusual surroundings and was totally absorbed into the book she was reading. I wondered about the book. I had noticed it when she boarded the bus. The title was *"Franny and Zooey,"* which I had heard or read something about but had not read myself. The woman had a lovely flowered handkerchief tucked in her hand and occasionally used it to dab her forehead and upper lip. She was wearing an aqua blue suit that looked very expensive. Her ensemble included a small matching pillbox hat. I thought to myself that this woman looked stunning but also very much out of place amongst the other passengers. Then I glanced down at myself and ran my hand across my worn solid black habit and thought

I probably looked even more out of place. A few people looked surprised as they passed by me searching for a seat. No one sat in the seat beside me. Some smiled as they passed and others made eye contact and then quickly looked away and continued toward the back of the bus. I wished Sam was here to fill the extra seat.

It was something that, although it had now been a couple of years, I had still not quite adjusted to; the averting eyes. My whole life, that is, life prior to entering the convent, I had always been that person who smiled and people smiled back. I was the only child of doting parents. I was the little girl that marched in the local parades with the Miss Sarah Jean Dance Studio, flipping cartwheels during one and twirling a shiny baton in the next. I was the high school cheerleader, band member and performer in the class plays. I was the girl who had a steady boyfriend in high school, a boyfriend that I loved with all my heart. A boyfriend that I hoped to have forever. A boyfriend who had strong convictions and felt after graduation that it was his duty to serve his country. A boyfriend that eagerly went to boot camp, served his country and bravely went to Vietnam. A boyfriend that did not come home.

Scott had been such an important person in my life. We had known each other through grade school, but it wasn't until our sophomore year that Scott became brave enough to no longer just hope at a distance.

It was fall and school had just started. It was football season and although he was one of the younger guys on the team, it looked like he would be getting some playing time on field. He finally felt he was able to calm himself and actually speak, not just as a friend but as someone with hopes of claiming a girlfriend. Unbeknownst to me, he had waited patiently throughout the day, waiting for the perfect time. He had coordinated it carefully in his mind. The plan was to try to catch me between classes, when he would be near the lockers exchanging books. He watched and finally I had come around the corner and headed down to my locker #174. He had approached quickly and tapped my shoulder. I remember I jumped. He quickly blurted out the words that were to invite me to the homecoming dance. I answered an empathetic yes before he had even a moment to stop sweating.

The dance had been an amazing night filled with glorious memories to savor. My parents had bought me a new brown plaid suit. It had a form fitted three-button jacket with a pleated skirt. I was allowed to schedule a hair appointment at The Last Curl. Stephanie was the best beautician in Landsten and had worked her magic. My long blonde hair had been taken and turned into an awesome up do, full of soft curls placed ever so gently around the crown of my head with about 1 million bobby pins holding them in place. My parents had told me I was going to be the prettiest girl of the evening. They took me to the school in time for the game to begin. Scott had been correct. He did play for quite a bit of the game that evening, but my mind was elsewhere. I could not wait for the game to finish and the dance to begin.

When the final buzzer blared, there were cheers all around. Landsten had won. I looked at the scoreboard and it read 28 – 21. Then I had looked at the field and the players were all huddled around the bench with the coach talking to them. I had searched the heads in the huddle looking for Scott and suddenly, I saw him. He was there in the back. He was not looking at the team or the coach. He was staring at me. I felt a rush go through me like I was being struck by lightning. It was a feeling that I knew I would never forget. And I never have. Remembering that night, I can feel the warmth of that bolt right now.

The night of homecoming was followed by nights at the library, nights at the Sweet Shoppe and nights with long walks. We fell in love quickly and deeply. In the years that followed, we were together as much as possible. Junior year came and went all too quickly. As our senior year came, classmates started making plans. Scott had his version of what would follow over the next few years, but it was very different from my vision. I worried, but my mother reminded me to trust in myself and in the Lord. She had said I should pray for guidance. I knew she was right, so that is exactly what I did.

Soon it was time for graduation. It was time to make those important future plans. What was it to be for each of us? I had been unsure of what I wanted from life, other than a life with Scott. It had always been so hard for me to realize the difference between us. I knew completely, with all my heart that I wanted to be with him. But, whether I wanted college or work was a complete mystery to me. I waited, but my prayers had not brought me an answer. I did know a couple of things for sure:

1. my parents had always envisioned me going to college and
2. Scott and I were meant to be together and that nothing would ever change that feeling.

It seemed to me that all 84 members of the Landsten graduating class of 1961 knew what their plans were after graduation, except me. Scott was so very sure. Since our sophomore year, he had repeated the same plans with every conversation when we talked about our future. Yes, we would marry, but he was always quick to say that things needed to happen in order. He was very firm about it. Before we would marry he would get his college degree. He wanted to be sure he could always provide for his family in the future. And before college, he felt a strong need to serve his country. He needed to be one of the strong and the brave just as his father had been so many years ago. He needed to commit to his country first and foremost. Then, after he served his time, he would attend college on his GI Bill and of course, then we would marry. Yes, those were his plans and his mind never strayed from them.

So, you see my dilemma. Everyone had a plan. Everyone was secure in exactly what they wanted to do after high school. I began to wonder about myself and my indecision. Why was I so unsettled? Was something wrong with me? Had I been lacking something in my life, something that didn't allow me to make choices? I hoped Sam would help guide me, but no whispers came to my ear.

My parents definitely wanted me to go to college. They made references of college from the early days of kindergarten and continued throughout my years of school. On any given summer vacation, if the road they traveled was ever in the vicinity of any college or university, the car followed a new path and an impromptu sightseeing tour took place. Over the years, many a college had been viewed, some more thoroughly than others, but all noted. Actually my father had kept a list and had marked the ones that were more favorable with a small star beside the name. As high school came along, he would often pull out the list he had compiled and make little comments about things he had recently read about one of the schools. Both of my parents had been giving me little hints and brochures throughout my entire senior year. They were not shy about insinuating that I should consider becoming a schoolteacher.

They had said, "It is a nice safe career with good benefits and summers off, what could be better?"

I thought if anything, a schoolteacher would be an okay profession, but my heart just wasn't in agreement. My parents blamed this indecision as Scotts' influence on me. I denied it of course, saying he had his own plans and they did not include limiting my choices. They listened, but I felt they had not ever changed their opinion. I guess it is always easier to blame the friends than to think your child has no dreams similar to your own. It was time to choose and let them breathe a little easier.

Finally, I opted to attend the small community college in the neighboring town. I was still unsure of what exactly I wanted to pursue, but I felt it would most likely be something that would allow me to work with children. So, my heart was not totally in it, but as September rolled around, I attended school. I settled on trying to get a degree in early education.

Feeling the freedom from school, rules and making important decisions, Scott and I knew we had until September to enjoy a glorious summer. The pressure was off. It was a carefree time and we took advantage of every minute. Don't get me wrong, we each had summer jobs. Scott worked for the city of Landsten. He spent most of his days mowing grass in the parks but also did other odd tasks, like trimming bushes and tree limbs as needed. I worked as a cashier at the Ben Franklin store in the plaza on Monroe Street. When there was no line of customers, I helped stock the shelves. It might sound boring, but my friend, Katherine also worked there and we had a lot of silly kind of fun together. The best part of both of our jobs was that we had our evenings free.

As mid-August rolled around, I started back into my panic mood. My worries returned. Summer had been perfect but too short. It was ending so fast, and I needed more time. In plain language: I was scared.

Scott had known all summer long that he would ship out for Boot Camp on September 5th. He was to be stationed at Parris Island in South Carolina. He was excited, actually excited. It was hard for me to realize that, but through many conversations over the summer, I came to accept it and see his excitement without feeling like he was abandoning me. I really did understand. He was following the path that he felt he must. If he swayed from that path, if he didn't follow things in the order in his head, then in his eyes, things would never be right.

One week passed, then two weeks passed, and now it was Labor Day and he would soon be gone.

We enjoyed the huge family picnic and as evening drew near, Scott said his good-byes and accepted his friends and relatives good wishes. Then he and I went for a long walk. We walked and talked about everything I could have imagined. We finally sat on the bench in the park. He reminded me of all of our dreams. He said I would never be far from his thoughts no matter what he was doing; climbing a rope, eating in the mess hall or lying in his bunk. My name would be constantly in his mind.

Then he reached into his pocket and pulled out a small silver jewelry box with a slightly smashed pink ribbon. The box was not the size of a ring box, more like a necklace or bracelet box. He handed it to me and asked me to open it. Inside was a small gold oval locket with a very fancy engraved "J" initial on the front. He said that the locket had belonged to his grandmother. I looked at him puzzled and he quickly pointed out that his grandmothers name was Jane. He reached for the locket and very gently opened it. Inside it, he had put a tiny picture of the two of us. It had been taken on our first date, the homecoming dance of our sophomore year. He told me that it had been the most precious night of his life because he had been with me. He said it was a night he would never forget and he wanted me to wear the locket until he came home. I cried as he hooked the latch at the back of my neck. I held the locket within my palm as he kissed me goodnight. Before we left, we repeated our promises to each other.

1. We would write letters constantly.
2. We would keep our pictures on us at all times.
3. We would say a prayer for each other every night.
4. And …no matter what happened, we would love each other until the day we died.

In the morning, he left. I was still crying as he waved good-bye. Now it was just me and Sam, my life-long friend. My friend who never judged me or expected anything more than for me to just be myself.

Each day, I lingered near the mailbox until I saw the postman walk up the sidewalk. Then I ran to meet him and anxiously shuffled through the days' mail, hoping to see my name on an envelope in Scotts' handwriting. His letters were wonderful. He shared everything about his new life in the military. I understood about his daily routine and all the rules he had to follow. He told me so much about other guys in his unit, I felt as though I knew each one of them.

After a very long 13 weeks, boot camp was completed, and Scott was able to come home for a few days, but just a few. His next orders were to report to Camp Pendleton in California. All I kept thinking was that California was very far away. Scott reminded me that he was happy for the assignment he received and felt lucky to be able to stay in the states. I did agree with that and he promised me he would be fine.

We talked about his time at camp and about how college was going for me. He saw his friends and relatives and I of course skipped a few classes and joined him at every gathering. Time went quickly and in what seemed like a blink of the eye, the days were done. Once again we were saying our good-byes and repeating our promises. I cried and he soothed. I was desperate to keep him close, but at the same time, I knew it was impossible.

Winter lasted a very long time. It seemed we might never see the trees turn green. Letters came in a regular pattern, at least three per week. My days were pretty routine. I studied and wrote letters. Most of my friends had gone away to college and the few that were here at the community college mostly had boyfriends in town. Those that did have fellas in the service were very dedicated to getting their courses completed, or were working and saving their money so a social life, even if I wanted one, was kind of out of the question. My parents tried to keep me busy on my down time, offering to paint my room or work on jigsaw puzzles.

Winter did finally pass and the signs of spring brought new hope. Soon, I would be on break from classes and hopefully, back to work at the Ben Franklin store. I wondered if Katherine would return this summer. She was away at Penn State studying American Literature. She had written a few times but never mentioned her summer plans. Sam was confident she would return.

Finally it was the end of May and classes were done. I had made it through my freshman year of college with a B average. Not too bad. My parents were happy and I was really looking forward to a break in my routine. I had written Katherine and good news for me, she was planning to return to Landsten for the summer break. I truly hoped we could both return to the store. I planned to stop in this week and ask about open positions.

Scott's letters continued to come without delay. He told me he had hopes of getting some time off soon and was planning a trip home. By soon, in military terms, he explained he was probably talking about August. I had to hold on until August. He said in the military some things happen very quickly and other things happen as though no one knows there was a plan for them to happen at all.

My summer days moved a little quicker with Katherine back home. She had broken up with her boyfriend in the early spring, so we were good company for each other. Time passed and finally August rolled around. Scott got approval for time away and was able to plan a quick trip home.

We had an amazing week together. I took the week off at the store and never left his side. We had a nice combination of quiet time for just us and family dinners and friends hanging out at local spots. The night before he was to return, he told me that he wanted me to be ready in case he had new news soon. He said there had been rumblings about possible orders for his unit to go overseas. He promised nothing was definite, so far it was truly all just rumors, but he wanted me to be prepared for the fact that it may happen.

And, it did. He was only back in California for 2 weeks, when the new orders came. His group was heading out to Vietnam. They were scheduled to leave on September 13th.

My heart felt broken. A fear like I had never felt before settled into my bones. Vietnam. It was such an unknown to me. How could Scott go there, a place I could not even imagine? A place where he wouldn't know the language or know who to trust. I just couldn't stand the thought of him being so very far away. Sam tried to console me, but I was distraught and not ready to listen.

During his time overseas, my life consisted of school, studying, writing letters and waiting for letters to arrive. There had been delays in the beginning and I panicked when I had received no word from Scott, but finally a letter arrived. Our connection was back in place but I soon found that there would be no predictable routine of arrival times of letters. Sometimes I would get nothing for a week, even two or three weeks and then I would get five letters all at once, each one showing the date written. I savored each letter and read them over and over to the point that I had memorized each line. I found comfort by placing the newest letter under my pillow and then as each new letter arrived, I would carefully place the previous letter into my special corsage box, where all Scott's letter were safely stored.

Time passed slowly, but it passed. School studies kept me busy followed by the same summer job and then school again. Letters continued and our future plans were always mentioned.

My nightmare started in August. I had gotten a letter, a very strange letter. One that was so foreign to me that if it were not for the recognizable handwriting, I might have guessed it was not written by Scott. His tone was different. He spoke more in anger than in love. I knew life was terribly hard there for him and my heart broke picturing him in unbearable situations.

> *You just don't know what it is like here. How can you even begin to say you understand? You can't understand. Unless you are here, living in filth like me, eating slop like me, you just can't pretend to know!*

I struggled to find a way to make sense of it all, but could not. Four days passed before the next letter arrived and seemed to have been written in that same vain.

> *Don't talk to me about what we will be doing in 3 years. Hell, I probably will never get out of here. Do you hear me? Forget me cause that is what I am doing, I am forgetting you. Go on with your goody two shoes life....do you hear me?*

I wrote back immediately and asked if he was alright? I was worried. I wrote and tried to ask him if something had happened? Sam reminded me of the horrors he might be seeing each and every day.

The letters that followed, never addressed my concerns. They described the violence he was witnessing. They explained his fears in one sentence and then his hatred in the next. This was not my Scott. I was frightened and there was nothing I could do about it. There was no way to reach him. There was no one else that I could ask. I didn't feel I could talk to my parents or to his parents. I felt so very alone.

I was so alone, except for Sam. I could always count on Sam, my dear sweet friend. A lifelong friend that I knew would always be by my side. I was blessed to have Sam in my life.

As each letter came, I hoped and prayed to open it and read something that made me feel like my old Scott was still there. I wanted so badly to hear him say he loved me. I wanted so desperately for him to come home so I could feel his touch against my cheek, his lips pressed against my lips.

I worried. I cried.

Then the letters stopped coming.

There were no violent letters.

There were no sweet spoken letters.

Everything just stopped. Even Sam grew very quiet.

Two weeks later, word came of Scott's death and my life stopped.

MITZI

Chapter 5 - 1968

It seemed like it was going to be a nice day. I had awoken early but the sun was already shining as I looked out my bathroom window. As I scanned the view of my garden, I could see I had some work to do and decided it would be best to get out there early before the sun got to its hottest time of the day. I thought to myself; maybe I could get Lina to help today. I was getting worried about her. She seemed to be in some sort of a slump lately, not wanting to participate in any of my daily activities. She was in tune only to her own little world and I didn't like it at all. As I peered further toward the window, I noticed also that there is no activity yet over at Elsie Becker's' house. I would have thought those children would already be up and scurrying around her house by this time of morning. I did see a big dog, a collie I think, resting on the back porch curled up against the screen door, shaded from the sun. My goodness, I wonder how Elsie stands it over there with all those children and pets underfoot. I guess it is a blessing at this point that Elsie's mind isn't working as it should that way she is hopefully oblivious to some of the commotion that surely is taking place inside her home.

I finished fussing over myself and headed downstairs. I went as I do every morning, straight to the kitchen. I made coffee, enough for both myself and Lina without our favorite brand, Maxwell House Drip. I must remember to get to the grocery today. I hate when we have to rely on our backup store brand, but mother taught us well to never be without coffee of some sort in the house.

Mother was good at keeping a well-stocked kitchen. Mother was good at lots of things. Possibly it was just that notion that had something to do with Lina and me never marrying and having our own children. Too many expectations to try to live up too. She and father were both perfectionists. This made our life as their children very hard. Of the three of us children, I imagine it was the hardest on our brother Henry Jr. Our father was not only a perfectionist, he was also a successful businessman and well-respected in the community. Henry Jr, as a young child, didn't try worth a rat's tail to please father and follow the rules. When he became an adult, well actually even as an adult, I think he only pretended to follow the righteous path but was much happier when he was living on the dangerous side.

How many times as a child did I remember father sitting Henry Jr down on the sofa after an embarrassing church service and telling him that he cannot continue to misbehave anytime but especially when out in public and extra especially during church service. He gave that same speech week after week. It began with him saying how we were a respected family in Pinesdale and others looked to us to set the example and being ornery was just not going to be accepted. It ended most often with a spanking. Lina and I would listen from around the corner, hiding from father's sight but staying close enough to see our brothers' face. Henry Jr. never showed any fear or dismay during his spankings. He made sure to walk away from the ordeal with his head held high and no tears in his eye.

We would watch father stare at him as he exited fathers' study and head up the stairs to his bedroom to finish his punishment. Our father always looked more distraught than Henry Jr. He often sat with his hands on his head and his head hanging downward after such spanking episodes. When he would finally rise, he would go over to his bookshelf, stare at a few titles and then bang his fist against the shelf. Eventually, he would straighten up, tuck his loosened shirt back into his pants and walk out and into the kitchen to speak with mother.

At that point, Lina and I knew it was safe to come out from our hiding place and scamper off into the parlor. It would be a spell before

Henry Jr was permitted to rejoin the family and when he did he acted as though nothing had taken place. Yes, our brother was tough from the beginning and that never did change. He was still that tough young man when he departed this earth in 1951. That was a sad day for Lina and I, yes a sad day indeed.

Lina and I were definitely different. We used to wonder as a child if we truly were all three children from our same parents. Henry Jr was so different from us, not in our looks. Dear no, not in looks. We all three looked similar. There was definitely a family resemblance between us, but by personalities, there was a major difference. Lina was soft-spoken and very artistic. Our father used to say Lina was just like his youngest sister, Olivia. Olivia had died at age 18 of the influenza. She had been a very shy young woman but father said she had quite a flare with her colorful paintings and musical abilities on the piano.

I resembled my mother with our hair coloring being the same. We looked so much alike that when I was in my late twenties, when I would be walking down the street or in the aisle of the grocery store often someone would yell hello to not Miriam or Mitzi as they call me, but hello to Pauline. I would turn and their faces would redden with embarrassment as they quickly corrected themselves. I never minded. I always thought our mother was a lovely woman and our physical shapes were very similar. Personality wise, I think we were different. Mother was very prim and proper and I had always been a tiny bit more fun loving.

Lina and I both loved our father dearly and would have been shaking in our shoes if we thought we were about to get a spanking. Thank goodness it only happened to me once when I was quite young. I was determined then and there to not get myself in a situation where that would have a chance to happen again. I don't believe Lina ever got a spanking, not even one.

It wasn't that we were so sheltered, it was just that we knew how to behave. Knowing that was one thing but not being able to stop being hit and abused by Henry Jr was a whole other story. He was terrible to both of us. I would like to think he was jealous of the attention mother and father gave to us girls but it was more than that. It all boiled down to this: Henry Jr had a mean streak in him and anyone in his path got to feel his wrath. Unfortunately, Lina and I were his main targets.

You often hear people say that it is "odd the things you remember from your childhood." Well when your childhood was like Lina and I's, I think it is pretty easy to realize why we remember the things we do. It is because they were brutal memories. We spent moments of everyday terrified of what our brother might be about to do to us.

Henry Jr was mean. Just plain mean. The kind of mean that was beyond pulling hair or pinching arms. He was more into tactics that caused longer lasting pain. Any chance he had he would trip us by sticking his foot in front of us or flinging a toy across the room so that it hit us while in mid-flight. He did the kind of damage that caused bruises and wasn't beyond causing mental pain too. He was more than mean, actually the better word was evil.

And every time; I mean every time an act of violence was witnessed by mother or father, he suffered a whipping from father. But that boy took every spanking as if he felt no pain. I often wonder if he really did feel pain or if his body felt no abuse. As a young boy and even later as a very young man, his bottom felt the wrath of fathers' hand and more than a few times father's belt but he continued to follow the wrong path whenever the opportunity arose. Stubborn and evil, yes those were both good words to describe our brother.

Life was very different for him than for Lina and I. We were listeners. Always were and still are to this day even as old as we are. I mean Lina is now sixty-one years old and I don't think she has ever broken a rule or spoken a mean word in her life. She is not simple but she stays very much to herself. She has always had that special artist touch and in times of trouble or worries, she turns to her art. She has been known to spend the best part of the day absorbed in her art studio painting, well just painting anything and everything. She says she never knows in advance which direction her art will take her, she just begins and follows its lead. I have always respected my little sister for her diligence. She never gave up on painting. It is her passion. She starts and simply continues to paint and repaint over some areas until it turns into something in which she is proud to sign her name. She is such a delicate person, maybe Olivia was also, but her quietness I am sorry to say made her even more of a target for Henry Jr. His punishing ways to her, with her being the youngest sibling, bordered criminal. Father tried his best to control him and protect us from Henry Jr, but it wasn't possible for father to be at our sides at all times.

It shames me to this day to think of the things he did to us. Although I was a year older than him, he was much stronger than myself and much stronger than Lina who was two years younger than him and had such a small bodily frame. Many a day, we would be outside playing in the garden and he would pull Lina toward the big garage with her screaming and thrashing to break free. I would run to get help but when help did arrive, they would find that he had her down on the garage floor, sitting atop of her stomach and holding her arms tight against the cold dirt floor. She would be screaming and he would be laughing as if he had not a care in the world.

He was smart enough to not instigate such acts when father was home so these types of attacks happened during our outdoor play times. Momma was usually slow to arrive, but Lina and I could always count on our neighbor, Tram Keller to hurry in and help. He would run up and start kicking and pushing at Henry Jr until he finally rolled off Lina. As Lina lay shaken and wiping tears from her cheeks, Henry Jr would jump up and start swinging his fists at Tram.

Bertram or Tram as we neighborhood kids called him was slightly shorter than Henry Jr but had never showed the least bit of fear in any situation that Henry caused at our house or anywhere in the neighborhood. He lived down the alley from us and was the oldest of 4 children of Bertram and Sylvia Keller. He was the only boy having three younger sisters, Jane and twins, Margaret and Mary.

But childhood history aside, it is just Lina and I now. We had an older sister Gretel. She was the first born child of our parents in 1902 but unfortunately she only lived to be 4 years old. She died after contracting typhoid fever in the fall of 1906. In those days, there was no proven medicines to give and many died. Our family was not the only one to suffer with this terrible disease. I was only two when she passed and have no recollection of her. There was only one photo taken that included Gretel. It was a family photo dated 1906. It includes our parents. Mother was holding Henry Jr as an infant, father was holding myself and standing in the front of everyone is little Gretel at age three with a shy smile on her face. On the back of the photo is written: The Henry Winter family: Henry holding Miriam age one, Pauline holding Henry Jr age three months and Gretel in front, age three.

We lost our brother Henry Jr in 1951 to a terrible tragedy. It is too sad to talk about so I will leave it that he passed away on a beautiful October Indian summer day when the leaves were just beginning to change into their beautiful shades of oranges, reds and yellows and the sun was setting against a pink and blue sky.

Yes, Lina and I found our way into adulthood and each took a very different path. Lina remained dedicated to her art and survived financially with a few stores in the bigger municipalities that offered to handle her work and keep a small commission when a client purchased a painting. She also has the trust that father left her and she has always lived with me here in the family home.

I on the other hand, accepted employment thru the Bell Telephone Company right out of high school. Being a girl, the opportunity to attend a college was never a consideration. As a female, my choices were made very simple for me. I, like every other girl in my class had two choices: chose to get a job or chose to get married. Many of my fellow female classmates graduated in May and by the end of June they were married. I wanted no part of getting married, so I got a job. Those were different times back in 1922 and the world has been slowly changing. There is now a movement called, "Women's Lib" that is in the process of changing or should I say demanding women have more rights in this world. It is all good, but it missed my youthful years and I was very limited to any type of real growth in the workplace. I am not complaining. Please do not see it that way. I was always very thankful that I joined a solid and profitable company right out of high school. I spent many years with Ohio Bell and I made many friends. It was a good job for the time, but I must say I am enjoying my retirement immensely.

Henry Jr was a different story. He was a young man. He had no choice in the matter. He was either to attend college or join the Armed Forces. He chose college and then did quite well in his business life, but poorly in his personal life and as I said earlier, he died in 1951. It was a tragedy and I don't like to even think about it. Lina and I never talk about it.

Back to me. Yes, I enjoyed my job with Bell Telephone Company. I was a telephone operator and I was a good one. No eavesdropping for me as I poked cords into a slew of different options on my switchboard. I did my job and transferred calls for 8 hours every day, 5 days a week for 42 years. There is no way of knowing for sure, because I did not eavesdrop, but some of my calls may have been major business dealings. It is hard to imagine how many very important people heard my voice say, "What City please?" during my many dedicated years. I just know I have now been retired for 4 years and life in retirement is good.

But, back to getting that coffee brewing. Lina will be downstairs shortly. If I want to try to recruit her help in the garden, I should offer her up a good hearty breakfast. Maybe some nice waffles today topped with some of Nell Taylors' raspberry preserves. Yes, that should do it. I hear her in the bathroom. I had better start mixing the batter.

MITZI

Chapter 6 - 1968

I had been right. The yummy breakfast I prepared for Lina seemed to have worked wonders on her. Truthfully I think it was Nell's strawberry preserves that pushed her over the edge. As we were clearing the breakfast dishes, and before I had the chance to even ask for her help, Lina willingly offered to help me in the garden. I made quite a fuss about being tickled to have an extra set of hands and about how much I hated to see the flowerbeds and the garden not looking their best lately. I suggested we begin right away so that we could get a lot accomplished before the sun peaked and roasted our old weary bones. Lina laughed and then went out to the back porch to gather her gardening gloves. I did the same and grabbed my straw hat and offered her the extra one which she took and placed atop her fair hair. Lina had not yet started to gray whereas I had quite a bit covering my head.

I kicked off my in-house shoes and put on my old dingy penny loafers that I have had for about 20 years and we headed out the back door. I was right, the morning air was still nice and cool. It was early enough that even the children were not outdoors yet so the only noise in the neighborhood was coming from a few of the neighborhood dogs as they scoured the alley looking for a stray cat to chase.

I told Lina we should probably start with the flower beds and then plan to work on the taller greenery along the trellis when our legs get too tired to bend. She laughed but agreed. We decided to start on the bed with the bright-colored Rudbeckia or as most folks call them, Brown-Eyed Susan's against the house; petunias in the middle and Myosotis, commonly referred to as Forget-Me-Nots, which is actually the name I prefer to call them, which lined the outer edge with teeny-tiny colonial blue blossoms. It is actually a very pretty flower bed; well-spaced and full of vibrant colors and I am very proud of it. I love looking at it and really wish we hadn't chosen for it to be on this east side of the house. It isn't the location. The amount of sun is perfect. It is the fact that this lovely flower bed faces the Becker house.

Elsie and I had never been the best of friends, just cordial and neighborly as is common courtesy. All of that politeness ended many years ago. In the beginning it was extremely difficult to see each other face-to-face; but many years have passed now and Elsie rarely comes out of her house. So, I sense the tension and probably always will but I don't have to deal with it openly anymore.

As Lina and I walk around the corner with our weed buckets in one hand and our trowels in the other I looked toward Elsie's window and hope I don't see a glimpse of her face through the window. So many times I look and she is there. This is starting out to be such a nice day that I just hope I don't see her staring back at me. I take a quick peek and I don't see her. I only see that old cat of hers and he appears to be asleep on the window sill. Yes, it is a glorious day.

Lina and I work quickly and pinch off the dead buds and pull out the scattered weeds we see popping through the ground. We tried so hard when we created this bed a few years ago to get every last weed out of the earth in the hopes of stopping future over-population of specific unwanted weeds; but alas it did not work.

I realize now that we have spent a good bit of time on this side of the house. I stand up to give my knees a break from routine. I lift my hat to give my sweaty hair a quick shake out. My eyes inadvertently glance toward Elsie's window and there she is staring in my direction. My initial response is to quickly turn away, as I have done for the past almost seventeen years, but today I will not look away. Today I decide to look right at her and nod my head in acknowledgement. I do. There is no reaction from her. She just continues to stare at me. The old cat appears to be sitting on her lap because I can only see his face and strange as this sounds, he is staring at me too.

She hates me. This is not a new discovery; this is a fact. I thought with time she would soften; I thought she would get tired of being angry and irrational; but she has not forgotten.

I have heard some bits and pieces from others in the neighborhood that has suggested that Elsie Becker is suffering from hardening of the arteries. I would imagine it could be true. Elsie is not a young woman like myself. She is at least twenty years my senior. I would guess her to be about eighty-five years old now. And unlike myself who was born into one of the elite families of the community, Elsie married into one. The Becker family had a long history of one of the finest families in Pinesdale. As my father always said it; "They were a pillar of the community." Yes, that was the phrase he always used when he spoke of that circle of families. The Becker family most certainly held a strong spot in that circle. And of course, my heritage, the Winter family was right up there with them.

Yes, in the 1940's, Otto and Elsie practically led the social circle in Pinesdale. They were at every dance, carnival, street fair, and sporting event. They held a chair on every committee; Otto on the business side such as town council; Knights of Columbus and Shriners. Elsie stayed very active with library directors meetings, church committees, and numerous women's club functions. Outside of Pinesdale, they traveled and held positions in groups of importance within the state. Yes, the 1940's were definitely Elsie and Otto's heyday. Once Otto passed away, everything changed and Elsie became practically a recluse. Many tried to reach out to her and she would accept guests at her home; I should clarify that to say, she would accept some guests at her home. I was not one of those people. I was never welcome.

From the day Otto died, she turned against me. I became her target of misery. I don't know why and I tried numerous times to talk with her about it in the beginning, but she would hear nothing from me. And one might say, she was a grieving widow and I should have respected her privacy and had sympathy for her loss. I should have given her time and space to allow healing to begin, and that may be true, but what about me. I also had just suffered a terrible blow. My only brother Henry had also just died. Where was her sympathy for me? I never was shown any sympathy from Elsie Becker. But I made allowance for that. I mean Henry died on Thursday evening and Otto Becker died the very next day. So strange two neighbors dying a day apart like that. Yes, it was very bizarre and more than one person in Pinesdale pointed that out to me.

But 1951 was a very long time ago for goodness sake. It is now 1968. Time to move on. But if what the neighbors have shared is true, maybe Elsie doesn't even realize it is 1968. Maybe in her mind it is still 1951 and she is still dwelling on Otto. On Otto's fall from that ladder. I shudder when I remember back to that day. That awful look on his face as he began to fall. I had hoped that someday, I would no longer remember that look; that I could somehow block it from my eyes, my head, and my thoughts. But alas, I much as I have tried over the years I have never accomplished that feat. It is all as plain now as the day it happened.

But, maybe things have changed for Elsie. If her mind isn't working right, then maybe she has forgotten.

Her former housekeeper, Miss Eulalie had always been very loyal to Elsie and although I would try to speak to her and ask about Elsie when I would see her at the grocery store or picking up items from her list at the drug store, Miss Eulalie would never say a word of a real answer about Elsie. All she ever offered were general statements in return to my concerns like; "She is just fine and I will tell her you said hello."

One day a few years ago, as Miss Eulalie was leaving at the end of the day, I approached her in the yard and asked if it was true that Elsie was losing her memory. It was a Tuesday evening and it was that time of day when it was almost dark, I guess I should just say it was dusk. I had just returned from a library committee meeting and saw her ready to get into her car. At first I just started to raise my hand from across the yard to say hello, but quickly changed my mind and instead started to walk in Eulalie's direction.

At first she did not realize I was coming her direction. She had already raised her hand in a slight hello type wave and had continued walking toward her car with her head downward. I continued across the yard and again yelled, "Hello Eulalie, can I talk with you for a minute?"

Eulalie reacted with surprise but did stop walking. She was now staring at me as though I was a creature from another planet and she could not imagine what I possibly needed from her. Since she did stop, I continued toward her but did slow down the pace of my steps. I was now close enough that I knew even if her eyesight was poor she could see my face, so I smiled her direction. Her facial expression did not change. She still looked at me with strange eyes.

Finally I was almost next to her. "Hello Eulalie," I said trying my very best to come across as friendly and cordial. "I just wanted to say hello and ask how you have been lately. Lina and I see you every day as you come and go, but just never get the chance to say anything more than hello. How are you and your family?"

She looked at me with distrust showing on her face and replied. "We are all just fine, thank you for asking." With that she turned as though she was ready to walk away.

"Wait just a second Eulalie," I say as fast as I can, "I had a quick question."

She stopped again and turned back to face me. This time she appeared to be annoyed as she said, "Yes Miss Miriam....what is it."

I was admittedly not surprised by her reaction but I tried to cover my true feelings and just ask my question before she really did walk away.

"I am sorry if I am keeping you. I am sure you are more than ready to go home for the evening. I am just concerned about Elsie. I have heard from other neighbors that she is having some health difficulties lately and I wondered if there is anything I can do to help."

Eulalie had a hard time hiding her true feelings. She looked at me more skeptical this time.

"Now Miss Miriam," she began, "we both know that what you really want are some answers but you also know darn well that Miss Elsie is never going to allow you to help her with nothing! So, I think we are done here. Good Evening."

"Please wait Eulalie," I plead. "I know you are aware of Elsie's strong feeling against me but she is wrong. I harbor no ill feelings toward her. This all stems from a misunderstanding so many years ago that it should all be forgotten by now. So I want you to know....."

At this point Eulalie interrupts, "Now just a minute Miss Miriam, I DO NOT think what happened is anything that I would consider a small matter or a forgotten matter. Now, if you will please excuse me, I must be getting home. Good evening Miriam."

With that she turned, got into her car, started the engine and left without looking back. I stood there in Elsie's yard and watched her drive away. Then, knowing I had tried and failed, I walked back to my house and went in for the evening, but not without looking toward that window and seeing Elsie.... watching me.

So, that was about 4 years ago and now Eulalie no longer works there and instead David and Ginger Holden have moved into the house with all their children and pets, so I think it is safe to assume that the rumors I heard were all true and that Elsie is failing in health. I am thinking she has done well to still be alive and it is time for the old girl to have some health issues. Some have insinuated she pretty much lives in a wheelchair. I am not sure of that. All I ever see in the window is her face and shoulders. I am not sure if she is sitting in an easy chair or a wheelchair.

Just like today, I see her. She is there. She is watching, always watching. I know she hates me and there is nothing I can ever do to change that. I tried in the beginning, but I grew tired of trying. She would never listen to reason. She had decided what happened and nothing I could say or do made her think any differently. My confrontation with Eulalie a few years back was my final straw. She could think whatever she wanted and she could sit and stare out her window at me from now thru eternity. I wasn't going to care anymore. Elsie Becker and her thoughts were not my problem. She could think whatever she wanted, because no one believed her then and no one would believe her now.

Anyway, it was now time for Lina and myself to give our knees that break and move to the back yard and work on the taller greenery. So if Elsie wants to get a nasty glitch in her neck watching us work, go at it Elsie. And you too Mr. Mertz!

61

SISTER JEANETTE

Chapter 7 - 1953

Susan's carefree existence changed on her 10th birthday. I guess I should say the news that she received on this special day affected her, but truly did not change her in the drastic way one might expect.

Life had begun for Susan as it does for many children. The only child of Ben and Frances Collins, she was doted on, but not spoiled. She was kept busy with both educational and social endeavors. For her young age, her parents were forward thinking and gave her the opportunity to consider many social activities until she found something that suited her perfectly. She tried becoming a Brownie you know, the younger version of the Girl Scouts. She enjoyed having her little friends from school there at the meetings and felt very official when learning the pledge. The Brownies did all sorts of activities like learning how to follow a recipe to bake buttermilk biscuits, making a red and green construction paper looped Christmas chain and little sewing projects like sewing on buttons and cutting out material with a pattern and then loop stitching the edges together with bright colored yarn. They were all good things for a little girl from the small town of Landsten to know but for Susan, it just was not a whole lot of fun.

By 1952, the country had come through World War II and was in many ways growing strong and in other ways, still mending. There had been so very many lives lost; so much sadness and struggling waiting to return to normalcy. Neighbors helped neighbors. However, for this little nine-year-old girl and so many others, this was just the world they knew.

Susan's memories did not include any vision of how life was before the war only of life during and since the war. As a child, she accepted things just as she saw them. She somehow understood without being told a back-story. She did not totally understand the reasoning for things. She knew her friend Sherry had only a mom and two brothers, no father. Her neighbor, Mr. Hughes walked with a limp but he still went to work every day at the Gilmore Machine Shop and mowed his own yard every Saturday. Mrs. Hughes went to work every day too at the Electric Company. Susan somehow understood that her own mother did not need or want to work outside their home. The world had changed and was continuing to evolve in many different ways. And the simple truth was this; Susan was okay with anything it wanted to do. And so was her little friend Sam.

Susan was an obedient child. She never gave her parents any reason for concerns. She did well in school, was attentive in church and was finding her own path with outside activities, such as dance class. Dance was her favorite after school activity. She excelled in many of the classes at Miss Sarah Jeans' Dance Studio. Recognized throughout the county, Sarah Jean was the best dance teacher. Her yearly recitals were legendary. She herself had been in and won many of the talent shows in the area while in her prime. In 1936, she had been named queen at the Sharrot County Fair. She opened her studio that same year and had immediately gained many students. Susan would have taken every class she offered but, due to the expense, needed to limit her lessons to tap, gymnastics and of course, her very favorite, baton.

On Susan's 10th birthday, after a busy day of celebrating with a party that included her five best friends and then a quiet family dinner, her parents asked her to sit and listen to her birth story. Susan listened attentively. Their news definitely had an impact on her, but one that she was able to somehow understand and accept. She of course had some questions, but they were ready with answers that they had been anticipating sharing for the past 10 years. Ben and Frances had long ago decided that age 10 was the ideal age to explain the truth to Susan. They felt that at this age she was old enough to understand the events that were her life and to realize how very much they loved her. As they all sat calmly talking on their comfy pale green sofa with Susan sitting between them in her special blue party dress with the lacy white pinafore. They were pleased with her composure. One would think that her parents totally understood their child. It was as if from her infancy they had known exactly how she was going to turn out, how her mind would think and consider things, how at ease she would be in difficult situations. It was as if they had somehow been given the power to see the future.

Yes, Susan had been adopted. And yes, it happened many years ago. Before Susan, Ben and Frances worried about the day when they would be given a child and need to face these questions. They wanted to be prepared. There had been years of hoping and praying for a child, but nothing had happened. Finally, Frances chose to consult a doctor. The news she had been given was devastating. She was incapable of conceiving a child. Both she and Ben took the news very hard. After some of the initial heartache was behind them, they decided to explore other avenues. They traveled into New York City and followed up on some names of organizations they had heard about that handled private adoptions. They felt most comfortable with a smaller agency located in Brooklyn. They attended instructional sessions and learned about caring for an adopted child, answering questions for the child and their rights as adoptive parents. They listened attentively, filled a notebook with information and when the sessions were complete they felt they were definitely in the right place. They liked their instructor, Nicole, who then became their caseworker. They had no hesitation. They felt they were ready and knew exactly what they wanted.

Susan had heard the name Nicole and gave her mother a sharp look. Frances looked to Ben and they both smiled.

Frances spoke. "Yes Susan, that is right. Her name was Nicole. And yes you are right to presume that we encouraged you to choose the name Nicole for your confirmation name because we felt so strongly about our Nicole from the adoption agency helping to bring you into our lives. It was as though she was helping God find you and connecting all of us together. Do you see why we felt that way?"

Susan nodded her head just enough to let us know she understood and that she was thinking about everything we were saying.

"Good," Frances said. "Should we go on?"

Again Susan nodded.

She continued telling the story. "We did not have a desire for a big family. We would not be greedy. We only wanted a child, one child. They wanted the opportunity to have a child to love. Someone to raise, teach, watch and enjoy their existence. Someone to encourage to follow the right path and to do good things with their life."

With their classes done and their minds set, they completed all the necessary paperwork. It was October of 1942 and a time in the world when interracial families had not yet been accepted. Their request read as follows:

Ben and Frances Collins: Interested only in a confidential adoption - newborn Caucasian infant, no preference as to boy or girl. Not interested in multiple births.

Things did not happen overnight. They knew to expect an amount of time to pass before things would start into motion. Something that they would have never guessed prior to the classes but that they now totally understood was that there were waiting lists of people eager to adopt, not older children but infants. They had been made aware that if they were willing to consider a child under the age of five, the wait time would be moved up quite a bit, but their decision did not change. If they were to have only the experience of raising one child, they wanted that experience to cover as much time as that life could offer. They would wait for a newborn.

The wait was not easy, but they waited. They used the time to prepare the nursery, in quiet shades of yellows and greens. They bought small items like blankets, sleepers, bottles, diapers, a few little stuffed animals and toys that all were fitting for either sex. They also put themselves on a strict monthly budget so they could set money aside in preparation of the additional expenses a child could bring. Things like more food, doctor expenses, and Christmas and birthday gifts. They even started an additional bank account that they deemed to be a college fund for their future child. They found all of the planning and saving helped to build their patience and pass the time waiting for things to happen. They often sat in the evenings and talked about what it would be like when they got the call…. their special call. They dreamed about how their lives would change in that moment. The time passed slowly but their dreams never wavered. Finally, the wait was over. The call came and yes, just as they had expected their lives changed immediately.

It had been extra hot and humid day in Landsten on July 8, 1943. The weatherman was predicting a storm to roll in later in the evening, so Ben left the office an hour early in order to get home and mow the yard before dinner and the storm. When the yardwork was finished, he came in hot and sweaty and told Frances he would jump in for a quick shower before dinner. While he was in the shower and Frances was mashing the potatoes, the telephone rang. It was their call. It was Nicole from the adoption agency.

Nicole's news was amazing. A baby girl had just been delivered at Brooklyn Hospital and while it didn't look like it was going to be a perfect match for them, things had changed and well, now it was….if they wanted the baby. The mother had just signed the official paper to say the little girl was available for immediate adoption. She weighed 7 lb. 2 oz., had lots of dark hair and appeared to be in good health. If they chose to adopt her, they could come as soon as they wanted to see her for themselves, but the child would not be able to leave the hospital until it had been observed for any possible problems over the next 24 hours.

Frances heard the words and her immediate thought was….IF? Had she just really said, "If?" Frances could not get that word out of her head fast enough. There was no "if", they wanted her. She wanted this baby. She wanted this little girl more than anything. And even more importantly, she knew in her heart exactly how much THEY wanted this little girl.

She hung up the phone and practically screamed for Henry. By the time she reached the hallway, he came running toward her wrapped in a towel and dripping water on the carpet, but neither cared. She had been yelling as loud as she could, "We have a baby! We finally have a baby!"

They were overjoyed. They held each other for a few moments and then Ben ran to get dressed and ready to go into the city. She and Ben did not want to take time to eat their dinner, but they inhaled quickly and set out for the hospital. It was about a 90-minute drive and the predicted storm had arrived just as the weatherman predicted. The storm slowed them down, but they made it by 10 pm. They were able to stand at the nursery window and view the babies but had no idea which one was to be theirs. They were able to pick out all the girls by the pink coloring of the blankets. There were 17 tiny little hospital cradles lined up in three small rows. All Ben and Frances knew at this time of night was that eight of the 17 were girls and one of those girls belong to them. One of those precious little girls was their baby.

They told this story to Susan and she listened attentively. They paused periodically to give her a chance to ask questions, but she just listened and waited patiently for more of the story.

Ben told her that they never met her birth mother, but were told a little bit about her by their caseworker. She was not married. She worked in the city. She was a good person. Very basic information like that. Nicole had told them that the mother did not know the father very well and he was someone who she had never planned to marry. She wanted, as all parents want that give their child up for adoption, a chance for the child to have a better life with two loving parents.

Again, Ben stopped and waited for any questions. Once again, Susan sat quietly with her hands still folded and she had no questions. They told her about choosing her name, Susan Marie, Susan after Bens sister and Marie after Frances' grandmother. They told her about the joy they felt when they first held her and how proud they were to bring her home. They told her about the happiness she had brought them over the years. They felt they had covered enough for today.

They thought there would be more questions after she had heard the whole story and had a few minutes to absorb all the information, but that time never came. Susan seemed perfectly content with the story and perfectly content with her life. She said she and Sam both understood and could they please play now. Ben and Frances had looked at each other in amazement and said, "Yes of course."

The little imaginary person named Sam had developed quite early in Susan's life. It was apparent from very early on that someone else had Susan's attention. She seem to be communicating in some fashion with someone. You often hear of small children being able to see spirits in the room that adults would never dream possible. They wondered. Was Susan speaking to someone from their past, possibly Marie, Frances' grandmother who had passed in 1940? Maybe the neighbor, Mr. Green who had just died last summer? It was a mystery and one they never solved.

When she was a wee bit older and able to talk, it was very apparent she had developed an imaginary playmate. She would often be sitting on the flooring playing with blocks and would look up toward the couch and giggle. Or be rocking her baby doll and look questioning across in space and then hand the baby forward as if ready to take turns sharing her doll.

As she got a little older, around the age of five, it became certain that the pattern was to continue. Ben and Frances became concerned that maybe they should be seeking professional help. They did locate a counselor. After a long session with much interaction by all of them, the counselor said there was no need to worry. It was a common childhood situation and eventually Susan would just let go and allow Sam to quietly disappear without any fuss.

On her 10th birthday, Sam was still present and was one of her honored guests at her party, but Ben and Frances did not care. Today had been very special. It had been a day that Ben and Frances had anticipated for the past 10 years and now it was over. The talk was now history. Susan accepted it and their explanation without hesitation. They had worried for years that they may not be able to answer her questions successfully. They never imagined her easy-going reaction. No questions ever came and the word adoption was not a word mentioned in the Collins household thereafter.

SISTER JEANETTE

Chapter 8 - 1968

Eight years later, me, little Susan Marie, graduated from high school and started college. Two years later I suffered a broken heart when Scott, the love of my life, died. I knew then my life as I had envisioned it in my dreams …. was gone. Nothing again for Susan Marie would ever be the same. My life not only felt lost….it was lost. I was lost. It was as though I was trapped inside a big transparent bubble with no desire to escape. I lived each day in my bedroom. During the day my head was filled with self-pity, my eyes with tears; during the nights my dreams were filled with Scott.

My parents tried to help. They kept telling me that "in time" I would feel better. "In time" my life would return to normal. "In time" I would feel like me again. They were very patient with me. They gave me "time." I knew I had to snap out of it and a change had to happen. I knew…. I had to return to life. And finally, one day I did. It had been a slow process and there had been no one thing that occurred that brought about the change. It was just as my parents had said; it just took time.

I finally woke up one day and felt a little more like myself, my old self. I didn't know a lot but I did know I could not just pick up my life where I left off. My world had changed and as I tried my best to move forward, I was wise enough to know I needed to create a new plan. I needed a new purpose. I needed a new focus. My heart had broken, my dreams had died and now my head had to seek out what my life could still manage.

Yes, I knew that a change was in order but what that change was to be was the hard part to figure out, but it was so necessary. I had returned to the real world, but still needed to find my new path. It took some time. I actually pondered for months. Unfortunately, even though I truly tried and spent many very quiet days sitting alone with my thoughts, my thoughts were still not focused. During this period of time, my parents suggested I consider some counseling sessions and I agreed. I knew I needed someone to help me sort out my thoughts and help me go forward.

In the end, the counseling was a blessing, but it had a rough start. I went to the Union Park Counseling Center. My counselor was an older gentleman named Lewis. He suggested I just start by talking about myself, and my life in general. As I talked he listened and occasionally he scribbled little notes on his yellow tablet. He very seldom looked my direction and when it came down to it, I just didn't feel comfortable with Lewis. Maybe it was my imagination but he seemed truly uninterested. I was brave enough to speak my mind at the end of the session. I explained how I felt and asked if I was able to request a different counselor for my next session.

To my surprise, he was very nice about my request. He even suggested a specific counselor and said he thought she would be a perfect match for me. I scheduled my session for the next week and realizing that this session had not helped me feel better at all, I prayed I would feel different after my next session.

The next week, I bravely walked in to meet my new counselor. Her name was Christine. She was a tall slender woman with blonde hair pulled into a loose ponytail and she had a warm smile. She shook my hand and I immediately knew this time was going to be perfect. She took a few minutes to tell me about herself. She was young, 29 and single. She too had experienced great pain early in her life with her own mothers passing when she was merely twelve, so she understood my pain. This time, the session went well and I felt a weight already lifting by the end of the hour.

I met with Christine twice a week for three months. We talked about everything under the sun and of course, eventually each conversation lead back to the root of my problem: what did I want from life and where should I search to find it? Through it all, she offered questions, but left the answers up to me to find. I left Christine's care feeling better about myself and knowing that I was strong enough to now move forward. My life was still important. I knew I had time on my side, some talents to rely on and now a new confidence. The decision was mine to make and I felt I might have already found my path.

I took more alone time and did finally figure out what I wanted to do and what needed to happen to make it possible. During this long process of continued self-reflection, I used what I had learned in counseling. I found the solitude I had endured over the past months had brought a peacefulness to me that was appealing. I also found that while I questioned my faith when I first got the news of Scotts' death, I now found that my faith was even more important in my life.

It was time for me to become a new and improved person. If Susan Maries' old life was over, then Susan Marie needed a new life. I was now someone that wanted a fresh start. I was now someone that wanted a reason to go forward. I was now someone that had a calling to not only help me but to help the world.

I had known it for quite a while. I think it had been in the back of my mind for a very long time. My new goal, my new focus, came to me very clearly one Sunday evening as I sat with my parents watching *"The Ed Sullivan Show"* and I had a strong urge to share my news with them. Truly, I am not sure why that particular Sunday evening it had suddenly become so important to burst out my news to my parents, but for whatever reason... it was and I did.

Surprisingly to me, I do not think they were shocked. I almost think they knew it already. I had chosen to enter the convent and I was ready to begin right now.

My parents had a firm belief in our Catholic faith and had always been very active in the church. I had attended catholic school through the eighth grade. The nearest catholic high school was almost an hour away, so I instead attended Landsten High School and I will never regret that part of my life. While the news did not shock my parents, they did as I would suspect all parents would do under the circumstances. They tried to offer thoughts about my expectations. It was a very big step, a big leap of faith as they say and they wanted to make sure I had considered every aspect of how my life would change.

I had given up a good deal of time wallowing in grief then coming to terms through counseling and finally through self-reflection I had chosen my path. I think it was time well spent.

So, within the next three weeks, things happened very quickly and I was soon off to begin my new life.

Through my studies at the convent I was able to come to terms with another loss. The person I was, Susan Marie, needed to understand it was time to end a very special part of my existence. I had to say good-bye to a dear old friend. A friend that I had felt had been with me since birth and had never left my side. A friend that had meant more to me than I could ever explain, even to those that loved me dearly. A friend that had given me strength and helped me never feel alone. It was time to say goodbye to that friend. It was time to say good-bye to Sam. My Sam. Never able to be seen, but always felt within my heart.

That remarkable little imaginary friend that had been so real to me that I could almost feel his warmth when he was at my side. My trusted friend that held my hand and helped me be brave; now I had to be brave on my own. It was time. Goodbye sweet Sam.

So, now here I am five years later. I am a new person. I entered the Congregation of the Sisters of Providence and allowed Susan Marie to fade away and Sister Jeanette to be born. Born to serve. My life now had a new purpose; a life to serve the Lord. Today, I am on my way to fulfill my role at St. Lucy's Catholic Church in Pinesdale, my 2nd assignment since becoming a nun.

This bus ride has been very long and my brain has had too much thinking time. My previous nights sleep had been restless and minimal due to my anticipation of todays' long journey and I found myself feeling very tired. More than once I suddenly awoke with a jerk of my head as it had been bobbing downward. Finally, I had given in to my tiredness, settled my head against the window and allowed my brain to forget about my surroundings and shut my eyes.

I had dozed off for I am truly unsure of how long and had been dreaming about being at some sort of a fancy social function. I had been wearing a lovely flowered summer dress with a full skirt and my hair was flowing down my back in loose curls. I had on pink ballerina flats, a pink pillbox hat and formal white wrist length gloves. There was soft classical music, Debussy I think, playing somewhere in the background and the faint sweet aroma of a chocolate cake baking in the distance. I was walking across a large dance floor through a crowd of very lively people. I recognized no one. There were so many people and some reached out for me but I kept walking as though on a specific mission.

I finally made it to the other side of the room and found myself walking into a dimly lit hallway. At the far end of the narrow corridor I could see two men stand talking. One was facing me but I could tell he had not seen me. He was a tall nice looking man with dark wavy hair. He had on a gray suit and looked to be about twenty-five or thirty. They were having a lively conversation and he was doing a lot of talking with his hands. The two continued talking as I continued to walk closer. I was finally very close to the men. The tall man, finally noticed me and with surprise, looked my direction. Just then, the other man also realized someone was behind him. He turned to look.

It seemed as though this next part happened in slow motion. His head and shoulders began to turn my direction. I was looking attentively at him. The side of his head was slowly moving my direction like an old wind-up toy that was running out of gas. And, then it happened. Our eyes met. The recognition was immediate and unbelievable. I stared. He stared. My heart melted. The shock began to pass. He took a step toward me and I just started to say, "Scott"……when I was suddenly jarred awake hearing the bus driver bellow, "Oak Mount City!"

I sat for a brief moment feeling unsure of where I was, where I was sitting. Then reality set in. I had been dreaming. But the dream had been so gloriously real. Scott was there. I was standing so close to him...I was almost close enough to touch him....almost. Why did I have to wake up at that moment? Everything had seemed so real. I could still feel myself there....in that hallway. I reached down and ran my hand across my habit realizing there was no flowered summer dress. There were no pink ballerina shoes. I was still dressed in black. I wondered where I had been in the dream and more importantly, why I had such a dream. I thought about my time in counseling. Christine had warned me about times when stressful moments may make me fall back into safe moments.....happier times.

Yes, my new assignment, saying good-byes to friendships made at St. Agatha's, and the long bus ride all had brought about enough stress to cause the dream. It was just a dream. I was fine. But it had been lovely to see Scotts' face.

I quickly took both hands to my face and lightly patted my cheeks to finish awaking my hazy mind. Preparing to depart this bus and the fragmented seat that my body had somehow seemed to adjust to over the past seven and three-quarters hours, my heart was once again lifted with anticipation. My new adventure was that much closer to beginning. I had finally reached Oak Mount City. My itinerary said I should expect to be met by Lucas Evans, the custodian from St. Lucy's Church. He would be driving a brown Ford Station Wagon and may possibly be accompanied by Sister Charlotte.

People were busy departing the bus, bumping others legs with their smaller bags as they hustled along the narrow path between the seats. Most walked directly past me without as much as a look my direction. Finally, a gentleman wearing a slightly crumpled brown suit stopped at my seat and motioned for me to enter the passageway. I quickly rose to my feet, grabbed my small satchel, nodded a thank-you gesture and exited the bus.

SABRINA

Chapter 9 - 1968

The cleaning fury continued throughout that first day with much being accomplished. We all worked very hard. Of course, I think I was working harder than my sisters because I was the most excited. Through these days, our "Nancy Drew" threesome sister bonding was growing more and more as our room was becoming a reality.

This afternoon, I spotted my record player inside one of the many boxes sitting in the room. I snatched it and set it up in our storage corner of the room. JoJo helped me dig around a few other boxes until we finally found my Frankie Avalon record case, the one that held all my precious 45 rpm records, all 10 of them! We slid Chubby Checkers', "*The Peppermint Twist*" record onto the base and set the needle down carefully on the edge. The music started and we all immediately began dancing and twisting around our big open space. Holly, who in the beginning had been so worried about the room, was now giggling more than the rest of us. She was even trying to twist her way down to the floor and up again. We were just starting to slow down when Momma appeared in our landing with Mr. Mertz slinking behind her. He was a finicky old cat but seemed to love Momma. I guess he realized who was now in charge of the kitchen. He used to cling to Aunt Elsie and he did still love his old mistress, but he was a smart old cat and now acted like he was also Momma's long-lost best friend. He knew who was filling his food dish!

"What are you girls doing in here?" she said as if she was mad. "You have the whole house shaking!" We all laughed and started dancing again. Momma watched for a few minutes then she laughed, threw off her apron and starting dancing the twist with us. We had a grand time. She is amazing. I love my Momma.

The next few days went by very quickly as we continued to work not only on our room but the whole house. I got into the habit of working hard for an hour or two then I would head outside and take a little break.

Today, I really wanted to read more of the journals, but JoJo and Little Miss Munchkin were always around so I had no privacy. Instead I worked on organizing my drawers and then headed outside. The neighborhood was somewhat quiet but at the same time full of movement. I liked watching everybody and getting a feeling about who my new neighbors were and how their days get started. Aunt Elsie had an old porch swing on a frame that sat right outside her back door. It had some rusty spots that made it look old and in need of repair but it was sturdy. I imagine when Daddy gets some time he will spiff it up and repaint it. By the time he is finished it will look new again. I cannot remember ever seeing Aunt Elsie use the swing, but I had seen Miss Eulalie on it many a time, probably when she needed a "mental" break from Aunt Elsie.

I didn't know many of the neighbors except that I had talked a few times to old Miss Winter and her sister, Lina when we visited Aunt Elsie. When I got bored with the big peoples boring conversation indoors I would go outdoors and walk around. Miss Winter was often out in her yard working on her flowers and she would talk to me. She was nice but also a little bit creepy. She reminded me of one of those old movie stars, you know the ones I mean. The ones in those old silent black and white movies. The ones where they put on way too much make-up and their faces looked exaggerated.

Miss Winter and Lina looked a lot alike except Lina was a tiny bit shorter and so was her hair. Miss Winters' name was Miriam, but her sister and I guess maybe all her friends called her "Mitzi." I think Mitzi is a funny sounding name for a really old woman. I thought it sounded more like a perfect name for a dog or cat. However I guess you get a nickname when you are a kid and it sticks with you. I imagine that someday when I am all grown-up and walking down the street with a new fella, I will not appreciate someone passing and saying, "Hello Stinkweed" to me!

Miss Winter told me that she retired a long time ago from the Bell Telephone Company. She said she worked there for forty years; 1915 to 1955. Forty years! Man that is a l-o-n-g time. She still liked to talk about the old days when she was a very proper telephone operator. She assured me that unlike some of her co-workers, she never eavesdropped on any private conversations. She said many times it was the younger newer operators that broke the rules. My best guess is she is now about eighty years old. Even though I know they are not twins, only sisters, they sure do seem to do everything together.

This morning they are not outside. From the alley that runs along our back yard, I can see all the backsides of the houses that are behind ours on Elm Street. The garage door was lifted, but Pastor Mason's car was still inside, so I knew he was still at home. I thought it was somewhat funny that Pastor Mason lived on Elm Street right across the alley from the Friends Church that sat right beside Aunt Elsie's house. However, Pastor Mason was not the parish leader at the Friends Church; he was the leader at the Methodist Church that was over on Birch Street. Momma told me she had heard he is a good pastor and that they have lots of kids, maybe four or so, and maybe one of them will be the right age for me, but I don't see anyone moving around over there yet today.

On the same side of the street as us, on the other side of Miss Winters' big white three-story house, is where Nell Taylor lives. Her house is nice. It looks like it has just been freshly painted this spring. It is a beige color with a pale green trim around all the windows, not just the front windows but all of the windows. She is already outside hanging damp but clean white sheets on her clothesline. Momma told me that Mrs. Taylor is a widow, so it makes sense that there is only one set of sheets and a few towels on her clothesline. She had been busy pinning, but now that everything was clipped and hanging, she looked over my way and waved hello before she went back inside the house. I waved back.

A minute later, I saw a kid coming down the alley on his bike. I noticed him slowing down and watching me as he was passing by the yard. Then I heard a door slam and just that quick, Mrs. Taylor was back outside. It looked like she was just dumping her kitchen trash into her big garbage can.

It had been a nice break on this still cool morning, but just about when I thought I should probably get back inside I see the bike coming back around. This time, he came riding it right up through the yard and toward our swing.

"Hey," he says quietly as he brings his bike to a stop right in front of me. "Are you the new family that is moving in here with Mrs. Becker?"

I looked him over. He was a little shorter than me and probably younger too. He had kinda light brown, no, I think his hair was more of a reddish color. It was the kind of hair that couldn't quite bring itself to lay nice on his head. It popped up a little right in the very front. I think Momma calls that a cow-lick; yes a cow-lick. He had a few little speckles on his cheeks and I thought to myself, boy I bet he hates those freckles. Then I noticed his eyes. I never saw eyes like his eyes. They were a cloudy gray color like when you look up at the sky as the evening sun is setting and the blue clouds have slowly started to change their color and switch over to a soft fluffy gray. Yep, his eyes were different than anybody I knew, so I knew I never saw him at school.

Now I notice his bike. His bike was a sight. It looked like it had made it through about 15 years of people riding it, wrecking it and then wrecking it again.

"Yea I am. Who are you?" I said trying to act casual.

"I am Knox; Knox Little. I live right over there," he said as he pointed across the alley. "We live in that little gray house right next to the Masons'."

"Oh," I said nodding. "Ok, that's nice."

Then we both just stared not knowing what else to say. Finally, just to say something, I snickered a little and said, "Nice bike."

He laughed and said, "Yea right.....it's a piece of junk. It was my sisters and she must have terrible balance because she wrecked it about 100 times. However, the wheels still spin and the seat is still in the right spot, so I ride it. And, yea I know, it's a girls' bike. I call her Betsy. And it is better than walking. I was kinda hoping for a new one for my birthday in March but my mom couldn't really afford to buy me one, so Betsy is what I've got."

Now he looked kind of embarrassed and I felt a little bit bad. We were back to just staring again.

"Ok, I gotta go," he said as he started getting back on his seat.

"Ok," I said. "I guess I will see you around."

I got up to head back in the house. I took a step or two and started to turn, but he was already heading back toward the alley. Two seconds later as I was just about to open the back door, I heard a rough scratching noise and sure enough, his chain had slipped off. He looked really frustrated. I headed toward him and bent down to check out the problem.

"Well," I said, "Looks like it is time to do a little work on Betsy" and we both laughed.

By the time we got the chain back on, our hands were filthy and I would say we were friends. I found out that he was 10 years old. Close enough to my age to not act like a baby and tough enough, well, lets' just say I wasn't totally sure yet about that part of him, but I had hopes that he was tough enough to "hang out" with this summer. I mean, I loved my sisters, but they didn't always enjoy the same things as me. Holly loved to play with dolls and JoJo liked to do the things that Momma did like sewing and baking, you know girlie stuff. JoJo was actually a lot like Audrey in that way. She and Audrey looked alike. They were both beautiful and they liked doing the same things.

I was kind of the misfit, I guess. I liked to be outdoors. I liked to dig into things and solve puzzles. I loved a good mystery and I liked to... well, I liked to explore things. Things like new neighborhoods and new friends. So my hope now is that Knox and I will be friends, good friends. I could use a good friend in the neighborhood.

I told Knox I had to get back inside to finish the cleaning as tomorrow was the big day to complete our move and I still had work that I needed to finish. He said OK and he would see me around. I started to walk back toward the house and then suddenly turned around and said, "Hey Knox.....wait a minute."

He stopped and waited for me to come back to him. I looked him in the eye and said, "What do you know about that old guy that hangs out at the Winter house?"

He stared at me for one second and said, "I think he is a creepy dude and I would love to know what he is always looking for walking around in her yard and in her garage."

That sealed it. Yes, Knox would be a friend.

"Ok then," I said. "Maybe I will see you later when I get my stuff done."

He smiled and said, "I will be here. I got nowhere to go. I can show you a lot of stuff in the neighborhood. We have only been here a few months, but I have checked them all out and have met most of the people. I can help get you up to speed on the fun stuff to do around here, which isn't much unless you like to ride bikes and watch people take care of their houses and yards."

A few months I thought to myself. So I guess that is why I wouldn't have seen him in school.

"Why yes," I said smugly, "That is exactly what I like to do. I will be back outside later, when I get everything done. See ya Knox."

I started to walk away and then turned back to him. He was still standing there holding up his bike and watching me.

"You have a really cool name." I said. "I like it, Knox."

"Yea, I know," he said sheepishly. "My Mom did that to me. She used to live in Knoxville, Tennessee when she was a little kid and I guess she really misses it. My sister came first. Her name is Cordelia Dawn, so I guess my mom wasn't very homesick yet when she was born. So, I got to be the lucky guy who got the name. Believe me, I think my life would be a whole lot better if my name was Tom or Jack, but, I am stuck with Knox. My sister, she hates her name too so we all just call her CD. You will see her around once in a while but she spends most of her time over on Birch Street with her friend Ellie."

"Well, I like your name," I told him. "It sounds strong and makes you different from all the Toms and Jacks. I like it but I do understand. My mom named all us girls after Audrey Hepburn movies she liked, but it is ok."

I turned to head into the house.

"Hey!" he yelled. "You never told me your name. What is it?"

I said calmly, "I am Sabrina," then quickly added, "But you can call me Stinkweed. That is what my Daddy calls me and I like it better."

"Stinkweed?" he exclaimed. "I guess I am lucky to be called Knox," he said with a little laugh. "See ya later Stinkweed."

I did a little smile to myself that warmed up my insides and said under my breath, "Cool Beans! I think I made a friend."

When I got back to the third floor, I cleaned, arranged and straightened with a whole new mission. To get my work done and get back outside. Not only did I want to explore the neighborhood, I wanted to explore it with Knox. Things were definitely looking up on Maple Street.

I worked my butt off for the next three hours, only taking a quick break to eat a peanut butter and jelly sandwich. I walked out on the back porch as I was chewing, but I didn't see Knox anywhere, only Tiffany, our cat sitting lazily on that old swing. I looked across the alley to the gray house and saw a pretty calico cat running around but everything else looked quiet. I went back inside. Our room was really looking good now. All three beds were in place and although the bedspreads were not new and pretty, we each definitely had our own corners of the massive space with each definitely well defined as our own.

Momma had made us new curtains for the room. The material she chose had a soft blue background and small pastel colored flowers floating everywhere. She bought 4 yards while it was on sale at Perskey's so she would have enough for all the windows, including the four tiny ones that edged against the floorboard. We had decided to leave the floor just as it was (except now it was clean) and we each placed a small colored area rug alongside of our beds. Momma and

Daddy stayed true to their word and left us create whatever we wanted, within reason. So the last few days, we painted the walls.

We used whatever paint we had left over from when we painted the last time at our old house and what Momma and Daddy had used to paint at Aunt Elsie's. We did have quite an assortment of colors in our room. JoJo and I helped Holly decide what to use and helped her paint. We had portions of cans of white, blue, pink, yellow and green.

Since I was the oldest and got to pick first, I chose white for my corner and painted two sides of the walls. I came out just far enough to stretch past the length of my bed and a little bit beyond where my dresser would sit on the other wall. I knew it was pretty plain and simple, but it looked clean and that was what I wanted.

JoJo picked pink and did just about the same area as I did. When her walls had dried, she used a little of the blue, yellow and green and painted very simple little stemmed flowers along the baseboard where the wall showed and made it look like a little flower garden was growing. It really was kind of cute, if you like that kind of stuff.

Holly needed help, so JoJo and I both helped her paint. She said she wanted bright yellow just like Aunt Elsie's kitchen because it made her feel happy. So, bright yellow was what we used and she was right, her corner was super cheerful. We decided it would look perfect with her bedspread.

Then JoJo opened her big mouth and said, "Holly...wouldn't you like it if we added a few blue clouds and a few balloons on your wall by your bed?"

Holly was excited beyond belief. So, next thing I knew, JoJo was mixing a tiny bit of the white paint in with the blue paint and little pale blue clouds were starting to appear on her wall. Then she added a green and a blue balloon to make it look like they were floating up toward the clouds. Needless to say, Holly loved it.

Then we all worked together on the fourth storage corner of the room. We decided to just all three paint at once and see what we ended up with when it was covered. Well, I thought we ended up with a mess, but the other girls loved it and said it was a colorful masterpiece.

Now that the painting was done and it had all finally dried, we were able to bring in and arrange all our belongings. It took a little while, especially for Holly because she had so many toys and she wanted them all arranged just so in her corner. We spent most of the afternoon completing it, but when it was done, it looked darn good. I was proud of us. We set out to create our own space and dang-nab it, we did!

My vote for the prettiest corner would be JoJo's. Her bedspread was pink and she had her normal pillow on the bed plus some pretty puffy smaller ones that she had sewn long before the big move, but that I guess I had never paid much attention to until today. She had decorated her walls with some cut out butterflies that she had painted with watercolors. Her dresser was centered on the wall near her bed. Around the mirror she taped up a whole bunch of tissue paper puffy flowers that Momma showed her how to make. They were pink and yellow. Her small table held some of her library books and her own copy of "The Adventures of Bob White" that she had gotten on her last birthday. It also held a small table lamp with a pink and white shade. And then there were the painted flowers at her baseboard. Yep, hers was definitely very pretty.

Holly's corner was nice if you were 6 years old. She had that bright yellow on her walls with the clouds and balloons. Her bedspread was yellow with flowers on it but you could hardly see it for all the dolls and stuffed animals that covered the top. Her favorite doll, Shirley Temple dressed in her blue polka-dot dress, white ruffled socks and black shiny shoes, held the place of honor on her pillow. Her nightstand had a small lamp on it that Momma used to keep in her bedroom. Momma needed a larger one now for their big bedroom, so it was easily given to Holly. It was very delicate looking with a glass figurine on the base of a Dutch girl holding a tulip. It had a yellow lampshade, so it was a really good fit for Holly's corner. Yes, her corner was cute.

My corner was a little different. I had a plain navy blue bedspread and did not keep a lot of junk on my bed. I did have more furniture than JoJo and Holly. I had a small table to store my things. It held a plain pencil post lamp with a navy blue lampshade. I had my favorite Nancy

Drew books, *"The Hidden Staircase"* and her newest release, *"The Spider Sapphire"* sitting on it. They were the only two I owned, but I had read all the rest. I got them either from the school library or the Pinesdale Library and read them cover to cover. It also held two of my most precious items that I tried to keep out of Holly's hands. Those were my spyglass magnifier and the kaleidoscope that Aunt Fay gave me last year. The kaleidoscope fascinated me. I looked in it every night before I went to sleep just because I love the mixture of ever-changing colors and shapes. I figured it helped me have pretty dreams.

My dresser was really old and plain, but it held all my clothes. My most favorite thing in my corner was my nightstand. It was made of a real pretty wood, maybe teak, but I don't know that for sure. It has three small drawers and the top one actually has a lock. I hid my most precious things in there and hid my key so none of my sisters could get into it ever. Right now in that top drawer, locked up tight, is my diary and Aunt Elsie's old journals. Whenever I know everyone else in the house is busy elsewhere, I run upstairs, unlock my drawer, read a page of her journal as quickly as possible, and then lock it back up. I keep a bookmarker in place so I can get to the new page quickly. I am now on page 11. Most of what I have read so far is very sad. She wrote about missing Otto and what was she going to do with the rest of her life. She also wrote about Mr. Mertz, who back then was just a kitten.

I still knew in my head that my parents would be furious with me if they found it, but I know in my heart, I just have to read it. Anyway, about our room. My corner is, I guess you would say, just plain and simple. But that is me, plain and simple. I love it.

Our fourth corner is the one that would be in the southeast corner of the room. In that corner, we put our laundry baskets and a trash can. We had salvaged a few of the garment racks. We had to spend a little time cleaning them up, but once we did, they turned out to be useful. We used them to hold our dresses, sweaters and coats. We each kept our everyday shoes under our beds, but in the fourth corner, we had salvaged one of Aunt Elsie's old shoe racks for our Sunday shoes. We also emptied one of her old hat boxes to store our church things, like our hats, gloves and lace dollies. Of course, we tried on all of her old hats and Holly even kept a few to play dress up in before we gave the rest to the Salvation Army.

The room actually worked out perfect and we all agreed we loved it. When all our belongings were exactly where we wanted them, we proudly looked around and then had a spontaneous group hug. Then with excitement in our voices, we called our family to the third floor for our final unveiling. They had all of course seen it at all different stages of the transformation, but today was different. It was officially done!

The three of us stood on the landing and blocked the view until everyone had gathered and then on the count of three we all dropped to the floor to give everyone the full view. There was true amazement on Momma and Daddy's faces. Even Audrey looked impressed for about 5 seconds and then went back downstairs. Our cats, Tiffany and Sister Luke were curled up and napping on my bed, and Mr. Mertz was all sprawled out sleeping on my rug, so it helped the bareness of my corner to not seem so obvious. Davey was nonchalant about it all, but Holly's corner did catch his eye due to the toys. Holly was beaming as she pointed out the beautiful clouds and balloons on her wall as if my parents had not already seen them. But that was okay....I found myself smiling just watching Holly beam. I looked at her little face and remembered how scared she looked when we first walked into the space, how she had cried. And to think with just a little work, we had turned that all around. It was now a treasured room just perfect for three sisters with three very different personalities.

SABRINA

Chapter 10 - 1968

Today was May 31st. The day had finally arrived. Everything was done and we all knew it, but Daddy said that tonight after dinner we should all take a break from what we were doing and go out to the house one last time.

Momma started to prepare dinner. I did the few small chores she asked of me and then I scooted out the back door. I was hoping to catch a glimpse of Knox either in his yard or on his bike. I didn't see him anywhere, so instead I just hung out on the swing. It seemed like nothing big was going on in the neighborhood so eventually I became bored and started to mosey around the yard. There were small flowerbeds along the front entrance of Aunt Elsie's house and I could smell the beautiful fragrance of the Lilies of the Valleys. I loved those tiny little white blossoms tucked in amongst the large sheltering green leaves. Hidden little pearl sized bells protected as if they were a precious treasure. They had always been a favorite of mine. Once when we were visiting Aunt Elsie, Momma and I were outside and I told her how I loved the Lilies of the Valley. Momma said she liked them too. She said when she was little her grandmother told her a story about the tiny lilies. She told me that the legend says they sprouted from tears. She said there were two versions of that legend, both about biblical figures. She did not know which one was the truth or even if either was true. I asked her who the biblical figures were in each of the versions. She said one was of Eve crying while being forced from the Garden of Eden and the other was of

Mary crying at the cross. Each tells that their tears turned into lilies of the valley.

I am thinking about both Mary and Eve today. To me, it wouldn't matter which was the true story. I could see both of those women having such sad feelings and I like the idea that God made something precious and beautiful from their tears. So, my point is, it doesn't matter which story is true but it does tell me that I am right! These little flowers are truly precious.

Actually I have two favorite flowers, Lilies of the Valley and Violets. Both are so petite and delicate but yet never insignificant. I guess maybe it is that tininess that draws my eyes to them. I know they have to fight and squeeze to survive amongst the bigger stronger flowers in the beds. I appreciate their fight to survive. They are small but yet very strong. I suppose that struggle has a lot to do with my love for them but I have to also include the beautiful contrast in their colors. The lilies are so white and pure and the violets are such a deep, dark purple. They are beautiful and I almost forgot to mention, the violets are known in history for the love of truth.

As I sit here with the flowers I am thinking about me too. I do believe I always try to find the truth. Maybe in the way back part of my mind, the Violet has helped to influence that goal. I know I am not being truthful by secretly reading Aunt Elsie's journals, but I just have a super strong feeling that I will find something important in her words, something that she can no longer share with any of us, something that we need to know. I also know I could give the journals to Momma and Daddy and they too could read them and find any special information that may be hidden in amongst the words, but I cannot fully trust that they will think about all of the possibilities as strongly as I see them. The minute I touched those journals, my head started spinning with ideas of what I could learn from the things she took the time to write so many years ago. Even if there is one sentence that tells us something unique from her past, it is worth taking the time to read them all, every page, start to finish. Would Momma and Daddy feel the same? I just don't think so. It has to be me that reads the journals.

Aunt Elsie's front yard was okay, but other than the flowers, it was not anything grand. It had some flat grassy space and then fell into a small hill that went straight down to the sidewalk. I thought it was going to be a pain to cut the grass but Daddy seemed to do it without any problems. Across the street, there were only two houses and both were very nice and recently painted. I had no idea who lived in either one of them.

Now, I find myself studying the large sloped hill that led down to the towns' baseball field. I was noticing the freshly painted lines on the field assuming there must be a game there tonight when I noticed a small figure walking along the sidewalk. It was hard to make out, but from the clothing, I guessed it was my new friend, Knox. I sat down on the top step that led to the sidewalk and waited. Sure enough, as the character got closer, I could see it was definitely Knox. Instead of walking straight and coming up the alley, he turned and walked up Maple Street.

As he got within earshot, I went down the seven steps to the sidewalk and said "Hey."

He smiled and said, "Hey yourself."

"Where ya been?" I asked.

He looked downward at his bag and said, "My mom needed a few things from Gus's Grocery and then I went to the library."

"Oh," I said, "I was looking for you earlier."

"Sorry I missed you," he replied. "Did you want to do something?"

"I would like to, but I can't right now," I answered. "Momma has about got supper ready and then Daddy wants us all to go back to the old house one more time to check things out. You know, make sure we didn't forget anything."

"Oh," he said. "Ok. Maybe tomorrow?"

Without any hesitation, I said very quickly, "Oh for sure tomorrow! I want to get started learning about this neighborhood. I have many questions and maybe you can answer some of them.....or even all of them! What books did you get at the library?"

"My favorites," he said. "The Hardy Boys of course. I've already read all of them," he said with hearty enthusiasm, "but I like to reread them to see if I might have missed an important clue the first time I read them. Today I got, *"The Secret Panel"* and *"The Crisscross Shadow."* I love trying to solve a great mystery. What about you? Do you like to try to solve mysteries?"

"You know what Knox," I said with a smile. "There is nothing I like better than to try to solve a good mystery. When I go to the library though, I get Nancy Drew mystery books!"

He looked at me and gave me a nice broad smile.

"Yep," I said, "Knox....I think we are going to be the best of friends. See ya tomorrow, early....okay?"

"You got it," he said and then together we walked up my little hill and through the back yard.

"See ya," I said and headed inside for supper.

I watched him from the back door as he went walking through Aunt Elsie's' yard and headed for the alley. He was swinging his grocery bag and whistling some crazy tune. I knew I was right. This was going to be a good friendship.

Dinner was good. Momma was a good cook and tonight she made meatloaf, mashed potatoes, a mix of green beans, yellow beans and lima beans and chocolate pudding for dessert. It was a little bit hard to sit and watch Aunt Elsie eat. She took very tiny bites and chewed her food kind of funny. She also looked around the table and mumbled a lot. But overall, it went fine. We all helped Momma clean up and then Daddy told Aunt Elsie we would be back soon. We loaded into the car and headed for the house.

As we drove up the lane, our beautiful treed lane, I realized that it would probably be the last time we would do this as a whole family. Sure, we would be back for things like to collect the rent or to fix a problem, but probably never again as a whole family.

We did a walk around the house and it was odd seeing it so bare, just floors and walls. It lost some of its charm sitting there looking so empty. The kitchen needed our old oak table with the napkin holder in the center and Momma's pots and pans sitting on the stove. My room needed my treasured nightstand and my bed. The bathroom looked lost without the fluffy blue toilet seat cover and matching rug. We were all pretty quiet as we walked from one empty room and into the next. It was pretty sad. Nothing felt right. We were now back at the kitchen. We looked at each other and then one-by-one started walking toward the door.

Once we stepped outside everything was different. I was back at home. The porch swing was still there right where it had always been. The big sprawling oak tree was still right near the house with its massive branches covering the house and lane with its splendor. The barn and little out-buildings were still there and the few animals we had, they were there too.

Daddy said he was going to do a walk thru of the out buildings and do one last check on our animals. Mr. Gratton would be taking care of them as of tomorrow. Davey ran along with Daddy, grabbing a few sticks and playing around as they walked. JoJo and Holly ran over to their old favorite playing spot near the little chicken house and began chasing each other around the open field.

Momma sat down on the old swing and Audrey and I crowded up on each side of her. We sat quiet for a while just looking across the land and gently swinging. I was thinking to myself how on many a night, we had sat outside on this old porch swing just to enjoy the quietness of the night. Sometimes, Momma would tell us stories about her younger days. My favorite was when she talked about the sights she had seen on her trip to New York City so many years ago. She would always start by saying she remembers it like it was just last week.

"Momma," I said. "Will you tell us about your New York trip just one more time?"

"Yes, please," Audrey chimed in.

"Why of course I will," she said glowing. "I remember it like it was just last week," she said with a little laugh. Then she got quiet for a second, patted her hands on her lap, looked at both Audrey and I and said. "But first, I would like to talk about a serious subject with you girls, while your little sisters and Davey are busy elsewhere. Would that be okay?"

Audrey and I both nodded with approval. Momma turned her head to look at each of us. She gave us each a gentle smile and then lowered her head for a moment and stared at her lap.

"Girls," she started, "I want to talk to you both about a serious subject tonight. Some of the reason is because you are both growing leaps and bounds and becoming such beautiful young woman and I am so very proud of both of you."

I could easily imagine Momma saying that sentence to Audrey, she really is beautiful...beautiful just like Momma; but I was shocked that she was including me in that sentence. I wanted to say, "Momma..I have looked in a mirror and I am NOT beautiful;" but Momma was talking so seriously that I knew I should not speak.

"The other reason I want to tell you this story," she continued, "is because of our move. We have lived a tiny bit of a sheltered life living here on the top of our little hill. The location has kind of protected you children from some of the world. Well, now that is going to change. Pinesdale is a small town, but it is still a town. We will not live on top of a little hill but in a neighborhood...therefore, we will have neighbors," she added a small chuckle but then went right back to serious.

"Not everyone in the world is nice and I know you are aware of that truth; we all watch Mr. Cronkite on the nightly news. But I worry that you might think there is no need to really worry when you live in a small town....but I want you to know; there is."

Momma stopped talking and sat staring out across the yard at our little sisters playing near the fields.

Audrey and I looked at each other, arched our brows and each gave that look that silently says don't speak. So we didn't.

After another minute, Momma took and placed her hands, one on each of Audrey and my legs and patted them. She remained quiet and hung her head down just slightly nodding it like a runner does while in his stance before starting an important race.

Suddenly she lifted her head and said, "Yes there are evil people even in a small town and I know because a very long time ago, someone evil tried to hurt me."

Audrey and I both gasped and turned to Momma. She quickly tried to calm us.

"Now girls, please," she pleaded, "Please just let me tell you what happened....then you may ask questions."

"I am going back to a long time ago when I was 16 years old," she began. "I was never a shy girl. Actually in my day I was considered a strong willed girl, at least by my parents. They thought I was hard to handle, even though most of the time I followed all the rules. I did say, most of the time," she chuckled.

"I know that when we look back in time," she continued, "we sometimes do so by looking through rose-colored glasses meaning the truth sometimes get stretched, bent and turned sideways into a totally different story all together. But I don't have on any rose colored glasses right now and my memories are still very much intact."

"Admittedly," she said very quietly, "My teenage years were emotional to say the least. Simply said, I wanted a different life than the life my parents were showing me. I always wanted a different life from as far back as I can remember. I was never quite satisfied. I was always a dreamer. I did not like living on a farm. I did not like the daily chores. The chores like you girls know.... that never take a break, never take a vacation. We have a few small animals here but you girls know from some of your friends that have bigger farms. When you live on a farm, the chores involve animals that need fed, watered, brushed, let out to pasture, milked, well, you girls understand. No question about it. Chores were 365 days per year."

"So," she said, "as you can imagine, I disliked those chores as a child but as a teenager, I hated them. As each morning came, I hated them more. By the time, I was 16, my life became unbearable with my dislike for farm living. I wanted nothing to do with it, but my chore list grew larger instead of smaller."

She sat shaking her head back and forth like she was trying to knock a few memories around inside her head. I wondered if she was trying to push them out or push them back and out of the way. Finally she must have pushed them somewhere because she stopped shaking her head and continued.

"My theory back then is the same as it is today; there is a time and a place for everything. Well, way back in October of 1949, a whole 20 years ago, I had decided it was my time to break free and break a rule."

"Mother and Daddy always thought I could manage to do everything they felt was necessary on the farm and still keep up my schoolwork and after school activities," she said quickly and as a matter of fact. "Well, somedays I could....but not that day," she said and then looked like she was going to drift away. But she didn't. She continued.

"I had decided that they were just going to have to understand," she said empathically like she was also trying hard to convince me and Audrey. "After all, I could not be in two places at the same time, and at 16, I felt like I should get to do a little bit of picking and choosing as to which event was to take top priority."

"Maybe I was too much of a dreamer," she said as though rethinking it, "but I had thought this with all the confidence in the world. I was smart enough to know the potential and more likely, the predictable outcome. Yep, I would get in big trouble for sure if I didn't choose the plan Mother and Daddy had selected and today I would tell you girls I was wrong to disobey, but not back then. I was a determined young lady."

"I did so want to stay after school that day and help decorate the archway for the football game on Friday night," she said. "As I said, I was 16 years old. I was a member of the Pep Club and decorating that archway was one of the most fun functions of the club. It might seem silly now, but I used to love making those soft tissue paper puff flowers and arranging them around the tubing to form the colorful arch."

My mind immediately pictured JoJo's mirror in our room and those pretty soft tissue flowers Momma had taught her to make. But Momma was still talking, I made myself listen to her words.

"It was fun cutting and hanging all the crate paper streamers across the arch for the football players to go charging through at the start of the game and watch the streamers break free and twirl for a second or two in the air before softly landing on the grassy field," she was saying it so clearly that I could see her in my mind as a teenage girl watching it happen.

"It was usually a job saved for the upper classmen," she continued. "I had waited patiently for my turn and it was about to be the last home game of the season. So, if I have made my case well, you surely see my point. It just wasn't fair. Do you agree?"

We both silently nodded in agreement.

"Well I am sure you have already guessed my plans were once again taken out of my control by chores," she said. "Daddy needed me to clean out the shed that night! I don't know why it had to be that specific night. Did he really think the animals were going to notice? It wasn't like they were going to jump up and yell "Hip hip hurrah, we have a clean shed today?""

I started to chuckle, but Audrey looked at me in disapproval and I stopped.

"I might have been wrong, but I decided he was just insisting I do it that night to make me mad. I wish Mother would have just once spoke up and said, "No James, she has plans for tonight." But no; my Mother never said a word to Daddy."

She said it with such sadness in her voice that I wanted to cry. I put my arm up and around her neck and gave her a hug. I love my Daddy and think of him like my best friend. I felt so bad that Momma's Daddy was so mean sounding. I never met Grandpa Wolfe. He died before I was born so I never did know much about him. I don't think I would have like him.

Momma hugged me back, kissed my forehead and said, "Thank you Sabrina."

Yes," she said and again patted our legs, "From as early as I can remember, Mother always took a step back and became as mum as a church mouse when Daddy spoke to us children. He ruled the roost, that is for sure and all of us kids knew it. I want you girls to understand that it isn't like that with me and your Daddy. We share our ideas and make decisions together. I hope you girls realize that and know that when you grow up and get married, your husband must know that you have a voice and a mind and a shared responsibility in your marriage," she looked at both of us and stared until we realized she wanted an answer. We both promptly nodded our heads. Momma was pleased.

She continued, "Back in our younger days, before we totally understood my Daddy's ways, we tested him, well Freddy and I tested him. You could always count on my brother Freddy to stir Daddy up. That boy took more whippings than I would think a normal child could stand. But Freddy wasn't normal. He was as stubborn as Daddy, but without the entitlement. He was just a head strong young boy who was determined to not let his old man get the best of him. When Fred got older, he didn't get whippings anymore but Daddy had his ways of still controlling him. The car was a huge one. When Fred lost his driving privileges, he was isolated to the farm. When he towed the line and stayed on his best behavior; when the farm chores were done and the supper table was cleared; he was free. He could go into town to visit his girlfriend or hang out at the Five and Dime store downtown with his friends. That time of the day was precious to Fred, so he did tow that line much more willingly then when he was a head strong 13 year old boy."

"And then there was Fay," she said and laughed. "My sister Fay was always the obedient one. She never got into any trouble with Daddy because she did whatever he asked of her and she never complained. She was the smart one of us three. When she was 19, she got married to Tony Montgomery, her high school sweetheart. Within a matter of a few months, she was expecting her first child. They lived just down the road from our farm. Frank worked at Hastings Mill in town but helped Daddy out at our farm in the evenings. I guess she was happy. Maybe she was happy, or maybe she just chose to do what was expected of her. I often wondered but never knew for sure. She was a lot like Mother; always quiet and content to go about her work. Thinking back to when we were youngsters or even later during our teenage years, I realized she never talked about her dreams. It was like she knew her destiny early on and accepted it. No questions asked." Momma went silent again.

Aunt Fay lived about 30 minutes from Pinesdale but we didn't see her very often. I liked her but I also didn't feel like I knew her very well. I knew her mostly because she sent us gifts on our birthdays.

Kind of back from her dreamy state she said, "But that was not me. I always had a million dreams. Actually it is probably more like a million and one and I wanted to do them all! And I do still believe I will. Promise me that you girls will always have dreams. You simply must. Remember what Cinderella sings, *"A dream is a wish you heart makes!"*

We both nodded in full agreement and Momma smiled.

"Anyway, back to my story. So that night," she continued, "I told Daddy I needed to go to the library. Yes, I lied. I am not proud of it, but I did. Well, it wasn't working. He wasn't going let me go to the library even when I told him I needed to look up information for my school report. He seemed to think I should have had all the information in my head. I tried to tell him that I was not some sort of genius that was able to store every word the teacher said in my head. I reminded him that I could not possibly be expected to automatically know everything about Franklin D. Roosevelt without having access to the Encyclopedia Britannica, which we did not own but could be found at the library. I assumed he never heard a word I said. But, that time he heard and he did answer me back."

"He said," she said firmly in imitation, "and I quote, be home directly after school, no lolly-gagging on your walk home. Get here and get your chores done, help your Momma get supper on the table and clean-up and then we will see if you have time to get to the library. Fred can drive you."

"Then of course, Fred chimed in and said he had plans and absolutely could not take me," and she added, "I was really mad at Fred."

Remembering it exactly, she said "I said, then I will walk, and I waited for a reaction from my father."

"Oh I remember it so well," she said. "Mother looked at Daddy with a look of concern. I noticed Daddy didn't even look her direction. With his head still in the newspaper he said to me, "As long as your work is done, it is fine with me if you want to walk. If I remember correctly that library closes at 8:00. You best make sure you are back in this house by 8:25 and no later."

Momma laughed and said, "And that was all I needed to hear. I said, Yes Sir to Daddy before he could change his mind. If I remember right, Mother only looked his direction and stared for a minute, then turned back to the kitchen sink and continued to work on peeling her bowl of apples."

"So," she continued, "That is how it was that I was able to go back to the school for the Pep Club gathering. That is how I was able to make my soft tissue paper flowers and hang those streamers. That was why I was walking home, alone, much later than I planned. That is why……"

She stopped talking. She hung her head again and when she looked up a minute later, she had tears welled up in her eyes.

"Momma," I said when I saw her eyes. "Momma what is it, what happened?"

Audrey grabbed Momma's folded hands. "Mother please tell us what happened."

Momma wiped her eyes and gave us each a gentle hug.

"It is funny," she said, "How some memories are so vividly clear. I mean that really was 20 years ago and I just relived that day with you. And…it was very clear. But girls, I knew it would be because I have relived that day in my mind so many times. That day holds a secret. My secret. A secret that up until this day I have only told your Daddy. A secret that scared me 20 years ago and still scares me to this day.

"Oh Momma," Audrey pleaded. "What happened? Please finish your story. You said we need to know, so you must tell us."

Just then, Holly started to run our direction. Momma stared and I was just ready to yell for her to get back to the barn, when JoJo yelled, "I am ready!" and Holly turned and ran toward her.

Audrey and I both turned back to Momma and watched her face in anticipation.

"Alright girls," she said. "I have told you a lot about that day, but now it is time for you to hear the most important part. The part that I always knew I would need to share with all my girls when the time was right…and though I do not like the idea of reliving it, I know I must."

"I went that night," she said with more strength in her voice, "And I decorated that arch. As I said, it took longer than I thought it would because Ellie didn't come and help. When we finally finished and I looked at the clock as I was leaving it said 8:05. I hurried out and ran down Oak and Main Street. It was already getting dark and I knew my time was short, so I decided that the only way I would make it in time was if I cut across the field by Webbers Lake....so I did."

"I had never cut through Webbers Lake when it was dark," she said almost apologetically. "I had gone through it many of times during the day when the lake looked so pretty and peaceful and there were people mingling around fishing, picnicking or just enjoying the day. But this time, it was dark and I admit, I was immediately scared."

"There was taller brush than I remembered too," she said, "along the outer areas that the city workers usually kept cut and it scratched against my arms as I trudged through where the path was no longer clear. It was just plain creepy because it was so very quiet and so dark. As I was walking, I thought I heard something, you know like I heard something but not really. It was just a feeling; or at least I thought so. I worried but I kept walking. I was almost to the far side when I heard it again and this time I decided it was just the wind rustling against the grasses and....," she paused as though she was afraid to finish her sentence.

"But then I quickly realized this time, it was different." she continued, "I knew it wasn't my imagination or just the wind. It was another person. I heard it clearly and it was close to me. I started walking faster. I was almost doing a slow run when I suddenly felt a hand grab my shoulder."

I jumped but Momma was so deep in her thoughts that she didn't even realize it. Audrey looked at me and held her finger up to her lips, telling me not to speak. I obeyed.

Momma continued, "And just that quickly the other hand went across my mouth. I tried to scream, but it came out just a quiet muffle. I could feel him trying to pull me downward. I struggled and tried to straighten my body and lunge it forward, but he was trying to grip me tighter and ended up pulling at the hair at the back of my head. I tried to scream again and his hand slightly shifted. I tried to bite his hand but his hand was too large and his grip too tight. I could almost feel my lips bruising from his strength that forced against them. He was trying again to pull me down and his arm had slid tighter against my neck now."

Momma's words were getting so quiet now and I was afraid she was going to cry. I grabbed her hand and held it tight and then got scared that I was holding it too tight and she might feel like she did that night...so I loosened my grip.

Momma gave me half of a smile, dabbed her eyes and kept going.

"I started to clumsily fall backwards and I could hear him breathing heavily," she said while shaking her head as though she was in a trance. "I was so afraid and I couldn't think of anything to do but pray. His grip loosened on my mouth as I hit the ground. My mouth as finally free. He was now coming down on me from the front. I could see a shadow, a dark shadow of a tall man. He was heavy on my body and my arms were pinned. He was close to my face, so close I could feel his hot breath on my skin. He tried to find my mouth but I jerked my head to the side and felt the sting of his unshaved face brushing against my cheek. I could feel his hands beginning to grope me, tugging at my jeans. He was strong. I had no fight left in me. I was crying."

Momma was crying now too. She wiped her eyes and said softly, "I said they only thing I could think to say and I said it as loud as I could, "Jesus Mary and Joseph please protect me."

SABRINA

Chapter 11 - 1968

I was softly crying now.

Momma held me tight and said, "I know this is upsetting Sabrina, but please understand that now that I have started this, I need to finish it. It is important to me that my daughters hear this from me and though it is very difficult for me to tell it to you, I know I must."

I swiped my hands across my teary eyes and nodded my head.

Momma continued. "After I asked for protection, for about 3 seconds, he froze," she said remembering. "I had hopes that it was over. That he would leave; run off back into the weeds. I prayed that this was all just a bad dream."

She paused for a few seconds and then said, "And then, it was like he came back to life. He let go of my arms and put his hands on my face and yanked my head back toward him. It felt like my neck snapped. He pressed his lips hard against mine. I could feel his sloppy wet lips against my face and then he started to move his hands downward again. He yanked at my blouse as though he was trying to rip it off. I tried to kick at him with my legs, but he was too heavy on top of me. I couldn't get any leverage against him. He again pinned my arms and started to slide himself down my body. Now with his face was scratching against my neck and onto the top of my blouse."

"Suddenly behind him I saw another shadow appear," she said as though in another trance. "Another man came through the bushes and before I could even get scared that he might be another attacker, he grabbed my attacker by the neck.

As he struggled to pull and lift him off of me, he shouted, "Run girl. Run! Get out of here. Now!"

I was so petrified that at first I didn't move. I realized I was free. He had my attacker off of me. The two of them were fighting directly over me but it was as if I was glued to the ground," she said looking at us to see if we understood.

She said in a louder voice. "My rescuer screamed at me again, "Run girl!"

"I guess I was dazed," she said with her voice now trembling. "I remember just seeing two dark shadows wrestling now right beside me on the ground and finally my brain snapped back into reality and I tried to rise to my feet. The attacker sensed my movement and stopped going at my rescuer and lunged back toward me and caught my left arm, knocking me back to the ground. I could feel his strength as he clenched my arm and his nails dug into my skin. I screamed and this time, it came out loud and clear."

The other man got to his feet and I saw his arm swing directly into the attackers face. He flew backwards and my rescuer grabbed my right arm and pulled me to my feet and said, "RUN ...Now! And keep running. Don't stop."

"And I did. I ran and ran and never looked back until I was at the back door of our house. As I tried to compose myself before I went into the house, I realized that my clothes were filthy and my blouse was ripped at the shoulder. I tucked it in as best I could, pulled my hair back and smoothed it with my fingers and took a deep breath. I knew I was late, but I didn't know how much and hoped that Daddy was asleep in his chair. He often feel asleep while reading."

She continued, "I crept quietly thru the back door. I stood motionless. I listened. I could hear Daddy's quiet snore and knew he had fallen asleep while reading in his favorite chair. I could hear the steady clicking of Mothers' knitting needles working in perfect consistent rhythm and I thought I might be able to pass without notice. I moved on tiptoes across the kitchen floor and skipped quickly up the carpeted stairs to my bedroom. Our room was empty. I heard Fay in the bathroom with the tub water running, so I hurried and changed into my pajamas. I hid my torn and dirty clothes under my bed. It was only then that I sat on the edge of my bed, relived my drama and tried to realize I was safe. I was safe from the awful man in the dark at Webbers Lake and safe from the wrath of my father. I crawled into my small twin bed and pulled my flower quilted comforter up tight against my neck and closed my eyes, pretending to be asleep. I waited until Fay came into the room and Momma had come in to check on us. Finally when all was quiet in the house; I cried myself to sleep."

Her story was done. She had told us her terrible secret that she so desperately wanted us to hear. To her it was her way to protect us. She needed us to realize that the world isn't always nice. She wanted us to realize that every man was not like our Daddy. She needed us to know that bad things can happen but that like her, we are strong young woman and need to protect ourselves; from bad situations and bad people.

Her point was well made. It was something that I can easily venture to say Audrey and I will never forget.

I looked at Momma. She looked drained and I didn't know how to help her except to hug her; so I did.

"My lovely sweet daughters, I am sorry, I am so sorry to tell you girls this horrible story," Momma said as she cried from her memories. "But I felt I must."

"That man was evil and it was only by the grace of God that the other man came upon that attack and saved me. I shudder to think what might have happened to me if my rescuer had not came upon us that night. As far as I know, that man was never caught or ever punished for the crime he tried to commit. I lived in fear for a very long time. I worried that he was watching me. That he might try again to catch me alone. I tell you very seriously that night changed my life and my view of the world."

Now it was Audrey and I that were hanging our heads down. We were both so sad for our mother. How very scared she must have been and how did she ever feel not afraid again after that ordeal. She was so strong. I was so proud of her.

"I can tell you girls that it was harder when no one knew my secret," she confided. "I never felt safe. I hated to be alone. But when I was 19, I started dating your Daddy. Once I knew things were serious between us, I told him what had happened to me. He promised me then that he would always protect me and no one would ever hurt me again….and I believed him. Your daddy made me feel safe in a way that no one else ever could have done. He made me happy, he made me laugh and he made me feel safe. There is nothing better than that girls. Nothing in this world better than that feeling. Please if you learn nothing else from me, please remember that and find that for yourselves when the time comes."

"But, also remember my story and know that there are many wonderful people in this world, but there are also some that may try to hurt you. Always be careful. Know your surroundings and don't take silly chances. "Please," she said as she pulled us both in for a big joint hug.

"Now….we need to lighten our mood," she said as though now that this weight was lifted from her, we could all think good thoughts again. "How about we get your little sisters over here and do one last nice swing fest before we move into that big beautiful, well almost beautiful house?"

We both nodded in agreement and Momma wiped her cheeks and yelled for JoJo and Holly.

By the time they joined us on the swing, Momma was grinning at all of us.

"Oh my lovely young ladies," she said, "this will be our last time to have a nightly swing here on the hill. Before your Daddy and Davey get back over here, what shall we talk about?"

The swing was gliding back and forth and back and forth and I realized everyone was patiently looking at me.

I said, "Oh well of course we all want to hear you talk about New York City!"

Momma took her hand and cupped my chin and said, "Well, if I must!" and then laughed and said, "I love to talk about New York City just as much as you girls love to hear it. So let's see where should I begin?"

"Oh," she said, "I know….. I remember it like it was just last week," and then she laughed and we all laughed with her.

"OK," she said. "How about we really start with the people? I just loved being amongst the crowds of people, moving at a constant and rapid pace. But, I also know you didn't dare stop to look in a storefront window without working your way over to the outer edge of the crowd or you would get kind of rammed and bumped from everybody trying to get past you."

Holly said, "Were those people mean to you Momma?"

"Oh no Holly," she said. "I know not everyone there was cold and distant as New Yorkers are often described. There were always a few that would not look your direction even if you were on fire, but many more that would nod their heads as they passed by Aunt Helen and me, and then would just as quickly refocus on their next steps. There was something that was hard to do. That was crossing the street! It was more like a game to see how many could cross before the cars would start blowing their horns, shooing the crowds out of their way. It was a challenge."

"That was another point about the big city," she said looking right at JoJo. "The amount of noise. You would never be able to sit like we are now and just enjoy the quietness of an evening. I guess because we live in a sleeping little burg, just as I did as a youngster, the noise was totally unexpected to me. It never stopped. Never. It didn't matter what time you started your day, or ended your day, it was always noisy. Traffic noises included constant blowing of horns to alert other cars or people to get out of the way. Traffic cops bravely stood on the street blowing their whistles. Ambulance sirens, police car sirens, people talking, babies crying, street vendors begging it was never-ending noise."

Then Momma looked at all of us and smiled again. We knew what was coming next. She was about to tell us what she loved.

She continued, "But let me tell you about the amazing lights in the city. I loved the bright colored neon lights that flashed everywhere in the evenings to catch the crowd's attention. I never saw so many blinking crazy colored lights in my life. Every theater had a different shows name in lights with a hundred smaller bulbs flashing around it. Billboard signs, store fronts, traffic lights, and then add in the crowds of people, well it was more than my little small town eyes could absorb. But the night we walked to the Fulton Theater and I saw the huge word "Gigi" flashing, well, it just simply took my breath away!"

She paused for a bit, then blinked kind of funny, looking like she is lost for a second or so and then looked at all of us and started talking again.

"I even enjoyed, a little bit, the folks that stood on every corner, almost begging the walkers to buy whatever they were selling that day," she said. "They sold all kinds of items; purses, wallets, scarves, books, umbrellas, bus ride tickets and even fruit! They all had chanting-type messages they yelled out trying to get everyone and anyone's attention. Sometimes, if they caught you looking their direction, they would carry the item and follow you for a bit, chanting their message almost directly into your ear. They would offer to lower their price or give you two for the price of one. Anything to make a sale. I got a little bit scared and I would try to walk a little faster. Aunt Helen would then grab my hand and try to pull me further away from the seller. Eventually, they would give up, drift back and move on to another candidate using the same tactics."

Then Momma sat quiet again.

I loved listening to Momma talk about her trip, but I also loved the way she always ends her stories and I expect it will be the same tonight. She is still staring off. It usually takes just a few extra minutes as she looks out at our land and into the beautiful evening sky, then she is ready.

Tonight she gives us all a small smile and says, "And as wonderful as all of that was at the time, there is nothing that compares to the tranquility of the soft, almost whispering breeze that sweeps across this old porch swing at the end of a busy summer day."

Then she quietly and adds in a more serious voice, "I know our life is changing, but I want you girls to remember that change is good. It may take us a little while to get comfortable in our new surroundings and for us to get used to living with Aunt Elsie, but we are a strong family and we can do this. It is important to your Daddy to take good care of Aunt Elsie. You girls don't know it, but she has helped your Daddy and me a few times over the years. Truth be told, we would not have been able to purchase this precious farmhouse if it had not been for Aunt Elsie. We owe her a lot and this is one small way to help pay her back. So...no more sad feelings. We are changing but we are still a family. We are the Holden family. We are moving into a beautiful house and we should all be happy. So...when Daddy and Davey get back, let's show them we are HAPPY!"

We all agreed. Then we all sat very silent staring at the view of our land. After about 5 minutes, Daddy and Davey came whistling back toward the house.

Daddy said, "Well are my ladies ready for city life?"

We all gave him an empathic "YES" and headed for the car.

As we drove down the lane, I was proud that we made Daddy happy, but I was still kind of sad in my heart. However, by the time we reached Maple Street, my head was already buzzing with my newest mysteries:

1. What would I discover reading Aunt Elsie's journals?
2. Who was Tram and what was he searching for with his flashlight in the dark nights?

I did not know the answers to anything right now, but I knew I would figure everything out soon.....with the help of my new friend, Knox.

It was late when we got home. We sat for a bit with Aunt Elsie in the living room. She talked quite a bit about Uncle Otto and that they were getting ready to travel again. And then Daddy became the focus of her conversation. I was only half listening. I was still thinking about

Momma's story. I was still feeling her fear. Then all of a sudden I heard Aunt Elsie say something else to Daddy that made no sense. I still think she might think Daddy is Uncle Otto. The remainder of her dialogue was to Mr. Mertz, her cat. It was sweet watching her hold the old cat on her lap and talk to him as if he was her child or something. I figured she probably forgot we were even sitting in the same room. It was just her and Mr. Mertz.

Finally, Momma and Daddy said we kids were to tell Aunt Elsie good night. I was happy to go and be able to head upstairs. With Miss Eulalie being officially finished and Daddy arranging for just some part time helpers, Momma would be the one helping to get Aunt Elsie ready for bed now. She could still do some things for herself, but she needed prompting. She sat in the wheelchair most of the day, but her legs still worked and she could walk, she just didn't like too. I suppose Momma will eventually train Audrey and then I will be next. I wondered how long Aunt Elsie would live. I mean, Daddy said she is 84 years old now, but I did remember Daddy telling me he knew someone that lived to be 102 years old. That is quite old. I bet that person sure did have some stories to tell. I was thinking too hard and worrying too much. As I climbed the stairs, I decided I should try to empty my head of worries and call it a day.

I crawled into my nice clean bed in my beautiful new room and thought about everything that had changed over the past few weeks. I said my prayers and was ready to roll over and close my eyes. When I turned on my side, coming from the tiny window, I saw a light flicker against the wall. I waited a minute and saw it again. I waited for a reaction from JoJo or Holly, but they were both already asleep. I shimmied out from under my covers, crawled to the end of my bed and slid down to the floor. I did an army crawl around the frame of my bed and lined myself up to the edge of the window. There it was again, a quick flash of a light. I peered closer. It was coming from the direction of the Winter house. I could see it was now pointing down toward the ground. It was so dark. All I could see was the beam of the light moving along. It was swinging now. Someone was walking in the yard and carrying a flashlight. The light kept moving, now it was behind the Winter house and then it was flickering around Nell Taylor's yard.

I kept watching. I cranked my head further around and looked over toward Knox's house. The upstairs was dark. I wondered if he was watching too. Suddenly the light flashed in my direction again. I jetted back into the corner but kept my eyes focused on the light beam. The beam seemed to be getting bigger and I realized it was coming closer to my Aunt Elsie's house. Worried that I might somehow be seen, I leaned further back. The light disappeared for more than a few seconds. I leaned my face closer to the window and realized that the light was right below me and wide, so it must be right next to the house. I pressed my head directly against the window and tried to look down. Just then, the direction of the light turned. And then it happened. Then I had a better view. I saw him as the light shone directly on his face for a brief second. It was him. It was Tram!

The light then moved slowly across the yard and back into the patio/garden area at Miss Winter's house. I kept my face pressed to the window and watched Tram move along the back area with the flashlight pointed downward for a few seconds and then up again. He moved slowly. Then he stopped and stood still for a few minutes. I waited to see what he was going to do next. He was creepy. What was he possibly looking for in all of our yards? I had never heard him speak. I wondered what he sounded like. Was his voice deep and strong or was he soft spoken?

He was walking again. He went straight to the garage and went inside. From the side window, I could see the faint reflection of the flashlight. The flashlight went out and the inside garage light came on and my show was over. I looked again toward Knox's house. Now his bedroom light was on. Ah-ha, he was awake and I just knew he had been watching Tram too. This would be great for us to talk about tomorrow.

I crawled back into my bed. My mind was buzzing now with all kinds of thoughts about Tram, Mitzi and Lina. What was it like to live in their house? I wondered why it was Miss Mitzi and Miss Lina. I wondered why neither of the sisters had ever married. I wondered if they had any other sisters or brothers. I wondered why Tram stayed at their house. I wondered if Tram was one of their boyfriends.

These were questions I could ask if I became better friends with Miss Mitzi. Yes, that was my mission for tomorrow. I would fill Knox in on my plan and together we would set things into motion. Tomorrow would be Mission - Miss Mitzi!

With all my adrenalin still pumping, I could not sleep. Since the girls were sleeping and the house was quiet with the exception of music coming from the radio in Audrey's room, I dug out my key and unlocked the nightstand drawer. Very quietly, I pulled out Aunt Elsie's journal from under my diary and gingerly switched on my table lamp. I propped my pillow upward and got comfortable to read. I did a quick survey of the room and all was normal. I quietly opened the journal and carefully turned to page 12 and set about to devour Aunt Elsie's words. I pictured Aunt Elsie downstairs laying quietly in her bed. I wondered what she would think if she knew I had her journals. I felt very guilty for a minute but then rationalized with my original thoughts. This was a woman who has lost touch with reality and without the journals, I truly know nothing about her and her life. This journal was my path to know the woman she used to be before, well you know, before her arteries hardened.

October 23, 1951

Today is day 18 without my Otto and nothing has gotten any easier. I am still lost without him and finding myself accomplishing nothing in a day beyond eating and bathing myself. There is so much that Otto took care of around the house, the yard and the business. My head spins everyday just thinking about my new responsibilities.

So many business decisions must be addressed soon and I am fearful that I will make a mistake. So many decisions! I know Otto trusted Herman to run things in his absence, but those absences were ever only for a few days, not forever. I know Otto trusted his attorney, Owen Campbell, but I only ever met him at functions like annual meetings or the Christmas parties. I never had to deal with him professionally. Now, how will he treat me? Would he even contact me and fill me in on problems or important decisions? Otto did leave the business to me. I am now the boss. I would expect to be kept abreast of any changes within the company. I would expect Owen to respect Otto's wishes and treat me in the same way as he did Otto. However, would he really even consider informing me or would he think I know nothing and treat me as just an empty figurehead of the company?

Oh how I miss Otto. I saw that awful Mitzi working in her yard today with Lina. She was pruning back the fall flowers getting ready for winter as if nothing had ever happened. As if her life was the same, her days were the same. She went about as if not a thing had changed in her life. She must be a cold-hearted bitch. Her brother died. The next day, my Otto died. And today, she is working in her yard as if it is just a normal fall day and the world is no different. I hate you Mitzi Winter and someday I will figure out how to make everyone believe you did it and you will pay for your sins.

I think Aunt Elsie sure had a lot to worry about back then and things are very different in today's circumstances. I wondered if she ended up running the company. I would ask Daddy about that tomorrow, but I would ask my questions cautiously to not raise any suspicions as to why I had such questions. I turned the page.

October 24, 1951

Today I asked Eulalie if she could possibly work more than her normal 2 days a week. I do not like being alone all the time. She said she could and I asked if she would work Monday through Friday from 9:00 am to 5:00 pm. She said she could but she had one day when she could not stay until 5:00. On Wednesdays, she helps at her church, cooking diners for the less fortunate, so she would need to leave by 3:30. I agreed to her terms. I think it will help having someone in the house to talk with, at least most days. There has still been no mention of an investigation into Henry Winter's death or of Otto's fall. That stupid Chief is so willing to believe both were just accidents. That my sure-footed Otto just simple fell! They are all blind to the high and mighty Winter family. This town has always been blind to their ways. I will NOT let this drop. That Chief will hear from me every day. I will be the thorn in his side. My poor Otto.

Oct. 26th, 1951

I missed writing in my journal yesterday. This was not by accident but a planned action. I found at the end of the day I had nothing new to say. I sat and read my recent journal pages and I realized my life cannot continue this way, a life without purpose. I need to settle back into a new life. A life without my Otto. I will give myself a few more days to pine away and feel sorry for myself and then I will begin again. I will make myself start my new life on Thursday, November 1st, All Souls Day. It seems a fitting time. I will find my purpose and set about on a new path. I must. I am determined to keep my sanity. But I will give myself permission to feel my grief. To understand the depth of my grief. All of my life, I saw things happen to other families, things I knew caused them pain. I had older relatives die and I thought I understood the dimensions of grief. But I was wrong. I understood nothing. I now know true grief and I am miserable. To me; grief is when a light you once loved inside you burns out. Everything remains dark. Eventually you will see daylight again, but it is never the same. The bright light you lost will never glow again. Without that light, the world seems dark. Always dark. And you find yourself being swallowed by the darkness.

We all know we must find our way thru the darkness and find light again. But none of us realizes how very hard it is to climb into the light. It is not an instinct. No one has ever prepared you for the task. It is something that one must learn on their own and it is very hard to do.

She sounds so very sad. So alone. I feel so bad for Aunt Elsie.

I decided at this point to give myself a break from reading and try to get some needed sleep, but I just couldn't resist. I knew there would be no sleep until I got my answer. I just had to know so I turned the page to check on how Aunt Elsie's plan worked out. Sure enough, what I saw next was:

November 1st, 1951 –

My New Beginning – Being Alone....

I stopped there. She was a woman of her words.

As I went to close the journal, I was still leaning upright in my bed and I felt something move in the journal. I saw there was a brown edge sticking out on the right side of the journal. I touched the edge and then folded the pages open to the spot. It was some sort of an old folded newspaper. It felt very brittle. Just then Tiffany jumped up on my bed and scared the heck out of me. I shooed her away quickly for fear she would tear the paper.

I sat up straighter, flattened my bedsheets and carefully unfolded the paper. I saw a bunch of columns covering social news, school news, obituaries and scattered advertisements. I turned the sheet over and realized now that I was looking at the front page of the Pinesdale

Weekly Review. I remembered Daddy bringing it home from the barbershop, but I never paid any attention to it in the past. I saw the date was October 5, 1951. I was just starting to wonder why Aunt Elsie saved this, when I saw the headline. Oh My Gosh! I read the article. I looked at Tiffany who was staring at me from the rug below, meowing and begging to be given permission to jump back up on the bed. I shook my head no at the cat and then thought to myself; this is big.

Pinesdale Mayor Henry Winter found dead

Mayor Henry Winter was found dead in the garage of the home he shared with his sisters, Miriam and Lina Winter. A complete autopsy will be performed when Coroner Ben Gregory returns from his annual hunting trip at Cook's Forest on October 7th.

At 7:48 pm Thursday evening, a call to the dispatcher was placed by Miss Miriam Winter requesting an ambulance at her home at 102 Maple Street. She reported that her brother, Henry was in the garage and ill.

Patrolman Jim Dowdy was first on the scene. Upon entering the garage, he reported he found Henry's car running and Henry lying on the garage floor near the door. He was unresponsive.

Within minutes, the volunteer squad arrived and pronounced Henry dead at the scene. The body was taken to the Bricker Funeral Home.

The family will post a complete obituary. Henry Winter was 46 years old. He was a lifelong resident of Pinesdale. He was a 1923 graduate of Pinesdale High School with a business degree from Penn State College awarded in 1927. He owned and operated Winter Accounting Firm and became Mayor in 1944. In 1939, his family suffered a house fire that took the lives of his wife, Marie and son, Paul.

Further information and the official cause of death will be published following the autopsy.

I read the article and then read it again. My mind was buzzing with ideas but my body was tired. I finally convinced myself to sleep and study this information again tomorrow. I started to refold the newspaper. As I finished, I realized that there had been another clipping. Apparently, when I unfolded the large page, it must have slipped out and fell onto my bed.

I opened the smaller clipping. There was no date showing on this one. The paper had been carefully trimmed to include only the obituary section. I scanned the listed names: Sylvia Smith, age 78, Frank Weston, age 92 and suddenly, there it was: Otto Becker, age 66.

Otto Becker

Mr. Otto Becker of 104 Maple Street went to be with the Lord on Friday, October 5th when he suffered a fatal head injury from a fall at his home. He was born on September 3rd, 1885 the son of Herman and Myra Becker.

Otto lived in Pinesdale his entire life. He was a 1903 graduate of Pinesdale High School. He completed 2 years of service in the U.S. Army and later attended Fairlane College earning a dual degree in engineering and business in 1911. He was a successful inventor. He owned and operated Becker Industries serving customers across the U.S. and overseas. He was a member of the Pinesdale Sportsman Club and The First Presbyterian Church. He enjoyed gardening, fishing, traveling and spending time with his many friends. He leaves the love of his life, his wife of 40 years the former Elsie Louise Holden and a nephew of his wife, Michael, his wife Pearl and their two sons, David and Mitchell.

Calling hours will be held on Monday evening from 7:00 to 9:00pm at the Bricker Funeral Home. Final visitations and funeral services will be at 11:00 am on Tuesday with burial at Maple Grove Cemetery.

I slowly refolded the clipping and carefully placed everything back in the journal and placed it safely back into my nightstand drawer and locked it. I patted my bedspread giving Tiffany the okay to return. I laid down, but I did not fall sleep for a long time.

SABRINA

Chapter 12 – 1968

It felt a little strange, but this morning when I awoke, I was no longer in the small bedroom that I had shared with Audrey. Today, I awoke in our massive room where JoJo and Holly still lay sleeping. We were done. We had moved. We could now say we live at 104 Maple Street. Aunt Elsie's large home was now our home too. I was in my new room that was full with color. I was in our room that had many windows, oh yes, windows……journals…..and newspapers clippings.

I had suddenly remembered last night and the flashlight shining in the window. I remembered me watching Tram walk around everyone's yards late last night, Tram walking into the garage. I wondered, was he still in the garage now? The window! I needed to peek through one of those little windows right now. I crawled off the end of my bed where I could lay right in front of the tiny baseboard window again that faced the Winter house. I got comfortable. I lay on my belly with my face up to the window. I had cleaned them all carefully and had done a good job, if I must say so myself, therefore my view was clear. It was much clearer than peering through the window last night in the dark. Tiffany tried to cuddle up beside me curling her body tight up against rib cage.

I was immediately disappointed with my view. Nothing appeared to be happening in any part of the neighborhood. I decided to wait a few minutes. I tried to be patient but my empty stomach was growling. I decided to get dressed, go downstairs, gobble my breakfast as quickly as Momma would allow me and find Knox.

My plan was all go until I finished my breakfast, set my plate in the sink and started out the back door. Momma stopped me in my tracks with those eyes in the back of her head. I swear, she had her back to me and her head partially inside the freezer while digging around for tonight's supper, and she still caught me.

"Just where do you think you are going young lady?" she asked.

"Momma, I just want to meet some of the new neighbors," I pleaded and continued, "After all, it is the neighborly thing to do and Knox promised to help me. He says he knows most everybody here."

"And just who is this Knox person and how old is he?" Momma asked.

"Momma, don't be silly. You must think I am Audrey." I said with a smile.

"Don't you try to be funny young lady," Momma said and I realized she was serious.

I knew then, if I wanted any chance to be free this morning, I had better start talking and fast. "Oh Momma, Knox is just a little kid, I think he said he was 10," I said quickly without taking a breath. "He told me yesterday that he moved here a few months ago with his Momma and sister. He didn't mention a Dad. I wonder if he has a Dad. Well, that part I don't know, but he seems nice. He rides an old banged-up bike. He said his Momma couldn't afford to get him a new one. Yesterday his chain fell off and I helped him fix it. He likes to walk and go to the library. He likes reading the Hardy Boys books and since I like reading Nancy Drew, I figure we had a lot in common so I was hoping...."

"Stop, stop, stop" Momma said as she held up one hand to me and had a frozen pot roast in the other. "Alright.... just stop talking. You can go," she finally said. "Just stay within yelling range and if I call for you, you answer me. Do you hear me young lady?"

"Yes Ma'am, I said obediently, "Yes Ma'am I do. I will. I will listen for you to yell. Do you want to meet him Momma? If you do I will bring him over to the house."

"I do," she responded, "But how about not today. I still have so much to do here. I will meet your little friend another day. Now go on out the door before I change my mind and pull out my list and give you a few jobs to do." She said all of that than looked at me and gave me a big smile.

"Go on now, scoot before I change my mind!" she said to me and pretended to sweep a broom toward the back door. Gigi had been resting; all stretched out in front of the sink. Thinking Momma was talking to her; she tried to quickly move out of her path and made a dash for the dining room. Momma watched her flee and then looked at me and we both laughed.

Momma is a good Momma. She could be real strict at times, but she could also be a lot of fun. Daddy always says that Momma has a crazy silly streak in her and she is not afraid to show it. He is right. We get to see that silly side of her a lot. And she has a really happy laugh. Some people laugh and it doesn't make you feel any much different. When my Momma laughs, it causes everybody around her to smile. Everybody wants to join her; she sets people at ease.

Momma gives advice to all us kids just like any other mother would to help teach her kids. She doesn't try to talk to me too much yet about clothes and hair stuff, not like she does with Audrey. I know that day will come eventually. For now, Momma talks to me about how I should act, especially around grown-ups. Some days Momma tells me I talk too much but she says that happens because she thinks that I think too much. I never knew a person could think too much. My Daddy says Momma is wrong. He says that my brain works just the right amount, but Momma says that's cause he isn't home all day....watching it as it happens. That is true. She is right about that. Daddy works at his barbershop every day from 8:00 am to 6:00 pm except on Sundays. It was originally my Papa Holden's shop but when daddy got old enough, he started cutting hair there too. A few years ago, when I was like five-years-old, Papa died. So, now it is just my Daddy there.

Anyway, I listened to my Momma. I scooted out the door. Tiffany followed me out but was content to find a spot on the back porch to lie in the sun. I started to look for Knox. I didn't see him in his back yard or on his bike in the alley. I really didn't want to knock on his door, but it was looking like that was what I was going to have to do. I headed across the alley and as I walked past Pastor Masons' house, I heard him inside. He was yelling and it was pretty loud. It didn't sound good. I supposed he was yelling at one of his kids. No big deal, every kid gets yelled at once in a while, I just kept walking.

I got to Knox's back yard. There was a waist-high fence that needed painting around his back yard and a gate with a flip-up kind of latch. The fence ran right up to the edge of the alley. I noticed then that Pastor Mason had a garage and so did Miss Winter, but the rest of us along the alley way did not, just a car parked in a short gravel driveway. I opened the gate and walked toward the back door. Suddenly a pretty little calico cat went running across his yard. Knox came running out the door.

"Hey Stinkweed," he said with a big grin.

"Hey," I said back. "Is that your cat?"

"No," he said very casually, "just one of those cats that seems to belong to nobody and visits every house on the street looking for food. I think she is kind of pretty and I try to throw something little out into the yard every day for her to find." He was quiet for a few seconds and then added, "I call her Tootsie."

"Oh okay," I said, "Yea, she does look nice but listen; I have something important I gotta ask you. Did you see Tram out scouting around the yards last night?"

"I did," he answered back as quickly as I had asked. "He was almost right up against the side of your house at one point. If there had been one of those pull down fire escape gadgets, he probably would have climbed right up to the top."

"And if he would have," I said, "He would have been staring right at my face because I had my face pressed up against that window. So...what do you think he was doing? What was he looking for out there all that time? I swear, if I don't figure it out soon, I am just gonna ask him!"

Then I remembered the article from last night. I said to him, "Wait a minute Knox. I got something else I gotta ask you."

When I was sure I had his complete attention, I stared directly into his eyes. I pointed my left arm toward the Winter garage and asked him, "Did you know that Miss Winter's brother, Henry, died right there in that garage?"

Knox stared at me with shock on his face and I knew my answer. His eyes were about bugging out of his face.

"What?" he said in a way too loud voice.

I quickly hushed him, "Keep in down Knox. Not everybody along this alley needs to know what we are talking about today."

He spoke quieter this time. "I didn't even know Miss Winter had a brother," he said. "I thought it was just her and Miss Lina. Do you mean he died right there ....in that garage? The garage that Tram hangs out in every night? What did he die from, I mean how did he die and hey, how do you know this stuff?"

I told him about Aunt Elsie's journals and about reading the old newspaper clipping that I found tucked inside the pages. He was indeed fascinated. I could almost feel his brain working.

His head was hanging downward and then suddenly, it jerked back up and he looked right at me. He spoke quickly as though if he didn't say it fast, he might forget what he wanted to say.

"We need go to the library…. and we need to go today," he said excitedly. "We need to start digging around to find out what happened. Did the newspaper say what happened; I mean did it tell you how he died? We need more details. Wait, maybe we can ask some of the old people in the neighborhood. Maybe they can give us some answers. We should ask…."

I jumped in to stop his unending questions and ideas.

"Hold on Knox," I said in my best grown up, older kid voice. "Let me explain a little bit first."

I explained that the article did not say much except that he had died and his sister was the one who called for the ambulance.

"It did say there would be an autopsy when the coroner returned from a vacation," I said with my eyes rolling. "After his vacation," I repeated. "How crazy is that?"

Knox looked at me with surprise and said, "What the heck?"

"Well then," he continued, "That is where our search has to begin. We need to find the newspaper that gives the coroners answers. I wonder how long he was on vacation."

"I don't exactly remember what it said, but I do remember it told that answer," I said. "I will recheck the article tonight after my sisters are asleep."

"No," he almost demanded. "Go check it now so we can get started with our digging around! I am anxious to get going. I can be a real Hardy Boy. Don't worry Stinkweed, I am good at it. I never miss any clues in their books. My mind is always thinking ahead. I will help you solve this mystery. I LOVE it!"

He was almost jumping up and down. I smiled at him. He was kinda cute when he got so excited.

"OK," I said slowly and as calmly as I could. I was already pretty excited too; but he was already way too excited for both of us.

"I can't go check it right now," I told him and immediately saw the disappointment in his eyes.

His immediate response was, "What?....Why?"

"I can't go check it right now," I explained, "because I don't want any of my family to know I am reading Aunt Elsie's journals."

Once again, it happened. Knox looked at me with total confusion on his face.

"I was thrilled when I found the journals while we were all cleaning the attic," I said as part of my explanation. "But I quickly realized the potential information they might hold and I hid them by locking them in my nightstand drawer," I said with a feeling of guilt that I was sure showed on my face.

He looked at me with a puzzled expression. All he said was, "Why?"

I expected the question and tried my best to explain my reasons.

"Well," I said, "Aunt Elsie is my Dad's GREAT aunt. She is old. I mean she is really old. I think she is probably almost 100!

His expression quickly changed from questioning to shock.

I continued. "Not everything about her works like it used to when she was younger. For example, her legs don't work very well anymore; she mostly sits in that big old black wheelchair. She can use her hands a little bit to push herself, but to really move around, she needs one of us to walk from behind her and push."

He gave me a look so that I knew he thought that made good sense and said, "That is why I have never seen her."

"Yes," I said. "She never comes out of the house. And, even more important," I said slowly to emphasize the importance, "Her mind doesn't work too well. She forgets things. I mean not just little unimportant things like where is my coffee cup; she forgets many things; big things. Do you know what I mean? Do you know anybody that is like that?"

He shook his head to tell me his answer was no.

"For example," I continue, "she forgets Uncle Otto died a very long time ago and she thinks her cat, Mr. Mertz can talk." I wait to see his expression; to see if he is surprised.

This time I am surprised. Instead of looking surprised, he looks sad.

"Awe," he says with real empathy, "the poor lady. That would be awful."

"It is," I reply. "That is why everything is so hard. That is why we moved into her house, so we could all help her, well, mostly my parents. But that is why….why I want to read the journals even though I don't think my parents would approve." I stop and wait to see if he gets my meaning.

He is quiet. I can tell he is thinking so I continue.

"I want to read them," I said, "because I think she was a very smart woman in her day. I want to know about her and the life she used to live before she had to sit in that dumb wheelchair all day and talk to an old cat. I want to know her history. I mean, after all, she is my great, great Aunt. Her history is also a part of my history. I want to know it. I guess you could say….it fascinates me."

I stop and stare into space for a moment. Then I look at Knox. "Does that make sense?"

He nods a yea, but then asks, "Why do you have to hide them?"

Before I can answer, I see his expression change and I think he understands.

"Wait, I get it," he says. "Just in case." He looks me in the eye again. "Am I right?"

I smile at him. Yep, I was right about Knox. He will be a good match for me. He does understand.

"Correct," I said with relief. "I don't know what I will find in the journals. I mean the very first day that I started to read them I see about Henry Winter and then, oh yea, did I tell you this? This is really weird. The very next day after Henry Winter died....Aunt Elsie's' husband, Uncle Otto died! Isn't that strange? Two neighbors dying one day apart. I think it is really strange. And...Aunt Elsie hates Miss Winter. I think she doesn't think either one of the deaths was an accident. "

Knox looks like he is ready to go crazy. "What!" he exclaims. "Oh my gosh. This is wild! "

"Wait...now let me think a minute," he says. "So, Henry Winter dies and we don't know what caused it. How old was Henry anyway?"

I think quickly and answer, "I remember this! He was 46 years old. It happened in 1951, on Oct. 4th. And in case this was to be your next question, Uncle Otto was 66 years old and he died on Oct. 5th 1951."

I waited. His mind was still thinking.

Finally, he said, "OK. I got that. But I need to know a little more. I know you want to know about Aunt Elsie, but do you think there will really be things written in those journals that your parents don't already know? I mean, parents usually know just about everything that happens in the family."

I nodded. He made a good point. "I think you could be right, but I don't want to take that chance. Aunt Elsie really can't confirm any answers to any questions anymore; but I have a gold mine in those journals. She wrote every word. She wrote what was important to her."

"I mean," I continued, "look what I found the very first day! I would have never even known about Miss Winter having a brother without the journals. I hope to find out more answers. Who knows...maybe one day, one of those pages will tell me what Tram is looking for every night! Wouldn't that be something? Just imagine the things I might read about."

"That is why," I said softer, "I just couldn't take a chance with telling Momma and Daddy about the journals. They might not see it like I do, like we do."

I am positive they would have said: NO ONE SHOULD READ THE JOURNALS. THESE ARE AUNT ELSIE'S PRIVATE THOUGHTS.

"And I know I am probably doing wrong," I said sadly, "maybe in God's eyes too, but I started now and I mean to finish."

Knox stared at me like a judge ready to pass a sentence. Finally, he said, "Nope. You aren't wrong. You are doing the right thing! It is exactly what any good detective would do. Do you think Richard Kimble on *"The Fugitive,"* would skip reading something that he thought could help prove his case? NO! He would read every word and you have to do the same."

Then he gave me a quick little wink and said, "Enough of all this chatter, we got ourselves a mystery to solve."

He stuck out his hand to me and said, "On my boy scouts honor, I will not tell anyone about Aunt Elsie's journals. Should the information happen to get out into the world; I swear I will never tell where the journals are hidden."

I laughed, but shook his hand.

He got right back to where we had left off. "OK...first things first,' he said. "Did the newspaper clipping tell you how Uncle Otto died?"

I answered quickly, as if I was on one of those game shows and the answer might win me a thousand dollars. "Yes, it said he died from a fall at home causing a head injury."

"Yikes," he answered, "that sounds like a bad way to go."

I nodded in agreement.

"Ok, so back to Henry," he continued. "After the autopsy was done; when the guy got back from vacation was there any clippings with that information? We need to know if he was murdered, if he was sick or if he killed himself."

124

I held up my hands and said, "Ok Hardy boy, you need to slow down."

I told him that maybe we were getting carried anyway, how could it be murder, but he insisted that we needed to know the truth before we could worry anymore about Tram.

We had started walking now while we were thinking and we were heading back up the alley toward my house. I saw the calico cat again and wondered if she had found any food.

Knox had brought an orange outside with him and he had been peeling it while we talked. It smelled so good. When he finished he offered me a chunk of three segments and I took it. I took a big bite and juice squirted out and down my chin. Knox was watching, but he didn't make me feel stupid or like a pig, he just laughed.

When he finished laughing, he said, "Why don't we...."

I said, "Why don't we what?"

"Ask him," he said in a very matter of fact sounding voice. "I think we could. I have said "Hey" to him before when I was riding my bike. I mean he is creepy looking, especially walking through yards in the dark, but during the daytime, he isn't too bad."

"I don't know," I confessed. "This is all kind of new to me. I am just getting used to the idea of having neighbors so close. I haven't had much experience in making small talk with nice ones let alone creepy ones. And, furthermore, I have seen him in the daytime; I think he is creepy with a capital C."

Knox stared at me. "Alright," he said. "I see your point. Let's do this. Tram usually comes around at about 10:30 each morning. He is here for a while then he takes off and I never see him again until it is dark."

With excitement in my eyes, I interrupted Knox to ask, "What's he come for in the morning?"

"Not sure," Knox said in kind of slow motion. I haven't figured that out yet, but you watch, he will be here. What time is it now?"

"I reckon it is about 9:00," I said as if I was his able-bodied assistant." He didn't immediately respond, so I added, "So we have a little time. What do you want to do until he gets here?"

"Well," he said, "You said you wanted to get to know the folks along the alley. Let me give you a run-down on what I have learned about each house so far. I think it will be good for you as you try to match them up with their names, faces, houses and cars that come and go through this alley."

"Perfect," I said.

Yes, I was right about Knox. He might be a touch younger than me but he has a good detective head on those shoulders.

"Let's start with Nell Taylor," he said. "Mrs. Nell… that is what she told me to call her. She is a really nice lady, but I think she is pretty lonely. We can knock on her door and I will start by telling her who you are and where you live. That will work. She is a real good baker. Maybe she will give us a cookie or something. Everything she bakes is good. Sometimes, I can smell her baking from my back yard. I make up a reason to stop over. She always gives me something," he said with a big grin.

We crossed the alley and start to walk up through her back yard. Her house and yard were nice and neat. She had a small garden that went almost right up against the Winter garage. There were two windows on this side of that garage, but they were pretty dirty and I couldn't see anything. What I could see was that Mrs. Taylor had gotten her garden in on time and already had good growth showing on her tomatoes and green beans.

Knox grinned at me and said, "You smell that?" Then he knocked on the back door and it was only a few seconds before it swung open.

"Good morning Knox," she said with a smile. "I see you brought me a new friend. Is she someone that likes blueberry muffins and much as you do? They are due to come out of the oven in 5 minutes. Come on in."

I looked at Knox. He arched his eyebrows at me and flashed a huge smile and said, "Good Morning Mrs. Nell, I want you to meet our new neighbor. This is Sabrina, but she likes to be called Stinkweed."

Mrs. Nell was now the one arching her eyebrows, "Well then, Stinkweed it shall be although, I think the name Sabrina is just lovely. Your father has the barbershop downtown, is that correct?"

126

"Yes, ma'am," I answered and knew Momma would be pleased that I used my manners.

"So," she continued, "Your family has moved in with Miss Elsie to help take care of her."

I nodded.

"Oh my, that is wonderful. I knew Miss Eulalie was getting too far up in her years to keep trying to take care of both that big house and Miss Elsie. That is a lot of work. Thank goodness, it appears to me your Momma has plenty of built-in helpers. I have noticed quite a few youngsters moving about the house recently. How many children are in your family Sabrina, um .... I mean Stinkweed?"

"There are five of us Mrs. Nell and it is okay, you may call me Sabrina," I said.

"Here you go," she said as she pulled the hot muffin tins out of the oven. "These are about as fresh as they can be."

She smiled at us as she tipped the tin and emptied the hot muffins in a pretty icy blue ceramic bowl. "I am making these to take over to your Momma today anyway," she continued, "So, here you go. Have one while they are at their best - Nice and hot! And please, have a seat at the table. Oh and wait, let me get you two some butter to spread onto them."

While she scurried to the refrigerator, I looked at Knox. We both smiled and sat down.

She gave us each a small china plate with a colorful blue tiny flower pattern circling the edge of the plate. She set a muffin on each plate, cut it in half and gave us each a butter knife. While we got busy adding our butter, she poured us each a glass of milk and then sat down with us at the table.

There was a minute or two of awkward silence as we took our first bites of the warm muffins. They were absolutely wonderful! Big, juicy and warm blueberries filled my mouth and pleased my taste buds.

I looked at Mrs. Nell and said, "Momma is going to love them."

Mrs. Nell was pleased. "Thank you and I accept your compliment," she said proudly. "Truth be told, I am known in Pinesdale for my blueberry muffins. Knox here can tell you that. I think he has a keen nose because he tends to show up when I start baking."

Knox looked a wee bit embarrassed.

"So," she continued, "What are you two up to this morning?"

Knox stopped chewing long enough to answer. "I am trying to help Stinkweed learn about the neighbors. She is a lot like me Mrs. Nell. She wants to get to know everybody on Maple and Elm Streets. She lived in the country before and isn't used to having people so close by. I told her everyone here is really nice, but she has some doubts about old Tram."

Oh my goodness, what did he just say to Mrs. Nell. I glared across the table at him, but quickly stopped and flashed a shy smiled when I realized Mrs. Nell was now looking at me.

"Um," I started to say but realized I still had a mouthful of muffin. I chewed quickly but she jumped in.

"Oh Sabrina," she said quietly, "I can surely understand your concern, but I think Bertram is merely a harmless old man. He has been a part of this neighborhood for as long as I have lived here."

Now I was curious. I got brave and I asked.

"Mrs. Nell, do you know Miss Winter and her sister well? I guess I mean did you grow up here in Pinesdale? Also, I kinda wondered if you had ever met their brother, Henry?"

I tried to watch her face carefully as I asked my questions. She stared at me, but not like she was shocked about the questions, but more that she was shocked that those were the things that a little girl would want to know. She probably thought I should be asking about how she made her yummy muffins or what else did she have planted in her garden. I guess I have to admit that I was not your typical little girl. I glanced at Knox. He was looking at Mrs. Nell, like the Cheshire Cat in *"Alice's Adventures in Wonderland,"* waiting for a mouse to come out of hiding.

She sat quiet for a few seconds, and then she looked at Knox and then back to me. Finally, she responded.

"Yes, Sabrina," she said, "I have lived in Pinesdale my whole life. Well I guess I should not say that so quickly. For a very short time, I moved to the big city. You see it often happens that we young folks think there is something bigger and better out there for us and we have to learn on our own that the grass is not always greener on the other side. The best thing about that time of my life was that I met Mr. Taylor. When I lived in the city I used to spend a lot of my evenings in the library. It was huge and held more books than one could ever count. I loved it the library. You know the city was very busy with lots of hustle and bustle but the city never seemed to creep into the library. You could hear a pin drop in there. Everyone in there treasured the space, the books, and the history of it all.

"One night," she reminisced with a faraway look in her eyes, "I was sitting at a table on the second floor reading a book I had found in the botanical section. The next thing I knew a handsome young man sat down at the table, right across from me with a book about woodworking. After about 5 minutes, he cleared his throat rather loudly. I looked up from my reading and smiled at him. He smiled back and quickly, as though planned, introduced himself. Me being the shy country girl that I was, I nodded and went right back to reading. The next night, I was there reading but this time I was on the third floor and sure enough, there he was again. This happened again the next night and the next and each time we said just a little more than the night before. After a week, he asked me out to dinner."

She sat quiet for a moment as if she was picturing herself back in the day. Then she shook her head a tiny bit and looked back at us looking just a little embarrassed.

"Oh my, well I guess you didn't need to know all of that. It was a very long time ago. But to somewhat finish my story, we did marry four months later on January 1st, 1944. We continued to live in the city and spend some of our evenings reading in the library. As we settled into married life, I found I was becoming more and more homesick for Pinesdale and my mother, so we packed up and moved back home. Mr. Taylor and I bought a house on the outskirts of town in 1945. It was a very nice little house and we loved it there."

She got quiet again then slowly she continued. "Mr. Taylor, Curtis, died in 1953. He suffered a massive heart attack. One minute he was fine and working in the garden and the next minute he was gone… forever."

Again, she became quiet.

"Then," she continued, "So, I sold our small home and moved back in here with my mother. She passed away in 1961."

Again, she grew quiet as though she was still reminiscing. Then just as suddenly, she said with new strength in her voice, "In answer to your question Sabrina, yes of course I knew….," she paused and kinda slowly cleared her throat. She then finished what she was saying but was still talking slowly when she finally said, "Henry Winter."

I don't know if it was the look on her face, the expression in her voice or the combination of the two but it seemed to me like she didn't like saying the name of Henry Winter. I wonder why? My Nancy Drew brain started working in overtime.

My mind was busy but I suddenly realized that she was talking again.

"As a young girl," she was saying, "he spent a lot of time next door at his family home. I was nineteen years old when he had a house fire and lost both his wife and son. That was when he moved back into the family home with Miriam, Lina and their father. So you see, he was a neighbor. He was the town's mayor for many years. He died in the early 1950's. Why do you ask?"

Knox and I looked at each other as if we had just hit a lottery.

"Oh, we were just wondering. You know, learning more and more about the neighborhood." Knox said quickly.

Mrs. Nell got up then to get us more milk and the minute she turned her back to us, he winked at me. We knew at that moment Mrs. Nell would be our source. She would be our puzzle-solver. For one thing, she liked us and that was a huge help on its own. Then, she knew Pinesdale. She knew the neighborhood. She knew Tram. And big bonus for us….she knew Henry Winter.

Our next step would be to scour the library to do our own research, but at least we now knew we would be able to fill in any blank spots with the help of Mrs. Nell.

Knox had a huge smile on his face. I was beaming back at him realizing how happy he was and that he didn't even know about the fire yet, but Mrs. Nell did! I couldn't wait to talk to him about all of it when we get back outside. I noticed a quick movement in the kitchen window. Tootsie had jumped up on the ledge and had given herself a front row view directly into the kitchen. She went to work quietly cleaning herself and enjoying the warmth of the morning sun. She seemed to sense my eyes, stopped and stared at me. A couple of slow blinks and she returned to her grooming. She really was a very pretty cat with a mix of butterscotch and caramel coloring on her white fur.

I realized Mrs. Nell was now smiling at me. I took another bite of my muffin and decided I was right, today was going to be a big day.

SISTER JEANETTE

Chapter 13 - 1968

Since Oak Mount City was fairly large in population, the bus depot was a bit more substantial than the one from where my trip had begun. There was immediate bench seating lining the exterior of the north side of the building and two phone booths, both already occupied. The walkway was filled with people, some entering buses, some departing. I tried to scan the area looking to see if I could spot a brown station wagon parked anywhere close by, but seeing none, I worked my way through the crowd of passengers and waited for the porter to pull my small brown suitcase from the storage bin of the bus. Once I had all my belongings I walked into the depot carrying my satchel in one hard and my small suitcase in the other.

Inside was much quieter. There were people milling around, but without the quick bustle in their step. Apparently they were either trying to fill time while waiting for their departure or like myself waiting for their rides to arrive.

I spotted a seat in what looked to be a quieter corner of the depot. The hard wooden bench was occupied by just one young woman holding a small sleeping baby. She smiled my direction as I sat at the far end of the long bench. I set my suitcase on the floor and placed my satchel beside me on the bench, folded my hands into my lap and prepared to wait.

I truly did not expect the driver to be sitting here waiting for me. The bus had arrived 45 minutes later than specified. I was sure the driver had most likely left to do some sort of errand when he was told of the expected late arrival. I hoped the clerk had been able to give him an approximate time to return. Since I had already experienced a long day of sitting a wee bit more would harder matter. I could wait.

Truly the bench was hard; very different from the broken seat of the bus, but my time to sit I expected to be short so it did not matter. After about 5 minutes of crowd-watching, the sleeping baby awoke and began to cry. Her pink blanket and ruffled bonnet made me fully aware that the little bundle was a girl. She had whimpered softly at first but once raised up to her mothers' shoulder and able to survey her surroundings, she began to wail. Her mother tried to soothe her. I was about to offer my help to the young mother that looked so very tired, but just as I was rising from the bench, I heard someone call my name. I stopped, looked up and saw a young man walking toward me.

My first thought was that this gentleman had made a mistake. I had been told my driver was to be the church custodian, Lucas, and he may possibly be accompanied by Sister Charlotte. The person saying my name was very young and did not look as I had imagined the church custodian. He was a nice looking young man with dark wavy hair and deep brown eyes. As he spoke I heard a faint accent, possibly Italian.

He continued moving toward me and again was saying my name.

"Hello, I assume you are Sister Jeanette?" he said as he reached out his hand to me. "My name is Christian, Christian Naples. My father is Lucas Naples, the custodian at St. Lucy's Church in Pinesdale. There was a problem at the rectory today so at the last minute I was sent to deliver you back to the church. It was to my advantage that your bus was delayed and you did not arrive on time. I am afraid I am not familiar with Oak Mount City and got slightly lost."

I heard everything the young man was saying but my mind was still concentrating on the fact that he was not Lucas. The shock must have shown on my face because as I was staring at him, I suddenly realized that he was again talking.

"Are you alright Sister Jeanette?" he said with a worried look across his face.

Kathleen F. Ewing

I focused, calmed my mind and smiled his direction.

"Why yes," I said. "I am perfectly fine. It has just been a very long day and I am anxious to reach my destination. Shall we keep moving forward? I admit I am very anxious to finally arrive at St. Lucy's."

I reached for my satchel and suitcase but Christian moved forward quickly and tried to take both from me.

"Christian please," I said. "I appreciate you carrying my suitcase, but I can manage my satchel."

"Ok Sister," he said as he pulled his hand back. "The car is parked just down the street a short distance from the depot. You can follow me please."

I did. As we stepped off the depot platform and lost the protective roof, I could feel a slight sprinkle of rain. I lowered my head just slightly to shield my face and within a few steps almost tripped over a raised level in the sidewalk. Though ahead of me, Christian heard my scuffle, turned back toward me and took my satchel from my hand. This time I did not object. We walked in silence for about a block and a half and finally he pointed out the older station wagon to me.

"Here she is," he said as he opened the door for me. "My father calls her Ethel," he said with a chuckle. And then suddenly looked apologetic.

"I am sorry Sister, did you not want to sit in the front seat. If you don't I won't be upset. I just thought if you did we could talk on the long ride back."

"Thank you Christian," I said as I climbed into the seat. "Yes, I would enjoy a nice conversation on our ride."

Christian smiled. He shut my door and moved to the back of the car to store my suitcase and satchel.

Once inside he struggled to be free of the parking spot as the car that had parked in front of him did not leave much move for maneuvering out of the small space; but he managed to get us out and onto the main roadway.

He said he estimated the drive would take about 55 minutes provided he did not get us lost again. I settled in for a long ride and hoped for some good conversation as I had barely spoken at all on the long bus ride and since I had also napped, I was now wide awake.

He was a very friendly young man and started our conversation. I found he was very easy to talk to...about many subjects. He started by asking if I had enjoyed my bus ride today. When I described the conditions of the bus and the length of the trip he replied he felt sorry for me. He asked if I was hungry and would I like to stop for a bite to eat. I explained that while I was indeed hungry; I thought I was more anxious to see my new church and meet Father Weaver and Sisters Charlotte and Bergan, so I would prefer to just drive.

"Hey," he said, "That is fine with me Sister. I did bring something to snack on while I was driving and there are some left. Here, help yourself and have one. My Ma makes the very best pizzelles. I am not kidding around; hers are the best in Pinesdale. Go ahead, try one. These ones are not anise flavored, she used vanilla because that is my favorite," he said with a grin.

Since I was famished, I did try one of the round Italian cookies and Christian was correct to brag about his mothers' baking abilities; it was delicious. We continued to talk and he seemed to be having no difficulty with the directions back to Pinesdale and the time flew by quickly. I was almost sorry see the small sign he pointed out to me that signified that we had arrived in the town of Pinesdale.

As we drove down the quiet street that brought us in from the outskirts of town, I saw small but well cared for houses. There were nice well-kept yards with lovely flower beds and lots of trees. Yes, there were glorious trees lining the street. I saw children riding bicycles and a little girl pulling a wagon filled with her baby dolls. She looked up just as we were passing and held up her tiny hand and waved to me. Such a sweet little welcoming gesture. I saw dogs, some running freely; some being walked by their owner with a leash in hand and others chained to the outside doghouses. I saw cats sleeping on front porches and others racing across yards and chasing after little squirrels. I saw one house with two older women casually swinging on the front porch swing. The home had the most beautiful flowers. There were potted red geraniums lining the edges of the three front steps. Along the front of the house were carefully planned flowers, tall Brown-Eyed Susan's along the back, pink and red mini-carnations in the center section and a mix of red, white and pink petunias in the front with a small section in the corner of Forget-Me-Nots, noticed easily although they are so small because they are my absolute favorites. I made a mental note to remember to try to meet the lovely lady that planted and cared so much for her flowers.

All of the streets on our way through this quaint country town looked similar. I was impressed. It looked perfect to me and I knew I would feel completely comfortable living and serving in Pinesdale. Within a few streets and turns, we were passing through the main business district, which was admittedly very small. I was able to see where I would do my shopping, get my stamps, get books from the library and was pleased when Christian informed me that they were all in walking distance from St. Lucy's.

Christian continued west on Main Street and in the very next block, he gestured for me to look out the window on my right. I did and was relieved to finally see the church. St. Lucy's sat up from the street level, just slightly like it had been built on a small hill. The church was small but at the same time impressive. The bricks were an old burnt red color and the steeple was shining down at me through the lowering sunlight. It was a lovely church, small but full of character and what stood out to me were the magnificent stained glass windows. They were of bright beautiful colors depicting life-like flowers; lilies in white and pansies in deep vibrant colors. The church may have been small but it had the stained glass windows of a cathedral. I loved it and could easily imagine myself offering my service to the Lord and the people of Pinesdale at this church.

Christian had paused the car to allow me to get a good look at my new church and then he smiled at me and gradually moved the car forward. He pulled from Main St onto Renee St and around to the rear of the church and into the parking area. The other properties which were also brick, had been in plain view from the street but I had focused my eyes only on the church and now could see both the rectory, where

Father Weaver lived and the smaller convent I would share with Sisters Charlotte and Bergan. There was also a small school building that housed grades K-6.

Christian parked the car and then smiled my direction and said, "Well Sister, we made it. Welcome to St. Lucy's. That is my father, Lucas, over there by the back side of the school building mowing grass, and you will need to get to know him but I think I should first take you into the rectory and introduce you to Father Weaver. He is not just an OK guy; he is a great guy. I think you will like him. I know all the folks in town like him a lot."

He continued, "The priest we had before Father Bob was a tough old guy. Sorry to say, he was not too well liked. His sermons were the fire and brimstone types and he didn't have much patience for people. That isn't the way it is with Father Bob. He is really a good guy and even I like his sermons. He is down to earth and always willing to listen and hear both sides of any issue. We all hope he stays a really long time here at St. Lucy's."

I started to move to open my door and Christian panicked and said, "Wait a minute Sister."

With that he hopped out of the car, ran around to my side and opened the door for me. As soon as I was out, he shut the door and scurried to the back of the car to obtain my satchel and suitcase. He sat them both down near the back tire of the car and then looked at me and said, "Let me take you inside to meet Father Bob.....I mean Father Weaver."

We started to walk toward the back door, but before we had taken more than 5 steps, the door opened and a tall and strikingly handsome young man appeared wearing a large smile and an outstretched hand aimed my direction.

"Hello," he said enthusiastically, "You must be Sister Jeanette. Welcome to our St. Lucy family. I hope young Christian here gave you the grand tour of our fair city during your ride."

I am not sure what my facial expression said to him, but I know what my mind was saying to me. It was reminding me that you are a nun. You were sent here to serve the Lord and the people of Pinesdale. Put your feelings and thoughts aside. And then I did so immediately. At least, I tried too.

I finally spoke. "Thank you Father Weaver," I said calmly. "I am so honored to be here and a part of St. Lucy's. I have been told many wonderful things about your parish, many by young Christian during our ride. The church, well the church is just beautiful. I absolutely love the stained glass windows and am anxious to see the inside."

"Yes," Father Bob said, "We are known for our lovely flowered windows throughout this area. Even some of the larger churches in neighboring towns are a little jealous of our windows," he said with the most attractive laugh.

I must stop noticing these qualities about him. Ashamed of myself, I quickly said, "It has been a long day Father. Would it be possible for me to meet Sisters Charlotte and Bergan and get my bags unpacked?" Then I heard myself and thought Oh Dear Lord …..this made me sound so uninterested. Oh! Now I am so embarrassed.

"Oh my yes," he said apologetically, "Let me walk you over to the convent and introduce you. I am sure you are tired. Long bus rides are not usually on any of our lists of fun events and I know your trip started at the crack of dawn. Follow me. Christian, please hand me Sister Jeanette's' bags."

As we walked together across the well-manicured lawn, Father Weaver talked a little bit about the history of St. Lucy's. He was quickly filling my head with numbers regarding dates and population, but I was retaining nothing. Whether I could attribute my day-dreaming to myself being exhausted from the long day, the bus ride, or to my astonishment of my sudden attraction to this handsome young priest and that I did not seem able to push out of my mind....I am not sure. But I did know that I needed to get myself under control and be prepared to meet the other sisters.

My mind was still feeling scattered when I realized he was knocking on the convent door. I composed myself and my thoughts. The door was immediately answered by a younger nun that was a little on the plump side. She was probably close to my age. I assumed this must be Sister

Bergan. My assumption was correct as she quickly introduced herself even before Father Weaver could say a word.

"Hello," she said very quickly with her hand stretched out; grabbing my free hand and shaking it vigorously. "I am Sister Bergan and you must be Sister Jeanette. We have been expecting you. Please come in. Sister Charlotte is in our sitting room. Let me take you there."

I looked at Father Weaver who gave me a small chuckle and said, "Please go right in Sister. You are in good hands. I will catch up with you tomorrow after you have had a chance to rest."

And with that he began to walk back to the rectory. I watched as he walked back across the lawn. He really was tall, probably easily six-foot which is tall compared to my 5 foot 2. He had broad shoulders with that trim waist. He walked with quick steps making me wonder if he is a jogger. I watched another few seconds then turned quickly realizing Sister Bergan was already way ahead of me and went inside the convent.

Sister Charlotte was much older than myself and Sister Bergan. Upon quick observation, I guessed she was probably in her mid-sixties. She sat perfectly straight in a comfy looking maroon stuffed easy chair in a small room that looked like it had been composed of a collection of odd pieces of furniture that might have been donations from different members of the parish.

There were 3 other chairs positioned in each of the other three corners of the room. Each chair was a different color and was made from different types of materials. One, which was gold in color, looked the oldest and the most lived in from the sags that filled the seat portion. The other two looked like they might have come from the same home. One was light brown and the other green in color, with one being very straight backed and stiff-looking and the other similar but more of a smaller side chair. There were two end tables, both wooden that did not match in the least, one was light-colored, probably maple while the other was a dark wood, maybe a pine. The small round coffee table that was located near Sister Charlottes' chair was yet another shade of brown and had a few deep nicks on the surface. There were three lamps

139

in total, two table lamps and one standing lamp, with none matching. In the corner, I saw a very small bookcase which appeared to hold a variety of reading material.

Sister Charlotte did not get up from her chair to greet me but gave me a very friendly hello and welcome to St. Lucy's. I could see she was a woman of few words in comparison to Sister Bergan who seemed to almost ramble with her enthusiasm. Sister Charlotte did ask me to please have a seat. She spoke to me for about 5 minutes telling me a brief history of St. Lucy's, the school, Sister Bergan and herself. She let me know that at the end of the school year, all lay teachers were questioned and all planned to return to St. Lucy's in the fall. That left Sister Bergan and myself to take care of office duties, act as school nurse and to fill in during any teachers absences. Sister Charlotte was of course the school principal. She asked if I had any immediate questions that she could answer for me. I thought for a moment and then said I appreciated what she had already shared and had no other questions at this time. She nodded her head in expectation and then she very nicely offered that I must be very tired and hungry after my long day and Sister Bergan would now show me to the kitchen where they had saved me a small meal that I could have before I retire to my room and tomorrow we would start fresh.

In my head, I was dancing with the idea of just getting off to myself to unpack, bathe and sleep, but decided it would be good to get some food in my stomach. I thanked her and followed Sister Bergan through the small room, the hallway corridor and toward the back of the house to the kitchen. She switched on the light allowing me to see a small kitchen with only the necessities. I saw a small refrigerator, stove, sink and a few cupboards. There was a small kitchen table up against the far wall with three mismatched chairs and covered with a yellow plastic tablecloth. On the table was a cake saver with a clear cover and I could see what looked like a small portion left of a chocolate cake. On the countertop, I saw an older toaster and a tall silver percolator with a large can of Maxwell House coffee sitting next to it and was relieved to realize they were coffee drinkers.

Sister Bergan motioned for me to have a seat and she went to the refrigerator and pull out a dinner plate that was tightly wrapped in Saran Wrap. She removed the wrap and I could see what looked like a large piece of meatloaf.

"We had this for dinner tonight," Sister Bergan said, "and saved this piece for you along with a few scalloped potatoes. Sister Charlotte and I are not the best of cooks, but you are in luck. Our custodians' wife prepared this meal for us tonight. Her name is Julia and she is very kind to us. She also brought this chocolate cake."

"That was very sweet of her," I said. "I think I sampled some of her Italian pizzelle cookies tonight on my ride home from the bus thanks to Christian."

"Oh my yes," Sister Bergan said with a little laugh. "We absolutely love their entire family! You will soon meet Lucas and Julia and you will see what I mean. For now, go ahead and eat. I am sure you are tired. Just yell when you are done and I will show you the rest of the house. And by the way, we are very happy to have you join us here at St. Lucy's."

I sat quietly and ate my meal. I decided to pass on the chocolate cake for tonight. I carried my plate to the sink and washed it clean. Sister Bergan must have heard the water, returned to the kitchen and led me down the hallway and to the stairway. We chatted as we walked and within a few words were heading up the steps to my new bedroom. From the landing I could see there were four doors; three bedrooms and a bathroom that we would all share.

As we passed each door, Sister Bergan pointed out whose room it was and then led me to the last door on the right, saying this was to be my room. I peered in and tried to see but the sun had now gone down and the room was dark. I could tell that the room was small and the walls were covered with some sort of a small-patterned wallpaper. Once she flipped the light switch on the wall I could see the room and the wallpaper much better. The paper looked like it had seen its better days. It was a light gray background covered with small white and pink colored roses and a scattering of green leaves everywhere. It was actually rather pretty,

141

probably very pretty in its better days but just darker than I would have expected. There was a small twin bed with a pink quilted bedspread that appeared to have had a very long and useful life span. The nightstand held a small table lamp with a plain white lampshade and a Bible. There was an old wooden dresser with three large drawers and a mirror that had a small crack running along the far left side.

I looked back to Sister Bergan. She was watching me with expectation in her eyes. I said, "It looks perfect!"

"Well then," she said and paused as she stared at me, "then let me leave and let you unpack and get yourself settled.

She turned to leave my room, then quickly turned to say one more thing.

"By the way," she said, "I took a damp rag and wiped out the dresser drawers this morning so you could go ahead and put your belongings right into them. So, if you don't need anything else, I will see you in the morning for 8:00 am service. It is a small parish and few attend the morning service, but there will be a small handful and that is a nice way to start to get acquainted with the members." Again she paused and then said, "Ok then. See you in the morning. Sleep well."

She closed the door behind her and I heard her walk to her bedroom and shut the door.

It truly had been a long day. Now that my stomach had been satisfied I would have loved to just crawl into bed and go to sleep but my skin felt so sticky from the bus ride that I knew I needed to run bath water. I forced myself to leave the solitude of my bedroom and get it done so I could start fresh in the morning. As I sat soaking in the warmth of the bath water, I found my thoughts drifting back to Father Weaver, but mostly just in curiosity as to what drew him to the priesthood. I mean I knew the events in my life that changed my plans and led me to my desire to serve the Lord. I guess I just wondered if something similar had made him aware of his calling. And, it wasn't just my attraction to him, I wondered the same thoughts about Sisters Charlotte and Bergan.

I had a lot to learn about my new parish including my church family. But for now, I needed sleep. I went about the business of washing and shampooing my hair and then I quickly dressed and returned to my bedroom. As I knelt beside my bed to say my prayers, I was extremely thankful for my safe arrival and my new beginnings. As I crawled into bed, I found myself thinking about my parents. I wondered if I should have called to let them know I had arrived at my new destination. It was much too late in the evening now to call, but I would remember to connect with them tomorrow.

I lay thinking about my life, about letting go of Sam, about losing Scott. I found myself crying yet again. Starting in a new parish had caused some anxiety eighteen months ago and I was hoping to do better this time. I guess I assumed just because it wasn't my first assignment that this time would feel almost normal, but it didn't. It was still a new church, a new home, new roommates and a new city. That was a lot of "news."

I tried to shake myself out of it all. I tried to think of something pleasant. I thought again about the ride into Pinesdale. I thought about the beautiful flower gardens; the older women casually talking on the front porch swing and the little children riding their bikes and the tiny one pulling the wagon load of baby dolls. I thought about the lovely stained glass windows. I then thought about the service in the morning and my first chance to see the inside of St. Lucy's church. And then.... I thought about Father Weaver giving the sermon at morning mass. And then I saw his face as he had walked out the door to greet me. I felt that rush again that sent shivers through my body. I was immediately ashamed of my thoughts. I tried desperately to shut my mind off and just go to sleep. I had a difficult time. I did the only thing I could think to do. I got up from my bead, located my rosary beads, crawled back into bed and began to pray.

Usually when I say my prayers, I am praying for others, my family, my friends, my parish community, the world. But tonight I am devoting my prayers to me. I am praying that God will help guide me back onto my set course; my course to serve this parish and the children of this parish. To keep my faith strong, my role in this parish on track and keep my personal thoughts and desires of the flesh out of my mind. It took about 30 minutes of praying and then I was finally able to go to sleep.

MITZI

Chapter 14 - 1912

One would think that 102 Maple Street was the perfect place for a child to grow up. There were plenty of neighbors with well-kept houses and spacious yards for playing and gardens for tending. There were large maple trees for climbing and ropes looped and knotted over branches for swinging. The summer air was filled with the sounds of busy children and barking dogs. There were different smells in the neighborhood depending on where you were standing and which way the breeze was blowing. From across the alley came the smell of fresh clean linens rustling with the breeze from Mrs. Fraley's clothesline but from the west side of the house was the wonderful aroma of Mrs. Clark baking her bread. I chose to move closer to Mrs. Clarks' open kitchen window. I had already had breakfast, but hoped she would see me outside and invite me in for a nice warm piece of bread. No one spread butter on quite as thick as Mrs. Clark. I waited patiently, sang a little song just loud enough so that maybe she would hear me and sure enough, she came to the window and invited me inside. Her bread was the very best.

Yes, it was just your typical Monday on a warm July morning on Maple Street in Pinesdale. I finished my bread quickly and hurried back outside before mother or Lina came looking for me. Henry had left with father early this morning, so I knew I didn't need to worry about him finding me. It was always a blessing when father took Henry with him for the day. Lina and I could do our chores much quicker without the worry of whatever mischief Henry was up too or trouble he was causing to someone in the neighborhood. It seemed that Henry could not go a day without upsetting someone, especially me.

Mrs. Clark had said for me to come back anytime to visit. Before I went out the screen door I did get brave and asked if Lina might be allowed to come over for a piece of bread...while it was still warm.

Mrs. Clark laughed and then looked me in the eye and said, "Your dear little sister Lina is welcome to stop by anytime, but your ornery brother Henry Jr...now that is another story!" Then Mrs. Clark laughed again and winked her eye at me.

I was only eight-years old but I understood exactly what she was saying to me. I knew she was smiling a sweet-sweet smile but I also knew she was dead serious about Henry Jr. He was not well-liked in our little neighborhood. Actually he was known as "The Tyrant of Maple St." Most of the other kids cleared out when Henry Jr. wanted to join in whatever game we were playing. If the game was Red Rover – they all took off running. He could be a vicious maniac in that game. Dodge ball was another game where all the kids scattered when he arrived but he didn't care. He would go off and find something else to do where he could make trouble. I hate to admit this, but on days when Henry Jr. had no children to pester or if he was just bored, I think he was not beyond hurting animals. The poor defenseless little animals.

I was never quite sure but I was quite concerned it was happening. One day last week all was quiet in the neighborhood. Lina and I had chores to do for mother. Henry Jr. had been told to clean out the garage for father. My chore list included scrubbing the upstairs woodwork. As I started to wipe around the window ledge, I saw Henry Jr. in the side yard. He was sitting staring at the old tom cat, the one we called Jasper that was napping in the sun partially hidden under mother's beautiful pink peonies bush. I wondered why he was staring so intently and suddenly I became alarmed when I saw him beginning to creep toward Jasper. The cat was oblivious to Henry's presence in the yard. Henry was getting closer and I started to panic. I had noticed limping cats before and always feared it had something to do with my brother. Henry Jr. was getting too close to Jasper. I knew my fears were correct. My mind was racing. Jasper should hear him, why doesn't Jasper hear him? Inside my head, I was yelling….. Move Jasper…move! I had to stop him. I did the only thing I could do. I started banging on the window.

The cat immediately jumped up from his sleep, saw Henry Jr and took off across the yard. Henry had stood and turned sharply toward my window with a mean scowl on his face and shook his fist at me. At the same time, Mother had yelled from downstairs asking if everything was alright and saying it sounded like I was breaking the window.

I had still been staring at Henry Jr. but I yelled down to mother, "I am fine mother. I was just waving to Henry Jr. I am sorry if I scared you."

Mother had started to come up the stairs and stopped part way and headed back down as she heard my explanation.

"That is fine Mitzi. Please hurry up and finish your chores and then come down and help me prepare lunch. Lina, are you almost done dusting? Get a move on girls. We need to get finished here very soon. Your father will be home and hungry."

Lina was only five years old, so her chore list was always much easier than mine. She was mostly given duties such as pick up our bedroom or as today, dusting. I was given the jobs that needed more strength like scrubbing woodwork or vacuuming. But I didn't mind. I was mothers' big helper and I knew she appreciated my work.

Henry Jr. had finally given up staring at me and walked back toward the garage. I knew father would be home soon so I felt I was safe enough. I assumed by the time lunch was over, Henry would forget about Jasper and whatever plan he had devised in his head. And I had been right. That day nothing else happened. I mean nothing else that caused any commotion.

Tram Kellar was a friend, a good friend to everyone in the neighborhood. He was only 9 years old, but all of us kids knew he was our protector. He wasn't afraid of Henry Jr. Nope, not afraid at all. He fought with him on a regular basis, especially in the summertime. Tram didn't always win but he won enough times to make us all glad he was nearby. He seemed to always be within ear shot of our pain and it didn't go unnoticed.

One night at the supper table father had asked the three of us what we had been doing for fun on these beautiful summer days. Lina and I each listed two or three projects and games that we were enjoying with the other children. Father seemed pleased with our acceptable answers. When Henry Jr didn't answer and only provided a shrug of his shoulders, father became perturbed.

"I asked you a question," he said sharply, "and I expect a better answer than I shrug. So I will ask again. What have you been doing on these summer days....Henry Jr.? Henry did not look up from his plate, but he did answer father. He unconvincingly and quietly responded, "I have been playing with Tram."

It was unconvincing to Lina and I who knew very well that Tram was not a friend to Henry Jr, but our father was not home during our playtime to know that Henry Jr. had no friends.

"Tram?" father said questioningly, "Do you mean Bertram Kellar's boy? And you say you are his friend? Well, that is good," father said cheerfully. "That is very good news Junior. I am pleased. What sort of things do you and Tram do for fun?"

"Well, um, you know ...we just do stuff," Henry Jr said, "just ....stuff."

"I understand that you do.... stuff," father said rather dryly as he cut his pork chop from the bone, "my question was posed to find out what kind of ...stuff. I mean do you play tag? Do you play war? Do you play baseball? And please lift your head when you speak to us. It is very disrespectful to speak with your face in your plate rather than facing your family."

Henry Jr. was smart enough to obey father. He was enjoying his pork chop and knew if he didn't comply with fathers order, he would be sent to his room without finishing his supper.

"Yes father, we play baseball," he said with his face up and staring at father.

Father seemed pleased, but Henry Jr knew Lina and I knew it was a lie. He waited until father returned to cutting his meat and mother had gone to the kitchen to get more bread then he shot both Lina and I a

147

look that needed no words. We both understood the look. It was to keep our mouths shut or else pay the price. We said nothing.

It was during this same summer that father found out that Henry Jr had told a lie all on his own. The truth came from Bertram Kellar himself. It seems father ran into Mr. Kellar during the town council meeting. Both had attended due to a proposed zoning change that had been suggested and as it turned out, both father and Mr. Kellar opposed the change. It was after a heated debate and the favorable ending that the zoning change option was to be rescinded that Mr. Kellar and father spoke.

When father came home that evening, he went to the stairway and yelled for Henry Jr. to come to his study. Henry Jr. complied. Lina and I tip-toed down the steps and took our traditional hiding place around the corner so we could listen to father speak to Henry Jr.

Father was angry. He said he felt like a fool when he had suggested that Tram was a good friend and Mr. Kellar had quickly informed him that was untrue. He told father that Tram and Henry Jr had many scuffles and shared many blows.

Father said, "Can you imagine my embarrassment.... my humiliation? Can you?"

Henry Jr stood silent in front of father.

Father continued, "It is one thing to have trouble getting along with other children, but it is a whole other matter to deliberately lie to your parent and that will not be permitted. It will not be permitted at all."

I could tell father was extremely upset. I was afraid for Henry Jr. He had been spanked many times but I thought tonight he may get a real thrashing. But I was wrong.

Father sat in silence with his head hanging downward. Henry Jr stood in silence staring at the ceiling. It seemed to just be very quiet for a very long time. I was getting tired of waiting.

After what seemed like an eternity my father lifted his head and said, "Go to bed Henry."

That was it, just go to bed. No lecture, no whipping. Just go to bed. Henry Jr. promptly walked out of the study and up the stairs. He did not slam his bedroom door but shut it very softly. He knew. He knew he had been spared. He didn't know why, but he was grateful and went straight to bed without another sound.

I looked again at father. He was still sitting in the chair and his head was back to hanging downward. I felt very badly for him. I remembered all his speeches about our family being a pillar in this town, a respected family that people looked up to for leadership and I understood how father must have felt tonight.

Mr. Kellar was not a nice man or a nice father. I had heard him yell at his children and saw him shove Tram to the ground one day when Lina and I were pulling weeds in mothers garden. They were in their backyard and Mr. Kellar was trying to show Tram how to repair a portion of their fence. Mr. Kellar's voice had gotten much louder and I stopped weeding to look that direction. Just as my head turned that direction, I saw Trams' father strike him on the side of his head. The blow was hard enough that Tram lost his footing and fell to the side, hitting the other side of his head against the fence and landing on the ground.

Within a second, his father yelled again, "Get up you stupid, lazy boy!"

Tram tried to stand quickly, lost his footing and slipped downward again.

"I said get up!" his father screamed.

With that second command, Mrs. Kellar came out the back door with a look of horror on her face. She began to rush toward Tram, but before she could reach him Mr. Kellar stood and grabbed her. She struggled, but he held tight.

Tram said, "I am okay mother. Please go back into the house. I will be fine."

"Fine?" Mr. Kellar said mockingly, "Fine you say. We'll see about that. Get up you lazy good for nothing. Get up now or I will knock you down again."

Tram grabbed the fence and pulled himself up. Mrs. Kellar pulled once again trying to break free of his hold.

"Leave him be woman. He has to learn. He is a good for nothing boy. I will teach him if I have to kill him doing it!"

149

I will never forget him saying those words. "I will teach him if I have to kill him doing it."

No...my father should not feel humiliated by Mr. Kellar. Father is a much better man, a much kinder man, a much smarter man. I feel bad that father doesn't know how much better he is than Mr. Kellar. I need to find a way to let father know the truth about Mr. Kellar. I can help father feel better. I will do that, but not tonight. He is too upset tonight and I fear he wouldn't really hear my words.

Lina and I backed away from the safety of our corner and scurried up the steps to our bedrooms. Once inside we each closed our doors very slowly and without the slightest noise as the doorknob latched closed.

Before I crawled into bed, I looked out the window and look toward the Kellars house. It was all dark. I hoped Mr. Kellar was asleep and that Tram was safe. I hoped Mr. Kellar didn't get mad and kill Tram tonight while I am sleeping. Tomorrow I will tell father what I heard. Father will know how to help Tram. Yes, father will help Tram, I know he will. And I will make sure father will knows he is a better man than Mr. Kellar.

But when morning came and we were all gathered around the table for breakfast, I didn't know how to go about beginning to broach the subject with my father. My parents were enjoying idle conversation as Henry Jr. spread Mothers' rich strawberry jam on his toast and Lina lazily shuffled her unwanted scrambled eggs around her plate. I waited between my bites of egg and toast for my opportunity. I had just lifted my cup for a sip of my orange juice when the table finally became quiet. I quickly lowered my cup, swallowed hard and quickly cleared my throat.

"Father," I began, "May I ask you a question?"

"Why yes, of course," he responded very quickly. "What is it my little Mitzi?"

I was afraid to bring up the name, but knew I must. I was speaking slowly, "Do...you...know Mr. Kellar?"

"Yes of course I do, he is our neighbor. I have known Bertram Kellar for a very long time as we both have grown up in this very neighborhood," he replied. "His father and my father had done some business together way back in the good old days as they say. We were never the best of friends, but in answer to your question, yes I am quite familiar with Bertram. Why do you ask?"

Oh brother I thought to myself. If father and Mr. Kellar were friends, I don't think father would like to hear what I wanted him to know about that nasty man. I sat wondering with my head down and my eyes staring directly at my plate and my eggs which were now getting cold.

Father took another bite of his toast as he waited for my reply. When I said nothing, he asked again.

"Dear," he said very calmly, "Why did you want to know about Mr. Kellar?"

"Oh it was nothing Father," I said very sheepishly, "I just wondered." Father stared at me for a moment and then he looked at mother. I saw that they shared a look. Then father said, "Children let's finish up our breakfast and then everyone please take their plates and juice cups to the kitchen for mother."

Everyone else had finished their food and began to stand and carry out their plates, even Lina. I hurried to scoop up the rest of my eggs so as not to get a lecture from mother about the poor children that had no food to eat and began to stand when father stopped me.

"Mitzi," he said very calmly, "after you take your plate to the kitchen, please join me in my study."

I immediately froze. When it came to us children, being requested to join father in his study was reserved for lectures or spankings. I didn't think I had done anything wrong, so I did not suspect a spanking. I assumed I was about to get a lecture about being too nosey about the neighbors. I took my plate to the kitchen and placed it in the sink.

Mother stopped me and gave me a quick little hug; then patted the top of my head and said, "Off with you now. Your father is waiting." I paused. She gave me a quick wink and said, "It will all be fine. Go on now. Don't keep him waiting."

I walked slowly out of the kitchen, thru the dining room and headed into fathers study. He was sitting at his desk and look up at me as I entered.

"Come sit down Mitzi." He said very calmly.

I did as I was told. I made my way to the brown leather chair that faced fathers large wooden desk and sat down gently, scooting myself back into the chair until my legs were stretched straight out in front of me. I folded my hands onto my lap, swallowed hard and looked at father.

"Am I in trouble father?" I asked in a very small sounding voice.

"No child," he responded quickly, "Not at all. I just wanted to continue our breakfast conversation about Mr. Kellar and thought you might rather speak in private. Was there something troubling you about Mr. Kellar?" He asked the question and then watched my face very carefully. I was aware that he was concerned and didn't know if I should continue or not. I wanted so for father to know he was a good father, not at all like Mr. Kellar, but I still wasn't convinced I was approaching it correctly. I began to bite at the edges of my lips and father continued.

"Mitzi, my dear," he said softly, "it is my guess that you have either seen or heard something in regards to Mr. Kellar that you did not feel was right. Am I correct in that assumption dear?"

I lowered my head and after a few seconds, nodded a yes.

"Ok then," he continued, "I think we should talk about it. If it makes you feel better I would like to start by telling you that I have seen and heard a few things from Mr. Kellar that I think were wrong also, and I have seen it more than once."

I looked straight away at my fathers' face in disbelief. He slowly nodded a yes to me.

I leaned forward in the chair and positioned myself so that my legs now came forward with the bend of my knees matching up with the edge of the chair. My feet still did not touch the floor but I felt much closer to my father.

"Oh my goodness father, what did you see him do?" I asked still in amazement that my father already knew something about this mean man.

"Well Mitzi," he said very clearly, "let's just say that over the years I have seen him do many cruel things to many people. When I said before that we were not the best of friends, I should have said we were never friends just acquaintances. That is why I became so upset last evening."

Father began to shake his head and again looked downward. Then he lifted his head and looked at me. "Something was said by Mr. Kellar last evening that embarrassed me and I know it embarrassed me more than it should have just because, well just because I do not think very highly of Mr. Kellar and his beliefs," he said very quietly but firmly. "But," he continued, "What I feel and think is not what I need to talk about right now. I would like to know what happened, what you saw or what you heard that has you upset with Mr. Kellar."

I was now much braver than I had been at the breakfast table. Father had been right. It was better to talk in private. Father had shared with me and now I understood exactly why father did not spank Henry Jr last evening. He was more upset that Mr. Kellar had been the one to tell him that news; then that Henry Jr. had lied.

I was now ready to share with him. I quickly told him what I had both seen and heard when I was weeding the garden. I told him everything and when I was done father sat quiet. I was ready for him to explode and tell me that he would take care of it, call the police or at least report him to the police, but instead father just sat quiet. After what seemed like five minutes father spoke.

"Mitzi," he said. "Mitzi my child, you have done the right thing to tell me. I must say I am not surprised. Bertram has always had a meanness to his character and I do not think that will change. I fear that his wife and children will always be the target of his anger. I am sorry that you have had to witness this first hand and I pray that he learns to control his temper. Unfortunately there is not much else we can do. It is his family and he can choose to discipline his children as he sees fit. I will do my best to keep my eyes and ears alert to his poor family and help when I can. I will ask that you keep yourself and your little sister away from Mr. Kellar. Do not play near his yard. And ...maybe it would be best to not play with his children."

This last statement took me by surprise. "Oh no father," I pleaded, "You cannot mean that. We need Tram!" I said it so fast that I didn't realize the complications of what I had just said to father. Now I had said too much and there was no going back.

153

Father responded immediately. "What do you mean Mitzi? Why do you need Tram? You need to explain. I don't understand."

What else could I do? I had to explain. Father had told me the truth and I owed it to him to tell him the truth. I told him the whole story. I told him about how Tram protected us. I told him how when a bully was hurting us or the other kids how Tram stepped in and helped. He always helped. I told father how he was always nearby and how we counted on the fact that he was always within earshot. I told father everything... everything except who was the bully. Then, I waited.

Father had watched me intently as I told him about the Dodge ball games, the Red Rover games, the Hide and Seek, the Tag and everything we children did for fun that always turned scary and painful because of someone, but I never said the name of that someone.

Father was still staring at me, when he very slowly said, "Mitzi... the bully, the one that causes all the trouble, the one that Tram has to stop," he paused, lowered his head and then re-lifted it and sadly looked at me and said, "Is that person Henry Jr?"

I saw the terrible look of hurt on my poor fathers' face. It broke my heart but I knew he already knew my answer so I said it. "Yes father," I said with tears welling up in my eyes, "Yes father, it is Henry Jr."

My father dropped his head into his folded arms on his desk. I knew he wasn't crying but I also knew he didn't want me to see the pain on his face. I sat very still for a minute then I got up from my chair; walked around my father's big wooden desk and put my small arm over my father back and patted him as a mother does to her baby.

Father did not move and allowed me to continue to comfort him for a few minutes. Finally he lifted his head and straightened in his chair. He scooted back and lifted me onto his lap.

"My little Mitzi," he said, "We have more than a few problems to fix. I promise you today that I will begin now to fix these problems. You, your sister and the other children in this neighborhood should not have to play in fear of your brother."

"I appreciate everything you shared with me today and I assure you that it will be our secret." He said firmly. "I do believe these matters do not need to continue and I will do my best to make sure things change for both Henry Jr and Tram. Thank you again for sharing your concerns. They were valid points and you were right to come to me.

"Now," he continued, but with a little more bounce in his voice, "Now let's see if your sister has started her chores. We wouldn't want her to finish too far ahead of you!"

With that he gave me a smile and then shoed me out of the study.

I obeyed and headed out into the dining room. When I looked back and into his study, he had swiveled his chair and was now facing the window that allowed him to stare outward toward the Kellar house. I watched and he just continued to stare. Finally after a minute, he swung his chair back around to face his desk; pulled his papers closer and began to read.

I felt better. I knew father told me the truth. I knew he really would work on fixing the problem, both with Henry Jr and Mr. Kellar. I prayed he could fix it and I hoped Lina and I would not have to worry about our brothers' anger anymore. I headed to the kitchen now with a new worry. I needed to see what chores mother had added to my list while I was gone.

SISTER JEANETTE

Chapter 15 - 1968

The sun was barely up when I arose and realized I was at St. Lucy's. I could hear the other sisters downstairs already moving about. I checked the clock on the nightstand and saw Mass would be starting in 45 minutes. I hurried to dress and headed down the stairs. I was greeted warmly and reminded that after mass, we would start my tour of the school, the church hall and rectory. I asked if they minded if I went over to the church ahead of them, so I could take a few minutes to look around. They gave me their blessing and I left.

As I walked across the lawn and past the rectory, my mind jumped back to the moment I had seen Father Weaver. I immediately tried to distract my thoughts. I studied the lawn, the church steps with a few small cracks, anything to put a different view into my eyes. And then, I stepped inside the church doors.

I walked into the church, my church, St. Lucy's for the first time and stood in amazement as I studied each of the beautifully paneled stained glass windows. They were the most magnificent windows I had ever seen. So many details and such vibrant colors that had been chosen; they were just absolutely perfect. I was staring at them in wonder, still with plenty of time before mass was to begin, when I felt a tap against my shoulder. I turned to find a tall man.

"Good morning Sister Jeanette," he said. "I am Lucas. I know you met my son Christian yesterday and I wanted to apologize for not being able to deliver you from the bus station."

"Oh my," I said while shaking his hand. "It is so very nice to meet you Lucas. You have raised a wonderful son. He was very polite and cautious with his driving. Thank you for sending him. And also, I do believe I also sampled your wives cooking and baking yesterday. Please tell her for me that I enjoyed a few of her Italian Pizzelles and also her meatloaf."

He smiled and then excused himself.

A few members of the parish were starting to arrive. I started to move back down the side aisle and around to the back of the church to enter by way of the middle aisle. At the back of the church I ran directly into a woman possibly in her forties.

She looked up and said, "Good morning Sister. You must be our new nun here at St. Lucy's. Oh my, we are so glad to have you. You will just love our little parish. Everyone here gets along and we all just love Father Weaver. He is the very best priest ever."

"Oh my," she continued, "Where are my manners? I am Nell Taylor. If there is anything I can do to help you get settle, please do not hesitate to ask. I am a widow and have plenty of time on my hands. Do you like blueberry muffins? Muffins are my specialty. Now let me give you a chance to speak."

I was taken aback by all of her quick information.

"Well," I said, "First let me say I love muffins and blueberry happens to be my very favorite."

We both laughed and then she suddenly stopped and stared at me in a very funny way.

"What is it?" I said. "Is there something the matter? Do I have something on my face?"

"No," she said very softly. "No....it is nothing. You just reminded me of someone when you smiled, someone that I miss."

"Oh well," she continued now back in her cheerful voice. "I better find my pew and get myself ready for Father Weaver. I just love his voice and his sermons."

With that, she reached her hand in to touch the holy water, made the sign of the cross, walked down to the third pew from the altar,

157

genuflected and found her seat in the pew and began her morning prayers.

Slowly the church started to fill in around me, some folks stopping to introduce themselves while others scurried past me as if I was not even seen or possibly they were just feeling too uncomfortable to say more than even a good morning. I look around and realize that there are a good number of people present for a Wednesday morning mass.

Sisters Bergan and Charlotte arrived and together we walked down the aisle and found a pew, kneel and began our prayers. About 5 minutes later, Father Weaver entered from the side altar and mass began.

It was immediate. The minute he entered, my eyes were paralyzed on him. And then he spoke, and my heart melted. I begin to pray harder. "Please God, please help me control my feelings."

I made it through mass but not without much concentration and many prayers with closed eyes. I now must face the fact that Father Weaver will be waiting for me at the rectory to give me a tour of all of St. Lucy's. I should see if Sister Bergan would like to go with me.

As I leave my pew and walk down the center aisle I see a few of the congregation has gathered at the back vestibule of the church. I see Sister Charlotte has moved ahead and is mingling amongst the group and as I approach she comes forward and takes my left hand.

"This my dear friends," she says with a smile, "Is Sister Jeanette, our newest member here at St. Lucy's and a great addition to our church."

I am just ready to say thank you when I suddenly feel a firm hand on my right shoulder.....and then a voice, that voice, his voice.

"We are certainly delighted to have Sister Jeanette join our parish family," Father Weaver is saying, "It is a blessing indeed." Then he smiles down at me. Yes, I said down at me. That six-foot frame of his makes him feel very tall when at my side.

I say a quiet, "Thank you" to the group and my superiors. Before I can say more, Mrs. Taylor speaks for the group and says how nice it is to have a third nun at the church. She says that there is so much going on at the church every day of the week that a helping hand is exactly what was needed. She lets me know she is on the church council and was part of the team that made a request to Bishop Sevachko at the diocese.

"I told them that our parish was growing with more children attending the school and we needed more of a nun presence in the community. I think it was an easy decision for him. He is proud of St. Lucy's and wants it to flourish."

"As we all do," says Father Weaver and everyone claps.

Sister Charlotte now jumps back in to make introductions of the 6 or 7 members. I nod when she points out Mrs. Taylor and remark that we met briefly before mass. Sister Charlotte tells me that Nell Taylor will be a great resource for me when I am learning the ropes at St. Lucy's. She says she has been at the parish longer than most in Pinesdale and knows many of the answers to questions that come up from time to time.

Nell laughs and says, "Keep my number handy Sister Jeanette, it is IV2-2085."

After I have met the remaining parishioners, Father Weaver suggests it is time to now meet the grounds. He asks that I walk with him. As we walk through the church he points out the different windows and statues and gives a brief history of each including which families have made substantial contributions toward acquiring such beautiful pieces of art.

We leave the church through the side door which faces the rectory. As we follow the sidewalk around to the back door of the house, he asks what made me chose to be a nun.

"I came about my decision slowly and with the help of a therapist," I admit freely. "I had faced the death of someone I had loved deeply and for a long time felt as though I was lost. It is strange but although I knew I was lost, I also knew I would be found again. I was not able to visualize my future purpose, but I always knew I would find it. And then one day I just woke up and it was there. It was as though it was there all the time and I finally just opened my eyes wide enough and found it."

"So," I continued as we walked up the steps to the rectory, "I joined the convent and began my classes. And here I am. I spent my first 18 months at St. Agatha's and now this is my second assignment."

I looked up and he was smiling at me.

159

"Well," he said, "On behalf of everyone at St. Lucy's, we are thrilled that you opened your eyes just wide enough." With that he gestured for me to enter and I was given a grand tour of his office and the house.

The house was much bigger than the rectory at St. Agatha's or my home parish of Our Lady of the Lourdes. It was easy to see this was a parish that appreciated their priest. The house was well furnished with all newer and matching pieces of furniture in the living and dining rooms. The kitchen, I would not say would make the cover of *House Beautiful,* but it was in much better condition than the one in the convent. I did notice at the far corner near the side entrance of the kitchen there was a tennis racket leaning against the wall.

"Do you play tennis Father Weaver?" I asked.

"Sister Jeanette," he replied, "First of all in answer to your question, Yes, I do enjoy playing tennis and feel it is important to keep up with some sort of exercise. Maybe you would like to join me sometime. I am always looking for a partner. After all, it is very hard to play tennis alone. I have to do a lot of ball chasing when that happens," he says with a laugh. "And," he continues, "May I please ask you to call me Father Bob, as so many of the parishioners do around here? Father Weaver sounds so very formal. It sounds as if we don't really even know each other and that is not the case, at least I hope it is not."

As he said that last sentence, he scanned my face with those deep chestnut colored eyes and then smiled the sweetest smile. Oh Lord, I know I must have blushed. Oh dear sweet Lord. What was it that they used to say in the old days; Please Lord stop this burning flame that is glowing inside me. Please!

I tried desperately to calm myself and prayed that my cheeks had returned to their normal coloring. I wanted to tell him, yes, I am very good at tennis, some might say, even competitive but instead I say, "I have tried tennis, Father Bob, back in high school but found that I was not very good at the game."

The last thing I want to consider right now is getting away one-on-one with him.

He responded quickly, "Well please think about it. I do not proclaim to be anywhere close to being good at the game myself, but I do feel it helps us to release tensions, especially in our line of work. We carry a lot of burdens around for a lot of people. Having a way even if it is only for a brief period of time to release those stresses in our day is good for all of us. Sister Bergan joins me periodically, though I usually have to almost twist her arm to get her to say yes. She does freely admit to enjoying it once she is there in the park. So please think about it."

With that he turned to continue the tour and leads me out the back door and across the parking area to the school. It is older two-story red brick building. It appears that they have recently replaced the entrance doors, but this also makes the windows appear ancient. The window casings have small cracks throughout and many areas of chipped paint. This is sad to realize, but the building looks not out of the ordinary for catholic school buildings nowadays. Parishioners are beginning to lose sight of the value of having children attend a religious school. People are questioning the need when money has to come from their pockets to attend while they must still pay local taxes to support the public school system. Our attendance numbers across the state, across the country, are dwindling. Many small parishes, much like St. Lucy's, have already closed their doors on their school rooms and are renting out the space for club meetings and social gatherings. As I walk through the doors, I feel blessed to still be needed at St. Lucy's. The tour is short. There are seven small classrooms, two sets of children's restrooms, one on each floor, three small office spaces and a large hall with a side kitchen. The hall is used for all extra activities, such as art, music, physical education, indoor recess and of course, the lunchroom.

I assume the tour is complete as Father Bob walks me back toward the convent. The back sidewalk is made of the same old red bricks as the school building. It is rough and has many bricks that have raised up from their space and now make it difficult to walk. As we come to the back door of the house, Father stops and takes my hand.

"Sister Jeanette, I just want to say again how fortunate we all feel here at St. Lucy's to have you join our parish. We have a lovely community here and I feel you will fit right in and be so very helpful. Please take today to relax a little and get acquainted with the other sisters and your new home. If you need anything, and I do mean anything, please come to the rectory. If I am out, please ask Lydia Morgan, my secretary to reach me. She usually knows right where I am supposed to be. Oh and on Thursdays, Lydia is off and Mrs. Tawney volunteers. Esther is a wonderful older woman and she just uses her instincts to hunt me down," he says with a laugh. "She is quite something. She treats me like her grandson. But anyway, you get the idea. I can be found."

He releases my hand and starts to turn to go. Then stops and turns back toward me.

"Oh...and don't forget. We have a tennis match on Friday at 10:00. If you don't have a racket, don't worry, I have a spare." He again laughs and then walks away. As he walks and with his back to me he adds, "Please don't make me go alone. My legs are too tired to chase all those balls."

I stare at him until he turns the corner and is out of site.

I am so confused. My mind will not settle itself. I think back to my days when I was studying at the Sisters of Providence. We did many exercises while in preparation to become a nun. One such exercise was called, "Settle Your Mind." While I was there I was able to clear my mind fairly easily, but this past week nothing has been easy. I almost wish....no, I don't really. I released Sam from myself so very long ago, and I knew I must; but today, I would have loved to hear his voice inside my head. He would have helped me just as he always did. He always knew the right thing to say. He always guided me and I had learned to depend on him and his sound advice. I remember all the different conversation when those that cared for me talked to me about letting go of Sam. I realize that they all loved me and wanted the best for me, but it was so hard to say good-bye to Sam.

There was one person that never felt Sam needed to leave my side. That was Scott. Dear sweet Scott. Scott wanted only for me to be happy and he understood my connection to Sam better than anyone else on the planet. He knew Sam was my sounding board. He just knew.....

But I must not move backwards. I must think for myself and I will. I just need to settle myself. I will try!

I go in through the back door and find myself in a small dark laundry room where the washing machine is busy making churning noises. I continue past it and a very old looking dryer and find myself in the kitchen where Sister Bergan is standing at the sink busy preparing a small roast to go into a speckled roasting pan. I see she has four potatoes and a hand full of carrots resting in the sink to be washed.

I am not sure yet of the household duties so I ask, "May I help you Sister Bergan?"

She jumps just a little and I realize that with the washer running, she has not heard me enter the house. I quickly apologize for startling her.

"Oh my heart," she says and then smiles at me. "It is okay. It was a combination of both being busy with my work and with my thoughts that are flying around in my head." She returns to the sink.

"Sister Bergan," I say almost too quietly. "May I ask you a little more about the parish?"

"Why of course," she says as she turns back to face me. "How was your tour?"

I say it was fine; that I was both impressed with the rectory and the school though the school looks like it needs some work.

She agrees. "Good. I am glad. Now what can I tell you?" she asks.

"Well," I stammer a little, "I guess I don't know for sure. I want to learn all I can....about my church family and the parish members. I mean I want to do a good job here at St. Lucy's' and I know it takes time to learn.... I totally understand that.... but ....," I find myself trailing off course.

"I am sorry," I continue, "I guess I am just not sure what I am searching for right now. Could we start with how you made your adjustment when you arrived at St. Lucy's?"

She puts down her things and washes her hands. As she is drying them with the colorful kitchen towel, she comes over and sits at the small table and I join her.

"Sister Jeanette," she begins. "I totally understand your first day jitters. I had them too and probably so does every nun on her first week at a new parish. I will say that in my case, I had it much easier than you. When I arrived here in 1964, it was my third assignment and at that time it was just Sister Charlotte and Father O'Shea and a very small parish family."

She hangs her head downward a little then lifts it back up and stares directly in my eyes and says," Father O'Shea was not the most pleasant man. I think most of the parish would tell you he was a bit of a tyrant. He was very old-school and kept to himself. He was not a friend to anyone here, he was just the priest. He was definitely the man in charge and the members, even the council members had little to say about anything that took place here at St. Lucy's. Needless to say, he was not popular and unfortunately, the diocese left him remain here for almost twenty years. That was way too long. The parish suffered and membership steadily declined. This is a small town surrounded by other small towns. A family would leave and find their way to St. Charles or St. Ignatius in the neighboring towns. Then another family and another. When I was sent here, the parish was at least half the size it is today. There had been another young sister that was here with Sister Charlotte ahead of me. Her name was Sister Jessica and she left abruptly. The only thing Sister Charlotte shared with me was that there were problems that brought about her departure. She shared that one statement and then said, "Enough said." It was a very short and cold explanation. That mystery along with a very unfriendly and unwelcoming priest left me feeling full of questions just as you feel now. So, dear Sister Jeanette, you are not alone."

She continues, "I think we all feel this strangeness when we first arrive at a new parish. There is a whole history that everyone around us already knows that we must learn to fit into ... without the privilege of knowing how to fit ourselves inside the circle. It is a learning environment we each make with each move, so you see, I entered with the same thoughts as you are feeling now. And yes, they are hard to put into words."

"I guess you are right," I conceded. "I did have a different experience at St. Agatha's, but maybe I am just remembering it differently because it was my first parish and I expected to arrive with all my unanswered thoughts...just because it was totally new. I guess this time I expected to feel more knowledgeable and I shouldn't have had those expectations. You are right, with every move I will need to find my own way to penetrate the circle."

Now I smile at her and say, "Thank you!"

She smiles and reaches across the table and takes my hand in hers.

"You are welcome and please don't worry. This parish is now thriving and the members love it here. They will make you feel welcome. I could right now tell you the names of at least 10 women that would jump through hoops to help you with any projects you desire. They are super helpful and generous to a tea. You must remember, those families that remained faithful to St. Lucy's during that long twenty years with Father O'Shea, are so thrilled to have a happy parish where their voices now matter, that they want to help with everything and they do!"

"Just to tell you a little more of the history as I witnessed," she continued, "As Father O'Shea was getting older, the diocese made the decision to send Father Bob to St. Lucy's in 1965 to be the assistant priest. He tried to help bring change, the change he could see was so desperately needed but just like the parish members, his hands were tied. Father O'Shea still ruled the roost even though he was then at the point of letting Father Bob take care of most of the services including weddings and funerals. When word spread of this, a few members did slowly start to return but it was a slow growth. During the next year, Father O'Shea's health started to fail and he made the decision to request retirement. The diocese quickly responded and Father O'Shea said his good-byes to St. Lucy's."

"Once that took place," she continued, "and word spread that he had moved to Nazareth Village, a retirement home in New York for priests and that Father Bob was now officially in charge, previous members began to flock back to the parish. The atmosphere changed immediately without any plans or meetings by Sister Charlotte, myself or Father Bob. It just happened. It was as if we were all rejoicing an immediate transformation. We were still St. Lucy's but with a whole new attitude. It was glorious."

She smiled a very bright smile and said, "So you see. You are fortunate. You joined into a family filled with peace and happiness. You will break through that circle very easily. Just have patience and let it happen at whatever pace it comes. Follow your instincts and when the time feels right, jump inside!"

With that, she released my hand, grinned a little more in my direction and then returned to her work at the sink.

I sat there at the table thinking about all she said and knew in my heart she was exactly right. I will find my way. It may be tomorrow, next week or even next month, but I am positive it will happen. I make a mental note to contact the nice lady from mass this morning, Mrs. Taylor, and see if she can fill me in on what might be some of the current projects the Ladies Guild are working on for the parish. That would be a good start and maybe she can help me get my foot in the door with the other ladies.

And...I think that maybe these feelings I am sensing when around Father Bob, are just coming from his friendly personality as she described. I do sense his warmth and caring nature.

I tell Sister Bergan that if she doesn't need me, I will go up to my room and better arrange my belongings. She assures me to go and take my time as there are no plans for the remainder of the morning. I do remember that I am to meet with Sister Charlotte this afternoon. I excuse myself.

As I start to leave the room, I turn and say, "Sister Bergan, by any chance do you play tennis?"

She laughs a hearty laugh and says without turning, "Oh my no. At least not anymore. I did try but found that I was a terrible tennis player. Just ask Father Bob. He will tell you." And then she laughs again at herself and keeps working.

I smile to myself and head upstairs. So, I guess I will have to join Father Bob on Friday at 10:00. He is correct, tennis is a good stress reliever. And if Sister Bergan was as bad as she proclaims, then he will be pleasantly surprised that I can actually play tennis. Maybe I will even win!

SABRINA

Chapter 16 - 1968

That day sitting in Mrs. Nell's kitchen had been the little poke of the stick that Knox and I needed to get us moving in the right direction. Suddenly everything had seemed possible. We had Mrs. Nell on our side. She liked us and had no qualms about sharing old history of the neighborhood with us. We came out of her house that day as if a fire had been lit underneath our feet and we took off running to find answers. The first thing we did was find ourselves a little gathering spot. We needed someplace quiet to discuss our thoughts and hopefully eventually form some conclusions. It had to be a close place and an easy place. I had too many little sisters and a brother that would nag at us if it were in my backyard and since Knox's sister, CD, was always over at Ellie's house we opted for his backyard. His yard wasn't huge, but toward the back portion there was a rather tall rhododendron bush with beautiful rose colored blossoms that was pretty heavy with growth at the middle and top portions. It would provide an almost pretend-type roof; an umbrella over us if we sat on the ground beneath it. We scoured the rest of the yard looking for other possibilities. There was a large tree with branches that were too high, so forget that option. There was a small shed that was already filled to the hilt with odd tools, garbage cans and stuff being stored; so it was out. There was another smaller rhododendron bush with pink blossoms, but it wasn't big enough to cover us at all. Nothing would work as easy as the rose colored bush so it was an easy decision. We agreed and set up camp. We agreed to refer to our camp as "The Rose" in case we were ever around other people and needed to alert each other as to the need to gather and share an update.

The site didn't have to hold much, mostly just us and our brains that were already working overtime. I filled Knox in on information I learned from reading the journals, since I never took them out of my bedroom. They were far too precious and it was too risky to let anyone else know they existed. Whenever I was able to get a chance to read, I gave him a full report the next day. Sometimes, nothing written seemed overly important to our case, but you never know what I might have missed so it was always better to have two brains reviewing the information. In most cases, Knox agreed with me that there had been no new valuable clues, but we continued to do our own digging.

Sneaking a baked good and information from Mrs. Nell had become almost a morning ritual. Every day we casually walked by or hung around the back alley near her yard. If in a five-minute span of time, she hadn't noticed us, I usually began to talk a little louder and sometimes I had to even talk a little louder to one of the cats before she came to the door and invited us in. Every day we asked just another question or two, nothing too obvious to arouse her to question our need for the information, but enough to keep us going in the right direction. Sometimes her answer made us positively giddy and we had to excuse ourselves and get out of there before we exploded with excitement. Some days, she seemed to be in more of a faraway mood and talked a lot about the past; about her mother, her husband, her life in the city. Yes, we learned a lot about Mrs. Nell during those morning chats.

She worried me one day. She had been talking about her husband and their life in New York before coming back to Pinesdale. She had told us before that they never had any children. I remembered that because that didn't seem to be the normal thing in Pinesdale. Most every family I knew had kids. I remembered how sad she got the last time when she was telling us about how she met her husband, at the library in New York City. I guess she was sad because he died, but she seemed sadder than that, sad maybe about something else. I was not sure what, but I have been thinking about it. I think there was a hidden clue in her story so sometimes when I can't sleep and JoJo is still awake and I can't read the journals, I lay and wonder about Mrs. Nell's life. I will figure it out eventually. I will figure out what was missing in her story that made her so sad.

But back to today. Today was not one of those days. This morning we had learned nothing of value at Mrs. Nell's and we were doubly bummed because our trips to the library over the past few days had also gotten us nothing new. We had been digging thru the Pinesdale newspaper archives and found nothing new regarding the death of Henry Winter. It was as if it happened, a quick news release was written and then it was forgotten. We never did locate the coroner's final report. It was nowhere to be found. We even searched the Newport Beacon, a larger newspaper from the neighboring community, but nothing. It was a dead end. In regards to Otto Becker, there was no individual report of his accident, just an obituary.

The same was practically true of the Henry Winter house fire that occurred in 1939. You would think a fire that caused the death of two people, a mother and child, would be investigated more than just a quick decision of an electrical cause by the local fire chief. But that was all there was in the newspaper. One simple news story giving the facts as the fire chief reported and nothing more. A day later the obituaries of his wife, Marie Debo Winter and their son, Paul Winter and then again, nothing more was to be found.

At our huddle this afternoon, we decided two things:

1. It was time for us to bring up the fire with Mrs. Nell. That would be our goal for tomorrow, to see if there had been any speculations by the townspeople when suddenly Henry Winter became a young widower.
2. I needed to read as much as possible tonight from the journals. Lately the pages were a lot about Aunt Elsie's feelings and about how hard it was to pass her time being alone in the house. I needed to read further ahead to see if she branched out with other ideas or new thoughts.

I promised I would get reading as soon as JoJo and Holly crashed for the night and I would stay up as late as I possibly could and just read. I wouldn't worry about watching old Tram roam around the yards tonight…. I would read!

With those decisions made, we decided our next decision was an easy one: It was lunchtime and we were hungry. I asked Knox if he would like to come over to my house. I was sure Momma wouldn't mind, especially if we only wanted peanut butter and jelly sandwiches. He was in full agreement.

I knew better than to just walk in the door with Knox, so as we came toward the back porch, I asked him to wait outside for just a minute.

I smiled at him and said, "Let me just go make sure Momma isn't mopping the kitchen floor or something. I will be right back."

He nodded in agreement and started checking out the rusty old swing that Daddy still hadn't gotten around to beautifying.

I went inside and found Momma working at the counter with her back to the door.

"Is that you Sabrina?" she said without turning around.

"Yes Momma," I replied quickly.

"I figured it was getting to be about your hungry time of day." She said with a little chuckle.

"Your sisters want toasted cheese. Does that sound good to you too?" she asked while still running the hand mixer.

"It sounds really good Momma, but I was wondering, do you have enough to make an extra sandwich for Knox? I kind of invited him for lunch when I thought it was just a peanut butter and jelly day," I said apologetically.

At this, Momma finally stopped mixing and turned around. I think she was expecting to see Knox standing beside me in the kitchen. Instead she peered her head to look out the back window and saw him standing out by the swing. She was pleasantly surprised that I had at least remembered the rules and gave me a quick smile.

"Why yes Sabrina," she said with a big smile, "I do believe I have an extra piece of cheese or two for your friend Knox, so please invite him in. And this is a good day. I already made some of your favorite black cherry Jell-O this morning so it should be set and ready to eat and I have some whipping cream that I just finished mixing now to top it off.

I stood there smiling at her and she said, "Well, go get the little fellow!"

Knox ate two cheese sandwiches and had a large bowl of Jell-O, but he passed on the whipped cream which I thought was about the biggest mistake a person could make. I loved whipped cream! He got along with my sisters, even Audrey was pleasant to him and of course Davey thought it was super cool to have another boy at the table. Momma tried to ask Knox about what we do all day and what kind of detectives are we trying to be, but Knox was very good at keeping his answers vague. He kept making references to the Hardy Boys and the books he was reading and what mysteries they were trying to solve. He gave away none of our information.

I felt kind of bad, like we were tricking Momma, but I know in my heart that as soon as we solve the case and as soon as we understand how and why things happened, we will tell her all the answers.

We finished lunch and cleared the table and then Momma shooed us back outside. Today was her first time to host the Wednesday Afternoon Neighbors Social Club at Aunt Elsie's house. It was a big deal for her and we girls had been helping her do some extra cleaning the last 2 days to get ready for the event. Last night she made her famous Double Chocolate Cake and stored it away carefully to keep it fresh for todays' gathering. She wanted to make a good impression on these ladies which is why she offered to host the event so soon after moving in at Aunt Elsie's house.

Before we scooted out the door, Knox started to ask Momma a few questions about her event today. I wondered why he cared, but as his questions started coming out, I started to realize what he was fishing for and what he was hoping to gain.

"So Mrs. Holden," he asked, "Is it a large group of neighbors you are expecting today?"

"Oh," she replied as she continued to work, "I do believe there will be about 8-10 ladies here. Not a big gathering, but enough to make for a fun afternoon."

He continued, "What is it you ladies do at these kinds of gatherings?"

"Well," she responded, "I think it is pretty standard that we play card games. I think Euchre is the one that was mentioned. I mean the ladies have good intentions, but I think they usually play a hand or two and then the cards suddenly stop being shuffled and the afternoon become more of a gossip session," she says and then laughs. "I mean I think that is the way with most women's club meetings. I will be surprised if this one is any different."

Now she is offering information without Knox saying a word.

"I made my famous Double Chocolate Cake for the ladies," she says almost bragging. "I hope they like it. I usually make it even though it is a lot of work, just because so many people love it. The recipe came from my Aunt Alma who made me promise to keep it a secret and I always have; I have never shared it with anyone. I have had people beg me for the recipe but I always explain it is an old family secret and I can only pass it down to my girls."

"But," she says firmly, "I really must get back to my preparations. Those ladies will be arriving at 2 o'clock so you two run along now or I will tell JoJo that she has been relieved of "Davey Duty" and I will put you two in charge of entertaining him while the ladies visit."

With that last remark, we both scooted out the door....and then once outside looked at each other and at the same time, said "The Rose" ...and ran to our spot. Once under our little umbrella, we started bouncing ideas off of each other.

"Those ladies," Knox said, "They are going to gossip! Do you know how lucky we are that it is at your house today? We might be able to find some answers, if we can just eavesdrop a little."

"I know," I squealed back at him. "It's the kind of break we really need. All I can say is, "Cool Beans!""

He quickly hushed me.

"Not so loud Stinkweed!" he warned. "Do you want to tip off the ladies that we are going to be listening? Now, where can we position ourselves so that we can hear? We need to be somewhere close enough to be able to hear everything they say. Where do you think Stinkweed? Where can we listen?"

I suggested that maybe Momma would let us help serve the cake.

He groaned, "That won't give us enough time. We need to be around long enough to hear things, not just a "Thank you" as we hand them a piece of cake."

"Okay, okay," I said, "Let me think." We both sat quiet for a minute. I was trying to concentrate and think about my house but I couldn't help feeling like we had picked a good place. Our "Rose" was great. I loved smelling the pretty scent of the blossoms while my brain was trying to work so hard. Then I slowly smiled and Knox looked at me with anticipation in his eyes.

"What is it Stinkweed?" he quickly. "Did you think of the perfect way to hear everything?"

I nodded my head and said, "I bet since it is a nice day, not too sticky hot outside, Momma will leave the windows open. We can sit outside under the window and listen!" I said suddenly really believing it would work. "What do you think?"

Knox just stared at me. Then he finally said, "Well, I am not sure it is the best idea, but I think it is all we have to choose from, so it's a go. Okay... which window. I mean where will your Momma have those ladies sitting?"

"Well," I said, trying to think logically, "while they are playing cards, they should be at the dining room table, but I am not sure if they will move to the living room to gossip...or if they will stay sitting around the table. I think the only thing we can do is start at the dining room and move if we need to."

Knox nodded in agreement.

"So," he said, "We have about 90 minutes till Operation Gossip begins. What do you want to do until then?"

"I know," I said with excitement. "Why don't we go ask Mrs. Nell if she is coming to Momma's gathering today and see if we can get a jump on some of the gossip.... and maybe even add a few little hints to get Mrs. Nell thinking about some topics that...maybe she will talk about with the other ladies!"

Now we were both jumping up and down, so proud of this new idea!!

We almost run her direction...and without any hesitation, as we approach her door, we start knocking.

Mrs. Nell answers the door as though she thinks there must be a fire in the neighborhood.

"Oh my dear children," she says in an almost scared voice, "What is it, what it wrong?"

Knox and I look at each other and know we should feel a little ashamed of ourselves, but instead I say, "Hey there Mrs. Nell, we just wanted to ask if you were going to go to the Wednesday Afternoon Neighborhood Social Meeting today at my Momma's."

"Well, my goodness sake," she says shaking her finger at us. "You children scared me banging on my door like that. I truly thought something was the matter, like my house was on fire or something. Oh my.... now my brain is all confused. What did you just ask me?"

Now I was ashamed. We really did scare her.

"I am sorry Mrs. Nell.," I said truly apologetically. "We didn't mean to scare you. My Momma is just very happy to be hosting the meeting today, and we wanted to know if you were going to be there." I said it than slowly while lowering my head. I was waiting to both hear her answer and also I was praying that her answer was yes!

She stood quiet as though she was wondering what I was doing, then finally she said, "Well of course I am going. I am anxious to sit and chat with your Momma and get to know her better. Most of us do not really know her too well and are anxious to be good neighbors. I think most everybody in the neighborhood is coming. I was just upstairs getting ready and..."

Suddenly our idea didn't seem so good to me. Mrs. Nell had been nothing but nice to me since moving here and I felt bad like we were trying to trick her. I couldn't do it. I interrupted her. I jumped in and said, "OK then, we better get out of your hair so you can get there on time. I hope you have a good time at Mommas gathering today. Bye Bye."

And with that I scurried out the door with Knox tagging behind me with questions in his eyes.

"What was that? What just happened in there? What happened to our plan?" he said with such a sad look on his face.

"Oh Knox," I said, "I am sorry but I just couldn't try to trick her. She has been so sweet and did you hear what she just said about wanting to get to know my momma and being good neighbors?"

"Yeah," he said begrudgingly, "I know. You are right."

"But," I said in an upbeat voice, "That doesn't mean our whole plan is ruined. I will still be sitting under that window in exactly...." I stop and look down at my old familiar Dopey wristwatch. Usually it brings a smile to my face just to see Dopey's goofy but happy smile, but today my smile is all about our plan.

"In exactly 83 minutes!" I tell Knox. "83 minutes till Operation Listen! Will you be ready?"

"You bet!" he said. "Now...back to the Rose!"

Those next 83 minutes passed slowly, but finally the women started to gather at my house. Knox and I were outside swinging on that rusty old swing watching each one walk to the house. Some came from the alley and went to the back door, like Mrs. Nell. She looked real pretty and smelled good too. I was so used to her smelling like blueberry muffins or peach cobbler, that I was almost surprised when she walked past me and I picked up the scent of Lilies-of-the-Valley and decided that she must have on perfume. Others came from Maple Street and used the front door. My mom scurried back and forth and tried to greet each person at the door. She already knew most of the women, at least well enough to know their names, but she told me today was going to be her chance to get to know each of them a little better. I wanted to say that I was actually hoping for the same result.

Momma looked so pretty. She had on her lavender dress and pale gray ballerina flats. Audrey helped her with her make-up and hair and she looked perfect. Her dark brown hair was neat and just a little poufy at the crown of her head where Audrey had teased it and then carefully combed the top coat smooth. Earlier this week when she had come home from Sally's Beauty Shoppe, Daddy said she looked like an angel with her new chin length bob. Audrey used a really pretty shade of lipstick called primrose and then some pink petunia colored blush. I noticed Momma had on the pretty opal necklace that her grandmother gave her for her high school graduation and I am sure she had on the matching earrings too, but I really couldn't see them through her hair.

Her prized chocolate cake was prominently sitting on Aunt Alma's clear crystal cake stand on the kitchen counter with a stack of what used to be Grandma Holden's fine china cake plates in a pretty pink rose flowered pattern. Grandma Holden died before I was born, but Momma says she was a truly beautiful woman and she is an angel in heaven watching over me. Momma has also laid out ahead of time the coffee cups, napkins and silverware.

Aunt Elsie always naps around this time of day and she is a very heavy sleeper, so even if the ladies' conversation becomes too lively, it won't wake Aunt Elsie. Momma also planned ahead in case she did wake up early. She pulled out one of Aunt Elsie's special dresses and cleaned and pressed it so she would be ready to greet the neighbors if she had a shorter nap than usual. So…I think Momma had thought of everything, now let the gathering begin!

Mrs. Nell was the first to arrive and today she looked really happy. I knew Momma would love her and I knew they would have at least something to start to talk about since Mrs. Nell was beginning to know me pretty well by now. Within the next five minutes, two more ladies arrived; Elaine Mason, the preacher's wife and Anna Mobley. All they had to do was walk across the alley and they were there. Knox's mother wasn't going to be able to come. She was one of the few mothers in the neighborhood that worked during the day, but she was also the only young one with a dead husband. Knox didn't talk about his father a lot but when he did, his eyes got all teary and I could tell it still hurt him a lot. His dad was in the service, so he had never been around a lot, he was always somewhere else in the world. All Knox told me was that he died in an accident while he was away. I didn't want to upset him, so I never asked any questions even though I had a bunch in my head.

The next few arrivals came by way of walking up the front sidewalk and knocking on the front door. Audrey was helping Momma to greet the guest as Momma didn't want to be rude and leave anyone waiting too long to enter. Knox was helping me with some names. He said those two ladies were, Trish Gratton and Mindy Lee. He said the younger one was Mrs. Gratton and her daughter Sara was the same age as him. And then we saw another crossing the alleyway and I recognized her.

"That is Mrs. Tawney," I said proudly. "I met her one day when Daddy and I were here dropping off a load of boxes. She was leaving Miss Winter and stopped to introduce herself to Daddy. She seemed real friendly."

Knox nodded in agreement but I could tell he was bored with entrances, he wanted the gossip to begin.

I patted his arm, "Hang in their boy. It won't take them long to get past the formalities."

And it was as if I had said a magic sentence because just like that we heard Momma say, "Ladies. Hello ladies…. may I have your attention for a moment."

Everyone stopped their private conversations and focused on Momma.

"There now," she said very sweetly. "Thank you."

She cleared her throat and then continued.

"Well ladies," she said with a smile, "I want to thank you all for coming. I am so happy to see so many of you here today. I have been very anxious to get to know each and every one of you and to feel like I am a part of this wonderful neighborhood. I am guessing that just about everyone is here, but as I look around, I realize that I don't think Miriam and Lina Winter have arrived yet."

There was a little bit of a gasp from someone. Knox and I moved closer to the window.

I couldn't see any faces, but I expected that Mommas had a look of surprise and then I heard her say…

"Why do you all look so shocked?" Momma continued. "I mean Miriam and Lina live right next door. I have not formally met them yet,

177

but I have seen them working in their yard and they have waved. Is there something you ladies think I should know? If so, please share it with me. I do not want to seem a fool."

Oh man…. I sensed the gossip was about to fly. I knew about Aunt Elsie hating Miriam from reading the journals, but Momma didn't know anything about it, at least I didn't think she knows anything. I am about to learn cause now I hear her voice again.

"Please, someone," she pleaded. "Please tell me."

A woman is talking. I can tell it isn't Mrs. Nell but I am not sure who is speaking, but she is speaking!

"I realize that you are quite young Mrs. Holden," she says.

Mother interrupts and says, "Please call me Ginger."

"Fine," the lady says, "If you will call me Esther? Well Ginger, the reason you will get a friendly greeting from Mitzi and Lina, but that they will not join you here in your home is due to Elsie. There I said it and now the rest of you ladies don't have to be the one to do it."

She pauses and then continues right onward.

"Elsie and Mitzi have not talked for years," she says very matter-of-factly. "Well…. let me see, it has been," she pauses for a few seconds, "17 years to be exact. They have not spoken a word to each other as far as any of us know."

"Oh my goodness," my mother says. "Why on earth…. I mean …what could have caused such a rift to last so many years? What a minute. Seventeen years ago? That would be …… 1951?"

Momma pauses again and I can almost hear her brain working.

The ladies are all staying quiet and Momma continues. "When we were talking about moving here, David commented that Aunt Elsie had been alone since 1951…… Does this have something to do with Otto's death? I wonder…. I mean what possibly happened? From what David told me Otto fell…out in the yard. It was an accident. It involved a ladder. Are you ladies trying to tell me about that accident or did something else happen that I am not aware of? I am at a loss. Esther, can you please share a little more information?"

All of the women remained very quiet. Knox and I were waiting on pins and needles for someone to speak. Finally, Mrs. Tawney began.

"Well Ginger," she said very calmly. "This might take a bit. Let me make you a deal. How about we first sit down and enjoy of piece of that yummy looking chocolate cake I see on that gorgeous crystal cake stand. And I do believe I smell some coffee brewing. If that is alright with you, I think that would be lovely and then as a group, we ladies can share with you the details of a very long-standing feud from our eyes that are certainly not privy to all the inside details. Only Miriam and Elsie have that information. And from what most of us have gathered, Elsie is no longer in a capacity to share her knowledge, so if you need more details, you will have to speak to Miriam Winter."

"But now," she continued, "May we try your cake?"

MITZI

Chapter 17 - 1968

We were just sitting in the kitchen finishing one of my favorite lunches; tuna salad on a fresh bakery bun with a slice of American Cheese and a slim slice of tomato on the top. I had placed the open face sandwich on a cookie sheet on the top rack of the oven and used the broiler setting. I left it in just long enough to melt and brown the edges of the cheese and when it bubbled a tiny bit I knew it was ready. My goodness it is yummy. Lina likes it too but not nearly as much as I do. But anyway I digress.

I was just finishing the last bite of my sandwich when I noticed out the kitchen window Nell Taylor walking toward the back alley. I saw she was carrying her purse so I figured she was heading over to the grocery store or to her weekly hair appointment, but I thought she always had her hair done on Tuesdays and her hair looked very good. Usually when it is time for her appointment I can tell it is time because her hair has by then lost its neat appearance and there isn't much pouf left it in. Today, her hair looks great, so I am sure she did it yesterday. As I am still wondering where she is going I notice that she is not heading for her car, so now I am more interested.

I look at Lina who is still chewing on her last bite of tuna salad and I say, "Lina do you see Nell out there in the back yard? What is she doing? I have lost my view of her."

Lina bends her neck backward to look out the side window. Apparently, not able to see anything she actually lifts herself a tiny bit and scoots her chair back another inch or so then turns back to me and says, "She is walking."

"Walking where?" I retort very quickly.

"Well," she begins to answer in a very smart-aleck tone. "That I am not able to tell you since I do not have the ability to read her mind."

I am just about to reprimand her for teasing me, when I can now see Nell very clearly from the other window on the east side of the room.

"Never mind Lina," I say as I watch, "I can see her walking now. I wonder where she is off too...wait a minute, she is turning" .....I pause. "Well my goodness," I say as I look back toward Lina. "She is going into the yard of.....Elsie Becker!"

"Elsie Becker!" Lina says in surprise. "Well, I wonder if she baked something for the new people, the Holden family, you know as a welcome to the neighborhood gesture."

"No," I say quickly. "I saw her take something the other day. She is carrying nothing more than her purse today."

"Ok," I continue. "She is still walking right toward the back door. Now she has stopped and is talking to one of their little girls and that little boy from across the alleyway who is always running around. I just wonder...... Maybe you are right and she wants to meet the new lady of the house, but it isn't like Nell to visit another day so close in time and without a gift of some kind."

I turn back around now to face Lina.

"Well, she went inside, so I guess it is as you assumed..... another welcoming type visit."

I get up to start to clear away the lunch dishes and I see Mrs. Mason coming down her back steps and meeting up with her at the bottom is another neighbor, Mrs. Mobley.

"Lina," I yell. "Come back in here and look at this."

I get no response from Lina. I look again. The two women are now to the back door and heading inside the Becker house. I start to yell again to Lina and decide it better to just go find her. When I do, she is in the study, staring out the front window.

"Lina," I say, "I have been calling you. I wanted you to see that now Mrs. Mason and Mrs. Mobley..."

She stops me.

"Look at this" she says peering out the window without turning my direction.

I see 2 more ladies walking and talking almost directly in front of our house. I recognize one of them as being Mrs. Gratton, but can't really see the face of the other woman. And then Lina points her finger. I follow it and I see two more ladies walking slowly up the sidewalk, one of them being Esther Tawney. Each of the women appears to be dressed in one of their better summer dresses and are carrying only their handbags.

"Well my goodness," is all I can think to say. "It appears they are having a party without us Lina."

Lina stares at me and shakes her head in agreement.

"I wonder what the occasion is.....what is the date today Mitzi?" she asks.

"Well," I answer her, "today is Wednesday, June 19th.

Then I think about it for a minute. "I can think of nothing special today," I report. "Can you Lina?"

Lina shakes her head to register that she has thought of nothing.

"Well then," I say, "I guess they are having a party without us. Oh well, no matter. We are better off staying home today. We can get something done instead of sitting around with that group and sharing gossip."

"That's it!" Lina says suddenly.

"What?" I ask.

"That is what today must be," she says sounding confident. "Remember the neighbor ladies used to get-together occasionally to do exactly what you just said. To sit and gossip. And I do believe they called it something. What was it?" she asked.

"Oh, I do remember that and it was exactly as you say Lina. It was the ladies on our street," I say finally. "And they called it the Wednesday Afternoon Neighborhood Social Club...or something foolish like that."

I sat quiet for a minute. I looked at Lina and she was just staring back at me.

"I know," I say apologetically to her. "I know you have none or at least a very limited number of neighborhood friends and that is because of me."

"Oh hush Mitzi," Lina said confidently. "We both know that the main reason we have few friends on this street beyond Esther Tawney is more to do with our brother Henry than ourselves."

"No...no...no." I said firmly. "We cannot blame this all on Henry. Many of these neighbors have only moved here in the last ten years or so, so they did not even know Henry. As for those that have been on this street for a long time yes, they knew Henry. Yes, many knew Henry the man. But only a few of those on this street knew Henry as a boy. And many did not truly know Henry. At least not the Henry you and I knew. Oh my goodness, when I think back to the mean things that boy did to me...... and I am almost still too ashamed to think of the things he did to you. My poor sister! I do not know how you were ever brave enough to stay in this house knowing what he was capable of doing when he thought no one was around to stop him."

With my last remark, Lina lowers her head. I see the look of shame come across her face and now I feel terrible that I have brought old memories back to the surface.

"Oh Lina," I say with pure regret in my voice. "I am so sorry to have stirred up such memories. I know how much it pains you to remember."

Lina does not answer me. Her head remains lowered. I fear she is reliving some of those terrible times now. The times when father was not at home. The times when mother was busy running the noisy old sewing machine. The times when the house was quiet, in the middle of the night. The time when I heard a disturbing noise coming from her room late one night.

It had been just a normal day. Nothing unusual had happened. We had dinner as a family, cleaned up the kitchen, sat and listened to the radio and then one-by-one we were sent to bed at our usual times. I had read for a while and then finally drifted off to sleep but was suddenly awoken from some sort of noise. I listened for a moment and then heard it again. I couldn't decide what type of noise I was hearing but I definitely heard it and it sounded like it was coming from my sister's room. I left my room and quietly crept along the dark hallway without a sound and slowly opened her bedroom door. I mostly saw only shadows but I knew. I immediately knew what was happening.

I saw the figure of Henry Jr. on top of my sister on her bed. As I tip-toed closer I could see her night gown had been thrown up and his left hand was held tightly against her face covering her mouth. She was thrashing and kicking. He had his head up her gown.

I sprang into action. I lunged closer and started beating on his back. He had not heard me or seen me coming, so I got in my first blows without him realizing I was in the room. But then he knew. He fought back and he hit me hard. I had made a noise when I hit the floor. Realizing this, he jumped off the bed and ran quickly back into his room which was directly across the hallway from Lina.

I heard father's voice come from his room. He yelled out and asked if everyone was alright. I heard his bedroom door open and again he had yelled, "Is everyone okay? What has happened?"

Within a minute, he came into Lina's open door. He looked toward Lina, who had already straightened herself and was sitting on her bed. Next he looked at me. I was just standing there beside her bed. He was waiting. I started to speak, but Lina quickly jumped in and gave an answer.

"I am sorry Father," she said calmly. "I am afraid I had a bad dream. Mitzi apparently ran in to wake me and in my panic from my dream, I pushed her and she fell. Her fall woke me up. I think we are both okay now. Mitzi," she asked very calmly, "are you okay?"

She looked at me with pleading eyes.

"Yes," I said in a weak voice. "Yes father, I heard her fussing and came to check and....," I chuckled a little to make the story more believable, "and just like that she gave me a shove and I landed pretty hard...right there on the floor. But I am okay."

"Well, my goodness," father had said, "You girls need to get your beauty sleep. Let's all forget about bad dreams and falling down and such and get back to sleep. Tomorrow will be here before you know it."

As I was about to turn and leave her room I remember I looked at Lina sitting there on her bed. There was such a look of relief on her face. I felt so sorry for her in that moment. She had just endure a terrible attack, I suspect a sexual attack by our brother and she had felt there was nothing that she could do but protect our father from such news about his son.

Father had already returned to his room so I turned around and went back into Lina's room and stood by her bedside. She stared up at me. I saw the tears now in her eyes. I bent forward and gave her a hug and she held me tightly. When she finally let go I said, "May I sleep in your bed tonight?"

She quickly scooted over and made room for me. We pulled our covers up tightly and eventually fell asleep.

Today as I sit here and look at her I see those same pleading eyes. I remember that incident so well and know in my heart that there were probably so many more that Lina endured and I wonder if she still has nightmares.

Henry did vile things to me and often tried to hurt me, but he never tried any of his sickening sexual deeds on me. I was stronger willed and stronger physically than Lina. She was always so quiet and almost fragile. Henry understood her loyalty to father and the idea that we were a prominent family in Pinesdale and we needed to live as an example for others and blah, blah, blah. She believed everything father said and she would never hurt father. Henry was smart. He understood Lina and it made her Henry's target.

It was more than a week after that attack when Lina finally said something to me about what happened.

She knew she had to talk with me, to explain why she didn't want father to know what really happened. I already understood the "why" part, but Lina didn't know that I did. Finally one quiet rainy day when mother was over at the church with her quilting group and Henry Jr. had went to spend the day with father at work, she confided in me. Lina truly did not want to talk about it, I could tell, but she felt she must tell me some so I would understand the need to protect her secret.

She said Henry had often attacked her. It started with small things like hitting her, tripping her, just mean kids type things. But one day when they were outside it became more than those things.

She said she had been weeding the garden and Henry came along and hit her on the back of the head. She had taken her hand and swung it up at him to hit him away. Instead, he grabbed her arm and yanked it back causing her body to swing around. Still holding her arm, he had drug her into the garage. Her body hurt all over from scraping across the gravel stones in the driveway. Once inside he let go just long enough to swing the garage side door shut. She had tried to get up and run, but he dove toward her and ended up knocking her back down. He had laughed and then slowly lifted her dress. He was trying to yank down her petticoat when the side door suddenly swung open with a bang and he stopped. Tram was standing there. He immediately jumped on Henry back and the fight began. As Lina scooted herself out of harm's way, Henry Jr. and Tram wrestled on the dirt floor. When he could take a minute to breathe, Tram yelled for her to get out. As Lina tried to get past them, Henry Jr. reached out and grabbed her ankle. Lina screamed and Tram was once again able to break Henry's grasp. Lina was free and ran out the door. She said she went into the house and hid in fathers study. She said she was so afraid to move that she eventually ended up falling asleep and finally awoke when mother came home from the store.

She finished her story and waited for me to absorb the information. Those kinds of things keep happening. She said she didn't know what she would do if Tram didn't live so close by and watch out for her. Then she said the next sentence and I wanted to cry.

"But Henry Jr is very smart. He figured out if he sneaks in my room at night when everyone is asleep then Tram can't come to my rescue. No one can. So now he leaves me alone outside, but hurts me when the house is quiet. I hate it when the house is quiet. And I cannot say anything or have anyone help me because if father knew what Henry Jr was doing it would break his heart. I just know it would. So, please Mitzi, I beg you, do not tell father. He must never know."

I honored Lina's wish. I never told. But I did figure out a way to help her. I began with mother. I suggested that it would be lovely to have a sewing room. For about a week I talked about how we could store all of our beautiful fabrics and cut our patterns without making a mess for father to see. After I felt I had laid enough groundwork, I started to say, it could happen if I moved my bedroom. I could instead share a space with Lina. I said there was plenty of room for 2 beds in her room and that it would be nice to share a room with my sister just like mother had done with her own sister.

I was beginning to think my plan was not working, I had been talking about it for a good two weeks now and nothing seemed to be stirring in mother's head and then it happened. One day during lunch with father, mother said she had been thinking about having the two of us share a bedroom in order to create space for a sewing room. She said she felt it would make a nice close bond for sisters to share a room as she had shared a room with her sister, Violet and she was much closer to her than to her sister Gloria.

Father had listened to mother and then said, "It is certainly something to think about!"

It was three days later that my bedroom became the sewing room. Father and Henry did all of the heavy lifting to make the room change happen. Whenever he could do so without father noticing, he glared at me. I was not afraid, I glared back. I wanted to send him a message that things had now changed. Tram was Lina's protector during the day, but I was now going to be Lina's protector during the night. On our own, he was stronger, but with the two of us together, we were stronger. Lina would no longer be his easy target.

That was so very many years ago, but it worked. There were still nights when he tried to return to our room, but he didn't count on the fact that I was now smarter too. I slept with a small lead pipe under my pillow. With the slightest noise, I was awakened and swung the pipe hitting him on the back of his legs. He had run out of the room like a crippled old man. Those nighttime attacks eventually stopped against Lina. What I didn't know until years later, was when the attacks stopped against Lina....they began against other unsuspecting girls in our area.

As for us today, Lina and I have kept our bond close. If the neighborhood ladies want to gather without us, then so be it. Although I would like to be included, I am well aware that I will NEVER be included in any gathering that includes Elsie Becker and certainly not in her home. Esther Tawney is still a friend that visits occasionally. She will eventually come to visit and tell Lina and me all about this gossip session she is attending today. Esther's memory is fine. She will tell us everything and though I shouldn't be….I am anxious to hear it all.

SABRINA

Chapter 18 - 1968

Oh my gosh…..Knox and I can't wait for the ladies to finish their cake. Right now, I wish Momma wasn't such a good cook …. but I know those ladies are likely to eat every last bite of their cake. We figured we shouldn't walk away from the window at all because they are likely to begin talking any minute. And we were right. They did exactly that.

It was hard to tell sometimes who was talking, but we knew Nell's voice and now we knew Mrs. Tawney too. I was wishing right about now that I had a notebook and pen with me, so I could write down any key facts…..but we were just going to have to rely on our memories.

Momma kind of got things started.

"Ladies," she said, "I am sorry to have started off our afternoon together with such a sad topic as a feud, but I am really at a loss. I am totally feeling in the dark as to what possibly took place between my Aunt Elsie and Miss Winter."

"Well," said Mrs. Tawney, "as a group many of us know a good bit of the complete story while many of the younger neighbors may be more like yourself. They may know about the tiff, but not all of the details that caused it to begin."

Knox looked at me and made his face get all scrunched up and he raised his hand up by his face and was shaking it, I guess pretending to be a high fa-louting lady or some such thing.

Mrs. Tawney is continuing. I wonder if she will even let any of the other ladies speak.

189

"The feud started during 2 tragic days in the fall of 1951," she states very much like she is doing the voice over for a documentary movie.

"The first tragedy occurred at the Winter home when they found Henry Winter, the mayor of Pinesdale, dead inside his garage. Right there in that big old garage. It was never determined how he died so most of us assumed it must have been a heart attack."

The room stayed kind of quiet with this piece of information, so we assumed most everybody must have already known that information. After all, he was the mayor.

"The second tragedy occurred the very next day when Otto Becker died when he fell from a ladder right here in his yard on this side of the house, facing the Winter home. It was a terrible accident and both deaths shocked the town of Pinesdale," she now paused as though waiting for the question and answer portion to begin.

My mother spoke first.

"Alright," Momma said rather sheepishly. "I did remember both pieces of information that you shared, but I must say, I still don't understand how a feud formed from those two events."

Knox and I both nod our heads in agreement with Momma.

There was a little bit of rumbling agreement around the room.

Mrs. Tawney now spoke again in a louder voice. "Ladies....ladies please!"

"As I was saying," she said being very dramatic, "and of course there wouldn't be except for ideas that someone developed in her head. And then that same person wouldn't let go of those ideas ....no matter how much people tried to get her to be sensible."

"OK," I hear Momma say. "OK, I assume you are referring to Aunt Elsie, but what kind of ideas did she have?"

"Well," and it is Mrs. Tawney talking again.

"Well, Elsie got it into her head that Otto did not fall accidentally. Yes, that is right. Elsie decided that Otto was always very careful and he wouldn't have fell from the ladder. She decided that......," she pauses for effect. "She decided that he fell because someone ....."

Again she pauses and then rapidly says, "Someone shook the ladder!"

There was a gasp from about half of the room followed by a lot of murmurings.

Now it was Mommas' turn again.

"Oh my goodness. And did she think one of the Winter sisters…. shook the ladder?"

"Yes she did," Mrs. Tawney said very dramatically.

"But why," Momma said very slowly as if she was trying to think of a possible reason while she was asking the question. "Why would either of them want to hurt Otto?"

Mrs. Tawney once again paused before answering. I wondered if she thought someone else should have a turn to talk, but finally she spoke.

"The only answer I have or anybody has is pure conjecture. Nothing has ever been confirmed, at least as far as I know. Jim Dowdy, the patrolman who found Henry, moved out-of-state about a year of two after all of this took place. Sheriff Mace, well he passed away a few years back. So, to try to ask a question, we would have slim pickings. But I do have a presumed answer, one that Elsie foolishly proclaimed as soon as Otto died and everyone presumed she was just consumed with grief."

"I am sure a few of you already know what I am going to say," she says and there is enough of a pause that we assume she is looking around the room to some of the older ladies. The ones that were living in the neighborhood in 1951.

"Elsie said Miriam Winter shook the ladder…. causing Otto to fall to his death…..because Otto had seen her kill her brother Henry Winter the day before."

I looked at Knox and his eyes were about bugging out of his face. He also looked like he was going to explode. I understood. I felt the same way too.

I had heard a loud gasp and I recognized it has my mother. There was a lot of voices talking at once and then I heard my mother's voice come out strong sounding over the others.

"Oh my goodness," she said loudly. "Well no one believed that…did they?"

"Not a living soul believed that idea," Mrs. Tawney spouted as though she herself was the law. "The sheriff let her talk that first day and even for a few days afterward, but then she just wouldn't let it drop. She kept insisting it was murder and she kept calling the sheriffs' office. Finally he just flatly refused to talk with her about it anymore. He said both deaths were explained to his satisfaction and the cases were closed."

"Poor Mitzi," she continued. "Elsie never spoke to her again. And now, from what we hear around the neighborhood Elsie has gotten past the point of being able to sensibly talk to anyone. We are not sure if that is true, but it is all a certainly sad situation."

My mother must be still trying to regain her composure, because she doesn't answer.

Finally, Momma says. "Yes Elsie has had some memory issues. She has a few good days but more are bad than good now. We are here because she needs help. I am sorry to hear of the problems that were created due to her heartache from losing her husband, Otto, but I am sure she must have had some reason. But I also understand grief can bring about many things."

At that last remark, suddenly all the women are now talking, some louder than others. I listen and I can hear Nell's voice. I am sure it was new information to quite a few and I kind feel bad that it all had to happen during Momma's first meeting. She wanted everything to be perfect and now all everybody will remember from today is Mrs. Tawney telling the whole story about 1951.

I look again at Knox. He is giving me a funny look like he is wondering why I look so sad. He gives me a two thumbs up sign and I nod but not with the enthusiasm he is expecting. He gives me the high sign to head over to our huddle area. We certainly have a lot to discuss. We sneak out from under the window and dodge ourselves across the yards to get across the alley without anyone noticing us. Once in the huddle….we just stare at each other and Knox takes his hand together and pretends they are a firework going off….POW!

For the rest of the afternoon, we sat in our little hideout discussing the new ideas. More than ideas, I had lots of new questions in my mind but they were the kind of questions I didn't think Knox would be able to help me answer. I wasn't sure just who could answer them except Miss Winter and Aunt Elsie, if only her mind was still working. I wondered if maybe Mrs. Nell might know anything more about 1951. I mean at least know a few more things then were already mentioned today at the gathering.

I reminded Knox of some of the details.

"We already knew from the journals that Aunt Elsie hated Mitzi Winter," I said. "We also knew she tried to make the police chief investigate Uncle Otto's death and he had turned a deaf ear. A new piece of information was that we didn't realize that other people were aware of Aunt Elsie's suspicions. That presents a new factor. Now we know that NO one would listen to her."

I studied Knox's face. He was thinking.

I said, "And that is the part that is bugging me."

He nodded, "Me too."

I know he agreed, but I wanted to further my case.

"Think about it," I continued. "Not too brag, but Uncle Otto and Aunt Elsie were supposed to be kind of like "Big Wigs" in Pinesdale in their heyday. I wonder why nobody questioned his fall. I mean I know people fall all the time, but most people don't die! Uncle Otto was a wealthy man. He owned a business in this town. You would think SOMEBODY besides his wife would have questioned his fall!"

"And," I just couldn't quit thinking and talking, "if other people knew there was at least some question about Otto and how he died, you would think it would have created a certain amount of "buzz" or gossip around this town. I wonder why it didn't? I wonder if maybe people didn't like Uncle Otto and Aunt Elsie? Awe....I guess I just wonder a lot."

"No," Knox jumped in quick. "You are right. Exactly! Why DID no one question him dying?"

He hung his head downward for a minute then he looked up and said, "OK. It is time. We need to start asking the hard questions. We need to pull the truth from the people mostly likely to know the answers. We have been too nice. Too easy going."

"But how?" I asked.

"It is time to do what any good Hardy Boy would do," he said full of confidence. "1. We need to go talk to the people that really know or at least are most likely to know and 2. You need to read further into those journals."

I answered but with another question.

"I assume you mean talk to the Winter sisters?" I asked in a matter-of-fact sounding voice. "But how do we make them talk? And in regards to the journals, I have read October thru December of 1951 and have found nothing new. Just a lot of pages talking about her daily life, the antics of Mr. Mertz, watching Miss Eulalie do her cleaning and of course, her hating Miss Mitzi. What exactly are you thinking I am going to find?"

"I don't know, but there just has to be something in there to help us. You try tonight to read and read if you have to stay up all night," he said almost like it was an order. "Are you up for the ....Nancy Drew?"

"Well I can try," I answered thinking I had no other choice. "But if I keep my light on all night, Tram might decide to start watching me!"

I said that thinking I was just being funny, but Knox's face lit up like a Christmas tree on Christmas Eve.

"Exactly....Tram!" he said excitedly.

"What?" I asked. "What about Tram?"

"Don't you see?" he asked. "That is who we need to talk to...Tram. Remember, Mrs. Nell said he was here when she was a little girl. She said his family had owned a house at one time in this neighborhood. And there is some connection to him and the Winter sisters or he wouldn't always be hanging around their house. He will know! I just know it. He will know!"

"Ok...Ok," I said. "I get it that he might know. But what makes you think he will tell us?"

He kind of came back down to earth with that thought.

"Well," he said slowly, "We will just have to be very clever or very friendly...or both."

He smiled that silly but kind of cute little smile he does. I smiled back and slowly nodded my head in agreement.

"Ok," I said, "Then that is our plan. I will stay up all night reading and while I sleep in late in the morning, you get your butt over to Mrs. Nell's and beg for a muffin and get us some real answers.

"Yes," he answered obediently.

I continued, "Then about 10:30, I will meet up with you here and together we will go try to talk with Tram while he is out in the garage away from the ears of the Winter sisters."

"Is it a plan?" I ask.

"It's a plan," he confirmed.

"Alright then," I said. "So what do you want to do now? I have a good 30 minutes before I have to head home for dinner."

Now I am thinking about Momma. I actually wonder if she is cooking dinner tonight. After those ladies left today, I bet she just sat down to think. I bet right now she really wishes Aunt Elsie could tell her all the answers too. Poor Momma, her big gathering probably wasn't considered much of a success. Actually, now that I think about it, maybe I better just head home a little early and see if Momma is ok.

"Hey Knox," I said, "I think I will go ahead home a little early and see if Momma needs any help. She had a kind of rough day today. But don't worry, I won't forget our plan."

I got up to leave.

Knox grabbed my arm. "Hey there Stinkweed," he said rather grown-up sounding. "Good luck tonight. Even if you get sleepy, keep alert. Don't miss something important. Okay?"

"You got it Knox! See you at 10:30."

NELL

Chapter 19 - 1942

The day I turned twenty-one, October 23rd 1942, my mother wanted to have a birthday celebration. You know, the kind like you have as a child with your family gathered around you; a big birthday cake with everyone singing "Happy Birthday" as you blow out the candles. Those were great when you were a little kid but not when you are twenty-one and finally free to make your own choices and do whatever you want! I wanted to feel that freedom. I had my own life now, well almost my own.

A few months prior, I had finally quit working at Becker Industries. I was stuck in a dead-end job I had held since graduating from high school. I had endured the monotony of the production line for way too long with no immediate hope of moving into an office position. When I started working there I envisioned moving up quickly. I had hopes that someone would see me working hard on the line, recognize my value and offer me a seat in the billing or shipping office. I knew it was a dream but I really did think if I worked hard and waited patiently new opportunities would come my way. The opportunities never visualized and I grew weary of waiting.

As if an answer to my prayers, one day as I was coming out the back door of our house and starting my usual morning walk to work, out of the blue, our neighbor Mr. Henry Winter Jr. offered me a ride. The Winter family had always been our neighbors here on Maple Street. Henry Jr. had of course lived there when I was young child. When he married, he moved into his own home but there was a terrible tragedy which changed his life. After that he returned to the family home on Maple Street. A short time later his father, Henry Sr. passed away from a heart attack, I think. I just know he was standing right there in the back yard talking with Tram Kellar and suddenly dropped to the ground. My mother said he apparently felt one quick jolt like a strike of lightening and was gone. So now it is just the three Winter siblings living in the house; Henry and his two sisters, Miriam and Lina.

As I was saying, Mr. Winter asked if he could offer me a ride. I was not accustom to Mr. Winter remembering my name or ever speaking to me. He was a neighbor and he was polite, but he usually spoke more to my mother than myself. Even then the most he usually said was, "Hello Mrs. Jenkins" as he walked in or out of the house carrying his briefcase. He took me by surprise on this particular morning and even though it was already appearing to be a typical sticky-hot muggy July day, I said a quick, "No thank you" and continued walking toward the alley. I watched out of the corner of my eye and saw him go into his garage.

I was almost to the end of the alley when I saw his shiny blue 1940 Packard Touring Sedan pull up beside me going very slowly. I looked his direction and he stopped the car.

He rolled down the passenger side window and said, "Please let me take you this morning Miss Jenkins. I have something I would like to talk to you about and I would love to get an answer from you as quickly as possible. And, it is cool in my car. I have the air conditioning turned up on high."

I was not sure if I should, but he had now peeked my curiosity. Also I had never ridden in a car that had air conditioning and I was curious about that too. I opened the door and cautiously climbed into the front seat keeping myself practically right up against the door handle.

He was right, the car was definitely cool. He chatted about nothing much during the three-minute ride, but when he pulled into the parking lot at Becker Industries, I was surprised that he pulled far away from the entrance door; parked and then shut off the car. The cool air stopped. He rolled down his window and then turned my direction. I hurried and rolled my window part way down too.

He began by explaining that besides being the Mayor of Pinesdale, he also owned his own business, an accounting firm; Winter Accounting Firm. He asked if I was aware of his business. I said I knew it was on Pyatt St. in between the Fabric & Yarn Shoppe and the Dentist office. I wondered what he was thinking. Pinesdale is a small town with only a small handful of storefronts, so I had walked past his building many, many times.

Then he asked if I had any interest in finance. I admitted I had never considered it as an option. He continued to talk with me, trying to explain what type of work he did for his clients. He had a very strong and almost intimidating personality. I admit very freely that he scared me a little with his intensity. If I hadn't wanted off the production line so badly I would have never even considered his proposal. But I did want out and I listened.

He said the words. For some reason, Mr. Winter had decided he wanted me. He asked if I would consider being his receptionist. He asked if I wanted to step into the seat of Connie McFarland who he had to let go a while back because business at the time had been dwindling. He alone had been handling all the office duties for quite some time and he now found himself prepared to finally get the office back to being staffed.

He presented his offer of $3.80 an hour which was 17 cents less than I was currently making at Becker. He explained my work scheduled would be four days per week from 9 am to 4:30 pm with a 30-minute lunch. I would have Wednesdays off but need to work a half day every other Saturday. My job would include the standard duties of a receptionist and light cleaning at the end of each day. He concluded by saying he would like an answer now, as in right now. Then he just stared at me.

I needed to punch in at work in 10 minutes, or else be considered tardy. I had very little experience in job searches and interviews but even I knew this was a very strange approach to securing a new employee. He was staring at me waiting for an answer. It was rather rude; he was giving me no time to really think about any of the pros and cons, and I already knew there were some cons, probably more cons than pros. I thought fast. It didn't pay as well and it didn't sound like it came with any extra benefits like my job at Becker Industries, but I wanted out. I looked at him again staring at me. I was nervous. I was unsure but I decided to jump.

I thanked Mr. Winter and said I would turn in my notice today and be able to start in two weeks.

He stopped smiling and said, "No Nell that won't do. I need you to start in one week. Just simply give them one week's notice. It will be fine."

Some people might not have thought it was a very smart move. I knew my mother would be furious with me, but as I told her later that day, it is my life. Would I better off financially? No. But might I be in a position to meet eligible men who come in to have Mr. Winter help them find ways to make more money with their investments. Heck yes. And that can't be bad!

So, even though my mother was sure I was making a terrible mistake and my friends were sad that I would be leaving the line, a week later, I was sitting at my own desk answering phone calls for Mr. Winter at the Winter Accounting Firm.

The job as receptionist was not as glamorous as I had hoped. Mr. Becker definitely got many calls but it seemed to me not many were from new clients. He got calls from current clients questioning their investments and some that even walked in and demanded to be seen immediately. Although his office door was closed during these conversations, I could often hear raised voices and what sounded like fists pounding against the desk as they made their complaints. I admit I did not understand much on Mr. Winter's selection of stocks and investments he chooses for his clients, but I did understand when they were not happy with the results and that...seemed to happen frequently.

But I wasn't about to give up on my role. I wasn't sure that I was truly going to learn anything about investments as Mr. Winter never asked me to do any type of research for him. My job consisted of answering the phone, typing papers, creating and collecting the mail and cleaning up any trash at the end of the day. My job was pretty simple and for now, that was enough to keep me happy.

As for today, today was my birthday. How lucky was I to turn 21 on a Friday? Two of my friends from Becker Industries; Trish Mitchell and Mindy Gillis wanted to take me out after work. They said we would have a quick dinner at Starlings; I love their fish and chips, and then go out for a little fun, some dancing and such. Now that I was finally of legal age, I wanted to make sure I celebrated with a few fancy mixed drinks too. I knew my mother wasn't happy with my choice...once again. But I had made up my own mind and chosen my new career path in July and it had turned out pretty good. Now today, I intended to do the same for my birthday.

The day had seemed long. I had found it usually does when you have plans that you are eager to get started. The clock finally reached 4:20 and it was time for my end of day ritual. As I was cleaning up the trash Mr. Winter had come out of his office. He was usually polite enough with me, but he had still never been overly friendly and I still felt that intense presence whenever he was in the room. I knew he faced an abundance of unhappy clients each week and figured that I needed to cut him a little slack knowing he was probably pretty miserable most of the time.

Today was different. Today he stopped and as I was watering the plants, he was actually making small talk. He asked if today was my birthday. I was surprised that he knew and I guess he could tell but my expression that I was shocked.

He said, "Back in July, when you filled out your paperwork it had asked your birthday. For some reason I remembered the date."

That made sense. I smiled and said, "Yes. It is today." Then I offered, "I am finally twenty-one!"

"Well," he said, "Happy birthday to you. So what are your big plans for celebrating such an auspicious day?"

I was still shocked to be having a whole conversation with him. I said, "I am going out to dinner and a little dancing with some friends."

"Well now, that sounds like fun," he said. "I guess it is good timing that this is not your Saturday to come into work." Then he laughed just a little and said, "OK then...Enjoy yourself."

He started for the door. He turned the knob and opened the door just a crack and then turned back to me and said, "Where do you young folks go nowadays to do, as you say, a little dancing?"

I had already turned back to the plants. I looked back to him and said, "What?"

He repeated, "I asked, where do you young folks go to dance nowadays?"

Without even thinking about it, I answered, "Big Jims!"

He responded, "Oh of course... Big Jims. Well, good night. Happy birthday and have a fun evening."

The night had been perfect. Trish offered to drive and after dinner we went right over to Big Jim's and as was to be my luck, they had a local band, Leo's Gang on the small stage. The place was very lively and I was having a great time. We had a few drinks and danced as a group most of the evening. Mindy had met up with an old flame and motioned to Trish and I that she was stepping outside, if you know what I mean. Trish had ordered another round of drinks and then returned to the dance floor. Suddenly I felt a tap on my shoulder and turned around to see Tony Myers standing there waiting for me to I guess fawn all over him or something. I turned back around to face Trish and went back to dancing. He tapped my shoulder again, this time a little harder. I turned around more prepared this time and said, "Sorry, not interested!" I turned back to Trish ready to laugh but she had a funny look on her face. I shrugged my shoulders at her and started to get back into trying to dance when she gave me a look that let me know I needed to turn around and see what was happening.

I turned and was shocked to see Henry Winter standing there with Tony. It was noisy in the bar but it appeared they were having heated words. Tony didn't look happy but finally looked at me as though he was thinking, "What the heck makes you so special," before he walked away.

Then he yelled, "Enjoy the old guy!"

It was kind of embarrassing. There I was left standing on the dance floor with Henry Winter. My boss. He just stood there waiting. I didn't know what he expected. I was there with my friend and I was having a good time. I had a few drinks, but I wasn't loopy yet and anyway, Trish was driving so I was okay.

I knew I had to say something to him. The music was loud so I leaned forward and said, "Hey Thanks."

"It looked like he was giving you a hard time," he said in a cocky sort of tone.

"Oh, that was just Tony. He is an okay guy, he was just a little drunk," I answered.

"Well," he said as though he was in charge of me, "he needed put in his place. I told him to hit the road and leave you alone. He won't bother you anymore tonight."

I gave him a look, so I guess I must have been a little drunk too and then I said, "I don't think that was necessary, but thanks. Okay now, I gotta get back to my friend. See ya Monday."

"You go ahead and dance some more," he said as though he were giving me permission. "I will go to the bar and get you girls some drinks. A birthday celebration." And he walked away.

I turned back to Trish and shrugged. "Oh well," I said with a laugh, "I guess he is buying us a round." We went back to dancing.

Mr. Winter returned with drinks and motioned for us to join him at the table in the corner. Mindy was still outside but Trish was eager for a drink and grabbed my arm and pulled me along with her to the table. It was not your typical table. Two young girls with one older man. Mr. Winter looked different. I was only used to seeing him in his suits. I wasn't sure he was the type of man that looked "normal" in everyday clothes.

He talked to us as though we were all his best friends. It was strange indeed. He asked Trish about her job and if she had a boyfriend. He asked her questions about me, like how long had we been friends, did I like my new job and such. I was getting uncomfortable and asked Trish if she wanted to dance. She did and as we rose to leave the table he assured us he would go get another round. Soon he yelled for us to come back to the table when we were thirsty. I admit I didn't really want to, but the idea of another free drink was also appealing.

This time as we sat and talked, I knew I was feeling some sort of buzz because I was no longer upset or feeling strange about being there with him at the table. The night grew on and the room got warmer. An hour later, Henry, as we were now all calling him, said we girls looked like we had drunk a little too much and he had better drive us home. We resisted at first, but as we stood to leave I noticed I was having difficulty standing evenly on the floor. It felt as if my shoes were on the wrong feet or something. Though neither of us lived far from Big Jim's, it was far enough that we could run into trouble getting home. Mindy had apparently left with her guy because we had seen not hide nor hair of her since early into the evening. So against my better judgement, I accepted for both of us.

Henry helped us each into the car and then drove nice and slowly since he too had been drinking, but not nearly as much as we girls. He found his way to Trish's house first and walked her to her door. With her now safe at home, he looked at me and said, "OK, now let me deliver you."

Instead of turning onto Maple St. he instead went straight as though he were heading back to the small downtown section of Pinesdale. It was true that I was probably drunk, but I was not so drunk to not see we were going the wrong way. I started to ask and he instead told me not to worry, that he needed to pick up something at the office before going home. I was now upset and feeling very warm and was afraid I was going to be sick.

I said to him, "Please I need to get home. Stop the car and I will walk. I really think I am going to be sick."

He said, "No, no no. Now .... don't get sick. No, no don't get sick here in my car."

He reached his arm across me and rapidly rolled down my window. "Here now, get some fresh air."

I remember I was so scared that I might vomit that I practically stuck my whole head out the window.

A minute later the car suddenly stopped. I looked up and saw we were in the alley behind his office. I looked at him questioningly. He saw me and seemed to know I was confused.

"I need something from the office," he said calmly. "It will do you good to get out of the car and walk a bit. Come on inside with me. Come on, it's okay. The fresh air will help."

Next thing I knew he was out of the car and over on my side opening the car door. He reached his arm in and placed it under mine and helped lift me to a stand. We walked together the few steps to the back entrance of the office. He pulled the key from his pocket and unlocked the door.

The office was of course dark and I thought it was odd that he didn't immediately turn on the light. Instead he shut the door and I heard the deadbolt latch.

He still had my arm and we started to walk a few steps, I stopped and said, "Please turn on some lights Mr. Winter. I can't see where I am going."

He said, "It is only a few more steps, keep walking. I've got you. The paper I need is right over here."

I took the steps and I noticed he had shifted his arm and pulled me closer. His arm was now extended enough around me that his fingers were touching against of side of my breast. I pulled myself forward and tried instead to walk without his arm but he grabbed me back quickly, holding me tighter than before.

I said, "Please Mr. Winter, you can let go. I am okay now. I can walk without any help. Actually I will just stand here and wait for you."

This seemed to anger him as he quickly said, "No. I need to keep you here beside me. Let me help you!" and again he reached around putting his right arm across my back and under my right arm but this time held his hand completely against my breast.

"Stop that Mr. Winter," I said this time with some anger in my voice as I tried to pull away from him. He let go and without any hesitation slapped my face and then grabbed me by my shoulders. The next thing I felt was my back being pushed against the wall and his mouth pressed hard against mine while my face was still feeling the burn from his slap.

"Stop it!" I said jerky my head free from his sloppy lips and pushing my hands against his chest.

He immediately grabbed my hands and then moved quickly to pin my arms against the wall. I sensed I had no ability to pull myself free. He was strong, much stronger than I would have guessed. I had so badly wanted to have those drinks earlier tonight, to celebrate and now I was so unable to make my body follow any of my commands. I was trying to fight back and to be strong but my body had no control. He was maneuvering me like I was nothing more than a rag doll.

He leaned his body against my left arm to free up his hand and I felt it searching my chest, hurriedly unbuttoning my blouse almost ripping it in the process. In another second, his mouth was on my neck. I could feel his disgusting tongue rubbing against my skin and his warm breath rising up on my face. The smell of alcohol was so pungent it was making me physically sick.

Now he had lowered himself to my chest. He was immediately trying to get beyond my bra. He began biting at the exposed flesh and trying to pull my breast free of its covering. I tried again to move from the wall, but he pressed his body tighter against me. I felt his strength growing and knew I had to get some control quickly before he made another move. As he was concentrating on my chest, I was able to pull my left arm free and I tried to push him back just enough to get my left leg free to kick him but he was very fast. He grabbed my arm again and this time as he came back at me I could feel the lower part of his body pressing against me. I could feel now the hard rise in his pants and knew I had to do something quickly. Everything was happening so fast, but yet at the same time was moving in slow motion.

In the next second he suddenly flipped my body around and pressed my face against the wall, slamming my right cheek so hard into the solid wall that I thought for sure it had broken a bone. He had his knee pressed hard against my backside, so hard that I thought he might push me right through the wall. I felt him unhook my bra and the release of my breasts.

I cried out, "No...please no!"

He immediately swung me back around and again pinned my upper arms to the wall but kept his body close enough to keep my legs from movement. He paused for a moment. Total calmness. I could feel his hot breath on my face. I was so thankful that it was dark and I could not see him. I knew what was coming next and braced myself, but I wasn't ready. His mouth went right to my breasts viciously biting and tugging at me. I cried out in pain but mostly in fear. I knew there was no one on the street or anywhere close by to hear me, but it was my only option.

He swung his hand up over my mouth and as soon as it was securely placed, he started to pull me downward to the floor. I knew I couldn't let that happen. I had to stay on my feet if I had any hope of not being raped. I tried to pull my hand free. I felt my adrenaline kick in and give me a spurt of new strength. I got my right hand free and I swung it at him with as much force as I could gather. I connected on his face but the blow only increased his anger and his urgency to complete his deed.

He grabbed my hair at the back of my head and yanked me downward. I hit my head hard as my body meet the floor surface. I felt dazed. I felt him lift my skirt and the roughness of his hands as he yanked down my panties, but it was as if it was all a bad dream. I had no fight left in me. I felt the weight of his body across my legs as he sat upright. I heard the zipper of his pants. I screamed as he entered me. Then I felt the entire weight of his body land on top of me.

It was over. I laid there in silence. I kept my eyes closed tightly but I felt the release of tiny warm tears seeping onto my face. I smelt the disgusting stench of his heavy alcohol breath. I endured the sickening feeling of him still inside me wanting desperately to push him off but afraid it would cause another attack. I was already reliving this attack in my head and I knew it was something that would forever haunt me. I felt every pain he inflicted on my body, and most prominently I felt the humiliation.

A minute later, he rolled off of me and said in a voice of anger, "Maybe in the future you will consider not wearing those tight sweaters of yours in the office, shaking your tits and swinging your hips to try to attract my attention. Didn't your mother teach you anything? If you dress and act like a slutty tramp, you shall be treated like a tramp. Now, get up and get dressed. I will take you home."

He walked over, switched on the light, and went to his desk and started to go through papers. I flinched at the brightness of the lights and quickly tried to cover myself. It had been such a violent attack and now that it was done, he acted as though I wasn't even in the room. I turned my back to him and put my bra back in place and buttoned my blouse. I felt my cheek and hoped that no bones were out of place. I stood up and straightened my skirt and had to look around for my panties. I would have just left without them, but it disgusted me to think of him later holding them in his hands. He must have thrown them when he ripped them off because I found them in the corner near the wastebasket. I discreetly put them back on and seeing him still busy at his desk, I crept silently out the back door. If I had been drunk before I was now completely sober. The fresh air hit my face and I breathed it in. I started to walk down Pyatt Street.

A few minutes later, his car pulled up beside me and he said, "Stop being such a stupid girl. Get in the car."

I ignored him and kept walking.

He tried again. He said, "Get in his car now. I will take you home."

I looked at him and said, "No I will not. You will not hurt me again. Get away from me or I will call the police."

He laughed, "Call them if you want. Who do you think they will believe? Me, an outstanding businessman and the mayor of the city, or you a foolish drunk girl. So, yes go ahead and call them. I would like to see this." And then he sped away.

I walked home and hoped that my mother was sound asleep. I wanted to bathe, to clean myself in the worst way, but knew if I tried to run bath water she would wake and question me. So, I crept quietly into the house and went right to my bedroom. I lay there feeling so violated and so upset with myself knowing only too well how foolish I had been to drink so much and then be totally unable to protect myself. I vowed then to never drink again.

I also realized something else. He was right. His words were true. No one would ever believe me. This was Henry Winter. Mayor Winter.

Prominent member of the Winter family. A man who just a few years ago lost both his wife and child. The town was sympathetic to him. He was rich. He made decisions for some of the richest people in this town.

As I went over the evening in my head, I realized he had calculated everything. He knew it was my birthday this weekend. He knew I was turning twenty-one and I would be of legal age. I was now considered an adult. At work on Friday he had asked and knew about my plans with my friends. He knew he wouldn't have to face me this Saturday and probably thought by Monday, I would know I needed my job and would return to work and never speak of it again.

I also knew in my heart that I was not the first girl to suffer at the hands of Henry Winter. He went through the evening tonight as though it was a scripted program. And, he was right. Who would believe me? I might end up with a bruise on my cheek, but the other bruised areas would be hidden away and most would be found inside my heart, my mind and in my soul.

Yes, he was right. I myself had never heard of any other girls in Pinesdale being raped though I am sure they existed. No one went forward because Henry Winter was a powerful man. I would end up doing just like the others. I would not want to embarrass my family. I would suffer in silence and pretend it never happened.

It was my only choice. I would forget this night. I would block the whole thing from my mind. I would never ever return to my desk at the Winter Accounting Firm. I would go first thing Monday morning back to Becker Industries and pray they would take me back. I would be happy, or at least content on the production line for the rest of my life. And finally, I would try very hard to hide my feelings so that I never had to tell my mother that she had been right and that a birthday cake with my family singing to me now sounded like the perfect birthday.

As it turned out, I was fortunate. The bruise on my cheek was mild and I was able to hide it with some foundation. While I did have bruises elsewhere, like the defined finger-shaped bruises on my upper arms where he had squeezed them so tightly; they were all hidden by choice of clothing. I had stayed in the house all weekend to avoid seeing anyone especially from the Winter family. Mother and I celebrated my birthday, quietly on Saturday. She baked my favorite apple cake and sang "Happy birthday to me" while I blew out the candles.

On Monday morning I did not go to work at Winter Accounting. Instead I did as planned. I went to ask for my old job back at Becker Industries. My visit went well. My manager was willing to take me back on the line at the same wage I had been earning when I left in July. As I was leaving I passed Mr. Becker, the owner of the company in the hallway. I knew him well as Mr. Becker also lived in my neighborhood. I explained I had just been given my position back on the production line and I thanked him. He said that he knew I had tried working with Henry Winter. He also mentioned that since I had gained some office experience I should watch for an opening in one of those types of positions here at Becker Industries. I told him I would love that kind of an opportunity and I would definitely watch for any such postings in the future.

He smiled at me and then said rather quietly, "I would never ask you to say or admit anything, but I have my own his suspicions that Henry Winter would not be the easiest person to have as a boss. We are happy to have you back. I hope you will be happier here."

I thank him again for allowing me to return. I wanted to hug him and say he would not believe how correct that his statements had been, but I just smiled politely and again as I stood to leave, thanked him and said I would be back next week.

My mother was happy to hear I quit at Winter Accounting and she was thrilled that I had gotten my old job back. Everything was back on course for me to live my dull existence. I was here safely tucked away at my mothers' home in Pinesdale and for now I was simply okay with this plan.

Unfortunately, the plan didn't last long. By December I had missed two of my menstrual periods. I knew for sure that I must be pregnant.

It was 1942 and I lived in the small town of Pinesdale. Any pregnancy before marriage brought shame to the family, let alone my own type of shame. I knew what had to happen. I could tell no one, not even my mother.

I needed to move and move quickly before there was any suspicion of a pregnancy. A pregnancy that could not be explained by a man who I despised. A man who would never admit to what he had done to me. A man who had lost his only child and may at some point try to claim this one. I could never let that happen. Never.

I had to leave and go far away. I was too young and financially not in a position to raise a child. I felt I had one option. The only option that made sense to me. I would place this baby up for adoption.

Yes. That would be my plan.

My new plan.

My necessary plan.

I needed to move.

Move now, far away and give this baby to a family that desperately wanted a child.

A child who would then never have to know she was created by a monster.

My child that I had to protect in the only way I knew to be possible.

Yes, this was my plan: Tell no one. Move far away. Give my child up for adoption.

And I would never tell a soul.

NELL

Chapter 20 - 1943

By January first, my plan was in place. I told everyone that I had long desired to live in the big city. I told them that I had applied and gotten a job in New York City and would be leaving in two weeks. It was true, I had applied and I did have an interview arranged. It was difficult as I had no true work experience and could not mention my short time as a receptionist since I did not want anyone to ever contact Henry Winter for a reference or to my life, so I only applied for waitressing and store clerk positions. My interview was set for 10:00 on Tuesday morning, January 12th at the Mishkin Drug Store. I met with a small woman named Vera with a big strong personality and a keen eye for finding the truth. I was careful with my answers, explained I was a widow and somehow convinced her that I was the best person for the job and I was hired. I had already found a tiny walk-up apartment with a hot plate and a pull-down bed. They call them Murphy beds and they are fairly common in city apartments.

So my life began in the city. My new co-workers accepted that I was recently widowed and that my husband was killed while in the military. I went by the name Ivy Jenkins. Ivy had been a name I always liked and I knew even in a state of emergency, I would remember it. My stomach was changing sizes rather rapidly and within a matter of a short period of time, they realized I was pregnant. While I was well aware that everyone had noticed, no one outwardly asked any questions. I maintained that I was a very private person and they respected my self-set boundaries of sharing information. While they were not nosey, they were extremely kind to me always offering to help me lift boxes or reach for something that they thought might cause me strain. Yes, I decided God had placed me in this position at Mishkin's and I was very lucky indeed.

My next task was to find a doctor, I called a few offices and found that I qualified for reduced rates since I lived alone. I went to see Dr. Reynolds at Brooklyn Hospital. He was a kind older man and though the examinations were not ideal, I felt I was in safe hands. He asked about my menstrual cycles and after some calculations, he determined my due date to be July 23rd. Oddly enough, I had tried to calculate it myself and had been very close.

I continued to save every penny I could, limiting my expenses to food, rent, utilities and taxi fare to get me to my doctor appointments. The only clothes I purchased were those for my ever expanding body. I decided to use the alone time to improve myself and spent my free time at the public library slowly reading my way through any section that peeked my interest.

I wrote to mother weekly and described a life that I was not quite leading, but one that I thought would make mother feel much better about my abrupt move. I told her about the wonderful library that was at least five, six or seven times larger than the Pinesdale library and was in walking distance from my apartment. All of that was completely true. I told her about the amazing city; describing Broadway theaters, Macy's department store, Central Park; just anything to make her think that each night after work I was having a grand time. I hoped it was working. I hoped she smiled when she reads my letters. She has such a beautiful smile. I hated to think she was sitting in Pinesdale worrying about me.

In her return letters, she often asked if I had meet any nice fellows yet. She seemed concerned that at the old age of twenty-one, I had better get on the ball and find myself a man before I was declared an old maid. I assured her that while I had settled on no one in particular yet, I was on the look-out.

As time continued to march forward, and my stomach continued to blossom, I knew it was time for me to make another hard decision. I had always known I needed to put this baby up for adoption. I was in no position to try to raise a child on my own and the memory of this child's conception would always cause a pain, so adoption was the only choice. By my sixth month, I had studied any and all information I could find on adoption agencies and had narrowed my list down to three or four that I felt from their literature would be good choices. I had asked to leave work at 2:00 on Tuesday. April 13th for a doctor appointment, so I also set up an appointment for that same day at 4:00 with Nicole at *For Each Child* in Brooklyn.

My doctor visit had gone fine but he was quite concerned that I seemed to be growing so fast. He used his stethoscope and listened to my stomach longer than he usually did and did a lot of writing in my medical chart, but in the end said only that he heard a very strong heartbeat. I took a taxi from there to the Children Agency to begin my next process. Nicole spent a great deal of time with me and was wonderful and put me right at ease and by the time I left I felt very comfortable with the idea of her finding the perfect family for my baby. I knew I would have to attend a series of special classes to make sure I was certain of my decision and that it was a decision that I made for all the right reasons. I already knew it was the right thing for me, so I had no ill feeling about the classes. Over the next weeks, I attended all six of them and concluded my last class by signing my consent for Nicole to be ready to place my child upon delivery.

I felt physically good but I thought I was huge. I was only a few weeks away from my due date now. New York City was hot in the summertime and there was just no way to avoid it. At work there were fans in the store, but at home, I had none. I had grown so large and there were days when the heat seemed unbearable. I lay at home in the evenings with a bowl of water on my night stand and continuously placed a cool wet rag on my head while watching my stomach move under my skin. I decided I must be going to give birth to an acrobat.

I tried to picture what my child might look like, whether it was a girl or a boy and if it was under other circumstances, what I would name him or her. I had thought about this a lot and even though in the classes they said to never give your child a name. They said having a name made it harder in the end to give the child away. I still did it. If it was a girl, I would want a sweet name, one that was simple yet happy. I would name her Molly. If it was a boy, I would want a strong name. I considered a family name but then decided against that idea and I would want him to have his very own name. I decided on Michael. A strong name like Michael the Archangel.

As the time grew closer I found I had so many silly thoughts. Nicole had warned me about such feelings and I knew they were to be expected, but I also knew my original choice was the right choice. The weekend of July 4th the store was to be open for the holiday. I was scheduled to work but on Friday evening, Vera came to me and said I should now take some time off before I have my baby. I told her that wasn't necessary; that it was good for me to work; that I was fine, but she insisted.

She said, "Let's call it a vacation. You come back after you have your sweet little baby."

I accepted her offer and headed home. I hibernated in my apartment for a few days and suffered with the heat. Finally I could stand it no more. I thought it surely had to be better anywhere other than my small hot apartment, so I decided to walk to the library. I still had a few weeks and left the house without any worry. I got to the library and found I was right, it was a degree or two cooler. I found a book and lowered myself into a chair to read. I had been there about an hour when I felt a new strange sensation in my tummy. It was a pain that ran along my lower right side. I passed it off as the baby making a quick movement, a somersault so to speak, but about 6 minutes later the same type of pain struck again. I began to worry. I decided I better go home. My apartment was only seven blocks from the library but the pain hit again and then again. I realized I was in labor. I panicked. It was too early.

I was having difficulty walking now. I decided to make a smart move and instead I hailed a taxi and told the driver to take me to Brooklyn hospital. Once there, the driver helped me inside and the nurse at the desk got me a wheelchair. She took down all my information, in my panicked state I was proud that I remembered to say Ivy Jenkins when she asked my name. She took me upstairs to the maternity floor. As she wheeled me along the hallway, I head moans and cries coming from other rooms. I was scared. Then as though God was helping me again, walking out of one of the rooms, I saw Dr. Reynolds. I immediately felt better. He acknowledged he had seen me and the nurse took me into my room. The curtain was pulled, but it was easy to sense there was another woman in the room and I could see the shadow of a man standing through the curtain.

The nurse got me into the bed and brought a cool rag for my forehead. I handed the nurse Nicole's card and asked her to call her and explain what was happening. The nurse read the card and then looked at me with compassionate eyes. She patted my shoulder and said she would place the call.

My pains were coming more frequently; about every four minutes. About twenty minutes later, Dr. Reynolds came in and did an examination that was very painful. Again he used his stethoscope and listened for a long time. Finally he put it back around his neck and came closer to me.

"I wouldn't be surprised Mrs. Jenkins if you didn't get a big surprise today and find yourself with two babies," he said with a smile. Then he assured me, "You will be fine and so will those babies. We just have to be careful to get them both out as soon as they are ready. It shouldn't be long now. You are well dilated. I will be back to check on you in about an hour."

That next hour was unbearable. My body ached and I felt tons of spasms until I thought I could bear no more. The nurse said Dr. Reynolds was delayed due to another birth. When he finally returned he studied me and said he was afraid if we didn't do something soon that the babies might be in danger. He told the nurse to prepare me for a surgery.

I looked at the nurse in shock. She explained to me that he felt it was now necessary to perform a Caesarean Section. I had read about those in the library and understood the procedure.

The nurse held my hand for a minute and said, "Don't worry. Dr. Reynolds is a wonderful doctor. He is doing the right thing. Everything will be fine."

A few minutes later the orderly came in with a cart and they placed me on it and wheeled me into surgery. I was given a medication that put me to sleep. When I awoke a short time later Dr. Reynolds said he was correct and I had given birth to two babies. A very healthy little girl weighing 5 pounds 4 ounces and a little boy that was struggling. He weighed 4 pounds 2 ounces and was having a great deal of difficulty breathing. He promised that they were doing everything they could for him but wanted me to realize he was considered critical at this point and might not be strong enough to survive. I knew I could not say it aloud but I thought to myself, he is my little Michael the Archangel. He is a fighter. He will fight to the end.

I remember I had looked at the clock and it was 3:10 am and I knew my babies were born on July 8th. July 8th, 1943. I began to pray for both of the babies but extra prayers for little Michael. I knew it had been wrong to think of names for them but I had chosen the right names. They had been mine for almost nine months while I carried them inside me. While they were in my womb they were mine to nurture, to feed with my body, and to love with all my heart. Now that they were in the outside world, they were no longer mine and I knew that. I wanted them to survive. Both of them to survive. I wanted them to travel through this life together. Twins bond even in the womb I was sure of it. They needed to stay together. I would tell Nicole she needed to make sure that they stayed together. Together always. I prayed.

The nurse came in to check on me and told me that Nicole had arrived a while ago and was waiting over by the nursery. She said the girl was fine but that the boy was growing weaker and I should be prepared. She said she understood my plans and wondered if I wanted to hold my babies. I told her yes. She said she would arrange it.

About 10 minutes later she arrived with a little one wrapped in a pink blanket. Molly, my little Molly. A chill came over me but immediately disappeared when she very carefully placed her in my arms. She was precious. Absolutely precious. She had a soft pink complexion and tufts of dark hair. I opened the swaddled blanket and touched her tiny fingers. She instinctively latched onto my little finger. I looked at her and decided that was to be our bond. Short, sweet and limited but our moment. I looked up at the nurse and asked the question that my heart was already giving me the answer too, "And my little boy?"

She looked at me with sad eyes and simply nodded her head no to let me know he was gone. Not meant to live on this earth and already at heaven's gate and given an easy entrance. I nodded back to her to let her know I understood.

Our quiet exchange was so much better than hearing the words. But some words did have to be spoken. The nurse said someone from the hospital would be in soon to talk to me about my son but for right now, I should treasure my time I had left with the baby.

She left the room and I was alone with my little Molly. I knew our time would be short and tried to memorize every detail of her face, her fingers, her smell, and her touch. She was my living and breathing baby doll. I had treasured so many dolls as a child and now, here today I had my very own. Even if it was only for twenty minutes, I had my own.

The next person through the door was Nicole. She told me how sorry she was about the little boy. I thanked her. She told me that the little girl was beautiful and that she had already placed the call and a very hopeful and excited couple was driving to the city right now and should be here within the next few hours. She asked one more time if I was sure and I responded yes.

She reached to her clipboard and shuffled some papers. She explained that once I signed the form, this little baby girl would be available to go to the couple. She said the baby would remain at the hospital for 24 hours and then be able to go home with the couple. I agreed.

I signed, Ivy Jenkins.

She allowed me to keep the baby in my arms until everything was done. When it was time, she asked if I was ready. I nodded my head yes, then looked one last time at the tiny little face and leaned my head down and kissed her on her forehead. Then I handed her to Nicole.

As she stood by my bed with the baby in her arms, she said, "Ivy, you have made a very hard but a very good decision. This little girl is going to a wonderful couple and will have a very good life. They have waited a very long time and I know they are going to be wonderful parents. They even started a bank account for her and Frances has already been buying toys and setting them aside for Christmas."

I lay in my bed and realize she just said Frances. I don't think she is even aware that she said the name. My little Molly's mothers name is going to be Frances. It wasn't much, but somehow it made me feel so much better to know even the smallest piece of information about ....my daughter. Molly would also always have a guardian angel watching over her, lttle Michael, my archangel.

I watched Nicole walk out of the room and even though I knew it was right and had to be, I couldn't stop the tears from flowing. So many emotions flowing through my body. I felt lost in a dark space and it was as though I was unable to breathe. I tried to calm myself. I thought about what I had read in books about finding your own peace. I remembered the simple chants to repeat in your mind, "Peace is love, love yourself first and then all is possible." I repeated at least fifty times as I lay there in the hospital room. I was finally back to a calm state, but at the same time somehow numb.

It had been a very long day and was now well into the night. I was almost asleep when the door opened and a middle aged woman came through the door. She looked about as tired as I felt.

She introduced herself to me saying, "Hello Ivy, my name is Angela. I work here at Brooklyn Hospital in the Department of Human Services. I am here today in regards to your little boy and sadly, his death. I have spoken with both Dr. Reynolds and your nurse and I understand your situation."

I nodded.

"It is a very unfortunate circumstance on which we must meet," she continued, "but decisions must be made and by all rights, those decisions come to you first and foremost. I have a couple of decisions for you to make. Do you feel up to discussing them at this time?"

I again nodded.

"Good then," she said, "First, would you like to have any type of service for you baby?"

I thought for a moment and then spoke. "I don't want a service, but I would like there to be a priest present at the burial. One from St. Cecilia's Catholic Church if possible. It is the church I attend."

"Fine," she responded. "And where would you like your baby boy buried? I mean to say, in which cemetery?"

"I often walk by Holy Cross Cemetery, I would like to make arrangements for him to be buried there. I will find a way to pay." I was so happy to be able to have a say in this decision.

Angela began writing and nodding her head in approval, "That is fine. I will make some calls in the morning and get that started for you. You can think about and consider what type of marker you would like him to have at a later date.

I nodded again.

"I do have one final question Ivy," she said. She looked at me with very sad eyes. "I know it is always advised against thinking of a name for any child that is going to be given up for adoption, but I know from experience that every mother breaks that rule and chooses a name for their child. What name did you give to your little boy?"

I held my head downward for a second, then raised it up and said, "His name was Michael. Michael Patrick Jenkins."

Over the next few weeks my body healed, but emotionally I was still dealing with my pain. There was no one I could talk with, so I had to keep my pain inside. There was no option to return to Pinesdale at this time, so on July 23rd, which had been my actual due date, I returned to work at Mishkins. They knew that my baby Michael had died and that was all they knew. There was no need for them to know anything beyond that information. They understood my sad days and treated me as they would any grieving mother.

My life during this time and over the next few months was so very different but yet so very much the same. I went to work and continued to spend most of my evenings in the library. I tried to save all of my extra money so that I could someday purchase a headstone for Michael.

MITZI

Chapter 21 - 1968

The very next day, Lina and I decided to call Esther and invite her over for morning tea. I told Lina I would try to bake some muffins, maybe blueberry would be nice. Though I wasn't the best baker in Pinesdale, I knew I could whip up something half way decent if I followed Mothers' recipe. I truly believe that being a good baker comes more from patience than the ability to follow a recipe. The problem in our house is that when it comes to baking, Lina has no interest at all and I just simply have no patience. But, in order to find out some information about that gathering at Elsie Becker's house yesterday, I would try my best to have patience today and follow mothers' recipe precisely as it is written and hope Esther offers some tidbits of the newest gossip.

I asked Lina to call and extend the invitation while I went to the kitchen to prepare to start baking. I carefully browsed thru mother's old wooden recipe box and found the tattered card. Across the top, in our mothers perfect penmanship was written "Aunt Olga's Blueberry Muffins." Aunt Olga had been mothers' aunt; her fathers' sister. Mother was very proud of family and just about every recipe in this old box had a family members name listed in the recipe title. I hope some of both mothers and Aunt Olga's spirit would help me today to have the patience to follow the recipe with exactness and create something as mouth-watering as I remembered from my past.

The first thing mentioned on the card was: "When possible, pick or select fresh blueberries." It is still June and blueberries tend to get most plentiful in July so I didn't know if our small bush that is crowded against the side of the garage will have enough ripe berries to make a full batch. I may need to adjust the recipe to a half batch. I headed outside with my small colander and begin to search the berry bushes. It was still pretty early and the sun had not come out enough to take the dampness off the berries. I was right. There were some nice ripe berries but they were few and far between as my fingers searched amongst the bramble. I looked over at Nell's yard and knew I could get plenty over there as she had so many bushes, they practically lined her side yard. Wishful thinking on my part, so I continued to rifle through the bush. After about 5 minutes, I had slightly blue-tipped fingers and felt I had enough for a half batch and that would be more than enough muffins for three women.

As I was heading back to the house, Nell Taylor stepped outside with her washing in hand. She yelled a good morning and I responded accordingly, as if I had no reason to be the least bit upset about anything at all. Back in the kitchen I set my half-filled colander in the sink and turned on the cool water to rinse the berries. Next I shook off the excess water and then set the bowl on the draining counter to finish letting them dry. I began to gather all the ingredients that mother had listed on her card; Flour, sugar, baking powder, milk, salt, oil, and one egg. I think that is another reason that I don't enjoy baking. When you cook a roast or potatoes, you gather the roast and the potatoes. When you bake, you usually end up pulling out half of the kitchen cupboard; too many ingredients.

By the time I was ready to start mixing everything together, Lina returned to the kitchen to report Esther can join us but not until after she does her errands. She thinks that she can make it by about 10:00. I look at the clock and see it is now 8:10. I decide to wait a bit before proceeding with the baking. If I time it right, the muffins can be fresh from the oven when Esther arrives and that way, even if they are not perfect, their warmth will make them taste that much better. They only need to bake 25 minutes according to mothers' note, so I will time it for about 9:30 in the oven.

I have a little free time, so I pour myself a cup of coffee and sit at the kitchen table to think about what questions I want to ask Esther and soon

Lina joins me. We start to converse back and forth about inching our way into specific questions in the hope that after we inch a little, Esther will simply start offering information. As we sit at the table, I am now staring off dreaming about something, when I suddenly realize I can once again see Elsie sitting by her window. She is always just staring. I wonder at this point what she is capable of doing in her daily routine. Maybe Esther will be able to answer that too.

Looking at Elsie makes me think again of Otto and his terrible fall. Thinking of Otto makes me think of Henry. Oh my goodness, I do hope Henry made it into heaven. If God truly is all forgiving as is written, then I feel sure Henry is there. He certainly did live a life that would need an abundance of forgiving.

I look again across the table at dear sweet quiet Lina as she carefully sips her coffee. I am so very thankful that she has her artwork to keep both her mind and her hands busy. She has so much in her life that I wish she could simply forget, but I know just how hard that is to do. I can tell when she is painting that her mind is free from bad memories. It is as though when she paints she secretly enters into another world, somewhere beyond anyone's reach. A place where she is safe and can imagine any life that she desires.

Oh my, I have sat and sipped coffee for far too long now. I need to get the muffins mixed and into the oven. Esther will be here before I know it.

There is a knock at the door just as the timer buzzes to remind me that the muffins have finished cooking. While I grab my hot pad and open the oven door; Lina answers the back door. I think to myself perfect timing. We are off to a very good start.

Esther apologizes for being a few minutes late and then says how lovely the kitchen smells. Lina starts to pour the coffee. Earlier I had put Lina in charge of setting the table for our guest. I knew her artistic flair would pay off today. She selected a multi-colored linen table cloth filled with spring flowers in soft yellows, pinks and lavender shades. She placed the matching sugar and creamer pieces near the center and then positioned the 3 white china plates and a soft pink napkin by each. She arranged a small vase of flowers from our own garden and positioned them in the center of the table. It was filled with a mix of a colorful assortment from our flower bed on the east side of the house. Lina was definitely talented. She had tied a lovely dark pink ribbon around the vase and the ribbon draped so casually down the sides of the vase; it just looked so professional. Yes, she could certainly set a lovely table.

After Esther remarked on the beautiful table and she and Lina were seated, I placed our larger white china plate on the table filled with five large warm muffins. The muffins smell divine and looked picture perfect. The colorful blueberries were peeking through the sugar-crusted outer coating just as I remembered them looking when Mother made them. I was proud of myself but I admit, I was praying that they tasted as good as they looked. I reminded myself that I had the warmth factor on my side which would account for at least 1 point of my baking attempt. Before I sat down, I added the final plate to the table with some fresh butter. I amazed myself, everything looked perfect.

We pass the plate of muffins around the small table. Immediately after her first bite, Esther asks about the muffin recipe. I explain it was mothers from her Aunt Olga and before I can finish Esther begins to tell us about the wonderful chocolate cake she had yesterday and that Ginger Holden baked it but refused to share the recipe. As soon as she says it, she gasps a little as though she had planned to not mention yesterday's gathering at the Becker house.

"Oh dear," she says apologetically, "I am sorry girls. I did not mean to mention that at all. Silly me."

Knowing how polite Lina will be, I jump in quickly to keep that particular conversation going forward.

"Oh my dear Esther," I say. "Don't give it a thought. Lina and I saw everyone walking over and gathering yesterday afternoon and we certainly understand that Mrs. Holden wouldn't dare invite us into Elsie's home."

"Well no Mitzi," she replies quickly. "It wasn't that at all. Ginger Holden was expecting you two to attend."

Lina and I both looked at each other in shock and then looked back to Esther.

She nodded her head in a yes motion.

"It appears," she said, "that Ginger Holden knew nothing about the feud between you and Elsie. I was as surprised as you. I mean everyone was shocked. I can tell you that it did make up most of our conversation for the afternoon. There was not one single card played, it was only cake eating, coffee drinking and conversation. I think it was a first for our group. Not one single card!"

Now I am very excited. I need to play my cards very carefully and not make Esther feel she is being pressured to tell the tales of the neighborhood. Even though my body is filled with racing adrenaline, I mean as racing as it can be for a sixty-four year old woman, I wait until Esther has set her muffin back onto her plate and give her a millisecond to chew. Then I say as calmly as I can, "Well it looked like Ginger had a good turnout." And then I casually take a sip of coffee.

Esther, quickly swallows and says, "Yes I do believe everyone turned out. Well of course, you would expect that....I mean everyone probably wanted to get a little better acquainted with Ginger and wanted to see what she had done to Elsie's tired old house. And by the way, even though she has not completed all her new ideas for the house, it is already a hundred times better than it had been. It is shaping up very nicely. I was impressed. In a short amount of time she has accomplished quite a bit. Of course she has all those daughters to help her. The oldest one was there yesterday helping. Her name is Audrey and she is a very pretty little thing. Before we were all ready to leave, Elsie came out of her bedroom and that little girl Audrey was helping take care of her so that her mother could continue her hostess duties."

I sensed we should not speak so that Esther would just keep talking and we could just keep listening.

It worked. We remained silent and just kept looking toward Esther and sure enough, she continued.

"Elsie is in a wheelchair now," she said sadly. "And I don't think she ever goes beyond the house anymore. She didn't say much but she looked really nice. She had on a pretty dress that looked like it might have been brand new. Some of the women, like Nell, tried to go over and speak with her, but she mostly just sat quiet. She did say a few things to the Gingers' girl, but not to us. I had heard she was losing her mind. I sure do feel bad about that and it scares me to death that it might happen to me. I try to test myself every day. Every morning, I make myself say the day of the week and I mark off the date on the calendar. I read the Pinesdale Review and I get a book from the library every two weeks and make myself finish it no matter how bad of a book it turns out the be ..... and trust me there are some bad ones."

"Have either of you ladies read, *"Mindy Gets Married?"* she asks. We both shake our heads to confirm our answer is no.

"Well don't," she continues, "because it was very naughty. Actually, it was pure trash. Such a filthy book. I am truly surprised that it is allowed to openly sit on our library shelf! I didn't think I should finish it ...but I kept my promise to myself and finished it. I will just say this; it is lucky that Mindy girl got married.... if you know what I mean."

We again just stay quiet and wait. She picks up her muffin to take a bite and instead sets it back down.

"Did you girls know that St. Lucy's got a new nun? Yes, Nell was telling us that she just arrived and she met her yesterday morning at mass. She says she is very sweet and a quiet little thing. We certainly need another nun to help at the school. You know St. Lucy's just keeps growing and Sister Charlotte is getting up there is years just like us and probably could use the extra hands. I sure do like Father Bob. His sermons are so inspiring and often times even lively. I like filling in for the secretary at the rectory on Thursday afternoons. I must remember to head back home soon. I need to be there by 1:00. I wouldn't want to be late and disappoint Father Bob."

Now she does take a bite of her muffins and chews. The room is quiet for a minute.

Out the back window, I have been seeing quick glimpses of Tram walking around in the garage. I am not sure what he is working on today, but I make a mental note to set aside a muffin for him. He will have a hard time believing that I actually made them and that they actually taste good.

I decide to jump in and sway this table conversation back to us.

"So, just how did Lina and I come up yesterday at Ginger's gathering?" I ask.

"Oh yes," she says while still swallowing, "that was the funny part. Ginger wanted us to wait for you two to arrive before she cut the cake. She actually thought you were coming? Did I tell you the cake was wonderful? So moist and it looked so pretty on her crystal cake stand. I wish there had been enough for me to take home a piece for my evening snack, but I do believe we ate it all! Imagine that, we ate the whole cake!"

Now she is laughing.

I again try to lead us back the right direction.

"But you say she wanted to wait for us to arrive?" I say presumptuously.

"Yes...can you believe that?" She is still shaking her head when she says, "I mean to say we were all shocked is a huge understatement."

"So," I say cautiously, "who corrected her?"

"Well I did!" she proudly announced. "Everyone else was I guess in too much of a shock. I waited; no one spoke, so I did."

Then she laughs remembering.

"I told her that there was a long standing feud between you and Elsie and I would fill her in on the how and why but not until I had a piece of that good looking chocolate cake."

She laughs again and says, "Man it was good. And I did as I promised when we finished I told her about the feud. You didn't care that I told her did you Mitzi? I mean you would think she already knew about it, but as she told me, in 1951, she was only 18, well 19 that fall, but far too young to be concerned about things that didn't pertain to her. She knew David's uncle had died, but not a lot about ... you know .... the happenings."

"No ... no," I proclaimed, "I am not upset. As you say, it is old news. I guess I am just surprised that over the years there had been no mention of all the particulars to her....I mean she is married to Elsie's nephew. But I guess they didn't always keep too close of contact with her. Elsie did become somewhat of a hermit after...Otto died."

"Oh yes," Esther jumped in. "She surely did. No one saw her very often after Otto passed. I tried to knock on her door plenty of times when I knew darn well she was in there but wouldn't come to the door. After a while, I just gave up."

She took her last bite of the muffin and chewed for a minute.

She was quiet for maybe 2 minutes....then she said, "Do you girls remember, when she and Otto would go out all the time and the way they were always traveling. My goodness but they had a wonderful life those two."

Then realizing what she had just said out loud, she became embarrassed.

"Oh my goodness, I am sorry again Mitzi," she proclaimed. "That is not nice of me to be thinking about all these things while I am sitting here in your kitchen eating your muffins. And by the way, the muffins were just wonderful, but I really should get on my way. I don't move as fast as I used to, but you know I am seventy-three now. I guess I am allowed to slow down a little."

She stands to leave and we are saying our good-byes when she suddenly turns back to me and says, "You should go over and meet Ginger. She is a sweet little thing and she harbors no bad feelings toward you ladies. And I really don't think you need to worry about Elsie. I am not sure she would even know who you are nowadays. Well good-bye, thanks for a lovely morning."

"Good-bye Esther and thank you for coming. We need to do this again real soon," I say and then shut the door. Lina and I just look at each other and smile. We certainly did get our answers and nearly didn't even have to ask any questions.

The rest of the day moved smoothly. After lunch, Lina went into the study to paint and I decided to just sit and take it easy. I guess all my worrying about baking this morning and getting all the gossip updates had worn me out. I kept looking at the stack of papers and magazines by the chair and decided to sort through them. I knew if I got a decent size pile prepared, Tram would take them to the city dump for me when he returns later tonight.

I am now almost through the whole pile when I think about Elsie and Esther saying she didn't speak to anyone yesterday except one of David's girls. I wonder if she didn't want to talk with Nell or if she didn't recognize Nell. If she really was suffering from hardening of the arteries, then maybe she didn't recognize any of the women. It has been a really long time since she neighbored with anybody. Maybe I should get brave and just go over and knock on the back door and introduce myself to Ginger Holden.

I try to picture our exchange. I would say hello, I am Miriam Winter, the woman who Elsie blames for the death of her husband. And she would say something like, "well hello there and come on in. I will tell Elsie you are here."

I think not. But I would love to find out about Elsie. I would love to know if she still has those thoughts. If she still remembers.....if she would recognize me. She stares at me out her window, but now I wonder, is she starting at me, specifically me or is she just staring?

I think as I sit here in this big quiet house. I think about many things, but I think about staring and Elsie and all the trouble in my life. Thinking about trouble always brings Henry Jr. back to my mind. This time, I am remembering that day; the day of the tragedy. It was such a horrific day and a day that just continued to get worse and worse as the day went on. And I was remembering father, poor father.

Just as my thoughts were getting very deep, I was suddenly brought back to reality when I realized that Lina was shaking me by my shoulder.

"Mitzi, Mitzi," she was saying. "Mitzi, what is it? What is wrong? You look as if you have seen a ghost. My goodness, talk to me Mitzi."

I jerked back as though I had just traveled for miles in a time machine.

"Oh Lina," I say rather weakly, "I was lost in thought. Really lost. And yes, I guess you could say I did see a ghost. The ghost of Henry."

"My goodness sister" Lina said now even more concerned. "You scared me. You looked positively pale. I was worried that you were having some kind of a stroke or something."

"I am sorry sister," I said still very quietly. "I was thinking about 1939."

SABRINA

Chapter 22 - 1968

I was right. Momma was sitting at the dining room table looking a little down in the dumps. Actually, it was easy for me to feel pretty sad too. I was a little down in the dumps when I saw the empty crystal cake stand. No double chocolate cake for me tonight.

"Hey Momma," I said. "Are the ladies all gone?"

"Oh yes," she said in a funny kind of voice. "They are certainly gone."

I sat down in the chair next to her and said, "Are you okay Momma? You look kind of....weird."

"Oh Sabrina," she said waving her head back and forth a little. "I am okay, but boy oh boy, the neighbor ladies kind of shocked me today. Yes, it was a very strange first time meeting for me and one I won't forget any too soon."

I just stared at her and finally she spoke again.

"It seems," she continued, "that Aunt Elsie has had some differences of opinions with Miriam Winter."

"I think they call her Mitzi, Momma," I said trying to be helpful.

"What, oh yes," she said as though she was deep in thought, "Yes, I know they all call her Mitzi. But I guess that is the only thing I knew about her. It seems Aunt Elsie doesn't have a very high opinion of her."

"Do you know why Aunt Elsie doesn't like her Momma?" I asked innocently.

"Well....that is a good question, little one," she said. "I suppose there must be a very good reason and some of the neighbor ladies think they know the reason, but I am just not sure. I think it is something I will ask your daddy when he gets home tonight. He might be able to help me figure it out. At least I hope so." Then she stopped and smiled my direction.

"So," she said staring at me, "Did you and your friend Knox have a good time today?"

She waited for me to answer. She really wanted to know. She is a good Momma. Even after all the upsetting stuff that happened to her today, she still wants to know about me. Gosh I love her.

"Yea," I said. "We were busy with our detective work, looking and gathering clues. You know, the kind of stuff we both like to do. We have some new ideas, so we'll see."

"Good," she said cheerfully. "I am glad that you made such a good friend right here in the neighborhood. I like Knox. What is it you always say? Oh, I know…. "Cool Beans!"

And then she laughed a big laugh and started for the kitchen.

"I better get dinner started," she said. "By the way Grandma Holden called and asked if anyone wants to spend the night tonight. JoJo, Holly and Davey all jumped at the chance. How about you? Do you want to go too?"

I almost busted a gut with excitement. I composed myself quickly and then casually yelled out to her from the dining room.

"No, I don't think so. Those kids get pretty wild at Grandma's after she pumps them full of cookies and ice cream. I am kind of tired today," I said. "I think I will stay home and I might even go to bed a little early."

"Suit yourself," Momma said with a smile and then headed into the kitchen.

After our favorite dinner of Mommas' favorite easy-to-make dinner of hot dogs and baked beans, the little kids gathered their pajamas and off they went to Grandma's. When Daddy returned from taking them, Momma said her and Daddy needed to talk so they went to the study and shut the door. Audrey was helping to get Aunt Elsie comfortable and then Momma had said she could go over to her friend Suzi's house. So, it looked like I would be able to complete my reading mission without needing to stay up all night.

I cleaned up the kitchen for Momma and then headed up the stairs.

I knew I would need to be careful because at some point Momma would come up to check on me and to say good-night. I decided to put a few little items on the upper part of the staircase; close enough for me to hear Momma complain when she stopped to pick them up and far enough back to give me time to hurry and hide the journals in case I was still reading. I chose two from Holly's pile, her stuffed yellow bunny with a jingle bell on its collar and her baby doll that cries "MaMa" when you hold her a certain way. Then so Holly wouldn't get all the blame, I placed one of my Nancy Drew books and JoJo's pink hair bow. It was a decent size little pile and I knew Momma wouldn't be able to pass by it without picking it up.

I hopped into my pajamas, combed out my pony-tail, pulled down my covers and carefully unlocked my drawer. I lifted off the items over the journals and then decided to just take out one journal at a time. I made sure I got the next one in order of time.

I lifted the front cover and it clearly said, *January 1st 1952.* I had the right one. I placed my cover-up items back on top of the other journals and shut the drawer. I didn't lock it just in case I had to hurry and put the journal back inside. I switched on my bedside lamp and then went over and turned off the bedroom ceiling light. Tiffany was curled at the foot of my bed. I didn't even notice her when I first came into the room, but now she was purring at me. I sat and patted her head for a few minutes. Before I climbed into my bed to start reading, I crawled over to the little window at the foot of my bed and checked around outside. It was just getting dark. I looked for Tram, but decided it was too early. There was no movement in the garage and anyway, his car wasn't even there. I looked over toward Knox's house. His bedroom light was on. I started to wonder what he might be doing then quickly decided I had better get busy and start reading.

I crawled under my covers and got my pillow situated just right making sure my back was comfy. I gently picked up the old journal and then just as quickly grabbed my copy of Nancy Drew, *"The Hidden Staircase,"* and placed it right beside me in case I missed the clue and Momma showed up in my room, unannounced.

I was ready now to read.

January 1, 1952

It is the first day of a brand new year. I have promised myself that I will try to stay positive as this new beginning marches forward. Time has not stopped. Otto is not coming back. My life is very different than I expected but it is still my life. I am still alive.

My grief is still very raw and I do not know how to change that except to wait for time to help make it hurt less. I know that Otto will always be in my heart but I pray that the hurt will subside and allow my mind to branch out into new interests. I used to have many but those things have all faded away from me. I must learn how to pull them back into my mind, my heart, my life.

January 2nd, 1952

I made it through the first day and I think I did fairly well. Eulalie had the day off. My nephew, Michael stopped by with his family today. Michael is a good boy, well man now. His wife Pearl is a beautiful young women. Their children, David and Mitchell, well I guess you wouldn't necessarily call them children. They are, what did Michael tell me yesterday? I think he said they are now ages 21 and 18. They are handsome and well-behaved young men. David, I am told, has himself a young girlfriend, one of Naomi Wolfes' granddaughters and that he seems to be rather serious about her. Mitchell is still at that crazy stage of young adulthood when he has far too many girlfriends. But Michael says he will find the right one soon.

Anyway, it was a good visit with them and Pearl has offered to help me start again with my oil painting, but I assure her at this time, I still have not enough interest to start a new project.

This entry was fun to read. I loved reading things about daddy and momma in the journal. I was trying to picture them at the ages Aunt Elsie was referring too. I have seen both of their high school graduation pictures, so I guess that is about how they looked in 1952.

I continue to read but find that over the next few weeks of entries, I am finding little new information. She seems to be repeating her pledges to do better over and over again as if she is trying to reinforce herself that they can come true.

I would like to skip over a few weeks of pages and jump ahead, but I know Knox is right and I could miss some important detail or a tiny little clue, so I keep reading. Finally part way through February I do see something that catches my eye.

February 18th, 1952

I was not looking forward to today. At 1:00 I met with Mr. Campbell. He asked for the meeting as he was preparing the 1951 taxes and needed some permissions from me and a signature before he could complete them. As Otto's attorney, I trusted him. I had no choice. I did not know enough about the finances of the company and had little desire to learn. He presented me with page after page of data about Becker Industries. My head was spinning by the time he got through those papers. I must say, I am very grateful that he has the ability to keep track of all of this for me. Otto hired a good man.

I was a little perplexed when he presented me with a page of medical expenses for 1951. As I glanced over the items, I saw some medical charges that didn't seem like they belonged to us. I pointed out to Owen there was possibly a mistake. There were 3 listings on the page for Mount Sinai Hospital for April and May of 1951. I said to him neither Otto nor myself ever went to Mount Sinai Hospital. That Mount Sinai Hospital is in New York City and we had no reason to ever go there. Owen had then taken the papers from me and said quickly that I was probably correct and he would fix that prior to completing the forms. He may have said that but I wasn't sure I believed him. For a few minutes, I was afraid that something was maybe being hidden from me, but then I realized that mistakes happen and Owen had many clients to help prepare their tax information. It was just as he said, a mistake had been made. I was sure he would correct the mistake.

We finished going over every other paper there and finally finished at about 3:30. It had been a long meeting and I was very happy to return home.

I stopped reading there and wondered about it myself. I suppose a mistake could be made, but a lawyer was usually known to be pretty careful and I would be surprised if he made that kind of a mistake. If it were true, I wonder what Uncle Otto could have been hiding and then I wondered, how I would ever be able to figure that out.

I took out my special notebook and added the new piece of information:

Oct. 11ᵗʰ, 1951 – I shall never forgive Mitzi Winter – not ever

February 18, 1952 – Mount Sinai Hospital – 3 entries of medical bills- April and May of 1951

I got back to reading, but was disappointed that of the next 15 or so entries, I had learned nothing new. I did notice that she was now started to skip days more frequently in her journal writing. Sometimes she went a few days between and a couple of times it was a week before she wrote down anything. I guess she had gotten so boring that she even bored herself. Things seemed to pick back up when the weather improved and she was able to watch out the window and keep an eye on Miss Winter again. I guess hatred does strange things to people.

May 18ᵗʰ 1952

Today Mitzi must have had a free Saturday and she worked outside most of the day. Her and Lina planted flowers as they laughed and talked the day away. They took lots of breaks and often came back out of the house carrying cups of coffee or eating a cookie. I didn't see Tram until it was almost dark. Mr. Mertz sat on my lap most of the day.

May 25ᵗʰ, 1952

Another Saturday watching "them" play in their yard. This time Tram was also there, doing some of the heavier jobs like digging on the back side of the garden and mowing the lawn. Those two sisters are thick as thieves. I would bet Lina knows exactly what Mitzi did. Shame on you Lina.

June 1st, 1952

Children are out of school now, so the days are busy again with running, laughing, bike riding, and baseball games across the street. I love watching the children play. Michael's son Mitchell has graduated from High School and has invited me to his party. It is tomorrow, I must decide whether to go or just send a gift.

Today is almost over. I imagine, I should go to the party.

I guess I will go to the party.

June 2nd, 1952he party

So I did attend the party and I am glad I went. It was almost nice to get out amongst a crowd of people again. I have not been in a group situation like that since Otto's calling hours. It was nice to see some new faces, but so sad to be reminded of calling hours. That funeral home was packed with people. There were even some people that I did not know, probably business associates or folks that worked at Becker Industries.

Boy, I was bummed about this entry. I was hoping since she mentioned the party that she would at least say something a little more about party. It would have been nice to read a line or two about my family. Thanks a lot Aunt Elsie. Didn't even say if they served yummy food and cake!

June 7th, 1952

Today, since it was Friday, I thought Mitzi was at work so I went out into my back yard to enjoy a little time on my swing and let Mr. Mertz experience some outdoor time. It was a wonderful day. Not too hot and a nice small breeze. My little strawberry plants that I put under my dining room window a few years ago were in full blown with juicy red berries. Eulalie picked what was there and was planning to make a small shortcake for dinner tonight. I love strawberry shortcake more than any other dessert and am anxious for it to be ready. Even though she picked most of the berries, I can still smell them and it is heavenly.

Then, the spell was broken. I realized I had sat too long. Mitzi's car pulled into the driveway. I tried to get up quickly and get inside the house but Mr. Mertz did not cooperate. He would not move from the swing. Finally I tried to shoo him, but he just kept relaxing and when I tried to quickly lift him I must have scared him and he scratched me. I was checking the scratch when Mitzi yelled across the yard to me. I wanted nothing to do with her and did not respond. I sensed her starting to walk my direction and I grabbed Mr. Mertz and went into the house and shut the door. Hopefully she got the hint.

June 9th, 1952

Today I stayed indoors.

Wow, that was certainly a sad entry.

I have been reading now for an hour. I think I am going to go against what I think I should do and instead I am going to start glancing for words other than grief, lonely, sad, alone and cry and watch for any other words that sound important. I realize I may miss an important clue, but there are simply too many pages that truly tell me nothing.

I have finished two journals now, each time I slip them back into the drawer and get the next one out. I am onto entries from September 15th 1952, when I suddenly hear Momma complain and I hear the jingle of the stuffed bunny's collar. I hurry and slid the journal under my bed and pick up my Nancy Drew book and quickly open it to page 52. I lean back onto my pillow and continue to read. Five seconds later, Momma walks in and begins to put the two toys on Holly's bed, then JoJo's bow onto the top of her dresser and she begins to walk my direction with my book.

"Young lady!" she says as she sways the cover of my book my direction. "Did you happen to forget this was on the steps?"

I don't want to lie, so I avoid answering the question and just say, "Sorry Momma."

She smiles and hands me my book. "So," she asks, "Are you figuring out the clues?"

I get scared for a minute, then I realize she means in the Nancy Drew book.

"No Momma I am not," I say very honestly. I have not been concentrating very well. I guess I am tired."

"Well," she says quickly, "I happen to know a good remedy for that. It is called sleep. Maybe you should try it." Then she smiles a nice warm smile at me and pats my shoulder.

I decide to ask. "So, was Daddy able to help you get the answers you were looking for Momma?"

At first, she looks at me a little stunned. Almost like she forgot she mentioned it to me earlier today.

I continue, "You know about the stuff the neighbor ladies told you at the party."

"Oh," she said nodding her head. "Yes, I am pleased to say Daddy did have some of the answers. Not all of them, but he was very helpful."

"So, now do you know why Aunt Elsie had a difference of opinion with Mitzi?" I asked hoping to hear her say it.

"Yes," she said with a confused look on her face. "And I guess you are old enough to know some family history. Your daddy says he remembers his father telling your grandmother that Aunt Elsie feels Mitzi shook the ladder and made Uncle Otto fall."

Then Momma stared at me...like she was thinking to herself, do you believe that?

"But why Momma?" I asked. "Why would Mitzi shake the ladder? Why would she want to hurt Uncle Otto?"

"Well Sabrina, that part is more than just a little vague." Momma said.

I guess the family felt it had something to do with the death of Henry Winter the day before. Something happened on that day. Something that nobody seems to know the reason behind. No one except maybe Aunt Elsie and she never mentioned anything to anyone as far as your Daddy knows. I told him I felt a little embarrassed at my meeting this afternoon. Everyone seemed to know more than I did about every part of this saga. I was a little in the dark. But, all of this happened right after your Daddy and I started to see each other. And that was a long time ago, so you go to sleep my little miss and get some rest. You can work on your Nancy Drew clues tomorrow."

"Ok...good night Momma," I said and did really want to believe it. I was tired.

She gave me a hug, pulled my covers up closer to my neck, flipped off my nightstand light and headed back downstairs. I waited until I heard her bedroom door shut and then I waited 3 more minutes before I turned my light back on.

Okay. I think there was more than just a little clue in Momma's information. She said, "Something happened the day before. It probably had something to do with Henry Winters death. Probably nobody knows but Aunt Elsie. That has got to be it. But what happened?"

If Mitzi really did shake that ladder, then she must have thought Uncle Otto knew about something that had happened the day before. If she was concerned, then she must be guilty of something, but how? Why? What could she have done? If the man died of a heart attack in his/her garage, what was she hiding?

All I seem to do is create questions, questions, and more questions. I am tired of questions. I want some answers!

So...think Sabrina. Think!

I pull out the very first journal I had read and reread it. Nothing. Nothing new. Nothing I missed. I think some more. When would Aunt Elsie think to even mention was happened the day before if not right at the very beginning when it happened? And then, suddenly... ding, ding, ding. I knew the answer. On the anniversary.

I open the journal drawer and grab the one that I had been reading - September 1952. I flip past some of the pages until I see it. *Oct. 4th 1952.*

I say a quick little pray and begin to read. Just as I lower my eyes to the page, I see a flash of light coming through my window. Tram! As I crawl toward the window in my consistent army crawl, I wonder if Tram is part of the "what happened the day before" information.

Yep, it is Tram walking around the yard again. He is just like a sentry, guarding the post. But, what is he guarding ... the cats?

I crawl back into my bed, thinking about Knox over there sound asleep as I am possibly about to get some answers. I am ready. I open the journal back to Oct 4th 1952 and I read.

Oct 4th, 1952

One Year!

One year has passed and Mitzi has received no blame. Not for Henry Jr or for my Otto.

God knows Henry Jr was an evil man. He probably deserved what he got and I would have gladly told the authorities just that. Yes, he got what he deserved. Otto and I both agreed. I did not blame Mitzi or Lina and neither did Otto. We would have told Mitzi just that, but now...never. Not after what she did. She ruined my life and I shall never forgive her. Never.

So Mitzi or Lina was involved in what happened to Henry! But why wasn't she also mad at Lina? Why is Mitzi the only target of her anger?

So maybe Henry's death it wasn't a heart attack. New questions! I gotta grab my notebook again from my drawer.

I begin to add the new info:

Oct. 11th, 1951 – I shall never forgive Mitzi Winter – not ever

February 18, 1952 – Mount Sinai Hospital – 3 entries of medical bills- April and May of 1951

Oct. 4· 1952 - Mitzi has still received no blame, not for Henry Jr. or Otto.

> Henry Winter was an evil man and probably deserved what he got. I did not blame Mitzi and neither did Otto.

My notes are done. I found what I think I needed to know. I wish I had more facts, but this is it. I hope when Knox reads the notes it helps him to know what questions to ask when he talks with Mrs. Nell. Maybe, just maybe some more pieces will fit together.

All of that is good, but there is one know thing that I think I know for sure.

I think I need to get brave and finally talk to Tram.

Somehow, I think Tram is the one that knows all the answers.

SISTER JEANETTE

Chapter 23 - 1968

I awoke today with renewed purpose. After morning mass I made a point to reach out to Mrs. Taylor to see if she would be willing to spend a little time with me and help me learn more about the women of the parish, especially those who enjoy participating in the different meetings and committees at St. Lucy's. My time with Sister Charlotte yesterday afternoon was well spent. She gave me a good insight into the way things get accomplished at this parish and helped me understand the role that was expected of me by herself and Father Bob. By suppertime, I was feeling much more secure in my thoughts about my new church home and the other matter that was so very important to me; my ability to keep the vows as I had pledged them to God. Yes, St. Lucy's was going to be a good experience.

Nell suggested I come to her house at 10:30 today, so I definitely had a little time to complete some of my household duties. She insisted that I come to her home for our meeting instead of here at the church. She said since I told her I love muffins, she wants me to sample hers right out of the oven. She insisted her home was easy to find and Sister Bergan agreed, so I will take my first walk around town today.

My household duty list included amongst other things, completing the ironing for the household. Since Sister Bergan, who was in charge of the weekly washing had done so yesterday, there was plenty for me to get started on today. As I ironed the long black habits, my tedium of the chore allowed my mind to easily drift away from my task and land on a variety of subjects.

One was my meeting today with Nell. I was remembering the morning we met in the church vestibule and how she suddenly stopped laughing and the strange look she gave me. It was definitely unusual and I wondered what it meant. She seemed like a very nice woman and I hoped to form a good friendship with her, so I said a little prayer that today things would go well. I was also thinking about Father Bob's invitation to play tennis tomorrow. I wondered if I should try to make an excuse to not play this week. I could say I am so busy learning my duties, trying to fit everything in and needing to balance my time. I know I can get my feelings under control but I still think it might be best to try to avoid him for as much as possible this first week.

"Oh My!" I whisper to myself as I quickly lifted the hot iron.

I had held the iron in place way too long and almost caused a burn. That would have been terrible to explain to Sister Charlotte on my first week here. I need to concentrate. I finished the habit, thankfully without scorching it and then put the ironing board away in the hall closet and set the iron on the kitchen countertop to cool down. It was now 10:00 and I needed to leave now and find my way to Mrs. Taylor's house. She gave me very thorough directions: Go east on Main St. for three blocks. When I see Sally's Beauty Shoppe, that is Oak St and I should turn left. Go south on Oak St, past Pyatt St, past the railroad tracks, past Lee Rd and then turn left onto Maple St. Her house will be the third house on the right side of the street; 98 Maple Street; a beige house with green trim. It sounded easy enough, but I knew I still needed to leave shortly.

I found my journey down Main St to be quite interesting. I had tried to observe as much as possible during my ride through town with Christian the other day, but found it much more interesting as I slowly walked past the many attractive storefronts. The library had an appealing display in the window, declaring June to be Mystery Month. The large front window was stacked with a variety of different detective book series such as "*At Bertram's Hotel*" by Agatha Christie, "*The Doorbell Rang*" by Rex Stout, "*A Deadly Shade of Gold*" by John D. MacDonald, a few from the Trixie Belden Series by Kathryn Kenny, and representing the children's section; The Hardy Boys, Encyclopedia Brown and of course Nancy Drew.

243

I love to read. I would definitely need to stop in on my way back to get myself a library card. I am not so much a fan of mysteries but I would love to explore the many, many shelves inside filled with the classics, biographies and yes, even romance novels. Yes, that will be first on my mental list of stops to make on my way back at St. Lucy's.

I know I saw the Post Office and Gus's Grocery store the other day but I didn't really remember noticing Webber's Hardware. I peeked in the window and thought to myself, I would not want to try to organize all of those things. My goodness. It looked like every nook and cranny in the store was filled and over-flowing. A few more steps and I smell permanent solution. It is very easy to know I am in front of Sally's Beauty Shoppe and I should turn. I did so quickly. One smell from every little girls childhood that she never forgets is the solution used when doing back to school permanents. Stink...stink...stink! And then how appropriate...the very next storefront is Peggy's Bakery. I still smell the permanent solution until I am right in front of the bakery door, and now I smell something heavenly; cinnamon. I dream a little and envision cinnamon rolls covered in lovely cream colored icing.

Now this image makes me miss my mother. She is a wonderful baker. She certainly is a great cook too, but her passion for baking was easily apparent. When she baked, it was never just a combination of mixing together the standards of flour, sugar, eggs and butter. Her world of baking included adding a new ingredient into the mix to change it up, either a little bit or a lot. A pinch of a new spice, a new oil, an unthought-of fruit; anything to make it her own. And her instincts were usually right on target. She would bring something wonderful to the table and my father would take one bite and then look at her and say, "Write that one down!" I do miss that. Cooking in the convent usually tends to follow tried and true recipes. Oh well, for today, cinnamon somethings have given me good memories.

Across the street is the Pinesdale Movie Theater and the show playing this Thursday, Friday and Saturday is *Bonnie and Clyde* starring Warren Beatty and Faye Dunaway and advertised for next week is *Barefoot In The Park* with Jane Fonda and Robert Redford. As is with most small town theaters, last year's movies are the standard.

I cross the bumpy railroad tracks and Lee Road and continue south. A short distance ahead I can see what must be Maple Street. I am now walking past a baseball field with a small group of little boys practicing or maybe playing an actual game. Most look to be about age eight or so with a couple younger ones and there are about nine or ten of them all together playing. It appears as a small comedy of errors as I stop briefly to watch. I wonder if the batter is perhaps the little brother of the pitcher. The other boys are yelling rather cruelly at him as he swings and misses two decent looking balls. While the pitcher does look frustrated, he stops and walks over to the smaller batter. He puts his arm over the little guys shoulder and walks him a few steps away from the others. They stand huddled together for a few moments and then I see the little guy wipe his sleeve across his eyes, smile a little half-smile and then both return to their positions. The pitcher throws, the little guy swings and this time, he connects. The ball heads toward the third base line, but manages to stay in play. The batter dashes his little legs to first base and arrives safely. He is jumping up and down with joy. I look back at the pitcher and his face is beaming with pride. I decided my heart is happy too and start walking. One of the little boys waiting his turn to bat sees me and yells, "Hello Sister!" and I wave and keep walking toward Maple Street.

I turn and see the 3rd house that is beige with green trim and find myself there knocking at the door in only a few minutes. Mrs. Taylor had been correct. It was easy to find and I thoroughly enjoyed my walk. I wait in nervous anticipation for her to answer the door.

A second later the door opens to Nell's smiling face.

"You are just in time Sister," she says cheerfully. "The muffins are due to come out of the oven in 3 minutes. Come in, please come right in."

Inside I see a spacious home filled with small treasured pieces, not over crowded but tastefully placed to ensure their prominence.

Nell, as she has asked me to call her, says for me to follow her directly into the kitchen. The aroma as I walk through the house is wonderful and I tell her so.

"Your muffins smell just heavenly Nell," I say.

She blushes just a little and answers, "Well, thank you. As I told you, I do pride myself on my baking. From a very little girl, it has just always been something I have tremendously enjoyed. My mother could bake but didn't truly love it, but oh my, my grandmother, now she was quite the baker. She never ever followed a recipe. She used to tell me baking comes directly from your heart, not you head. I guess I have a little bit of her in me. I like to experiment, but once I have a recipe right, I keep it that way. Like these blueberry muffins, I perfected this recipe at sixteen and I have never changed it, not once," she says with a proud smile.

"Well," I said, "I cannot wait to try them. My walk has peeked my appetite and walking past Peggy's Bakery helped too. She was baking something cinnamon and it smelled divine."

"Oh my yes," she responded. "Peggy makes delicious cinnamon rolls. It is her trademark item."

The kitchen is painted a nice light yellow color and she has ample windows with minimal flower patterned valances that allow the morning sun to shine in and create a nice warm glow across the room. The windows facing the west and east sides of the house are open about 3-4 inches allowing just a little of the breeze to seep through and counterpoint the oven heat.

Her table has been set for our get-together and I see immediately that she is a fan of Fiestaware dishes. The table is adorned with a variety of Fiestaware pieces. A mint green teapot, with two matching cups and saucers. She has chosen two small yellow cake plates and has placed the most adorable matching cloth napkins with a flowered pattern including yellow daffodils and mint colored greenery. There is a yellow medium-sized bowl waiting on the table for the muffins and near it a yellow plate holding the butter. Her tablecloth is a solid pale yellow color. In the center of the table she has again utilized her Fiestaware collection to include a green bud vase. In the vase she has placed two artificial daffodils, since daffodils are a spring flower and have at this point into the summer already bloomed and disappeared. I remark again how special her table looks.

It is apparent that Nell takes great pride in her home. She has now poured me a cup of piping hot tea and has taken the muffins from the oven and placed them on a cooling rack.

"Give them just a few minutes to cool and let the berries settle and then we will give them a taste," she says confidently.

"Perfect," I say and then take a sip of my tea. "You have set a lovely table. I see you, like so many of my relatives have a love for the Fiestaware dishes. Your collection is apparent throughout your kitchen and is gorgeous. My father usually gives my mother a new piece every year for Christmas."

"Oh my yes," Nell answers quickly. "It is the same here. I guess it just kind of feels like it should be a part of my home. You will find many of us here in Pinesdale collect the pieces. But now, let's try these muffins."

She places about 5 of the muffins in the bowl and returns them to the table and then places one on my yellow plate. It looks so perfect that I hate to cut into it. The golden colored crust that has formed across the top with the bright blue of the berries and their juices bursting through looks delightful against the backdrop of the bright yellow plate and soft colored tablecloth.

I look at Nell and say, "I think we should take a picture of this beautiful setting before we eat the muffins."

Nell quickly agrees and hops up. "Wait!" she says, "You are correct. Let me get my camera."

I was only making the suggestion because the table truly was pretty, but she jumped at the idea. She zipped out of the room and headed into the next room on the left. I assume it is a study. She returns a few seconds later carrying the camera by its strap.

"This is one of those Polaroid Swinger Camera," she says proudly. "You get the picture immediately. I wish it was in color, but at least it will create a memory for us. Okay, now smile."

I do as I am instructed and she brings up the camera to focus it. She looks thru the viewer and then stops and lowers the camera. She is smiling at me as though I should be aware of the reason for her smile, so I continue to smile.

She lifts the camera again and says, "Ok Sister here we go, one, two, three."

And, snap. It is done.

"Now," she says, "We wait ten seconds and wa-la, we will have a picture."

Sure enough, the picture came out the side of the camera. She ripped it free from the camera and peeled off the backing and there I am, sitting at her table.

"Oh," I say "You are correct it is a lovely memory but wouldn't it be nice if it could have shown the vibrant colors of your table. Is there enough film that I might take a picture of you?"

"Oh yes," she says enthusiastically, "But wait just one minute."

She goes to the back door, opens it and looks out.

"Tram, Oh Tram," she yells, "Are you over there Tram?"

Almost immediately, I hear a man's voice in return.

"Yes, I am here Nell," he responds, "Is there a problem?"

"No Tram," she answers, "I am fine. I just wondered if you could come over for a very quick favor. I will pay with a warm blueberry muffin," she says with a little laugh and a look in my direction.

"Well I would have helped for nothing," Tram says as he comes through the door lifting off his worn looking hat, "But for one of your muffins, I will do at least 2 favors."

He then notices me at the table and quickly acts more formal.

"Good morning Sister," he says very politely. "I do not believe we have met."

Before I can answer, Nell jumps in and says, "Tram, please let me introduce you to our newest member at St. Lucy's. This is Sister Jeanette. Sister, this is Bertram Kellar, though he usually prefers to be called Tram."

"It is nice to meet you Sister, and yes, Nell is correct. Bertram was my father and not such a pleasant fellow, so please call me Tram." he says very respectfully. "I know you will love St. Lucy's, everybody does. I am not of your faith, but even I know Father Bob and think he is a great person. Pinesdale is small, maybe smaller than you are used to, but it is a nice quiet little town."

"It is nice to meet you, Tram," I say. "And yes, I think I will enjoy my time at St. Lucy's. As far as the small town, I might have been born in a big city, but I was only there for one day. I grew up in a small town, so again, I think I will feel right at home.

"One day you say?" Trams asks with a little humor in his tone, "I guess you made up your mind very quickly that big city life wasn't the life for you!"

Now I laugh and say, "Well, I am not totally sure about that idea yet. Big city life might be okay. I was only 1 day old. I was adopted and very quickly moved from the big city to suburban life. So you see my experience in the big city was limited to one day in a hospital nursery. My opinion just might not be totally balanced."

Now Tram laughs but Nell is quiet. Even Tram seems to have noticed the immediate change is her. He nudges her a little with his elbow and she quickly smiles again.

"Now Nell, what is this favor you need? I am eager for my muffin," he says and then laughs.

"Oh my yes," she says as though returning from a daydream. "Tram would you please use my new-fangled camera and take a picture of Sister Jeanette and myself here sitting at the table?"

As we begin to get side by side, she says, "As a matter of fact Tram, I will take you up on that second favor, please take two pictures and then we can each have a memory." She smiles a me.

We stand and pose. He takes the first picture. We wait for it to be released from the camera and he tears it off and peels the backing. Then he asks us to pose again and repeats the process. When the second one is complete, Nell places one on her counter and hands the other to me and then asks Tram if he has time to sit with us.

He politely declines her offer saying he has things to do next door. She retrieves a paper napkin and opens it. She carefully places a muffin in the center and wraps the corners around it and hands it to Tram. Then she reaches into the bowl and grabs one more muffin and hands it to him and says, "Enjoy this one now while it is warm."

He gives her a nice wide grin.

"And thank you Tram," she says cheerfully, "And I hope we didn't detain you too much."

"No, not at all Nell. It was nice to meet you Sister Jeanette," he says as he tips his wide brimmed hat and heads out the door.

Nell turns back to me, still looking just a little flustered.

Hoping to bring her back to our purpose for today I say, "Tram seems very nice. Has he always been your neighbor?"

"My neighbor...what?" She is still looking a little out of her element. "Tram, no, I mean yes, he has."

"I guess it is a long story, but I think I can explain it," she continues. "Tram grew up here...on the west side of my house, right where the Hill family lives today. But his family has not lived there since, oh let me think, probably since 1930, yes 1930. I remember I had just had my 10th birthday when his father passed away. He was correct when he told you his father was not a nice person. Even at ten years old I knew that. Tram was the oldest child of five children and he was horrible to Tram. My mother had said he was that way his whole life and I guess there are some things that do not change."

"How sad," I said in agreement. "But then Tram still lives here in the neighborhood?"

"No, well but yes, but no," Nell says and then shakes her head my direction. "It is a confusing history. Let me see if I can explain that part. The Winter family lives right next door, to the east of my house. That is Miriam, who we all call Mitzi and her younger sister Lina. They are the only two left from the family. The Winter family had at one time been very prominent members of the community, and still are, but things like that are not given the importance that they used to have back in the day. Their father Henry Winter Sr. had been quite the business man and came from a long line of successful men. You know, they used to call that type the pillars of the community."

I nod my head in agreement.

"In my hometown," I offer, "it had been the Adams family. Please go on."

She nodded and said, "Yes, then you know exactly what I mean."

She continued, "Well, Mr. Winter had another daughter that my mother had told me died as a very young child from one of the deadly viruses that swept the country. They also had one son, Henry Jr who is now deceased."

She cleared her throat, and then said, "Henry passed away in 1951, and as a matter of fact, we just had quite a discussion about him the other day at our neighborhood ladies group."

She paused a moment, as if in deep thought. "But anyway," she said suddenly and picked her conversation back up on topic, "back to Tram. Earlier on, he was just one of the neighborhood kids. Always around, you know what I mean. Well, he tended to cling pretty close the Henry Jr., but they were very different people. I never quite understood their friendship. To this day Tram is sweet, smart, sensible and very responsible. Henry Jr, was our mayor here in Pinesdale and had his own accounting business. I was even his receptionist for a very short period of time, but he was not a nice person. Clever yes, smart yes, but nice, no. He had many faults. Probably more than I even know. Now that I am a mature adult, I realize that I should have taken to heart my mother's perceptions and more closely followed her words. She was a very wise woman. I didn't always do that and I learned the hard way. She didn't trust Henry Winter and did not vote for him to be our mayor. She used to say to me, "that young man has tragedy written across his forehead and someday we will understand why."

She sat quiet again for a moment, then with that same strange face, she stared at me.

"I used to wonder what she meant," she said slowly, "but I guess tragedy can come in many different forms and mean something different to everyone."

Then she laughed and said, "To a small child, a tragedy is losing a favorite toy. To a teenager, it is developing a pimple before a big dance. To an adult, then yes, it can take many forms."

"You said Henry Jr. had passed away, almost 20 years ago?" I asked. "How did he die?"

"Now that too is strange," she explained. "He died right there in that garage," she said as she pointed out the kitchen window. "There was never a real investigation, but we all assume he had a heart attack."

"Well," I responded, "that is very sad. His sisters must have been devastated."

"My mother had told me that she saw Henry go into the garage. She had been taking the garbage out back to the trash can. She heard his car start up and said that while she was busy shooing the stray cat from our back yard, she continued to hear the car running. She returned into the house and was still working at cleaning up the kitchen when she saw Mitzi walk toward the garage from the window. She said she did not return for a few minutes, but when she did it was her and Lina was walking back into the house with the look of fear on her face. Within five minutes, my mother heard a siren coming closer to our house. It pulled into the Winter driveway and my mother stepped outside. She said she saw the policeman opened the garage door and Mitzi and Lina crying. In the next five minutes an ambulance arrived and when it left there were no lights and siren."

"So," she said, "Mother assumed he must have died from a heart attack. The newspaper did not say anything differently and as far as I know, that is how it was left."

"Tram has since that day spent much of his time still at the Winter home. He comes over every morning and returns in the evening. He helps Mitzi and Lina keep up with the house and yard and spends a great deal of time in the garage. He usually eats his dinner with them. I am not exactly sure where he actually lives," she concluded.

Her story told, she now seems to be more back to present day thinking, "Oh my, how did we get on such a subject?" Sister Jeanette, please now lets' talk about what you wanted to discuss. But first, please tell me what you think of the muffins. I noticed you have tasted them. "

During Nell's story, I had begun to nibble when I could on my muffin and she was correct, it was delicious.

"Oh my yes," I said empathically, "Just as I expected, they are heavenly! I am totally enjoying every bite."

"Well good!" she said. "Now it is your turn to talk and I will nibble on one myself."

"Well," I began, "Nell, I was told you are about the busiest member of our church community and that if I wanted to know anything about the going-ons at the church, I should ask you."

Nell laughs a little and says, "Well, if Sister Charlotte or Father Bob gave you that information, I will take it as an extreme compliment."

"Then," I offered, "It should be a compliment because they are exactly who told me to contact you."

She offered a sheepish grin and said, "Well then good! How can I help?"

"Exactly the word I needed," I responded. "Help...please!"

"Of course, I can help you dear sweet girl," she said without hesitation. "We can start by you attending every meeting and sitting close to me so I can introduce you and then quietly remind you of who the ladies are, I think that will be helpful in the beginning, don't you?"

"Oh yes," I answered sincerely.

"Then as we move forward," she continued, "I will keep you updated of the things we have tried in the past and if they were unsuccessful and not to be attempted again, or just the opposite."

"We have six different committee groups; the School Committee, the Funeral Committee, the Church Decorating and Cleaning Committee; the Bingo Committee, the Luncheon Committee and of course the Ladies Auxiliary which picks up any other responsibilities that there isn't already a committee to cover," she says with a laugh.

"I am a member of each committee which is probably why Sister Charlotte led you my direction," she says proudly. "But it is easy for me to stay very active. I am alone. My husband passed away in 1953 and my mother in 1961. God bless both of their souls. I was never blessed with any children. And I did work for a short time in my younger days, but my husband left me not a wealthy woman, but with enough to get by on without any struggles. After he passed, I sold our home and moved back in with my mother here on Maple Street. I was an only child so when mother passed, she left this house to me. So, you see my demands are simple and I like to keep my life that way too, simple."

"Back to the committees," she returned to her helpful hints, "Some are all business, like of course the Funeral Committee. But some are a combination of both work and fun. Like the school committee for example. It is mostly a fund raising committee, but we also get to do some fun projects with the children in the process. Another of those types are our Luncheon Committees. Some important luncheons are once again to raise monies for the church, but we also have luncheons that are just about fun and fellowship. One of those occurs the first Monday of the every month; our birthday luncheon. We keep it very light. A simple luncheon of soup and chicken or tuna salad and of course, we bake a cake to share and sing Happy Birthday. While I am thinking about it, let me grab my notebook and we can add your name to the birthday list."

"Yes," I said immediately, "I would love to be on the Luncheon Committee."

"Well," she said as she reentered the room with her notebook in hand, "You can be on any committee you wish, but I meant I wanted to add your name and birthday so we could celebrate your day when it arrives."

She was busy opening the trapper type notebook and sorting through the many different tabs. Apparently, she keeps all her information for all the committees in one large notebook. Very organized I decided.

"Now then" she said as she stopped flipping pages. "I am in my Luncheon committee section and now here is my list of members and birthdays. OK Sister Jeanette what month is your birthday?"

"Well, my birthday is very soon," I answered proudly. "It is in July."

With this information, she now began to flip pages again. Seven flips and she had arrived at July and began to write my name.

Without looking up from her book, she said, "And Sister, what day in July?"

I answered, "the 8th."

She starts to write and then stops suddenly. "Did you say the 8th Sister?"

"Yes," I respond.

She never looked up at me but asked another question, "And what year were you born Sister?"

I answered, "1943."

Nell sat quiet for a minute, maybe two and I was beginning to wonder if she has had a stroke. She has stopped writing and is just staring at the notebook.

"Are you okay Nell?" I ask. "You look a little pale. Should I call for Tram?"

'No," she responds quickly. "Please No, I do not need Tram. I am fine ….really. I am just tired."

Now I am embarrassed.

"Oh I am very sorry Nell," I say. "I apologize. I have taken up too much of your time. Let me be on my way."

She is quick to say she has loved having me over for tea and there is a knock at her back door. Still somewhat flustered she gets up to answer it.

There is a young boy standing there. He is a cute little fellow and looks to be about 9 or 10 years old.

"Hi Mrs. Nell," he says cheerfully. "I thought I smelled some blueberry muffins!"

"Oh," she says not overly welcoming, "Good morning Knox. Yes I made muffins. Come on inside."

She looks back again at me standing by the table. She walks over and grabs my hand.

"Sister Jeanette," she in now smiling. "This young man is Knox, Knox Little. He lives right across the alley from me and he has a keen nose when it comes to my baking."

I am happy to see her acting more like herself again.

"Hello Knox," I say "It is very nice to meet you. I am Sister Jeanette and I am new here in Pinesdale. Nell has just been helping me learn a little bit about the community and I have taken up enough of her time. I need to head back to St. Lucy's. I hope to take a minute to stop at your lovely library and get myself a library card."

"You will love our library Sister," Knox offers. "This month is Mystery month and we have a ton of good books with detective stories. Those are my favorite. I love solving mysteries."

Nell and I both smile at that one. Nell tells the boy to go ahead and have a seat and enjoy a muffin. He immediately does as she suggests.

"That is wonderful." I say to Knox. "It was very nice to meet you. Now Nell, I really must be on my way." I reach down and pick up my picture from the table. "Thank you again for the picture."

Knox was already busy buttering his muffin.

I say to her more quietly as we walk through her house to the front door. "Thank you so much Nell for all of your help this morning. I really do appreciate it and I hope you feel better. I was worried there for a minute."

"I am perfectly fine Sister Jeanette," she says with a new zest in her voice. "Actually I am more than fine. Actually, I think I am pretty wonderful right now, and I think that is because of you!" she says with a smile that makes her whole face light up.

I think to myself. What an amazing difference from five minutes ago. Now I at least I feel better about leaving her. The young boy Knox could run for help if she has any trouble. The neighbor Tram is still close by.

I have made my connection to Nell and it was a good visit. I know she will help me build my comfort zone amongst the other members of the committees. My mind and my heart rests a little easier.

Now, off to the library.

MITZI

Chapter 24 - 1939

Henry Jr had always had a great many faults, but I can honestly say that the birth of his son, Paul Henry Winter on February 26, 1936 was the day his persistent cold heart melted...just a little. On that day little Paul became forever destined to be the bright spot in Henrys' life. He loved that little boy and truly became a different person when he was with him. Lina and I had both immediately noticed the affect Paul had on Henry. There was no way to describe it other which than just to say he was a tiny bit calmer and showed a little more patience. As a matter of fact on some occasions he even smiled which we both enjoyed seeing even if it was only ever directed toward Paul. Yes, he was just a different man. It was as if after 34 years a small soft almost invisible spot had finally opened in his once extremely cruel and cold heart. The splinter sized opening may not have been quite big enough to include the rest of us, but it was big enough for that tiny little boy and that was a start. A start that had given myself and Lina a tiny glimmer of hope. Unfortunately that miniscule ray of hope only proved to make the reality that much more disappointing when in time we came to understand that little Paul was not able to change Henry enough....not nearly enough.

In 1939 little Paul was already three years old and only on a few rare occasions had I been asked to baby-sit. This was odd to me since there was not an abundance of female relatives in young Paul's life. In our small town most family trees were connected to each other in some sort of fashion. I mean for example when a cousin of Linda so-and-so married a cousin of Polly so-and-so, well then before you know it – it has formed this new blossom with more relatives that bloom and at the next big family reunion, that family has sprouted and grown. It happens more than you think.

But I guess we, the Winter family, are the exception to this pattern. Paul simply had three aunts, just three. There was myself and Lina and Henry's wife Marie, had only one sibling, a sister Veronica who lived three states to our west. The poor little guy had no living grandmothers. Maries' own mother, I think her name had been Anita, passed away when Marie was just a young girl though I had never heard any of the pertinent details. I just assumed that she had probably been a sickly woman since she had passed at such a young age. And of course our own dear mother, God rest her soul was never the healthiest woman. Unfortunately not long after some of the shock and panic of the Great Depression of 1930 had finally begun to settle, she developed a cough that just would not go away. Although many remedies were tried, nothing changed. Dr. Mace finally diagnosed her with tuberculosis. She remained ill and bedridden for a long time with father spending every free hour at her bedside. He remained devoted to her and her healing. Nothing helped mother and in October of 1931 she died. It was a terrible blow to all of us but father was totally lost without her. The once strong figure, gradually dwindled in strength and lost his will to excel. He was able to maintain his business but no longer felt the same strong sense of pride in his endeavors. He was content to just go through his daily rituals. Life did change a little for him when Henry had his child and named him Paul after our mother, Pauline. He had a grandchild; his first grandchild. Father finally seemed to regain a little of his spark. He doted on little Paul and a new cheerfulness was inside him again. He still wasn't the father that we knew, but he was close.

I had told Henry and Marie many times that I would be happy to help with little Paul but well I guess Marie liked being at home and there had been little need. As far as babysitting, although I was the busy working gal in the family and Lina was usually at home; having Lina babysit was not an option. Lina never told our parents anything about Henry Jr.'s menacing acts against her, but she also never put herself in a position to ever be alone in a room with him. Once he married and purchased his own home she began to relax and had some moments of peace beyond her painting time. But do not get me wrong, she still would have preferred that he never be inside our home, though she would never ask father for such a request. When he did visit she made sure she was never in the same room with him for too long of a period. She usually excused herself and went to her art studio. Too much damage had been done in the past and Lina, now 32 felt she could never trust Henry Jr. She had no faith in the old Henry or the new Henry. In her mind, trust wasn't an option with him. I know our father sensed this strained relationship between his children and possibly even knew small details of some of the cause, but if he did it was never mentioned. He never questioned Lina or her abrupt exits. Their unusual relationship had just become acceptable.

Our Sunday brunches following church service were the exception for everyone. We gathered together and actually acted like a family. Brunches always included myself and Lina, father, and Henry Jr, Marie and Paul. On some occasions even Tram joined us. I think because there were so many of us present, Lina felt more secure and father felt more like the old days.

These days were relaxing. Our choice of food was simple. The menu wasn't anything new and exciting or complicated. We stuck with the traditional offerings of ham and eggs, a fruit cup and usually one of our mothers' recipes such as peach cobbler or apple cake, either of which father very much appreciated. If the weather was nice we usually filled our plates and went outside and sat amongst the flower garden. Little Paul would run and play and study each of the different colored flowering blooms. He would periodically swing past his mother to get a quick bite of his scrambled eggs and then run to play again. They were pleasant, leisurely days for all of us just sitting back and watching the happiness of a small child enjoying his freedom to run, play and explore.

On this particular Sunday Tram had not been able to join us though I don't remember the reason. We filled up on the food, played with Paul and walked about the yard. Eventually we returned to our sedentary positions and just simply enjoyed witnessing Paul's never-ending curiosity about the world. The silence was broken when Marie casually mentioned her up-coming doctor appointment and asked if Henry could watch Paul for about an hour or so on Thursday morning. Henry had agreed without giving it much thought. He had said that it would not be a problem. He would simply go in to work a little later than usual. Much to Paul's dismay, after another ten minutes of play Henry said it was time to leave. Paul fussed a little, but Henry scooped him up and tossed him into the air. He was just slightly above Henry's head but Paul roared with laughter. Henry repeated this two more times and then lowered Paul to the ground and told him to say his good-byes. Little Paul was still full of giggles as he ran and gave kisses on the cheeks to all three of us and added a special hug to our father. He ran back to Marie, waved to us again as she put him into the car and they drove away.

Since Lina and I had not yet married we continued to live at the family home with father and performed all of the cooking and cleaning duties. When not at work, father spent most of his time either in the living room or upstairs in his bedroom. He was now 61 and trying to retire from his business. He had happily given his study to Lina a few years ago so that she could use it for her art studio. She had started to sell some of her work on consignment to a few exclusive decorating stores in larger cities. There was the hope that this trend would continue so she spent a great amount of time every day in the studio creating new pieces and father was very proud of her artistic talent.

It had been a busy morning so father said he was going up to his room to read and also possibly nap. Lina went in to the study to paint and I was perfectly content to clean up the kitchen and then sit enjoying the quiet of this peaceful afternoon and some reading.

The next evening while I was busy peeling potatoes and Lina was setting the table in preparation for our dinner, Henry's car pulled into our driveway. For a few moments, he stood outside talking with Tram. I noticed two of the cats were slowly slinking across the grass and heading toward Nell Taylors' backyard. I looked over to see Duchess, our newest indoor cat who had been peacefully sleeping under the table now had her ears perked upward. It is funny but somehow all of the cats, even though they are a whole new generation of cats from those of our childhood, they still scatter and hide in Henry Jr.'s presence. I guess they pick up his scent and whatever that scent is, it must terrorize them. In the same fashion as the cats, Lina moved to the window and studied Henry's presence in the backyard. She turned and looked at me with a combination of questions and a bit of fear in her eyes. Her fears came honestly from old memories. She would forever remain uncomfortable when Henry Jr was in the house, especially for an unexplained visit such as today. She set the remaining dish on the table and left the kitchen. Duchess followed. I knew they would both make themselves scarce until they heard his car leave the driveway and I totally understood. Finally Henry entered through the back door.

"Well hello," I said. "To what do we owe the honor of a visit two days in a row?"

"Well," he said, "It seems I have a problem for this Thursday morning. I have a very important new client, Fritz Herman coming in to discuss opening an account with my firm. I did not know that Connie scheduled it for Thursday at 9:00 and I had her call his office this morning to try to change it, but his secretary said after Friday, he is going out-of-state for the next two weeks and I didn't want to put it off that long. He has the potential to be a very big client …he has very deep pockets and I could use that in my firm, especially right now. I don't want to lose him."

I had listened and now waited for him to say more. He didn't, he just kept watching my face.

Finally I said, "OK….that sounds logical. Did you need something else?"

He looked at me like I had just grown a third head.

"You had said if I ever needed you to …. you could watch Paul," he said with a bit of annoyance sounding in his voice. "Can you do that for me?"

Then it all came back to me. The conversation from yesterday at brunch. Marie's doctor appointment. The need for a baby-sitter.

261

Kathleen F. Ewing

"Oh," I said now recovering. "You want to know if I can watch Paul then…on Thursday….in the morning?"

He nodded his head in affirmation while still looking astonished that I did not seem to automatically recall the conversation. I hated this pompous better and smarter than me attitude of his and I had about enough of his impatience with me too.

"Listen," I said firmly. "I do remember the conversation from yesterday. The problem occurred because you didn't feed me much background information to know what you were referencing, so don't be so mean! For goodness sake Paul, try to calm down."

"Alright….Alright!" he said angrily. "What do you want me to say? I'm sorry. OK! I am sorry. But geez … I am sitting on a hot seat right now. I have a lot on my mind. Marie said she couldn't move her appointment and they said Fritz couldn't change his appointment, so I am behind the eight ball. Everything is a mess and I am upset!"

I don't like it when I see Henry get this upset. It is never good when Henry is angry. Usually bad things happen. I am very happy that Lina is beyond earshot right now. This display would make her very nervous. Now that I understand the request, I felt I could answer.

"OK Henry. Please calm down. I can put in a request for a personal day tomorrow and I am sure it will be approved. Yes, I will watch Paul," I say as calmly as I can.

"Alright then," he said curtly. "Alright, I will tell Marie it is all taken care of for Thursday."

I see he is starting to calm down now. I hear the change in his voice. I notice his breathing is now slower and steady and his facial coloring is back to normal. He actually looks like he is realizing the tension is leaving his body and he slowly lowers himself to a seat at the kitchen table.

"Are you ok?" I ask in the calmest voice I can muster.

"Yes, yes of course," he says almost in slow motion. "It has just been a long and stressful day."

I sit down at the table too. He looks at me as I sit at the table across from him.

He stares for another moment and then he says to me, "Where is father?"

"Father?" I say. "He is still at the office. He will probably be home within the next half hour or so. Why?"

Henry got that I'm in trouble look on his face. He started his attempt to explain.

"Things have not been the best at the firm for the past six months or so," he said. "Money is tight. I mean money is tight everywhere. Clients are few and far between. It isn't all my fault.....the world is still trying to recover from the depression. People still don't have a lot of trust in letting someone else manage their money."

He looks pretty sad and then says, "I actually have been considering letting Connie go. She is a great worker, a trusted employee, but you don't need workers when you have no work."

He looks very discouraged. I feel bad but I don't understand the world of finance and therefore can be of no help to him.

"Henry, is it really that bad?" I ask.

He only says one word. "Yes."

"As for Connie, you are right," I say and I mean it. "If things are as bad as you say, then yes unfortunately you probably need to let her go. But remember this: she is smart and dependable. She will find another job.

"And," I ask rather slowly, "Marie certainly understands...right?"

"She doesn't know," he informs me.

"Oh Henry. You need to tell her. As you say this condition is not your fault it is the whole nation. Many are still in tight times. She will understand and ...." I pause hoping to think of something else, something more optimistic to say.

"Things will start looking up soon," I finally say. "You have a new important client coming. Don't despair. If you don't want to tell her, Marie will never need to know because things will change. You will see, very soon things will change," I say trying to smile.

He shakes his head. "I think they better change," he says still solemnly.

Then he looks at me and tries to form his own small smile. Very quietly he says, "I believe that Maries' doctor appointment this week is to …. confirm that she is ….. or might be expecting our next child."

I am shocked. Happily shocked, but shocked. Paul is three years old, and that is plenty of time in between children, but somehow I always assumed they would have just one child.

"Oh Paul," I say happily. "That would be wonderful. Paul will be such a sweet big brother. If it is so .. then it is a gift Henry. You must think of it that way. It is a gift from God. And things will start to turn around for you. You will see. Many good things and blessings are coming your way. You will see."

He shakes his head at me and smiles and says, "You women. Always looking for the bright side."

Then he stands. "OK then," he says with new strength in his voice. "You will get Thursday off work and watch Paul?"

"Yes," I say.

"And hopefully," he says as if my boss, "you understand to not mention the news I shared with you today. Not any of it to anybody. Not even Lina and especially not father! Do you understand?"

He is being very bossy. He is making me angry but I decide to go the other direction and make a joke of his order. I put my hand across my heart and I say, "On my code as a professional telephone operator, I will not divulge any of the information that my ears were able to hear today." Then I laugh and he smirks too and goes out the door.

He looks back and says, "Not a word…to anyone! You got it?"

I nod my head to show agreement.

The next day, I requested the day off and as I expected it was approved. I was actually looking forward to Thursday. I was thinking about what Lina and I might do with the little fellow. Maybe a trip to the park or a long walk around Webbers Lake might be nice. Now that he was three, he got around pretty good and Marie had said he loves to swing.

Another plus of the day was to be that I could sleep well past my usual 5:45 am alarm. I did not need to watch Paul until right before

10:00, so the morning time was just for myself. I could either sleep in or get up just a little later than my normal, and enjoy a leisurely morning in my pajamas. It sounded like a heavenly day to me.

By Wednesday evening, I had decided to spend the morning lounging in my pajamas until about 9:00 and then I would get ready for Paul to arrive. I stayed up a little later than normal with the new book I am currently reading, *Of Mice and Men* by John Steinbeck. Actually I read so long that I feel asleep in my reading chair in my bedroom. I think I awoke about half way through the night and crawled into my bed.

When I awoke in the morning, I looked at the clock and when I saw it said 8:10 at first I panicked, then I quickly remember it was my day off and relaxed. I knew I still had some time to be lazy before I needed to get myself ready for little Paul. Lina had already eaten, so I made a new fresh pot of coffee and had a piece of toast with orange marmalade jelly. After sitting and enjoying my breakfast, I went upstairs to get dressed. I was still combing my hair when the telephone rang. I looked at the clock, it was 9:22.

Lina yelled for me to come to the phone. When she handed it to me she said it was Marie.

"Hello Marie," I said and before she could respond I added, "Is little Paul ready to come over to see his aunties?"

"Actually no," she said. "That is why I am calling. I don't feel very well all of a sudden and I don't think I want to go out today. I called and rescheduled my appointment for next week. I am so sorry I troubled you and that you took the day off of work."

"Oh my goodness," I said quickly. "Please do not worry. I totally understand. I am disappointed. I was really looking forward to a play date with Paul. I had lots of things planned for us to do. Maybe I should still come and get Paul so that you can rest?"

"Oh," she said. "No, that isn't necessary. He still takes a morning nap some days and today he was up extra early. I will have him lay beside me and we will read books until he falls asleep. I really am sorry about today but anytime on the weekend, you may take Paul for an outing, so that you don't have to miss work. Just let us know when.

Again, I am sorry. I am going to go lay down now and see if I can convince this little guy to take a nap with me. I am sure I will feel better later. Thank you Mitzi and again I am sorry."

"No worries my dear. We can talk later when you feel better."

And with that we hung up the phone.

I thought to myself that maybe Henry was right in his assumption that she might be expecting a baby. Tired and not feeling well. Sounds like it is a good possibility.

I knew Lina had returned to the study. I yelled, "Well it seems we now have a free day. What shall we do?"

Lina and I decided there was nothing high on our list to do today, except maybe later take a ride over to Antonio's in Oak Mount City for dinner tonight. It was a little bit of a drive but the food there was wonderful, it was a lovely day and we had plenty of time. So as for right now, my lazy day was to continue. I puttered around in the kitchen for a bit and decided to mix together a small coffee cake for our noon dessert and popped it into the oven. I looked at the clock. It was only 9:50. The cake would be done by about 10:20 so with nothing else pressing to be accomplished I decided to sit and enjoy my hot cup of coffee and do a little more reading. I had completed two chapters when I looked at the clock and realized it was time to get the cake from the oven. It smelled so good. The combined cinnamon and nutmeg aroma filled the kitchen. I wanted to nibble on a small piece while it was still warm, but just as I reached for a knife, I jumped when I heard the fire siren begin to roar.

Pinesdale is a small town with an undersized volunteer fire department so the whistle tended to howl for a good bit of time before everyone finally got assemble and ready to travel. I did as I always do when the siren blows and I said a quick prayer for the safety of the volunteers and for whoever was in need of their assistance.

The siren had been blaring for about a good three or four minutes when the phone rang. It had startled me. I composed myself and answered it by the fifth ring.

"Hello," I said.

"Hello there Mitzi, may I talk to Paul?" It was Henry and he sounded very chipper.

I answered with my first instinct. "How did you meeting go with Fritz?"

"What?" he said. "Oh, Fritz, he cancelled first thing this morning. Said he'd get back with me in a few weeks, but my guess is he found another firm."

"Well, that certainly wasn't nice of him after all the trouble you went through," I said. "But maybe he really did have a conflict just like he said. It could all be very true. Things happen. We shouldn't assume it was a lie."

"Well, at this point I am not worried." he said very casually. "So is Paul being a good boy?"

"I am sorry Henry," I said while trying to press my finger against my other ear. "What did you say? I couldn't hear you very well, the fire truck just went down the street and it was extremely loud."

"I asked if Paul is being good for you, but instead just let me talk with him," he repeated louder this time.

"I'm sorry Henry. Paul isn't here." I said thinking I would have thought he had already spoken to Marie and would have known that information.

"Where is he?" he asked. "Does Lina have him outside?"

"No Henry," I explained. "He isn't here because he didn't come today. Marie didn't feel well and called to ….."

"What!" he was almost yelling. "Mitzi, what are you saying? Where is he? Where is Marie?" "Oh my God…where is he?" Now he was screaming.

"Henry," I said sternly. "Calm down, they are fine. They are both at home probably sleeping. Marie called earlier and said she didn't feel well. She cancelled her doctor appointment and said they were both going to lay down and take a nap."

The next thing I heard was a thump like the receiver had fallen and hit the floor. I waited. There was no sound.

"Henry?" I said into the receiver. "Henry, are you there?" "Henry …answer me!"

Again, no response.

I waited another minute, then I hung up the phone.

"Lina," I called. "Lina! Can you come here please?"

Lina came walking into the living room wearing her painting smock and carrying a wet brush in her hand.

"What is it Mitzi?" she asked.

I repeated the conversation I had just had with Henry, trying to remember his exact words.

She looked as puzzled as myself.

I asked her, "What do you think? I am somehow both unsure of what I think but I know I am frightened," I said. "Henrys' frame of mind has not been good this week," I told her. "I think he has been carrying some burdens we are unaware of sister."

Lina remained quiet. She left the room and came back a moment later without her smock and brush. She lowered herself into the chair across from mine and we sat and stared at each other.

Finally I said, "Should we call father?"

Lina responded quickly, "No, I don't think so. I think we should wait. Father is not as strong as he used to be. The worry would not be good for him. And...as of this minute we do not know what there is to worry about so I feel we should wait."

I agreed and said, "Well then let's hope he will call us back. I am sure he will call us back."

We waited in silence. Our eyes went from the clock to the phone and back to each other in constant repetition. No call came. Five more minutes passed. Then fifteen more minutes passed and finally at 10:52 the phone rang. I grabbed the receiver quickly and said, "Henry?"

It was not Henry. It was Walter Schnell, a gentleman that I did not know very well but I did know he lived only a few house down the street from Henry and Marie. Walter called to inform us that there was a fire at Henry's house. He said Henry was there and he didn't want to elaborate, but he felt we should come right away. He mentioned that he had first tried to reach our father but was told he was unavailable and just thought someone from the family should come. I thanked him and said we were on our way.

Lina and I ran to the car and I drove us to Henry's home which was less than a mile outside of town. It was a lovely two story, three bedroom house with a nice sized yard. There was a huge oak tree on the north side of the house that held Pauls' rope and tie swing. Behind that was Marie's beautiful garden. She seemed to have a golden thumb when it came to flowers and plants.

As I drove all I could think about was Marie repeating that she and Paul would take a nap. I prayed that they got out of the house quickly without any injury. I looked over at Lina and she was wiping away silent tears. I knew she was thinking the same thoughts as me. Then I thought about Henry and his quick temper. Was he there at the house and upsetting everyone, placing blame before he had any details? Was he scolding Marie in front of the fireman? Was Henry being Henry?

Then my thoughts jumped quickly of little Paul. How scared he must be seeing a fire. The poor little dear. I tried to clear my head of all bad thoughts and just drove as quickly as I could to get there and find my answers.

As we drove, we could see smoke rising in the distance. When we finally reached his driveway, we saw much commotion was still going on at the house. The fire department was still there although it looked like the worst of the fire was extinguished. The men looked exhausted and dirty. Our immediate view was only of the front portion of the house. The front entrance area had some damage, but it looked like the main structure was still in place.

Everyone was walking about outside the house. They studied both of us as we got out of the car, but no one said a word to either of us. We started to walk toward the house, both of our eyes searching for any sign of Henry, Marie or Paul. We didn't see any of the three. We did notice a lot of movement coming from the back side of the house so we walked that direction.

The back side of the house was horrific. It was almost gone. It looked as if the fire had just climbed straight up the walls. There were people and volunteer firefighters moving about and once again, my eyes started searching for a familiar face. Finally I found him. He was on the ground curled up almost into the shape of a ball near the northeast corner of the house, close to the maple tree that held Paul's swing.

I saw him and I immediately felt a rush of grief fly though me. Something was wrong, terribly, terribly wrong. I looked at Lina. She was already crying with her head hung downward.

We walked slowly toward Henry, praying with each step that Marie and Paul had already been taken to the hospital in Hudson. That we had just missed the ambulance that transported them both to get the best care. Hoping with each breath that this was all a bad dream and trying desperately to wake myself up. But then we reached Henry. He saw our shoes and slowly lifted his head.

He looked pitiful. His face and white shirt had black soot smudges and his hands showed signs of reddened burns on his skin. His gray suit jacket was ripped on the right shoulder and had speckled burn spots where I assume ashes landed when the fire was still burning. His eyes were bloodshot from both the heat of the fire and the crying that had since occurred. He looked lost, totally lost.

I bent down to his level. I took his hand into mine. Tears were rolling down my cheeks and I said softly, "Henry....Henry what happened?"

He stared at me with his face full of agony.

Then quietly, so quiet I almost didn't hear him speak, he whispered, "They're gone."

And then he spoke again but this time he almost shouted at me emphasizing each word as he said, "They are both gone!"

And then his head fell back down and he moaned as though he was ready to die himself.

I was froze to my spot, kneeling on the wet ground my body shaking with pain. Henry was right beside me but unreachable. He was totally lost in grief. I tried to calm myself and think what I should do. I so wished father was here to handle what needed to be done. It was too much. I didn't know what to do.

I looked over expecting to see Lina right beside me, but she wasn't there. I looked back a few yards behind me and saw Lina talking with the Fire Chief. I got myself to my feet and walked over to join them. Lina was crying and had her hankie out dabbing her eyes.

"I am sorry Miss Mitzi," he said. "I was just telling Miss Lina when we arrived the back of the house was fully engulfed. We didn't know if anyone was home at the time. We tried to get guys in through the front door. They searched the downstairs and yelled names, but we didn't hear no one. We finally were able to get a guy up the stairs and he found them both. Looks like they had been sleeping in the main bedroom. Smoke probably got to them before they even realized there was a fire. It is a shame, a dam shame.

Just so you ladies know, Mr. Bricker from the funeral home has already come and taken the bodies. There was no sense waiting. Henry is in no shape to make any decisions today. We tried to reach your father to come, I guess Richard told you that already. So Mr. Bricker just said to have you folks come by the home tomorrow to make the necessary arrangements."

He stared at Henry for a moment then he continued. "Your brother is pretty broken up as anyone would expect," he said still staring at Henry. "We don't have any idea yet as to what started the fire. If we can't figure it out we will call in the fire inspector, but in most cases, it is electrical."

Someone yelled his name and he said, "Well ladies it seems I am needed. If there is anything you ladies need, just give us a call. We will be cleaning up here and we will keep the truck here for a while yet to make sure nothing else starts up."

With that, he walked back to his men and continued to do what fireman do, watch the structure.

We went back over to Henry. He was lying on the ground, still sobbing. We tried to talk to him, encouraging him to come home with us, but it was as if he couldn't even hear us talking. We each took an arm and tried to help him stand but we could not lift him. He was too heavy even with both of us trying and without some assistance on his part, he was just too heavy for us to lift. One of the fireman saw our dilemma and walked over.

He said in a very low voice, "Come on Henry. Let me help you up buddy. There is nothing you can do here. Go on home with your sisters."

Henry started to try to help just a little. He allowed his knees to straighten, but still kept his head hanging low.

"That's it. That a boy....just stand right up there. Let me help you walk to the car," he said with a very gentle voice.

And he did. He got Henry over to the car and opened the car door. We all tried to persuade Henry to climb in but he instead started leaning against the side of the car and sobbing again. The fireman attempted to shift his body toward the back seat and aim him into the car. Just as we finally got him inside and shut the door, Tram pulled up along the road. He parked and looked in amazement at the scene. He ran over to our car.

He looked at me and then at Henry lying across the back seat and said, "What on earth happened?"

I said in a hushed voice. "It is terrible Tram, both Marie and little Paul are gone. Oh dear Lord!" And I put my face into my hands.

"Mitzi, slide over." he said. "You are in no shape to drive."

I obeyed without question and slid over closer to Lina and grabbed her hand. Tram jumped in and started the car. We slowly pulled away from the house. Listening to Henry sob in the back seat. It was the longest mile in my life. By the time Tram pulled into our driveway, Henry had started to quiet down. Tram let the car idle a moment or two, looked across the seat at Lina and me and then turned the car off.

"Now comes the hard part," he whispered to us. He climbed out of the car and Lina and I did the same.

Tram opened the door to the back seat and said, "Come on Henry. Time to get out. Come on in the house now."

To my surprise, Henry listened to Tram and did just that. He slowly lifted his head and started to slide across the seat. His legs seemed weak, but with Trams arm around him, he was able to stand and slowly walk into our house. Tram kept him walking right through the kitchen and took him all the way into the living room and helped him set in the comfy blue chair.

Henry leaned back into the chair and with sad eyes looked up at Tram. To my shock and horror the next words out of Trams' mouth were not gentle or consoling. There were said in a calm but angry tone: "Why did you do it?"

I gasped as did Lina. I spoke first, "Tram….No! Tram…Henry would never, no he would never hurt his family. Please Tram, don't even say such a thing….."

Tram quickly put his hand up to me and said "Stop! For God's sake …. Stop Mitzi and let Henry answer. We have to get the answer. We have to know what he has done before anyone else comes here with these same questions. I cannot help him if I don't know what was done. He has to answer me."

I hated it - but I understood. With a broken spirit, I nodded my head in agreement with Tram, all the while silently praying I did not hear what I was dreading.

Tram got down on his knees so he was face-to-face level with Henry. He waited until Henry made eye contact with him and then he demanded an answer.

"What did you do?" he said with clear anger showing on his face.

I began to cry even thinking that Henry might have been involved. Oh dear Lord, please …please…let him say he did nothing.

And then I saw his eyes. For the first time in my entire life….I saw in his eyes….real pain, real torment.

The words came out quietly but totally legible. I heard them and wanted to just curl up in a ball and die.

Henry stared right into Tram's eyes and said, "I thought they weren't home. I thought the house was empty." Then he started to cry again and repeated even louder, "I thought they weren't home!"

Then he threw his head into his lap and sobbed.

SABRINA

Chapter 25 - 1968

Knox had gobbled the entire muffin by the time Nell returned to the kitchen. He noticed she seemed to be in a very good mood and knew it was going to be a good day to get some answers. But right now, she had gone right to the kitchen window and was looking out at Tram as though she had forgotten Knox was even sitting at her table.

Knox got up and went to peer out the window too. "Whatcha' lookin at Mrs. Nell?" he asked. "Is something wrong out there? Is Tram OK?"

"Oh my yes, Knox," she said. "No worries my little friend. Today is a perfect day. I mean today is just a wonderfully perfect day." She said it with the biggest smile I had ever seen on her face.

"Wow Mrs. Nell," he said. "You sure are happy. Is it cause I came to visit or did Sister Jeanette do something to get you so giddy, though I don't suspect a nun could do much to get a person giddy?"

"Well Knox, you would be quite surprised," she said cheerfully. "But," she continued, "let us just say it is the combination of both of you. Now did you enjoy your muffin? Would you like another one? I have plenty to share."

"No thank you," he said and then quickly tried to lead right into the subject matter. He cleared his throat and then jumped right in saying, "there sure were a lot of you ladies gathered at Mrs. Holden's party yesterday. Did you have a good time?"

"Oh my yes," she said as she busied herself putting plates into the sink. "Ginger is a lovely young woman and oh my but she served such a wonderful dessert yesterday. She does make a very good double chocolate cake. It was heavenly. A few had a second helping and I think when the meeting was over, there wasn't a piece left."

Knox made another attempt. "So," he said rather slowly, "Do you ladies actually have a meeting, or do you just play cards or even just chit-chat?"

"Well actually Knox," she said, "we usually do a little of all of that, but not yesterday. Yesterday it was an odd gathering. We got off on a different subject and I guess you could say, we got stuck on it."

"Wow, what was the subject you ladies got stuck on?" Knox asked innocently.

"Well, it is a long story young man," she said while kind studying the young boys face. Then she talked kind of slow while still watching. "And it had to do with something that happened a long time ago."

"Oh!" Knox said. "Did it have anything to do with Tram?"

"Tram?" she asked. "Why would you think it involved Tram?

"Oh, I don't know," Knox said while scratching his head. "He is just a creepy kind of guy."

"Tram?" she asked in disbelief. "Oh my no Knox. You are wrong. Tram is one of the nicest people you will ever meet. Why Tram has been a fixture in this neighborhood since before I was born. He has always been nothing but kind to me and he always was helpful to my mother. My dear mother was a very good judge of character and she always had nothing but praise for Tram Kellar. What was it she used to call him? Atlas. Yes, that is it, she called him Atlas."

"Why did she call him Atlas?" Knox asked.

"Well," she offered. "If you know anything about mythology, Atlas was at one time given a punishment. He was made to hold up the heavens on his shoulders. So, in a way, he carried the weight of the world on his back. My mother knew of Tram's good heart, his loyalty to his friends and his sense of decency. So, if you think about Tram's life that is exactly what he has done. He worries about all of us and watches over everyone; people and animals. So you see he carries the weight of our world on his back."

275

Knox thought for a minute and then asked, "Well, who exactly is he or was he always helping? And why did you all need so much help?"

This time, Nell stopped fussing about the kitchen and sat down at the table. She folded her hands together and studied his small face.

"It seems you really want to know some history about ALL of us," she said teasingly, "so let me jump backward in time and tell you a little bit about what I know. Maybe I can clear up some things for you."

Knox was pleased and said, "Wow! I was gonna ask if you could tell me some things today about this neighborhood from back in the old days and here you are ready to do just that! This is great. Go ahead Mrs. Nell. I am listening."

Nell smiled at the young boys' eagerness.

"Knox," she continued, "I am more than happy to tell you what I know but I am curious as to why you are so interested. I mean to say, Tram is now an old man. Why do you have such an interest in his past and the past of others?"

"Ah Mrs. Nell," Knox answered, "It is just the detective in me. You know I want to be just like the Hardy Boys. I would just love to solve a mystery! And my friend, Stinkweed. She is the same except she needs to be Nancy Drew. We both like it. We both like to read the mysteries. And…. don't tell her I told you but we kind of have our own detective club."

He was still in a very excited mood when he asked, "Mrs. Nell, do you think there is a mystery to be solved here in Pinesdale? He paused then added, "And even one right here on Maple Street?"

"Well," she said thinking to herself about how her thoughts and her life had changed over just the past few days, "First of all, I commend you both for loving to read. I have spent a great deal of time in libraries myself. And, I guess I could help a couple of budding detectives. Unfortunately, I don't think there is much of a mystery going on here in our little neighborhood, but let me tell you what I know and then you can decide."

She began talking right away. She started from her beginnings; telling him she only had her own view of the world to share, but that her view she felt was pretty good. She told him about life along Maple Street alley as it was during her childhood days; naming all the families that lived in these same houses.

She said, "Families came and went, but the houses stayed all the same except for a few new coats of paint."

In the meantime, Sabrina had been hanging around the nearly empty house waiting for the time to meet up with Knox. Since her younger sisters and Davey were still at her grandmothers and Audrey was, well who knows where Audrey was, the house was pretty quiet. She knew if she tried to hang out with her mother, she would end up being put to work on a task and then wouldn't be able to get free in time to meet with Knox, so she carefully avoided her right now. She opted to go into the study and just kind of hide for a bit. Instead, she was surprised to see Aunt Elsie in there sitting with her wheelchair propped up near the window. Mr. Mertz was curled onto her lap and seemed to be in a deep sleep. The thought entered her mind to quietly tip-toe back out of the room, but Aunt Elsie looked her way and called to her.

"You there," she called, "Child, come here. Yes, you. Come closer to me."

I obeyed and walked over to her.

"Which one are you?" she asked. "There are so many of you now moving about the house, I just can't keep you straight in my head. Are you Jane?"

At first, I just felt bad and wanted to say once again, no Aunt Elsie, I am Sabrina, but then I remembered reading about a Jane in her journal. Jane? Yes, it was Jane. It was when she had been reminiscing about her childhood she talked about a girl named Jane. I can't remember the last name, I would have to look it up, but yes, it sounded like Jane was someone she liked. She only mentions her one or two times. I wondered what had ever happened to Jane.

"No Aunt Elsie," I said, "It is me, Sabrina. I am David's daughter."

"Whose daughter?" she asked

"David," I answered. "I am David's daughter. I live here now. I live with you."

277

"Ok then," she quickly answered as though she had not really heard me speak. "Sit down here and talk with me."

I did as I was told. There was no chair close beside her so that she could hear me, so I pulled one of the tall straight back chairs over close to her wheelchair. Mr. Mertz did not appreciate our conversation or the dragging of the chair and he stretched himself on her lap, shook a little and then climbed over to the window ledge and repositioned himself. Before he closed his eyes again, he looked at me as if to say, "My eyes might be shut...but I am watching you!" I sat down and waited. I was just beginning to think she forgot I was there when she began to speak.

"I am surprised that I am still alive. I never would have guess I would live this long. It doesn't really seem fair that I am still here waiting and Otto has been gone for so long."

I was surprised that she remembered that Otto was gone. Maybe she is having a good brain day. I waited to see what would come next from her. She remained quiet again for a couple of minutes. She did notice Mr. Mertz on the ledge and tried to call him back. He ignored her. He opened one eye, closed it again and just ignored her.

"That is alright boy. You just stay there and keep an eye out," she said while nodding her head. "That old man over there at Mitzi's house.... you just watch him. Don't you let him hurt Jane. That's it, you just keep watching. You are a good cat Mr. Mertz. Yes, a very good cat."

I wondered what she was talking about. Why did she want Mr. Mertz to watch Tram? I thought it was Mitzi he was supposed to watch? I sat there for another ten minutes and she never said another word. She actually fell asleep while I was there so I quietly crept out of the room and worked my way right to the back door without Momma even noticing me.

I looked over to Knox's yard, but he was nowhere to be seen. I went ahead over to "The Huddle" and sat down to wait. I guess you could say I was very impatient today. I could not sit still. It wasn't that I had startling news to share, but I did have a little bit of something to share. After a few more of "waiting minutes," I decided to go find him.

I headed right for Mrs. Nell's house. As I walked up the backyard, I saw Tram was out by the garage at Mitzi's house. He looked over at me and started to wave, but I darted my head quickly the other direction and hurried to her back door. Tootsie was sitting on the ledge sunning herself. She meowed as I came closer. I peeked in and saw Nell and Knox sitting at the kitchen table and I decided I couldn't wait. I knocked on the door.

I saw Mrs. Nell look my direction and then smile. She motioned for me to come inside and I did. Knox looked surprised to see me.

"Good morning Stinkweed!" Nell said with a hearty voice. "Come in and join us. Would you like a muffin?"

"Yes ma'am," I answered.

As she got up to get me a plate and a muffin, Knox gave me a look as though he was saying…. why are you here?

I shrugged my shoulders at him and sat down.

"Here you go Sabrina," she said as she set down a scrumptious looking muffin on a bright yellow plate. As she was getting the plate of butter to the table she said, "You enjoy. Your friend here was just explaining to me that you two are budding detectives."

I shot Knox a stern look.

He grinned and said, "It's ok Stinkweed. Mrs. Nell likes that we both read detective books," he said nodding his head like crazy. She is going to tell us some stories. Old stories about this neighborhood and she is going to tell us about Atlas!"

He said that last part like it was very important and I was just plain confused. He saw my confusion and said, "And guess who Atlas is Stinkweed?"

I looked at him like he was plum crazy.

Mrs. Nell jumped in and said, "I just told Knox that my mother use to call Tram Atlas because he carried the weight of the world on his shoulders."

"I see," I said very slowly because I really didn't really see at all!

Knox jumped in and said, "Go ahead Mrs. Nell. Go ahead and tell us more. We want to know everything."

She looked from Knox to me and then back to Knox.

"Children, you certainly are curious," she said very much like a school teacher, "I think I have a better idea."

"What!" Knox said in shock. He was almost pleading. "No Mrs. Nell. Don't stop. Tell us your stories. Go ahead and tell them."

Now it was me looking from one person to another. I was all of a sudden worried that I arrived and ruined everything. Knox was going to be really mad at me if she changed her mind. I put my head down and bit into my muffin.

"Now hold on there Mr. Knox, a.k.a. Frank or Joe Hardy," Mrs. Nell said. "I didn't say I wasn't going to share my stories," she said a little softer, "but that I think we might do this in a better way."

Knox looked still upset. He rolled his eyes at me and then focused back on Mrs. Nell and in a creepy way, just kept staring at her.

I wanted to yell to him … "Blink Knox!"

I think Mrs. Nell had something very important on her mind that she wanted to say and she was busy just getting the sentences in order inside her head because she didn't even see Knox staring at her. She was focused too but in a whole different way.

"Recently," she said still speaking softly but definitely in an "I'm in charge" kind of way, "I have come to realize that secrets……well, that secrets are just not good. They can be hurtful and cause a lot of pain for many people. Sometimes even to people we do not even know. Do you understand what I mean?"

We both just stared at her.

"I mean to say," she continued, "a small secret to one person can be …. Well, it can be life-changing to another person."

She went on to explain. "You asked me earlier Knox if Pinesdale had any mysteries to solve. I don't truly know if things could be considered a real mystery but Pinesdale has had many secrets over the years. Some that I know and others that I am sure I would have never dreamed possible."

"Maybe you children are on the right path," she continued. "Yes, I do believe … you … are on the …. right path." She looked at both of us like she had just discovered America and said, "Yes! It is time to get rid of secrets!"

"Great!" yelled Knox. "I love that idea. Go ahead and tell us!"

"Well, I am glad you agree Knox," she said proudly, "but my idea comes with another thought."

"Oh no!" he said as though someone had just burst his balloon.

"It isn't bad," Nell said. "I just think that if you young detectives really want to find some answers to your questions about this neighborhood, then we need to involve more people."

Now even I was confused, so I asked this time.

"Mrs. Nell," I asked carefully so as not to appear bossy, "just who do you think needs to join in on this talk about secrets?"

"I think you want to know about neighbors, so to get answers, we need to invite the neighbors," she said in a very matter of fact voice. "Maybe you will find out all the things you want to know if we really get people talking. Just like at the meeting at your house the other day Sabrina. Your mother learned lots of new information."

"I guess so." I answered. "She did tell me a little bit about what she learned and she was kind of upset."

I looked downward and shuffled my muffin around on my plate and then added, "She said …. she was embarrassed," I added softly.

"There now," Nell said reaching over and gently patting my shoulder. "You see," said Nell. "That is what I mean. So, secrets no more. I am going to call a special neighbors meeting. Let's see who all should we include? Sabrina, your parents for sure. And because they got left out the other day, we need to ask Mitzi and Lina to come. I would also like to invite Sister Jeanette. Does that sound like a good group?"

I looked at Knox. Our expressions mirrored each other. We shook our heads no.

"No?" Mrs. Nell asked.

"No," Knox said, "We want another person to join the group. You forgot about Atlas!"

SISTER JEANETTE

Chapter 26 - 1968

Friday morning arrived. The sun was already shining brightly as I walked across the lawn to attend morning mass. I could see the usual devoted group had already settled into the pews with Nell Taylor noticing my arrival and making a point to acknowledge me. This time when Father Bob entered from the side altar, I was able to look at him and accept the fact that I found him to be a very attractive man. Yes, I am a nun and made a commitment to God that I shall not break. But, I was also still a young woman and I understood that from time to time I would have such feelings of attraction because I am human. It did not mean I was an evil person. It did not mean that I would ever act upon those types of feelings. It did not mean I would ever give up my devotion to God. It simply meant I was human.

I prayed now that during my time at St. Lucy's I would love my church. I would love my role at this parish. I would love working with and getting to know all of my new church family. And I would love my life.

I reflected. I did love the life I had chosen. But I also often wondered how different my life would have been if Scott had not gone into the service. Would we have married? Would I have become a mother by now? Would I have been happy? Questions to which I will never know any answers.

I had also been thinking about Sam. I think I was feeling guilty that I had allowed him to resurface so easily back into my life. I was supposed to move on alone. I was supposed to be strong. But, it wasn't right. He was supposed to be with me. I knew that in my heart. I suppose he resurfaced due to all of my crazy feelings lately. New anxieties tended to bring back points of comfort. I had tried to listen and tried to push Sam out of my head, knowing God should be enough, but I still needed Sam. Trying to picture him being gone was never something I could handle. He was still with me. Silent but always there. Always there.

Was it my momentary infatuation with Father Bob that was still troubling me? Those thoughts running around in my head, the worry of the harm I would bring to my life if I acted on those thoughts? I didn't think so, but at the same time I could not answer the questions. Was I scared? Was I feeling lost? Was I seeking something more, something new, something?

I had apparently been very deep in thought because I suddenly snapped back to reality and realized the closing prayer was being recited. I looked at the sisters to my right and both were deep in prayer.

As we walked down the aisle at the end of mass, Nell Taylor came up to me and remarked she had so enjoyed our little get-together the other day. I agreed that it had been very nice. She asked if I possibly had time later today to meet with her again. She said she had some other committee notes to go over with me and some other items to discuss. She asked if 5:00 would be okay. She offered that she would make dinner and having no other commitments, I whole-heartedly agreed.

Walking back to the convent with the other sisters, we heard Father Bob holler our direction and stopped.

He approached us and asked with a big smile on his face, "OK, so which of you is up for a game of tennis on this magnificent summer day?"

We all chuckled a little before Sister Charlotte said, "Well certainly not me. I don't think I have enough energy in these old knees. They are feeling their years lately. I will pass."

Sister Bergan jumped in next. "Now I have tried the game and as you know Father Bob, the good Lord did not give me much talent in the way of a strong back swing. I think it is best if I stick to croquet. When you want to have a rip-roaring croquet match, then you come find me. Maybe Sister Jeanette is your candidate today."

With that, everyone laughed and then both she and Sister Charlotte started off again toward the convent.

"Well then," said Father Bob, "I guess that does leave you Sister Jeanette. Are you feeling up for a match today?"

"I actually think I am," I said with a little bit of confidence. "I didn't mention it before, but I played a little in high school and my coach thought I was pretty good. Now, I might be a little rusty but I am willing to try."

"That is great," he said with a huge smile. "I have a few things to get done this morning. How would 1:00 be?"

"It would be fine for me," I said. "I have a meeting at 5:00 with Nell Taylor. But I was wondering, where do you play? I have only had a chance to explore a small bit of the town, mostly Main St during my walk over to Nell's the other day."

"Oh good, then you have already been to Nell's house. I know she was anxious to spend some time with you. Did she make you her blueberry muffins?"

I nodded a yes. "She certainly did and they were delicious."

He jumped right back in. "Yes, aren't they great?" I love when she invites me over. She always bakes something delicious."

"OK then," he said. "We can play today at Webbers Lake. There is a couple of tennis courts there. Have you seen the lake yet? If not, come a little early and we can take a little walk. I think you will like it. It is very peaceful there. I have some things I need to get done. See you at 1:00."

We parted and I returned to the convent to catch up on more of my household duties. There were three of us in the house, but Sister Charlotte did not carry the same work load of chores since she had many other church related tasks to care for each week. I was not complaining. I liked keeping busy and my chores were a good way to keep my mind occupied.

By 12:30, I had everything done that was necessary for the day. I went to get ready for the match, hoping I would not embarrass myself.

As I was heading up the steps there was a knock on the door. It was Father Bob.

"Sister Jeanette," he said with apology already showing in his eyes, "I am so very sorry but I need to cancel our tennis game for today. A parishioner has called the office with a major personal problem and needs to see me for counseling today, like today in a half an hour."

"Give it no thought at all Father Bob," I answered immediately. "I will give myself permission to try to get a little more in shape so that I will be better prepared to win upon your next invitation." I gave him a silly grin.

"Well," he said, "I do not expect this session today to take the entire afternoon. Can we still plan to take our walk around Webbers' Lake and then I will drop you off at Nell Taylor's for your dinner tonight? Does that sound okay?"

"Yes, that would be very nice." I agreed.

"Okay then," he said, "I really must go now. Can I come pick you up say about 3:30?"

"Perfect," I said.

And he was off, almost running back across the lawn. So now I had time to spare. I went up to my room. I wrote a letter to my parents and then settled down to finally try reading. I had gotten my library card the other day and found the book "*Franny and Zooey*" on the shelf of newer releases. I remembered it from seeing it on the well-dressed woman's lap during the long bus ride. Now I had enough time to get a good start on it. I read a little and then found I had fallen asleep. I awoke at 2:45 with plenty of time to get ready and enjoy a cup of coffee.

It was about 3:20 when Father Bob came for me and off we went to Webber's Lake. He was correct. It was wonderful. There was of course a beautiful lake, with two or three docks. It was not quite big enough for motor boats, but a great space for a couple of canoes with a few people fishing. There were lots of trees, scattered picnic tables; two tennis courts and a basketball court. I could see there were marked areas with walking paths that lead you deeper into the treed areas.

It was both beautiful and peaceful. There were couples with blankets spread in the grassy area with picnic lunches. Others were sitting quietly and reading. In general, it just looked like a perfect place to relax.

"You are so right Father Bob," I said while still taking in all of the lovely scenery, "It is just perfect here."

"I agree," he said, "But may I ask a favor of you?"

I nodded my head a yes.

"May I say it is not necessary for you to call me Father Bob …. I think just Bob will do," he said with a grin.

"Well," I said, "I am not too sure about it, but if you insist, then just Bob it is. So … Just Bob, what would you like to do?" I said and then we both laughed.

We walked around the lake and talked about so many things. The church, why he became a priest, why I became a nun, what towns we grew up in, what are goals are for the future. You name it, we discussed it. We also talked about some of the church members, people like Lucas Naples and Nell Taylor.

While talking about Nell, he said, "She is truly a wonderful woman and she has not lead an easy life."

He looked at me like he was waiting for a response from me. Being new to the area, I of course knew no one's history and didn't feel comfortable asking any questions … at least not yet.

"I don't know anything about the life Nell has lead, I mean I barely know just a few basics of her life at present." I told him. "When we met the other day she did fill me in on some of the church committees and what happens in some of them. She asked that we meet to cover more information today."

"It just so happens that I know about her meeting with you today." He continued, "I mean to say, she did share some of the information that she wants to cover with you. It will be a very worthwhile meeting."

He had said this with a kind of sheepish tone in his voice. I felt as if he was saying the words but trying hard to sound like he wasn't saying the words. I was confused as to why this very confident man now sounded like an unsure messenger.

"OK," I said, "I will." He seemed so concerned, so serious that I said it with a little laugh trying to once again lighten the mood. "I promise."

It worked, he smiled again.

Suddenly he looked at his watch and said, "Oh my goodness, it is 4:45. We have to get you over to Nell's."

As he pulled the car into her driveway, he said, "I hope your evening goes well. I know your dinner will be great but afterwards, please listen with an open heart. Let her speak her peace. Give yourself time to let it all sink in before you react. We learn new things every day. Today might just be your day."

I looked at him and I think he saw the worry in my eyes.

"My goodness," I said. "What on earth is she planning to discuss with me? I am not sure I am up to it. Is it a counseling session she needs?"

"Yes," he said empathically. "Yes, think of it that way. A counseling session for Nell. Yes, and do your best to hear all of her words before you form your opinion. Yes, do that!"

I stared at him and again he saw the worry in my eyes.

"Go ahead in Jeanette," he said softly. "Trust me, you will be fine."

He looked confident but I wasn't so sure. I got out of the car, walked past her little garden and to her back door. I took a deep breath and I knocked.

Nell answered the door immediately and welcomed me in. Her table was set once again showcasing her colorful Fiestaware collection, this time with a rainbow of colors displayed amongst the plates, bowls and serving dishes. She welcomed me and then said her dinner was ready to come out of the oven. She grabbed her pot-holders and pulled out a large roaster bearing an arched lid which hid the contents. She set it on top of the stove and lifted the lid. A mouth-watering aroma immediately filled the kitchen and I could see the food she had prepared looked wonderful. She had made one of my favorite meals. There was a large pot roast surrounded by roasted potatoes, carrots and celery resting in an amazing brown broth that she was now already gathering to make her gravy. Already on the table was homemade chunky applesauce with a sprinkle of cinnamon on top and warm homemade yeast buns. Over on the other side of the counter I could see what looked like a homemade apple pie resting on a cooling rack. It was my idea of a perfect meal and it reminded me so much of home.

All I could say was, "Oh my heavens Nell, this looks amazing. It reminds me so much of home."

"Well that is a wonderful compliment," Nell said with a smile.

"Sister Jeanette, please sit here" she said tapping the top of the chair, "Will you please say grace and then we can enjoy."

"Most certainly I will!" I replied and did.

Everything tasted wonderful. I thanked Nell numerous times. Once or twice during our meal; again while eating the scrumptious pie with her luscious freshly whipped cream and finally again while I helped wash and put away the dishes.

Admittedly, I was a little uneasy about what was to come next in the evening. This counseling type session that Nell apparently wanted to have after our dinner had worried me. I hoped that I was a good listener and was able to give adequate advice once hearing her problem. While I was nervous I was also anxious to begin, if that makes any sense. I knew Nell was a very special member of the St. Lucy parish and I didn't want to let down Father Bob or Sister Charlotte. I sat back down at the table and waited for Nell to open up the discussion.

She started by saying, "I assume that Father Bob told you that I had something I want to discuss tonight?"

I was unsure if he was supposed to alert me, so I timidly nodded my head in agreement.

She then asked if it was okay to sit right here at the kitchen table or if I wanted a softer chair we could go to the living room. I offered that I thought her kitchen was a great spot to talk. Her kitchen was full of warmth and honesty. She agreed and sat down but then she quickly hopped back up and said she would be back in 2 minutes.

My hands had started to get fidgety so I clasped them together. She returned to the kitchen carrying a rather old looking, heavily filled 8X10 manila envelope that was clasped shut. She set it on the table. I could see on the top left corner was written, Ivy Jenkins. I decided it was best if I didn't ask any questions and I let Nell begin the conversation.

"Sister Jeanette, I want to start by saying just how happy I am that you have recently joined the St. Lucy parish and by doing so you have given me the opportunity to meet you." She now paused as though trying to determine what to say next. I could tell she was struggling.

I jumped in, "Well I have to tell you Nell that I feel the same way. St. Lucy's has turned out to be just wonderful. I have met some delightful people and I have you right at the top of my list."

With that she nodded and then lowered her head. When she raised it a few seconds later, I could see the beginning of tears in her eyes. I reached my hand across the table and held hers.

"Dear Nell," I said with true compassion in my heart, "I am so sorry that something is troubling you so deeply. Please take your time. I have nowhere else I need to be tonight. I can stay for as long as you need me to."

With that she looked up at me and though she was smiling, even bigger teas were forming. She let go of my hand and immediately re-held my hand this time with hers covering the top of mine. I smiled.

She let go to wipe her eyes with the N initialed handkerchief from her apron pocket. Realizing then that she still had her apron on, she rose to remove it, laid it across the back of her chair and sat back down.

She began.

"Sister Jeanette, tonight I was hoping to tell you a story about my life. It is a story that I have only shared twice in my life. The first person I told was Curtis Taylor after he had proposed marriage to me because I just knew it was something he needed to know before I could knowingly accept his proposal. He was a wonderful and kind man and my story did not change his opinion of me or his feelings for me. We married on January 1st of 1944. The date was our idea to begin our life together with a fresh new year. And we did have a good life together. Unfortunately, the Lord called him back far too soon. He died in 1953 and I miss him deeply."

She had paused and I could see the hurt that still lingered in her eyes.

"You two must have had a very special love for each other," I said. I smiled at her but also felt the hurt in my heart. I had known that kind of love too, so long ago with Scott.

She brightened, "We did. We did everything together and never grew tired of each other's company. Maybe it was supposed to be that way since God did not see fit to give us any children. Not many people were aware but I did become pregnant twice. Each time I suffered a miscarriage about as soon as the doctor determined I was with child. It was very hard on both of us. We wanted children. We had prayed for a family; it just didn't happen."

We looked at each other, but I knew that I should not speak. She had more to tell and needed to keep going.

"The other person that now knows my story …… just learned of it over the past 2 days. That person is Father Bob. It is actually my fault that he cancelled your tennis match today. I am sorry, but I really needed to speak with him." She said this and then looked to see if I was surprised.

I sensed this time, I should speak. She was waiting for me to speak.

"Please do not worry about our tennis match. I assure you it wasn't going to be much of a match. And, you are correct. Father Bob asked if I was coming to see you tonight," I said cautiously. "He did say that when I come tonight I should listen with open ears so to speak. He insinuated that it was a delicate matter that we might be discussing and that you might be looking for some feedback from me."

I continued, "I promise you Nell that I am here tonight only to help you. I promise I will keep your story safe in my heart."

Now Nell was smiling and crying at the same time.

"Nell, please, what is it? You need to allow this story; this burden you are carrying to release. I can see how upset you are."

She sat and faced me and shook her head no. Then she spoke.

"No…no…no you dear sweet girl," she said softly. "My story is different now. It is different since meeting you. It is no longer a story of burden but of joy. My tears now are happy tears."

I wanted to be helpful to Nell, but I was admittedly lost now.

"Nell," I spoke very carefully now, not wanting to upset her. "I must admit that I am now confused. I am not sure if I am understanding. Maybe we should…."

She interrupted me. "You poor child. Yes, I have confused you and I will make a new attempt at explaining and go in a more logical order now instead of starting at the beginning and then jumping to my end." She smiled and I breathed easier.

I truly did not want to fail her. I wanted to be able to console her or guide her whichever was needed.

"OK," she said, "now let me continue, this time from the beginning."

"One night very long ago, as a young single woman I went out with friends to celebrate my 21st birthday. I was admittedly very foolish and had too much to drink that evening. I did realize afterward, when it was much too late, that the person that was buying me those drinks had a specific reason in mind." She looked at me now with some shame on her face.

"This next part is very hard to say," she continued. She paused and took a deep breath. "That evening I was raped." She kept her head down now as she said, "It was a vicious attack by a much older, very prominent man in the community. Afterwards he called me a tramp, which I wasn't!" she proclaimed very quickly.

I grabbed her hand again and said, "Oh poor Nell!"

She shook her head and said, "He warned me that no one would believe me if I told. Actually, he dared me to report it. He was such an evil man. It will be easy for you to know who he was when I say this next part and he is dead now so he can bring no harm to either of us. He was a business man and the mayor of Pinesdale at the time."

My immediate thought was not about the fact that he was the mayor or that he was dead, but why had she said he could not harm us?

"Please ...continue Nell." I said

"I didn't tell. I didn't tell anyone. Not my mother or my friends. I quit my job, oh, I forgot to say that he was also my employer. But, yes, I never went back. I returned to my former job and was just going to forget it ever happened. But as life often does, 8 weeks later I was surprised when I realized I was pregnant."

"Oh my, that must have been terrible to deal with on your own." I said.

"It was," she responded. "It was 1942. It was a time when a good family didn't dare say their daughter was in a family way when there was no husband. It just wasn't accepted. At least not in Pinesdale. I did the only thing I could do. I left. I left Pinesdale. And so my life of lies began."

She continued, "I told everyone I had always dreamed of moving to the Big City and that part was actually true. I did have at times aspirations of living amongst a large crowd of people, sharing the hustle and bustle of daily life and enjoying the evenings under the neon marquees lights.

But, I digress. I had secured an interview there and much to my relief, everyone believed me. So on January 8th, 1943, I moved to New York City. I was still unsure of acceptance even in the city of an unwed woman, so I assumed a new name and made up a story of a military husband and of recently becoming a widow." She said this part with a complete look of shame on her face.

Very quietly, I said, "Ivy Jenkins?"

She nodded a yes, patted the stuffed envelope and continued.

"It was the only thing I thought I could do. I had to find a way to make a living. I had found a very cheap, very tiny apartment, but in New York, nothing was too cheap." she said. "I worked at Mishkins Drug store and I swear if it had been any other place, I probably wouldn't have survived. They were so kind to me both before and after my pregnancy."

"I did all the necessary things," Nell said with some pride in her voice. "I found a doctor and when the time was right, I also sought an agency that I felt I could trust to handle the process of finding a good home for my baby." She now stopped and studied Sister Jeanette's face. Nothing appeared abnormal so she continued.

"As time grew closer," she continued cautiously, "my doctor had concerns about my pregnancy, but didn't voice them to me until the very end." She paused.

Sister Jeanette looked at her sympathetically, "Was there a problem with your baby?"

"There was," Nell answered. "At the last minute, my doctor decided they needed to arrive quickly and my labor wasn't moving fast enough, so a caesarean section was performed." She sat quiet for a minute. "You see it was a complete surprise to me…. but I was about to have twins!"

She spoke now with more anxiety in her voice. "I began to pray that they would both be born healthy. Then I worried about my adoption plan. I wanted to make sure that they stayed together. I would tell Nicole that they had to stay together …always. I would tell her that she must find a family that would love them both and promise to always keep them together."

The memories were rushing back to her now so quickly. I could almost feel Nell's panic. I could understand how difficult it had been for her being alone and facing giving up not a child but her children. I sat very still and waited for her to continue.

She spoke. "The surgery took place and I did give birth to twins, a girl and a boy. The girl, who I had called during my pregnancy, Molly was fine and healthy, but there was a problem. My son, Michael as I called him was struggling. He was not breathing normally. The doctor prepared me that it was touch and go for him, but that they were doing their best to keep him safe. It was 1943, medicine had not yet advanced to where it is today. I imagine there was not a whole lot they could do for him."

"Did he survive?" I asked quietly.

"My son, Michael Patrick Jenkins did not survive." she answered with sadness still in her voice.

A minute later, with a slightly brighter voice she added, "But, my daughter did. My Molly did."

It was now my turn to say something of wisdom. Words escaped me. "I am so sorry Nell about your dear little Michael, there are no words. But having your little Molly was such a blessing."

"It was very bittersweet," she said honestly. "I was able to hold her in my arms and touch her tiny fingers and kiss her soft pink cheeks, but only for a short time. It was while I was holding her that the nurse let me know that Michael had died. And ten minutes later, they handed me the papers and took her from me to let her meet her new family."

Kathleen F. Ewing

Now Nell sat very quiet. I felt deep sympathy for her and her story, but I wasn't sure what my words were now to be. How could I help her? I had only words to express how very sorry I was and how I wished her story had a different ending.

I spoke. "Nell, I am very sorry about the circumstances of your pregnancy, but I am sure you understand that God is not vengeful and he was not punishing you in anyway. Michael was just not meant for this earth. He was meant to be one of God's special angels."

She spoke now with a small trickle of tears on her cheeks. The memories had hurt her deeply.

"Don't you see sister," she said. "I had tried hard to do the right thing for my family and for my child. The only thing I asked for me was that God keep my babies together....and that didn't happen. Molly went to a family, a good family, but a part of her was lost forever."

I did not know how to respond to this, so I just sat quiet.

Nell sat quiet too, reflecting I imagined. I knew I needed to say something. I needed to help her finish her story. It was apparent from her face that she had more to say, more burden to lift and whatever it was, I needed to help her get it out.

I then asked, "Nell, what is in your envelope?"

She wiped her tears and then reached for the enveloped and unclasped the top tab.

"I saved everything important," she said as she began pulling papers free from the package.

I could see many small mailing envelopes, pictures, pay stubs, rent receipts, a library card, a birth certificate, and some very formal looking papers.

She started to sort some of the papers.

"These," she said as she gathered all the small envelopes and stacked them, "These are some of the letters that my mother wrote me and then there are some in here that I wrote to her. I found them in her vanity drawer after she died. She saved them all. For all those years, she saved them."

"Oh, silly me," she said. "You are going to think soon that all I do is cry if I don't stop."

"Please Nell," I said, "You had a very sad story to tell. I would probably wonder more if you had not cried tonight!"

"OK then," she said. "I have other papers here too. Some are receipts, I think it is funny to realize how inexpensive some things were compared to the rates today. "I also have here Michael's birth and death certificates and the paper I signed allowing for the adoption of my Molly."

With that she slid the birth certificate over facing me so that I could read it. I looked up at her and I could see she was waiting and expected me to read the document.

So, I read it.

Across the top it said: State of New York, Division of Vital Statistics, Certificate of Live Birth

City: Brooklyn New York County: Kings County State: New York Hospital: Brooklyn Hospital

At this point, I stopped and said, "Hey Nell, I was born at Brooklyn Hospital too."

Nell just nodded.

I continued to read. Child's Name: Michael Patrick Jenkins Sex: Male

A box was checked to show he was a Twin. Next was Date of Birth: July 8, 1943

I said, "Oh my goodness Nell. July 8th 1943 is the same day I was born. I must have been at the very same place as you that day.

She nodded again.

Father of Child; was left blank Mother of Child: Ivy Nell Jenkins Age at time of birth: 21 years

And then I stopped reading. My mind was racing and at the same time trying to stop to think it through calmly. There was no calmly. I looked at Nell with shock on my face.

She nodded again but this time with tears in her eyes. She said, "I think so"

'What," I proclaimed. "But how? How did you know? I mean what made you think?"

I had too many questions. I panicked now thinking this can't be true and what is this doing to Nell. If it isn't true now, it will crush her. I have to calm down and think about this logically.

"Nell," I tried to say with a voice of reason. "It can't really be true...can it?"

"I think it is very true," she said calmly now.

"But Nell," I said again. We cannot rely on just a birthdate. Imagine how many babies were born on July 8th 1943 in Brooklyn. I could imagine there were many."

She smiled at me and then reached under the pile of envelopes. She pulled out a scrap of paper and then said, "Before I show this to you, I want you to know this is something I wrote down that day in the hospital, the day my little babies were born and both taken from me. I saved it so that I would always remember it."

Then she slid the paper across the table for me to read. It said across the top: July 8th, 1943. Under that it said: In the excitement of the moment, my caseworker Nicole said to me: She is going to wonderful parents. They even started a bank account for her and Frances has already been buying toys and setting them aside for Christmas.

My eyes stopped reading after I saw the name Frances.

Tears were now flooding my face. I couldn't stop. Nell stood up and came around the table and hugged me.

She said, "I have been waiting a long time for my second hug from you." She continued hugging me. "This is a blessing I never expected to know and I thank God with all my heart. It was God that brought you to St. Lucy's. God wanted me to find you."

It was still unbelievable to me. I looked at Nell and this time I really studied her face.

"How did you know? I mean, what made you even think it was possible? I just met you a few days ago."

She looked at me with such love in her eyes. This time there were tears, but they were tears of joy.

"It was so very easy" she said. "It happened the very first day. Remember the day I met you when we were at morning mass. We talked and all was fine. But then I said something and you and you smiled. Then you laughed and I saw it. I saw the face of my mother. It was your smile. I thought I knew right then and there that you were my Molly."

I didn't know what to say. I think I was still in shock.

She continued, "And then when I invited you for the muffins, you mentioned your birthday. And then when we had Tram come in to take the picture of the two of us side by side. I could see even more resemblance. You didn't know me when I was young, but I was pretty, just like you."

"So much of it does make sense I agree, but," I added, "Nell.... are we both just wishing more than we should?"

"I wasn't sure either and I didn't want to make you think something if it wasn't true." she said. "That is why I went to Father Bob today. I knew he would look at it logically and if there was something I was missing; he would find it. I told him my whole story and showed him all the papers, just like I showed you. He found it remarkable. I asked him if there were any pieces of information from the diocese that might help to confirm any part of my thoughts."

She continued, still staring into my eyes. "He confirmed the diocese provides a file of necessary paperwork on each of their church personnel. Father Bob stood very still for a moment. Maybe he was just thinking, saying a prayer or maybe just weighing his reasoning. Then he walked over to the file cabinet in the corner of the room and unlocked the top drawer. He quickly slid his fingers along the top of the many files until he found the one he needed and pulled it out. He came back to his desk and held the closed file on his lap. He looked at me, staring straight into my pleading eyes and then looked back to the file. He slowly opened it. I sat quiet for a few minutes which felt more like an eternity as he read through the paperwork. He closed the file and studied it again and then looked very seriously at me as I sat waiting."

"He said he shouldn't share your information without your permission," she said hesitantly. "He also said he knew how very important this was to me and said he felt deep in his heart that when all the answers came out, you would understand and forgive him. So please Sister Jeanette, Susan or Molly....please forgive him."

She continued a little faster now, like she couldn't wait to share whatever was to come next. "He read me some pertinent pieces of information. Key things like your given birth name: Susan; your birthdate: 7-8-1943; your birthplace: Brooklyn Hospital, New York City. All of those pieces matched perfectly into my history too. But there was more."

She kept talking, "There were other vital pieces that were interesting for me, but did not help confirm anything, like the name of the town where you grew up, certifications you received and then the conclusive piece that told me and Father Bob that I was right. It was your emergency contact numbers. We were able to know your parents' names! It said Ben and Frances Collins. It was Frances! "

She took a breath and waited for me to react. When I didn't immediately she said, "Father Bob and I decided our best approach would be to contact them and ask some questions."

Then she took another deep breath and with a teary voice, she said, "And by the way, I was able to speak to your mother. She loves you very much. After she heard all of the details, she said she was truly grateful that we had found each other. She said she always felt bad that Susan's birth mother would never know what a wonderful person she had become. She said, now her heart is full. She is a lovely woman."

I nodded my head and tears dripped from my cheeks.

"Your mother confirmed their caseworkers name was Nicole. Your parents had no idea that you had been a twin, but after thinking for a while your mother did remember something that she now understood had been important. It was a statement that Nicole had made to her during that initial phone call. She said at the time, it had made no sense but she just felt that maybe she heard her wrong in all of her excitement about getting a baby."

She told me the whole story. "She said they had taken their pre-adoption classes and when it came time to complete the final paperwork, they had applied for a newborn child but were very clear that it did not matter if it was a girl or a boy. They had also been very clear that they were not interested in multiple births. They wanted only the opportunity to raise one child. She said that the night they got the call, Nicole had said, "A baby girl had just been delivered at Brooklyn Hospital and while it didn't look like it was going to be a perfect match for them, things had changed and now it was."

"Oh my goodness," I said as I quickly understood the implication.

"Yes," Nell said. "It just seemed that everything we heard and found today, pointed to it being true. The Lord took my Michael, but now after all these years, he is giving me back you!"

It was a shock. How could it be that I was sent to this small town and within a few days I have been given this gift of finding my birth mother? I mean I was never even looking for my birth mother. How does something like this just....happen?

And then my mind paused for just long enough to allow me to truly think about everything she had told me. My birth, the hospital, a twin! And suddenly I knew! It was true! It was really true! Oh my goodness, I had been a twin!

Just that quick, all those little pieces of my life made perfect sense. I just knew she was right .... I knew it was true. I looked at Nell and said exactly what I felt.

"Nell," I said softly, "this is all giving me chills."

"I know," she said, "I felt exactly the same way." "But, I am worried," she said with concern on her face and fear in her voice. "I know this has all been a shock to you. I understand you must feel confused. But my dear, your face, it is suddenly so pale. Are you okay?"

I looked up to the heavens. I clasped my hands as if in prayer and I tried to get my words out very carefully.

I opened my mouth. "Nell, I know now it is true. It is all true! I mean I know now the other part ...... I mean I know now why I...," I stopped. This was important. I needed to rethink my words and say it just right.

Nell was still staring at me waiting to hear whatever it was that I so badly wanted to explain to her. She was being so very patient. So, motherly. I knew that what I was going to say in the next minute was going to bring her a new relief. I needed to make sure she understood exactly what I was telling her.

I could feel the words trying to form a sentence but I knew they were rolling around all jumbled out of order and making no sense. I stopped and looked again into Nell's waiting eyes.

I spoke slowly so that she would hear each word.

"Nell, I know now. I mean I understand about your Michael," I said.

Nell's expression of concern now changed to questioning. Her eyes were searching my face, eager to hear the next words.

"Nell," I said with compassion. "All those years ago. God did answer your prayers. Your Michael, he has been by my side. He has been there with me all of my life. He has shared every moment. He has helped to guide me. He has helped me make choices. Nell....he has been with me!"

"You see Nell, God did listen to you," I said with full confidence and reached for her hands. "He heard your prayers and he made sure that even though he needed your Michael in heaven, he allowed him to still be a part of me."

Nell was still staring at me. Seeming to slowly absorb what I was saying as tears were filling her eyes.

Taking her hand and holding it up to my heart I continued. "He was always here Nell, tucked inside my heart. The only difference was …. I didn't know him as Michael. I have always called him Sam."

SISTER JEANETTE

Chapter 27 - 1968

Tonight at Nell's house, my life changed.

My world as I had known it for the past 25 years, was just turned upside down and inside out. It was all good, actually it was all amazing; but it was new and I needed just a little time to adjust.

I had been Susan for 23 years; the dutiful daughter of Ben and Frances Collins.

I recently had become Sister Jeanette; a member of the Congregation of the Sisters of Providence.

And now I know that had circumstances been different at my birth, I would have been Molly.

My mind was still spinning with all that I had learned in the past 24 hours. I wanted to talk to my parents, to Father Bob, to Sister Bergan, to everyone and anyone who would listen, but I knew the right answer was, not yet. For now, just breathe. I needed to give myself a little more time to think it all through. I wanted to have a clear mind about all of it before I started to share it with others.

I needed to talk with Sam or should I now think of him as Michael. My brother Michael! My twin that I had shared space with inside our mother's womb. And I also needed to give myself now permission to know that all this time, I had not been crazy. I was not imagining that there was someone there deep inside me. Someone always helping me, guiding me protecting me.

I loved my adoptive mother, but to now have the opportunity to know my birth mother was such an amazing gift. I was treasuring every minute we spent together. I had a million questions I wanted to ask Nell. Our time together the day she told me went so fast but we had promised to continue forward this new journey and never let it go. I was pleased that Nell had asked me to be included in the neighbors meeting she had planned. I knew that I would not know many of the people that would be attending and that some might even be a little put-off by my being in attendance, but it was very important to Nell and I didn't want to disappoint her.

Nell had mentioned it was her opinion that it was time to end all secrets and she hoped to have that happen at this meeting. I knew that Nell was making reference to her own secret about having a child, having me, but I was not at all sure what other types of secrets might be discussed. Nell had just told me to expect an interesting afternoon.

Tomorrow, I knew I had a few things beyond my normal household chores that I must accomplish. I needed to talk with Father Bob and I needed to talk with my parents. I expected both to be lovely, happy conversations so I was anxious to make my connections. For now I needed to make myself a nice hot cup of tea and sit quietly in my room and reflect upon my day.

I was up late into the evening but still awoke at my usual time to the sun was shining brightly through the side window of my room. I quickly dressed and prepared for morning mass. The church seemed fuller than usual or maybe it just appeared that way because I was in such a glorious mood. Father Bob was still breath-taking and his sermon strong and on-point.

When Mass ended I took part in the usual chatting to the congregation paying special attention to Nell. We shared a secret now that only we and Father Bob knew, so I tried my best to act in front of the parishioners as I had always acted in the past. It was not up to me to reveal anything. That would happen only when Nell felt it should and not a second before.

We did share a little hug after most of the others had walked away and Nell re-confirmed that I would be at her house at 3:00. I promised I would be there and suggested I might come a few minutes early to help her with any finishing up duties. She nodded in appreciation and scooted out.

I noticed Father Bob was talking with a church council member near the stairs that lead to the choir loft and it looked as though their conversation was about to end. I stood for another moment or two and had time to think about my day. Ideally I would see Father Bob this afternoon and wait for the cheaper after 5:00 phone rates to make the long-distance call to my parents. I was still thinking when I realized that Mr. Candle had already left and Father Bob was walking toward me.

I asked Father Bob if he had any free moments today that we could have a brief talk. He looked at me sheepishly, like a small child does when he thinks he might be in for a scolding. I quickly smiled and assured him that I only had good things to discuss, but that I would like to do it in private.

Father Bob had made it all possible for Nell to confirm her suspicions and I wanted him to know that I was not only not upset but I was overjoyed. Nell had said he predicted my feelings and he had done so correctly, but I still wanted to make sure he knew how I felt and how happy I was that he read those papers to Nell.

Father Bob smiled and invited me to join him in his study. Together we walked through the church and out the side door that was closest to the rectory. As we followed the stone-tiled path I kept thinking about his sheepish looking face. He truly was a handsome man, but a devout man. I remembered our talk that day at Webbers' Lake. His story about how he made his decision to join the priesthood was inspiring. It is often times a troubled beginning that leads us to our spiritual awakening. His purpose was real and would sustain him for a very long time. I hoped mine would do the same.

We went inside and he went directly to his study. He sat at his desk and I in the chair across from him. I was ready to begin, but when I looked at him I saw his eyes, those beautiful, soulful eyes were focused in the corner of the room. I turned my head to look behind me and saw a file cabinet. Then I remembered Nell saying "He locked the cabinet and rifled through the files until he found it."

Sensing his worry, I spoke quickly. "Father Bob I just wanted to thank you, to thank you from the bottom of my heart for helping Nell to confirm the details so she could feel sure before she came to me. It was such a shock, I think I am still shaking."

Father Bob's expression immediately changed from concern to excitement.

"I know," he said quickly. "I listened to her and it did all make sense but in my heart I thought what is the chance of it all being so very simple. We were fortunate your mother was at home when we called. And after she spoke with your mother for a few minutes, and Frances is a very kind woman by the way, there was no other possibility but that it was all true. When I think about the steps that put this into place it is truly a miracle."

He continued, "I mean as a nun, you could have been sent anywhere for your next assignment and how it just happened to be St. Lucy's....well I just don't know other than to say that God had a hand in you finding Nell!"

His face was so much more relaxed now. He was at ease and I was glad. I did not want him to ever think I was upset with him. I was happy he shared my information with Nell. He did the right thing and I wanted him to know that was exactly how I felt. I smiled at him and studied his relaxed face. Before I could say anything, he jumped back in with his own thought.

"I did want to explain that under any other circumstances, I would not have shared any of your personnel information without your permission. I knew it was....."

"Please Father Bob," I said quickly before he could go any further. "Please do not apologize for giving me such a gift."

His facial expression told me I had spoken well and that enough had been said. We talked for about fifteen minutes about Nell and how my life had now changed and would continue to change. In the end, he once again asked about a tennis match.

"So Sister Jeanette," he said coyly, "I think you still owe me a tennis match. How about this afternoon?"

"You are correct," I replied, "I do but this afternoon won't work for me. Nell has asked me to attend a neighborhood meeting that she has planned. I am not sure what all is going to be involved but it seemed very important to her that I attend, so I did already commit."

"Are you free anytime on Monday?" I asked.

"Why yes," he said grinning. "I do believe I can keep some time open in the afternoon. How about 1:30?"

"I think 1:30 sounds fine," I said. "I will be ready. And now I better get back to the convent. Sister Bergan will think I am neglecting my chores."

I returned to the convent and finished all my household duties but when I sat down for lunch I began reflecting again on what had happened over the last day. I wanted to share my news with Sister Bergan and even Sister Charlotte but I knew it was too soon.

And then I thought about the big meeting that I would be attending in just a few hours. What did Nell have planned for this neighbors meeting. I knew by the look on her face when she spoke about it that things were going to be brought up that might shock some people. Well I knew her news about me alone was going to shock people....but what else was going to be said at this meeting? I decided my brain wouldn't rest until this meeting was over.

THE MEETING

Chapter 28 - 1968

Not everyone was in full agreement. Some had some pretty serious reservations about this so-called meeting Nell had arranged for today, but when three o'clock arrived, everyone came in the door. Since it was being held at Nell house, she had baked for the occasion. She made a peach pie that had just come out of the oven about 45 minutes before the neighbors gathered, so it was cooled but just barely and was going to be very hard to resist. And for those that didn't appreciate a good pie she also made a fresh strawberry shortcake. She did not make but purchased a half gallon of vanilla bean ice cream to be used as the finishing touch to both of her desserts. Earlier today, she had prepared a pitcher of ice tea with a sprig of spearmint for flavor and just now, she had a pot of coffee percolating.

She wanted this meeting to go well and she knew fully well that it always helped to feed your guests with something appealing for their sweet tooth for the best outcome.

She was still floating on cloud nine over her discovery of her "Molly" or as she was better known amongst the others in Pinedale, Sister Jeanette. After Nell had revealed her news to Jeanette and Jeanette had come to realize it was all true, they had spent the next three hours sharing information with each other. Nell wanted to know everything about Jeanette's life. She had only her own imagination to rely on for so many years and now she finally could hear all the details from her very own daughter and she wanted to hear it all. She now had the opportunity to do just that!

She could see her, hear her and reach out to touch her. She was not only a beautiful young woman but she also had a heart of gold. She could see "Molly" resembled both herself and her mother with her lovely smile and coloring. She was not tall at all, so in that way she was just like Nell. From Nell's eyes, Jeanette was absolutely perfect! But there was so much else to know. She now had a good start. She was learning bit by bit; piece by piece. With every sentence spoken came another tiny part of the puzzle. Their long discussion the first day, built some of the frame of the puzzle. And with some topics, small sections started to fit together, but there was so much more, so many more pieces to try to match and fit into the frame and Nell wasn't sure if they spent every day together for the next full year, if she would have all her questions answered. Her mind bounced from one subject to another and the questions kept resurfacing about every topic. What were her likes and dislikes; goals, dreams and fears? She wanted to know all she could about everything she could and the same was true for Jeanette.

Jeanette was the first to arrive, but in all honesty, not really. Nell had set the meeting for Sunday at 3:00 pm but Knox had come knocking on her backdoor at 10:15 am ready and raring to sit the people down and talk. Nell had been kind. She knew he was full of nervous energy and if she sent him away, he would just turn around and be back again in another hour, so she found some little odd jobs for him to do to occupy his time and his thoughts. She had just run out of ideas when she had another knock on the door at 11:45 and found Sabrina on her doorstep. Luckily, Sabrina was only there because she was looking for Knox, and off they went across the alleyway with their two heads whispering together sharing who knows what kinds of secrets. All Nell knew was they were both out of her hair for a bit and she could really finish preparing for the afternoon.

Now that Jeanette had arrived a tiny bit early, she was also helping Nell with her last minute touches. She had just finished arranging the fresh flowers Nell had cut from her garden and had placed one small vase on the kitchen table and another larger one on the coffee table in the living room where Nell had hoped to have everyone gather. She had just placed the vase in the living room when she heard a knock at the back door. In the kitchen she found Nell talking with Mitzi and Lina Winter. She was just about to introduce them to Jeanette when there was another knock and it was David and Ginger Holden. Nell had them all standing in the kitchen and she was making introductions to Sister Jeanette when Knox and Sabrina returned.

Nell laughed and said, "Well now that my two little detectives have arrived, I think we can get this little party, I mean meeting, started."

Ginger looked surprised. She looked at Sabrina and Knox and then back to Nell and said, "Detectives? Do I have a detective living under my nose and I do not even know it? Should I be worried?"

Nell laughed again and said, "Oh my yes, these two do some of the best detective work this side of the Rockies! But as for the need to be worried, no my dear Ginger, I think you are safe."

Looking around the now crowded kitchen, Nell said, "Shall we move into the living room and if it is alright with everyone, I think we should just get started and save some of the desserts for when we need a little break."

With this statement, Knox cleverly cleared his thought rather loudly. Everyone stopped and looked his direction.

Nell said, "Is there a problem Knox?"

"Um...," he said now just a tiny bit embarrassed as everyone was looking right at him, "I think we are missing someone. Tram isn't here yet."

"You are correct Knox," Nell said. "Tram did say he would join us but also said he might be a few minutes late. How about we go into the living room and have a seat and in the meantime, I will go ahead and serve everyone a yummy dessert. By then, Tram should be here. Would that be a better option Knox?" She gave him a quick wink.

"Yes ma'am," Knox answered quickly. "That sounds to me like a great option."

Nell took orders for pie or shortcake and Jeanette and Ginger offered to help get the servings ready and scoop the ice cream. Sabrina helped to pass out the plates. She could hardly wait to finish serving so she could cut into her own piece of warm peach pie. That velvety vanilla ice cream melting down over the pie looked so good, she hated to hand it to her father but did and then hurried back to the kitchen to grab her own. It melted in her mouth. She was very proud of her friendship with Nell and knew her mother would be impressed with her desserts.

Everyone seemed to be enjoying their desserts, but still no Tram. Nell and Jeanette were starting to gather plates and were now taking orders for coffee or ice tea when there was a knock again at the back door. Knox flew past the others and into the kitchen to open the door. He said hello and then yelled to everyone, "Tram is here!"

Tram came into the room and looked first to Mitzi and Lina, acknowledged he had already met Sister Jeanette and allowed Nell to introduce him to David, Ginger and Sabrina.

"Tram," Nell said, "these fine folks are the Holden's. David, our local barber, I think you probably already know."

Tram stuck out his hand while nodding his head and gave a hearty handshake to David.

Nell continued, "And this is David's lovely wife Ginger. I am sure you have probably already seen her in the yard since she now lives right next door to you folks."

Tram took off his hat and said, "I don't believe I have Mrs. Holden, but it is very nice to meet you now. I am so pleased that Elsie has family living with her now. It has to be a comfort to her to have other folks within her house. I hope you like it there and here. It is a nice quiet neighborhood."

He and Ginger shared a cordial smile and then he focused his eyes on Sabrina.

"This is our daughter Sabrina." Ginger said as she wrapped her arm around Sabrina's back.

"Well, hello Miss Sabrina," Tram said. "I do believe I have seen you scurry across the yard and riding your bike here with young Knox, but it is very nice to finally meet you."

"Hello Mr. Kellar," I spoke but it came out kind of soft and shy-like.

"Please," Tram said. "Please just call me Tram. Everyone does."

"Ok," I said with a little more confidence, "Hello Tram. It is nice to meet you."

"There now," Nell said. "Tram, let me get you a dessert. Everyone else has already finished. And then if you don't mind, we will get started while you nibble on yours. May I offer you peach pie or strawberry shortcake?"

"Or if you are smart," Knox added, "You will ask for both!"

Everyone laughed. Tram asked for pie. Nell got his plate ready and everyone else found their seat again in the living room.

Nell entered, delivered her pie plate to Tram and then stood looking a touch nervous. She cleared her throat and then smiled at everyone and began.

She began. "I have asked you all here today for a very specific reason. It all started with these two young detectives, Knox and Sabrina, asking me questions about this neighborhood. Their questions were fine and I enjoyed sharing some of what I know with these children, but the more they asked and the more I answered... I came to realize there are a lot of questions yet to be asked and answered and I did not feel I would be capable of providing.... all of the answers."

Everyone looked a little uneasy and looked to Nell as if they didn't quite understand what she was expecting today.

Nell seemed to sense their worry and knew her explanation had not yet answered their questions.

"Please.... let me try again," she said calmly.

"Recently, very recently," she said, "I have discovered something absolutely amazing. I will share it with you shortly, but let me first tell you something about me and my life. I have had a secret that I have kept for the past 27 years. A secret that I always felt I must keep. I secret that I had promised myself that I would never tell another living soul."

Now the room went totally silent as if no one was even breathing and many had looks of concern on their faces.

"Well," she continued, "let me tell you.... that secret has caused me to have a very different life then I was meant to live. It denied me of so much joy. My poor, poor mother, she never even knew...."

At this point she had to stop and pull her hankie from her pocket and wipe her tears. She looked toward Sister Jeanette who was also dabbing her eyes.

Nell sniffed and then pushed her hankie back into her pocket.

"Folks," she said trying to come across with a little more strength in her voice, "over the years I have cried many, many tears of sadness, but over the past few days I have cried only tears of joy. Joy because my secret, my secret that I felt I needed to keep hidden inside my heart for all these years is now free and overflowing with happiness."

The room was still confused, but everyone was back to breathing normally again.

Nell gave everyone a gigantic smile and with a heart full of pride she said, "Let me just tell you this way. Everyone, I would like to introduce you to …. my daughter."

Everyone gasped. Everyone was in shock. But then Nell walked over and stood right beside Sister Jeanette.

"This is my daughter, Sister Jeanette," she said proudly. Sister Jeanette stood up in her long black habit and head covering and hugged Nell.

My first thought was; do nuns really have mothers? But then I about kicked myself in the behind. Of course nuns have mothers, duh!!

My mother was the first to stand and walk over to Nell and congratulate her and Sister Jeanette. Mitzi and Lina followed while Tram and my dad remained seated. But next the questions flew and Nell told the story of seeing her in church, recognizing her smile, hearing her birthdate, and confirming both the hospital and the name of her adoptive mother, Frances.

The women talked and asked questions for about 10 minutes straight. When they finally got done being bubbly over those pieces of the puzzle, then Nell knew it was time to finish her story.

"The hardest part," she said slowly, "is the memory of how I came to conceive this blessed child. It happened a long time ago, well 26 years ago and it involves another portion of my secret. You see…. I went out to celebrate my 21st birthday and ended up accepting a few too many drinks from someone I thought I could trust and not realizing until it was too late that he had a plan in his head for how the evening would end."

Poor Nell was now lowering her head as though it hurt her to remember. Mother looked at me and Knox and asked us to go out into the kitchen until she called us to return. I so badly wanted to disobey and stay but I knew my mother and I knew she was being very serious. We left the room.

Mrs. Nell went on to tell her story. Mother will never know, but we could still hear Nell from the kitchen and we also peeked from around the doors edge. Everyone was so wrapped up in hearing Nell speak that they paid no attention our direction.

"I won't call him a gentleman, but this man offered to drive me and my friend home that evening. After he dropped her off, he made an excuse to make another stop on the way home and while at this place, he attacked me. It was a vicious attack and in the end, he raped me."

There were gasps from all the women, especially Sister Jeanette.

Nell was determined to say her piece and kept right on talking.

"He offered that I could report him but in the same breath assured me that no one would believe me....and sadly, I believed him to be correct," she said. "That was my first mistake. A few months later, I realized I was pregnant."

"It was 1942," She said as if that would make some sort of sense to everyone. "A young girl that was pregnant without marriage brought shame to her family in those days. I couldn't do that to my mother," she said now almost crying again. "So I did the only thing I thought I could do. I planned to move away and give the baby up for adoption. And I had to do it quickly before anyone suspected. Within a few weeks, I was moved to New York City. I called myself Ivy Jenkins. I got a job and let my employer and co-workers think I was a war widow. Then 6 months after arriving there my babies were born."

She stopped talking. Looking around the room for questioning looks, she saw them and continued.

"Yes," she said sounding almost like she was kind of happy again. "You heard me correctly. I said babies. I gave birth to twins. The agency suggests you don't think of names for the babies but I did. In my heart I called them Molly and Michael."

She pointed in Sister Jeanette's direction, "Molly...who you see here with us today was born very healthy and was adopted by a wonderful couple named Ben and Frances. My little Michael was not as fortunate. He was born with a breathing defect and survived only a short amount of time. I named him Michael Patrick Jenkins. He is buried at Holy Cross Cemetery in New York City."

"Up until this week," she continued, "I only shared my story with one other person, my husband Curtis. He was such a sweet and caring man. As my wedding gift, he purchased the headstone for Michael's grave." She dabbed a tear again.

"My point in telling my story to all of you today is," she said now sounding very strong, "that my secret caused me a lot of pain and by not even trying to press charges against that man, my secret allowed him to continue his terrible life. When I think of how many other girls I possibly put in harm's way, I just want to shudder."

She said all of this and slowly sank into her car and just stared at everyone. A minute or two passed. Everyone was quiet for a moment. I wondered if they were thinking about poor Nell, about the poor baby that died or about all the other girls that bad guy might have hurt.

Suddenly we heard Tram's voice. He spoke loud and clear.

"Secrets.... yes...too many secrets," he said slowly.

He lifted his head and looked right at Nell. "You are right Nell. It is time to get rid of secrets."

It seemed he had made up his mind to be the one to speak next.

"I am sorry to say this here today in front of everybody and I am sorry for you Mitzi and Lina, but Nell is right," he said. "Secrets are, well they are just not good and I think amongst our couple of houses here, there have been a whole lot of secrets."

"Nell," he continued, "You are a very brave woman and have endured more than a person should...and I want to thank you. Your story has inspired me to rid myself of some dark secrets that I too have held for many, many years. Unfortunately, I have more than one to release."

Now it was Tram who looked uneasy and was breathing hard.

"Ok," he said rather slowly, "let me start with you Nell. I know it was Henry Jr that raped you."

Not everyone knew who Henry Jr. was, so there was no gasped, but I looked directly toward Mitzi and Lina, and they had their heads looking downward.

Nell answered him directly. "Yes, Tram you are correct."

Then Nell looked over at both Mitzi and Lina. I could see that she was sad for them.

"Girls," Nell said, "I am very sorry that you have to hear this about your brother.

Now everybody understood who Henry Jr. was and now I could see faces changing expressions.

"He was an awful man to me." Nell said softly. "It was very hard for me when I came back to Pinesdale to live and I had to see him and then later when he moved back into the family home and I had to be his neighbor again. But I missed my sweet mother and I was determined to not let him take her or anything else away from me."

Mitzi and Lina kept their heads done and had their hankies to their faces.

Tram said quietly, "I knew Nell because Henry bragged to me about how he had tricked you and what he had done. You are right Nell; he was an evil person. In their own way, Mitzi and Lina know that is true. He was their brother, but I think they both know that is true."

Tram was on a roll and continued talking.

"When you left town Nell, "he said, "Henry guessed that you might be having his baby. He wanted to hire a detective to find you but he didn't dare. I told him if he even tried to find you, I would make sure he was never ever able to hurt anyone again. He knew I meant it."

Nell nodded her head and spoke in a low voice, "Thank you Tram."

Mitzi looked up and finally spoke.

"You are right Tram and Nell; Henry Jr was not a good person. He never was for even one day of his life. Every thought in his head had an evil connection attached to it. Often times Lina and myself were his targets. We learned how to hide and protect ourselves, but it was an awful way to live. I know his actions practically killed our father. Father was at his wits end on how to handle him, his own son."

Now Nell was asking, "Tram, you are such a good person. I told the children the other day how my mother called you Atlas. By the way Ginger, please let the children return. Sabrina ...Knox...come back please."

We came flying back into the room and planted ourselves right in front of Tram.

Nell waited for us to catch our breath and then continued.

"It is by your questions," Nell said, "that we are finally able to open up these secrets. You should be here to get the answers."

My mother smiled at me.

Nell continued, "Tram the children are, as most children are...curious. They have many questions about you. And as I was saying, I myself always wondered why you remained so close with Henry Jr? You two were such opposites, like Good and Evil."

Tram nodded his head but also hung it downward.

"The answer to that question," he said, "involves another secret. But I guess like we have said it is time to get rid of the secrets. A very long time ago, Henry Winter Sr. came to me and said he needed a favor."

He looked directly at Mitzi.

"Mitzi, we have never spoke about this but I think you know exactly what day I am talking about."

Mitzi looked at Tram and with a small smile across her face, she nodded her head.

He smiled at her and continued. "It was a very long time ago, I was just a young pup and Henry Sr. came up to me while I was outside working in the back yard. I think he knew my father wasn't home. Well, to make a long story short, he explained about his problem with Henry Jr and him hurting the other kids. He said that Mitzi told him I protected her and the other kids from Henry Jr. He asked me if I could keep doing that. He said if I would help him he would help my Mother with groceries in return."

315

Tram looked really sad like the memory was too much to bear.

"We shook on it," he said, "and I tried to never let him down. I did as much as I could but there were times when I just didn't know or see ahead enough to be able to stop Henry. One of those times…. was you Nell, and I am so very sorry."

Nell walked over and gave him a hug.

Tram looked up and gently nodded his head toward Nell. Then he shocked me by looking directly at my mother. "But you Ginger, I was able to stop him from hurting you that night at Webbers' Lake."

My mother looked shocked and I saw tears immediately build up in her eyes and then she just released them and burst out crying.

"That was you Tram?" she cried. She looked from Tram to my daddy and then back to Tram.

"All these years," she cried. "All these years …. I have wondered … all these years who that brave man was that night. I was never able to thank you. I never knew who attacked me. Now I know it was Henry Winter. Oh my…David. It is over. I got answers after all these years."

Then she buried her head in my father shoulder and cried. I ran over to hug her.

I remembered her story from the night on the swing. I remember how scared she had been. Then I started to think about how I had said Tram was a creepy old man. How I was kind of scared of him. How I watched him at night. Now all I wanted to do was hug him for helping my Momma. I wondered how many other women he had helped. Nell was right. He was a good man and he was really an Atlas.

I looked over at him and our eyes connected. He smiled and it helped make me feel brave. Brave enough to talk to him.

I asked, "Tram, why do you walk around the yards at night shining your flashlight?"

My father said, "Sabrina — hush now child. That is none of your business or our business."

But Tram stopped him. "It is alright David," Tram said. "Let her talk and ask questions. It seems to me that these children have started something good here today. My heart is feeling lighter and better already."

"Young lady, I think I have heard Knox call you Stinkweed when you are outside playing. May I call you Stinkweed too?" He asked teasingly and I nodded yes.

"My answer is pretty simple," he continued. "My deal with Henry Sr was to keep my eye on Henry Jr. and I did that for a lot of years. But Henry Jr. not only hurt people … he also like to torture the poor innocent cats. So, I got into the habit of checking on the cats nightly too …. to make sure they were put in the garage for the evening. Henry Jr has been gone for a long time, but the cats kind of got to where they depended on me and as each new kitten came along, I just kept watching out for them. Did I scare you? If I did I am sorry."

"Nah," I said bravely. "That's okay. I am glad that the cats can count on you!" I looked over at Knox and he was smiling too.

My momma was done crying now and had now got herself in better control where she could think like her normal self.

"Tram," Momma said as though her heart were breaking, "I cannot thank you enough for protecting me. I only wish I had known it was you all this time."

"That's okay," Tram said. "He used to like to hang around Webber's Lake for a couple of reasons. It was always dark there in the evenings and when they didn't keep the grass cut down, it made it way too easy for him. He often went there pretending to be fishing."

Tram kept on talking. It was as though now that the burden of secrets was lifted, he had to let them all flow freely.

"Mitzi and Lina," he said, "I know you ladies have endured your share of pain from Henry and I know some of those pains run very deep, but the man has been dead for a very long time. It is time for more to be released and I think you will both feel better."

Mitzi and Lina looked at each other in shock. None of us knew what they were thinking but the horror in their eyes told us it wasn't something that would be easy to share. What could he possibly want them to tell? They stayed silent.

"Ladies I am just going to say it," he said. "In 1939, before many of you were alive or old enough to know what was happening in the world there was a fire at Henry Jr's home. That fire took the life of his wife, Marie and their son, little Paul. That fire was not an accident. It was set by Henry Winter."

"Oh my," Sister Jeanette said and then immediately started to pray. She had been very quiet up until this point. I realized now that this bad man that everyone was talking about ...was her father and I bet she had already figured that out too.

Tram continued, "This time, it was not intentional. Henry truly thought they were not at home. He set the fire by pouring gasoline on the back of the house and then simply lighting a match. He needed to collect the insurance money because his business was in deep financial trouble. And you are right Nell about him not getting into trouble. No one even questioned him about any part of it. Then just wrote that the fire was due to electrical problems."

Tram hung his head again and let it sway back and forth in disbelief.

My daddy was finally ready to ask a question. He made a strange sound like he was trying to clear his throat and everyone looked at him.

"I was wondering," Daddy said, "I know Henry Jr died right before my Uncle Otto, but I never did hear what he died from, I mean...what happened?"

He waited. We all waited. Everyone looked toward Mitzi and Lina, but they both sat quiet. Nell finally spoke and repeated the story that her mother had told her about seeing him go to the garage and not come back out.

Nell said, "Mother assumed he must have had a heart attack."

Again, the room stayed quiet probably waiting for Mitzi or Lina to confirm, but they sat quiet in their chairs. It was Tram that finally answered.

"That was another of the great Henry Winter Jr. quiet mysteries," he said. "Once again, no one really investigated what happened. It was marked a closed case the same night it occurred. Cause of death was listed as heart attack on the police report."

The room was way too quiet now. No one knew what to say to Mitzi and Lina.

Tram took another deep breath and said, "Now, if you folks will indulge me, I have one more secret to share. This one is one of those secrets like Nell's...one that I have told no one. Two other people knew it, but they have both passed long ago."

"The day that Henry Sr. came to talk with me," he said, "we also talked about other things. We sat in the back portion of the yard for a long time. It was about 2 years later, one of many days when my father had drunk way too much and came home and started beating on my mother. I stepped in to stop him and it did work, he stopped hitting my Mum and started whipping me."

Another very deep slow breath. "He usually couldn't last too long and then he would pass out. It was after one of those beatings that my Mum took me out into the yard away from the sleeping drunk and told me that she wanted me to know, that I would never be like him."

He looked at the group and everyone nodded their heads in silent agreement.

He continued, "She told me that I was strong and kind and I had fine character.... just like my father!

"I looked at her like she had taken too hard of a blow to her head," he said with a chuckle. "That was when she told me. My father was not Bertram Kellar. My father was Henry Winter Sr.!"

Mitzi and Lina both looked like they had just seen a ghost. Mitzi spoke first.

"Tram.... really?" was all she said.

"For a long time," he said, "I thought my mum might have just said it to make me feel better. You know how Mum's can be, wanting their kids to think better about themselves. But it was true! Years later, Henry Sr. told me so himself."

"It was 1930," Tram said as though he was in a story-telling mood. "My father had just died. After the funeral, Henry Sr. asked me to come to his office. I sat down and he told me everything. About how sickly your mother got after your sister Gretel's death. How he and my mum had been friends in their childhood. How it started as a comfort thing and just went too far. He said my mum understood he could never hurt

319

his own family but that he would always lookout for me financially. And he did."

"That day in his office," Tram continued "he wanted me to know that he had bought me land in the country and would help me to build a house. And he did. He was always there to help me if I needed it. He was a great man."

Mitzi and Lina were now smiling at Tram.

Mitzi spoke first.

"I remember a day, very long ago when I was just a little girl. I went to talk with father in his study and I asked him to help you. You see, I had seen your father beating you and I was very upset. I remember how very distressed my father had become too. It all makes perfect sense now Tram. Father loved you too."

Now Lina finally spoke. It was soft, but loud enough for all to hear.

"And in father's last will and testament," she said, "I remember a small section so clearly. It said, "No one lives their life without a secret. I have a secret and someday my children will learn of it. I hope when they do, they accept it and know that with all my heart, I did the best I could to make amends."

Mitzi and Lina hugged each other. Then together they got up and walked over to Tram and hugged him too.

Mitzi looked at him and said, "And you have continued your promise to father by watching over us all these years Tram. Your mother was right Tram, you are a good kind man and you are so much like our father. And your mother was right too Nell. He is Atlas. He has carried the weight of the world on his shoulders.

The secrets were all out. Nell asked everyone to stay and have another piece of pie and people started to mingle freely and talk to each other.

Suddenly Knox said, "Wait a minute. I still need one more answer."

Everyone stopped talking and looked at Knox.

Now Knox looked kind of worried.

"Well," he said carefully, "I just wondered why Elsie Becker is so mad at Miss Winter? Miss Winter, do you know the answer?"

Mitzi held her breath and looked around the room. No one spoke for a second and then suddenly, David spoke.

"I think I can answer that one," David said. "Aunt Elsie is a lonely old woman who sadly misses the love of her life and wants to blame someone. He fell. We all know that. He just slipped and fell."

As the grown-ups talked further about the secrets, Knox and I went and found our own quiet corner of the room and sat down with our second pieces of pie.

"I don't know Stinkweed," Knox said, "What do you think? Do you think we heard everything there was to tell?"

I shook my head to respond no. "I was watching the Winter sisters faces," I said in my very serious voice. "When you think about it, every secret discussed today involved the sisters in some way or another, yet they hardly spoke a word."

"Yep," I said looking very seriously at Knox. "They were too quiet. I don't like it. If I were a guessing girl, I would guess they have a secret that they were afraid someone else might know, might bring up. I think they were keeping quiet because they are set on keeping whatever that secret is...a secret."

Knox nodded approvingly at me.

"Our work is going to need to keep going. We don't have all the answers!"

LINA

Chapter 29 – October 4, 1951

The day had started like so many other fall days. The weather was pleasant and the neighborhood had become almost quiet by 8:30 am when the children had finally all made their way to school. Mrs. Jenkins had her laundry hanging on the clothesline bright and early so now the bedsheets seemed to already be dry as they flapped in the breeze. Esther Tawney had taken her noontime walk around the neighborhood that she claimed her doctor had suggested was for exercise. Mitzi and I felt this short walk was more so to make sure she didn't miss anything that might be going on in the neighborhood and to ensure no new gossip got started without her being one of the first to hear the rumor.

Otto and Elsie Becker had left together earlier today but had already returned this afternoon and were now busy working outside in their yard. Mitzi and I always enjoyed our spring and summertime yards when they were filled with bright, colorful flowers; the lovely aroma which comes from their blended fragrances and of course the buzz of the necessary but bothersome bees. But in the fall, there was still much beauty to be found with the sturdy greenery, the ever-hardy mums in vibrant colors with yellow being my favorite, and the continuously changing colors of the leaves on our many assorted trees in our yard.

Mitzi still worked but I so enjoyed the days like today when she took a vacation day and was able to putter at leisure in the yard with me. We easily found plenty of small activities that we could accomplish in our

322

yard and then without feeling any sense of guilt, other projects that we could set aside for another day. Truly, just any other day would be fine!

For our neighbor Otto it was a completely different situation. He was still very active with his work owning more than one business and having many responsibilities to himself, Elsie and to the many people in his employment. I greatly admired him. He had always excelled in school and now he did so in both his work and his life. He had married his sweetheart Elsie Holden and remained to this day dedicated to her. I always wondered why they had no children; whether it was that Elsie was barren or whether it was their choice to live their life as just a couple keeping them free to work, travel and do whatever came their way at the spur of the moment. Either way, they were a model couple here in our small town.

My point of saying all of this about Otto and Elsie is to remark that today, Otto has been outside working in the yard and on the house as though he is the only one that can possible get the work done. He is a very wealthy man and could easily hire these types of services to be done for him, but he does not. He wants to take care of his own belongings and Elsie is much the same way. They are committed to their life and in the same way to their home. I myself think it is refreshing to witness.

Mitzi and I are fortunate that we have Tram who has been a loyal friend throughout our lives and is always willing to lend a helping hand when we have tasks that we as women cannot quite manage. Many times between the two of us, we still do not have the required strength to complete certain tasks and Tram is always nearby. Henry Jr could help us, but he will not. Henry is of the belief that many tasks are beneath his level. He has never been one to get his hands dirty, at least not in the true sense of the word, meaning his hands show the physical signs of true work, dirt, sweat and grit. When that is needed, Tram steps in and it gets done. Actually, Mitzi and I prefer our days much better when Henry is not at home. We love the days when he goes to his office at 7:00 am and doesn't return until 8:00 or 9:00 in the evening, often complaining of being so tired that he goes right to his bedroom. Those are good days for us.

Today Henry left early, but returned home at about 5:30, changed from his suit into more casual clothes and then left again saying not to hold dinner for him. As he was leaving I watched from the kitchen window. I saw him go into the garage, then from the side garage window, I could see him lifting his fishing pole from the hooks on the side wall. A minute later, I heard the garage door lift and saw his car leaving. He went down the alley. I assumed he was heading over to Webbers Lake.

I let Mitzi know that he was gone. We could now prepare our supper and not worry about him sitting at the table grumbling about the world of finance, about our repeated meal of chicken yet again, or about the world in general. He certainly was an unhappy man.

We did as we usually did and prepared chicken for dinner. Tram stopped in a little earlier than usual and we invited him to join us. He asked about the whereabouts of Henry and I told him that I felt he had gone fishing. I was a little concerned because Tram immediately changed his expression. He asked if Henry had told me he was going fishing and I said no but that I had seen him put his fishing pole in the car. Tram asked if we had noticed if he was in a good mood.

I looked over at Mitzi who was peeling a few potatoes and then said, "No, but then again when was Henry ever in a good mood?"

Mitzi shook her head in agreement. Tram thanked us for the offer of dinner, but said he had something that needed his attention and he had better get to it. After he left, Mitzi and I decided that maybe everyone leaving us at dinnertime did have something to do with the frequency of our serving chicken.

After we had eaten and the kitchen was back in proper order, Mitzi said she had changed her mind and was going to attend the library committee meeting tonight after all. She remembered a few of the issues that were brought up last month and did not want to give Esther Tawney a chance to push them through without a proper number of votes. So, she changed into presentable clothes and headed out.

I decided I would go into the study to work on my latest project. A customer at Willow-Bee's Emporium had commissioned a watercolor piece to include hummingbirds and the color blue. Their order as relayed to me by the shop owner had said it was not to be just any shade of blue but they specifically requested azure blue. I had started to create the vision that appeared in my mind two days ago, but was still adding tiny flecks of light green to the mix, trying to create the perfect blend of colors. My favorite of our cats, Scooter, had joined me in the study and was patiently sitting in my favorite chair in the corner of the room, maybe watching me work or maybe just sleeping. It was hard to tell. As with most cats, I was not impressing him with my colorful artwork.

I had been in the study about 20 minutes when I heard the back door open and slam shut. I knew it was Henry. I stood very quiet and hoped he would go directly to his room for the evening. I heard him open the refrigerator. I heard him set a bottle against the counter and I could hear the sound of the bottle opener clanking against the glass followed by the pop of the bottle cap and then it spinning against the countertop before it dropped into the sink. I knew he was taking a swig and then the bottle landed hard against the counter. I heard his footsteps.

He yelled as he walked, "Mitzi, Lina!"

I set down my brush and without making a sound, backed myself away from my easel and into the far corner of the room. My hope was he would look into the room, not see me and go to his room for the night.

I knew he was probably drunk. I knew what he was capable of when he was sober let alone drunk. I had lived this same scenario many times in my 44 years of life as his younger sister. I had suffered his abuse before and I was determined not to suffer it again today.

I was not so lucky. He entered the room looking agitated. He came all the way in and yelled my name. Then looking past the serene ivory colored walls, he looked directly at me. I had a full view of him now and could see he was a mess. His clothes looked like he had already been in some sort of a battle. There was a penetrating rage in his eyes. Knowing he had me cornered, he started slowly walking toward me. I could see by his fumbling walk that he had definitely been drinking.

325

I was determined to sound strong and unafraid. I yelled out, "No Henry. Not today. Mitzi is upstairs. She will hear you and be right down here to push you away. Get away from me. Do you hear me? Get away! I will call for Tram. Do you hear me?"

My words came out strong, but he didn't stop. He came at me. He was right in front of me now.

He smiled a wicked smile and said very smugly, "Go ahead, call for your precious Tram. He won't be coming. I made sure of that."

And with that he swung his hand with all his might and slapped me across my face. Luckily, he lost some of his balance as he swung and the force of the blow wasn't as brutal as I have felt in the past. As he tried to regain his balance, I ducked around his left arm and tried to run, but he grabbed the back of my sweater and pulled me back against him.

"You make me sick little sister," he whispered into my ear. I could smell the overpowering odor of the beer and felt droplets of spittle on my neck. I pulled to free myself but he wasn't loosening his grip. He spun my body around and pushed me against the wall.

I had no one to help me. Mitzi should be back soon, but right now, it was just me. I was never able to fight. He was always too strong. I was ready to give up. I was ready to just close my eyes and let it happen again. I had endured it before. Maybe it was better to just let it happen now rather than have my body battered and have it still happen anyway.

He still had a tight hold on me but I was letting my arms go limp. He spun me toward him and there was that memorized look of pure evil showing on his face.

He took his hands to my shoulders and said, "Ready to accommodate me dear sister?"

I closed my eyes tight and braced myself for yet another attack of humiliation. His hands started to slide down my sweater and then there was a scream and they were gone. It happened so quickly that I almost didn't realize I was free to escape.

The scream...it was Henry. The reason....it was Scooter. Scooter had freed me. Scooter had jumped up onto Henry's back and dug his claws deep into his skin. Henry had cried out with pain, but Scooter hung on. God bless Scooter.

I ran. I ran up the stairs and into my bedroom. I locked my door and braced my desk chair under the doorknob, a trick I had used many times in the past and found it to be effective. Then I sat on the edge of my bed and prayed that he had given up. I prayed that he was still laying on the floor of the study and that he would fall asleep there. I also prayed that Scooter had run and hid out of Henrys reach.

I would watch out the window for Mitzi to return from the library. I would see her in plenty of time as she walked down Pyatt St and would warn her to come in very quietly.

Five minutes into my prayers, I heard movement. I panicked thinking I would soon hear his heavy footsteps coming up the stairs to begin beating on my door, but the noise didn't come closer. The noise moved further away. Then with a loud bang, I heard the slam of the back door. I was still fearful and stayed in my room. When nothing else happened after a few more minutes, I decided to move over and into father's old bedroom so that I could view the backyard.

I loosened my desk chair and slowly, very slowly and without making a sound unlocked my door. I turned the knob and allowed the door to let in a small beam of light. Again there was no noise and the hallway was now in full view and I saw no one. No one except little Scooter. He was lying right at the top of the stairway as if he was standing guard. He turned his head to look my direction, but didn't move any part of his body. God bless that beautiful cat.

I quickly ran into my father's room and again locked the door. There was no chair to brace against the doorknob. My eyes searched the room and seeing nothing other than the small antique dry sink that I knew I could slide, I put my weight behind it and pushed it until it was in front of the door.

Feeling a little more secure, I then went to the window that faced the back of the house and peered out from the corner. I could see the back yard and did not see Henry. I had hopes that I would see Tram knowing he was usually here at the house by this time of day, but he was nowhere to be seen. Remembering the remark Henry had made earlier in the study I now worried about Tram.

Suddenly, I saw movement in the garage. I saw Henry. He was in the garage. I saw him walking around, almost pacing. What was he doing? I wanted to watch but at the same time I was so afraid that he would look upward and see me. I quickly moved my body far to the right side of the window frame allowing myself only to lean just enough for my left eye to peer outward to watch his movement. Yes, I could still see and felt much better about being more hidden from his evil eyes.

Just then, he opened the driver's side door of his car, got in and shut the door. I felt immediate relief. He was leaving. I knew he should not be driving since he had been drinking, but I didn't care. I just wanted him gone. But, he wasn't going. He was just sitting there.

Five minutes had now passed and he was still sitting. His head was resting against the wheel with his arms stretched up and over the wheel too. Was he actually feeling remorse for what he had done? Probably not. More likely he was sleeping. I knew he had been drinking but I had no idea as to how much he had drank. Was he passed out? Would he sleep there all night? I didn't know anything for certain. It was like I was once again a part of a game of cat and mouse and at any given minute that cat could spring up and pounce again. This mouse had been caught too many times and was still too scared to move. I hated myself for always being so afraid. I had spent my entire life being a part of this cat and mouse game and I was very tired of the outcome. I wanted to be brave. I knew I needed to be brave but the reality is that it is very hard to be brave.

I concentrated very hard on being brave and when my fears finally quieted down and my head was thinking more clearly I recognized how dark it appeared in the garage and realized Henry had not opened the garage door. So, he wasn't planning to go anywhere? He never opened the garage door. Was he asleep now? Was he so drunk that he had fallen asleep so easily? Why did he go to the garage if he was just going to go to sleep?

Another five minutes had passed. He had made small little shifts to his body while sitting in the seat but still looked to be very much asleep.

I was feeling much calmer now. I went to the door and slowly pushed the dry sink back to its original spot and unlocked the door. Not totally trusting yet, I returned to the window to make sure Henry had not moved. He was still in the car.

I went into my room, looked out the front window and could see Mitzi crossing the railroad tracks. In about ten minutes, she would be home and hopefully Tram would not be far behind her. I returned to father's room one more time to check Henry and yes, he was still there. I tip-toed down the stairs and saw Scooter was now waiting at the bottom of the stairs. I picked him up; hugged him and called him my brave protector. Together we went through the rooms to the kitchen door and peered out the window.

Yes, the garage was definitely fairly dark inside and I could see the car and the top of Henry's head. I decided he was probably out for the night.

I looked at Scooter and said, "We can be brave together!"

I opened the back door and followed the walk to the back of the garage. I looked around but no one was outside tonight. I would have felt so much better if Tram or even anybody else were in their yards but felt strongly that Henry must be very sound asleep by now. As I got closer to the garage, I held Scooter tight. He meowed and I realized that I was squeezing him too tight. I loosened my hold. I went to the side garage door and peered through the glass window. It allowed me to look right in and see Henry with his head on the steering wheel, sound asleep. Yes, I breathed a little easier, he was asleep.

I am not sure why I did this next thing, but I did. I slowly and quietly opened the door.

The car was rumbling. Oh My God, the car was running. It must have been running this whole time. How long had it been? Ten or fifteen minutes. What was I going to do?

Scooter immediately sensed something was wrong. Something turned him from my brave protector to my terrified cat. He tried to jump from my arms. I had been holding him tight and as he scrambled to run free his claws scratched my arm and I let out a cry. I was scared.

Without truly knowing what I was doing, I slammed the door shut and then froze with my face peering in to watch his head.

And just like that, Henry moved. He slowly lifted his head from the wheel. He appeared dazed. He looked like he was having a hard time breathing and he moved as if his body was stuck in the seat. The car door slowly crept open and his body seemed to almost fall from his steadfast position. His head and shoulders hit the dirt floor first and his hips and legs tumbled after them. He looked like a worm as he squirmed to get himself turned around. His head slightly lifted and looked toward the door. He looked right at me, but I wasn't sure if he really saw me. He started to try to crawl toward the door.

I would have been more frightened had he not looked so incredibly weak. Everything seemed to be happening in extreme slow-motion. Right lower arm and elbow drug two-inches forward, a shifting of body weight, left lower arm and elbow drug two-inches forward, another shift of weight. And couple of inches of progress. And then it repeated but he seemed to be a tiny bit more determined now. The shifts of weight seemed to be happening with a little more strength, but not enough strength yet to scare me.

He was now almost to the door. I watched as he looked up at me and realized I stood on the other side of the door. He tried to lift his body. He wants to reach the door. He is trying to reach up to get a grip on the door knob. He wants desperately to be able to pull himself upward. His eyes are pleading with me to help him.

He doesn't know it yet, but on the other side of this door, I have a tight hold on the doorknob. I can see how weak he is right now and I flashed back to when it was me that was the weak one and he had me pinned down on this same cold garage floor, hurting me in ways no brother should ever hurt his sister. I see myself sleeping in my bed and being attacked in the dark of the night. I remember each and every time he grabbed and terrorized me when he thought I was alone and helpless. I remember it all. And now the table is turned. It is Henry who is helpless and I have the control.

I understand now that he was not just asleep. I understood what a running car inside a closed garage does to the air. Whether he was too drunk to know what he was doing or whether he was fully aware of the situation he put himself in I did not know. But I did know about me. I did know that I was not about to let go of the doorknob.

My opportunity had finally come. I finally had my chance to be free. I had suffered at his hands for 44 years and my chance was now to quit living in fear. I was being brave. I was grabbing my chance.

He had now lifted his body high enough to be partially on his knees. I could see by the slow rise and fall of his chest that his breathing was extremely labored. I knew now for sure that he could see my face through the glass and he was using every bit of the strength he had left to pull on the knob. His face showed pain and I thought again about all the pain and humiliation he had caused me and others throughout our life. His face was pleading and I remembered all the times I begged him not to hurt me but he did and laughed. His face shifted to fear and I thought about the fear Marie and little Paul had to have felt when they awoke to not being able to breathe. The reality that Marie must have known when she heard the roar of the fire and saw the dense smoke. His face showed hurt and I remembered all the hurt he had caused my poor father.

I was deep in thought to all those terrible memories when I suddenly looked again at Henry and realized something had changed. His face now showed defeat. He looked up at me and for a split second I thought I saw remorse. Then just as quickly he closed his eyes and his body sank back to the dirt floor. There was no more movement.

I was still holding the knob as tightly as ever when I felt a hand on my shoulder. I turned to see Mitzi. She had tears in her eyes. I tried to release my fingers from the doorknob but I had been gripping it so tightly for so long, that I could hardly get them to loosen. Mitzi saw my white fingers and helped to pull them from the knob. As soon as they broke free, I swung my arms around Mitzi and sobbed.

She held me tight for a minute and then said, "It is alright now, he is gone. He won't hurt you anymore?"

I nodded my head with a yes.

"Mitzi," I said as soon as I had gathered my tears. "Mitzi, I did it," I said with shame in my voice. "I killed him."

"No," Mitzi said with resolute, "you see, the car is still running. He killed himself."

"No Mitzi," I continued, desperate to explain to her what happened. "I killed him. He was trying to get free. He woke up, he changed his mind. He was trying to get the door open..."

"No," Mitzi said firmly. "He died from carbon dioxide. He started the car and he stayed in the garage because he wanted to die."

"But no Mitzi," I said, "He was trying to get out. I stopped him. I did this to him. I killed our brother."

"No Lina," Mitzi said softly. "Listen to me. He did this to himself. But if you want to think of it your way, then …. we both killed our brother. I was standing right here behind you."

I gasped. "Oh Mitzi," I said, "Were you really? How long were you here?"

"Long enough," she said. "I came home and found the house empty. I was of course worried when I couldn't find you. I was calling your name and you didn't answer. I was scared. Then I saw the open beer bottle on the kitchen counter. I knew then that he must have come home. I knew in my heart that he must be here and hurting you. I came to find you."

She stopped for a moment, as though everything was just now catching up with her. "I did find you." she said rubbing my back. "I found you here holding the doorknob …. protecting yourself. I heard the car running. You appeared to be in some sort of shock as though you were in a hysterical trance."

She took a deep breath. "Then Henry raised up and I saw him," she said with empathy. "I realized what was happening. I saw the condition he was in and I knew what was about to happen and…… I wasn't going to stop you."

She was staring at the door again now and I began to softly cry again.

"He looked up," she said, "and he saw both of our faces staring at him. He knew then that we had won this time. That is what finally did it. For the first time in his life..... he realized that we had won and he gave up."

Then as if she herself had snapped out of a trance, she opened the garage side door. His body lay motionless on the floor. She carefully stepped over it; walked the few steps to the car, reached in and turned off the still running motor. She shut the car door and then turned to the side window of the garage and lifted it up about 6 or so inches. Then she went around the front of the car and over to the other side and again opened the window to about the same height.

She walked back over to me and said, "That should create enough crosswind to clear it out before anyone else arrives. We wouldn't want to bring any harm to anyone else today. Leave the door ajar and let's go into the house and call the constable."

She said it all so calmly that I was amazed with her.

As we walked together, I happen to look over toward the Becker's house and saw Otto standing in the window. I quickly put my head downward and went inside the house. Mitzi placed the call to the police station.

Deputy Dowd arrived within minutes. We were waiting outside for him. He went into the garage. A minute or so later he came out to us and asked, "Did he have a heart attack?"

We answered that we had been in the house and when he didn't come inside we came out to look and found him just like he is now, lying in the garage.

He said, "OK, we will get an ambulance here. You ladies can go inside. We will take care of it from here."

We did as we were told. We went inside the house. The ambulance came barreling into our driveway with lights flashing and enough noise to wake up the entire neighborhood. Next the police chief arrived. Within a matter of a few minutes they had loaded the body into the ambulance and they pulled away slowly. No flashing lights or siren needed.

The police chief came into the house and asked a couple of questions; what time did he come home, were we aware that he was in the garage, had he been drinking, did he have a heart condition?

We answered everything and acted like grieving sisters should act. The chief seemed satisfied. He offered his condolences and turned to walk away, but in a few steps he stopped and looked back at me.

"Miss Lina," he said very matter-of-factly, "What did you do to your arm there? Looks like some fresh blood."

I glanced down at my arm and saw what he had seen. Two pink scratches, each a few inches long with some red trickles of dried blood scattered along the lines. So much had happened that I totally forgot about my scratch.

"Oh that," I said casually, "that would be from my favorite cat, Scooter.

He nodded his head in full belief and with a little chuckle in his voice he said, "Well then, I guess that answers my question. No need for me to ask the cat! Good night ladies."

The door closed and we watched as the cruiser pulled away.

Mitzi looked at me and said, "Well then sister. I think we are going to be fine."

I in turn looked at Mitzi and said, "We might have one problem sister. Otto Becker was watching out his window."

EPILOGUE

Secrets......

We all keep secrets. They may be tiny secrets that we easily rationalize and say to ourselves .... this would be of no interest to anyone beyond me, so no need to share. But yes, without another thought ... that little piece of information becomes a secret.

Sometimes we keep a secret to protect a family member, a friend, a co-worker or and this one is kind of important, ourselves.

Some people feel relief when their secret is freed. For Nell Taylor releasing her secrets had brought her a new life filled with joy. She had many good years with her daughter before the ugly cancer diagnosis came and took her life in 1982.

The diocese moves church personnel every so many years to allow the church environment to constantly grow and move forward. Father Bob and Sister Jeanette enjoyed many tennis matches up until 1974 when he was transferred to a larger church to once again try to rebuild a dwindling congregation. Sister Charlotte remained at St Lucy's until her health began to fail and she was moved to the closest retirement village. Sister Bergan had been promoted to a higher level position at St. Agatha's and Sister Jeanette, being an exemplary nun, requested and was given special permission to remain at St. Lucy's to be close to her mother.

Sabrina and Knox did try to continue their search for answers following Nell's meeting. They had been smart children and knew the Winter sisters were holding back, keeping their secret. They never did figure out that one last secret but they continued to find more problems in the small town of Pinesdale to keep their minds busy for many a summer.

Sabrina eventually left Pinesdale to attend college. Her early detective skills had helped in her decision to study psychology where her final thesis was titled, *"How Keeping A Secret Affects the Mind."* As you have probably already guessed, Aunt Elsie's Journals played a big part in her topic and her theory. She now lives in the big city where she is a psychologist in private practice and spends one day each week listening to and guiding prisoners at the state penitentiary.

Knox surprised everyone, especially his mother when he chose to follow in his fathers' footsteps. He joined the Marine Corp immediately following his high school graduation. He was given the opportunity to become a pilot, loved it and turned his four-year stint into a lifetime career.

But back to those secrets. How many secrets end up bringing about a change that affects other people's lives? Those few people that truly have no idea that there even is a secret. I suppose many.

In the case of Henry Sr and Mrs. Kellar they kept their love affair a secret for a combination of reasons. One, to protect themselves and another to protect their loved ones. Mrs. Kellar had to know that there was a certain possibility of not surviving the violent side of her husbands' wrath if he learned the truth and she also had to protect her young and impressionable son. Henry Sr. kept his secret to protect his lovely wife and to keep shame from falling on his family. That type of shame even for a man in the early 1900's would bring a risk to his standing in the community. Each eventually only told one person during their lifetime and it was the same person for both, their child Tram.

For Elsie Becker, a secret caused yet another casualty to not one life but two. Elsie spent 17 years despising her neighbor Mitzi Winter. Mitzi Winter spent 17 years not knowing why Elsie Becker hated her with such a passion. Both women spent those 17 years with a certain amount of anxiety that all stemmed from one secret. A secret that neither woman even knew existed. Only Otto Becker knew and he had taken that secret with him to his grave. If only he had not tried to spare his wife of that one secret, both women would have lead a much different existence.

You see on October 4th 1951, Otto had seen Henry Jr. stagger into the garage and he heard the car start. He continued to pay close attention because he knew that Henry Jr looked like he had been drinking and was in no condition to drive. When the garage door did not immediately open, he decided not to worry and went back into the house. He had gone into the living room and noticed a short time later Lina walking to the garage. He knew from the past how violent Henry Jr could become, especially when he had been drinking so he watched as Lina almost tip-toed around the garage. He was still standing at the window when he witnessed Lina take hold of the door handle on the side door of the garage. He stood frozen in his spot, unable to pull his eyes away as he continued to watch and saw her straining to keep hold of the handle. He could see the tension in her arms, the fear on her face, and the rigidness of her body.

He called Elsie to the window. Both watched small, frail Lina standing there with her body shaking. Both saw Mitzi later come from the back door and walk through the yard to Lina and silently stand behind her. Both were watching when Mitzi helped pry Lina's fingers from the handle. Both saw Lina collapse into her arms, weak with what they assumed were both pain and guilt. As the sheriff and ambulance came and went, Otto and Elsie discussed what to do and had quickly decided, almost too easily, to not say a word. Otto had been a good friend of Henry Sr. A close enough friend that Henry Sr. had shared with Otto some of his disappointment and heartache concerning his son's violent tendencies. Otto had also heard many rumors and believed them to be true.

So when Mitzi saw Otto working outdoors the next day she hoped to approach him to see if she could find out what he may have witnessed the day before. When she had finally built up her courage and walked across the side yard he was already up on the ladder cleaning gutters. When Otto heard her voice, he knew why she was there. He knew he needed to ease her mind and he started to climb down the ladder. He was still a few steps from the ground when she begged him to stop saying she didn't want to disturb his work. He knew how hard this conversation was going to be for Mitzi and stopped as she requested.

She began to speak but he wanted her worry to end and interrupted her. He spoke softly and told her that both he and Elsie had seen what happened at the garage last evening. She gasped and lowered her head. He quickly continued and said they had both decided to not say a word, not a word to anyone.

Mitzi had felt immediate relief which was apparent to Otto by the expression on her face. Otto went on to say they felt it was not their business. He told her that he had at times had quiet conversations with her father and understood the tortured life they had lead with Henry Jr. and his cruelty. He assured her that she and Lina had nothing to worry about and they had both he and Elsie's sympathy.

Mitzi had been much relieved and was anxious to share this news with Lina, but Otto had continued with their conversation. He had begun to talk on a lighter subject about the pregnant cat, the one Tram called Buttercup, and Mitzi felt it would be rude if she didn't stand and visit with Otto. So, she responded that Tram would soon have more kittens to care for and as Otto began to laugh, he suddenly gasped and grabbed his chest. His face changed to an expression of panic and pain. He had only been about five prongs up from the ground but as his entire body went suddenly rigid he began to waver on the ladder. Then it all happened so quickly but yet it felt to Mitzi like it was happening in slow motion. Otto's body began to topple forward causing his head to hit hard against each prong as his stiff body slid downward banging against each step of the ladder as he passed and finally landing hard against the sidewalk.

Mitzi had screamed and then ran to her house to call an ambulance. As she was almost in the back door, she saw Elsie running to his body, screaming for help. She went inside and called the fire department. The whistle blew and within a few minutes a crew arrived with the small truck, but left slowly. Otto had died instantly.

And that was it. Elsie never spoke to Mitzi again. Elsie believed in her heart that Mitzi feared Otto was going to talk to the police about what Lina had done to Henry Jr. and that she had shaken the ladder to cause Otto's fall.

But that wasn't the case. Six months before Otto's fall, he had been a patient at Mount Sinai Hospital. He had told Elsie he was going on just another of his business trips. While there, he had been told by the best doctor he could find that there was nothing they could do for his heart. He had an enlarged heart. His heart had been growing slowly over the years, but at a steady pace. In 1951, there had been no research or medical equipment that had yet to be found that would allow a surgeon to go inside and try to remedy the situation. He had sought the best and they had nothing to offer him, not even a prediction of how much time he had left. They had sent him on his way telling him to live his life in the present and enjoy the time he had left.

Otto knew if he told Elsie his news that the time he had left would be of her suffering each day watching and waiting for any sign of a problem. He resolved to keep his health problem a secret. He wanted her to tackle each day with the same zest for life that she had shown since the first day he met her. He prepared quietly, making sure all legal papers were in order and that financially she would never have a thing to cause her any worry.

It is ironic that he tried so hard to make sure Elsie's life would go forward easily, but his secret caused her world to stop and never again allowed her to have peace of mind.

Sabrina read those journals and read them more than once trying to unravel the mystery of Aunt Elsie's reasoning, but she never found the answer because the answer just wasn't there to be found. Sometimes even the best minds cannot find answers when secrets are never set free.

Secrets....

Until the day, or should I say the evening of Tram's death, he continued his vigilant nightly stroll to make sure the neighborhood was safe. On the evening of September 24th, 1976 while David Holden was sitting in Aunt Elsie's old favorite spot watching a brand new television show called, *"Charlie's Angels,"* he suddenly saw the flashlight dart past his window aiming upward. He jumped up to see Tram lying on the ground. He rushed outside as Ginger called for an ambulance. They arrived in a flash and he was transported to the nearest hospital. He had suffered a heart attack. He spent the next two days there before his weakened body gave out and he passed peacefully in his sleep. Atlas was done protecting the world.

Mitzi and Lina continued their same rituals at the family home on Maple Street as the town of Pinesdale continued to grow. They had chosen to not divulge their secret at Nell's big neighborhood meeting that day and they never did tell a soul. Not even Tram. As they had spent their entire life together, when it came time for their deaths they practically did that together too.

Mitzi and Lina had both gotten pretty far up in years and were no longer able to care for themselves. Together they moved into Miss Hilda's Boarding Home on Mitzi's 88th birthday. They shared a small room and spent every day in each other's company. Mitzi passed at the ripe old age of 90 on a hot August day. Lina lasted only two months without her sister and died peacefully in her sleep on Oct. 4th 1994. Ironic that she died on that specific day.

Throughout their lives, the sisters had only ever lived with two options:

Year after year of enduing hurt and pain ....and then after 1951, year after year of carrying guilt.

In truth, telling their secret would not have changed any lives but their own. They chose to live with their secret forever. A secret held and kept by only the two sisters ... and of course, a cat.

About the Author —

Kathleen F. Ewing is a wife, mother, grandmother, ophthalmic technician, and a former piano teacher for many, many years. In the past few years she has added writer to her list of loves.

In other words, she is your average American housewife. She is a person who loves to be creative and busy and most people just call her Kathy.

She lives in a small town in Northeast Ohio with her husband, Handsome Harry and their very old and grumpy little Bichon dog named Bartlett. Her family provides her with an abundance of antics and new ideas that she safely stores in the back of her mind for whenever that next book starts to get an itch to be created.

There is never a dull moment in her daily life or within her mind so get ready, that next book is already itching to be written.

I hope you enjoyed reading, Ask The Cat and I hope I have another new tale ready for you soon. Kathy